Daniel Defoe, Henry Morley

**The Earlier Life and the Chief Rarlier Works of Daniel Defoe**

Daniel Defoe, Henry Morley

**The Earlier Life and the Chief Rarlier Works of Daniel Defoe**

ISBN/EAN: 9783337424749

Printed in Europe, USA, Canada, Australia, Japan

Cover: Foto ©Andreas Hilbeck / pixelio.de

More available books at **www.hansebooks.com**

# THE EARLIER LIFE

AND

# THE CHIEF EARLIER WORKS

OF

# DANIEL DEFOE

EDITED BY

H E N R Y   M O R L E Y, LL.D.

PROFESSOR OF ENGLISH LITERATURE AT UNIVERSITY COLLEGE
LONDON

LONDON
GEORGE ROUTLEDGE AND SONS
BROADWAY, LUDGATE HILL
GLASGOW, MANCHESTER, AND NEW YORK
1889

# CONTENTS.

# THE EARLIER LIFE

OF

# DANIEL DEFOE.

———+———

## CHAPTER I.

### (1661–1689.)

DANIEL FOE—afterwards De Foe—may have been born in the year 1661, in the parish of St. Giles's, Cripplegate. There is no evidence of the date of his birth beyond a passage in a pamphlet of thirty or forty pages, published by him under an assumed name in November 1727.[1] The writer says that he is in his sixty-seventh year. Daniel Defoe died on the 26th of April 1731. He had been named Daniel after his grandfather, of whom we learn accidentally, from a passage written in 1711 in the seventh volume of Defoe's "Review," that in the time of Charles the First he kept a pack of hounds, and farmed his own estate at Elton, in Northamptonshire. James, son of Daniel Foe, a younger son, with steady character, found a way to success by bringing cattle from their grazing grounds to the London meat-market. He became a citizen of London, trading as a butcher

---

[1] The pamphlet was called " The Protestant Monastery ; or, A Complaint against the Brutality of the Present Age. Particularly the Pertness and Insolence of our Youth to Aged Persons . . . Concluding with a Proposal for Erecting a Protestant Monastery, where Persons of Small Fortune may End their Days in Plenty, Ease, and Credit, without Burthening their Relations, or accepting Public Charities. By Andrew Moreton, Esq., Author of ' Everybody's Business is Nobody's Business.' "

in Cripplegate, till he retired from business. He was alive in
1705, and in 1708 was spoken of as dead.

On the 19th of May 1662, when Daniel, the son of James
Foe, was an infant, there was passed "An Act for the Uniformity
of Public Prayers and Administration of Sacraments and other
Rites and Ceremonies, and for establishing the form of making,
ordaining, and consecrating Bishops, Priests, and Deacons, in the
Church of England." By that Act every minister was bound,
before next Bartholomew's Day, the 24th of August, to declare
his assent to everything contained in the Prayer Book, on penalty
of forfeiting his benefice. On that day, accordingly, while seven
thousand of those who had taken the covenant conformed, two
thousand of the most honest of the clergymen, whose bias was
Puritan, accepted the forfeiture of their livings. In that manner
the foundations were laid of English Nonconformity.

In 1664 a "Conventicle Act" came into operation against the
Nonconforming clergy, which prohibited the meeting of more
persons than five for any form of worship except that provided
by the Book of Common Prayer.

In 1665 a "Five-Mile Act" required the Nonconforming ministers to swear "that it is not lawful upon any pretence whatever
to take arms against the King," or "to endeavour any alteration of the government of Church or State," and that they "will
not at any time endeavour any alteration of government, either
in Church or State." Whoever had not taken that oath was forbidden to go within five miles of any borough, or any place where
he had been wont to minister.

The Vicar of St. Giles's, Cripplegate, whom James Foe regarded
as his spiritual guide, the Reverend Samuel Annesley, was one of
the two thousand clergy who were driven out of the Church in
1662. His age then was about forty-two. He had been born at
Kellingworth, near Warwick, and was a nephew of the Arthur
Annesley who became first Earl of Anglesey. Samuel Annesley
was a young child when his father died, but his mother gave much
care to his education. He was sent to Queen's College, Oxford,
in 1635. He proceeded in due time to the degree of M.A. and

to ordination. He served on board a man-of-war as chaplain to the Earl of Warwick, Admiral of the Fleet under the Parliament; and he afterwards occupied the place of a minister who had been ejected by the Parliament from his living of Cliffe in Kent. He preached the Fast Sermon before the House of Commons on the 26th of July 1648. The University of Oxford gave him the honorary degree of Doctor of Laws; he went to sea again with the Earl of Warwick; and he resigned the living of Cliffe after he had won to himself the attachment of a congregation that at first regarded him as an intruder.

Samuel Annesley was one of those Presbyterians who had a strong feeling of loyalty to the Crown. He refused to supply a horse for service against the King at Worcester; and that there might be no use of his church in thanks to God for Cromwell's victory, he sent a servant at night forty miles to lock the church and bring away the keys.

It was in 1658 that Richard Cromwell presented Dr. Annesley to the vicarage of St. Giles's, Cripplegate, which was confirmed to him by Charles II. in 1660. After he went out of the church in 1662, Samuel Annesley preached, and suffered penalties for preaching, at a meeting-house in Little St. Helen's. James Foe was of the number of his people who had followed him thither. At this meeting-house young Daniel Foe first joined in public worship.

Dr. Annesley was a grandfather of John Wesley through Ann Annesley, his daughter, who became the wife of the Rev. Samuel Wesley, and was John Wesley's mother. The good pastor died on the last day of the year 1696; and in 1697 Daniel Foe expressed his affection for him in verses entitled "The Character of the Late Dr. Samuel Annesley, by way of Elegy."

We should not, he said, yield to a passion of grief when the death of an honoured friend shows us that—

> " The World, whose nature is to fade and die,
> Must change, and take up Immortality;
> And Time, which to Eternity rolls on,
> Must change, and be Eternity begun."

We should rather take example from the dead, and be warned by the witness to us that

> "The Best of Men cannot suspend their Fate ;
> The Good die early, and the Bad die late."

Daniel Foe's verse tells how Annesley was vowed from childhood to the service of the Church, and from the first was worthy :—

> "His pious course with childhood he began,
> And was his Maker's sooner than his own ;
>
> .    .    .    .    .    .
>
> The Sacred Study all his thoughts confined,
> A sign what secret Hand prepared his Mind :
> The Heavenly Book he made his only School,
> In Youth his Study, and in Age his Rule.
> Solid, yet vigorous too, both grave and young,
> A taking Aspect and a charming Tongue ;
> With David's Courage and Josiah's Truth,
> All over Love, Sincerity, and Truth.
> As the Gay World attacked him with her charms,
> He shook the gaudy Trifle from his Arms.
>
> .    .    .    .    .    .
>
> His native Candour and familiar Style,
> Which did so oft his Hearers' Hours beguile,
> Charmed us with godliness, and while he spake,
> We loved the Doctrine for the Teacher's sake.
> While he informed us what those Doctrines meant,
> By dint of Practice more than Argument,
> Strange were the Charms of his Sincerity,
> Which made his Actions and his Words agree
> At such a constant and exact a rate
> As made a Harmony we wondered at.
>
> "Honour he had by Birth, and not by Chance,
> And more by Merit than Inheritance ;
> But both, together joined, complete his Fame,
> For Honesty and Honour are the same,
> And show, when Merit's joined with Quality,
> The Gentleman and Christian may agree.
>
> .    .    .    .    .    .
>
> Humility was his dear, darling Grace,
> And Honesty sate Regent in his face :

Meekness of Soul did in his Aspect shine,
But in the Truth resolved, and masculine ;
A pleasing Smile sat ever on his Brow,
A sign that cheerful Peace was lodged below.
If e'er his Duty forced him to contend,
Calmness was all his Temper, Peace his end ;
And if just Censure followed the Debate,
His Pity would his Zeal anticipate.

" A Heavenly Patience did his Mind possess,
Cheerful in Pain and thankful in Distress ;
Mighty in Works of Sacred Charity,
Which none knew better how to guide than he ;
Bounty and generous thoughts took up his Mind,
Extensive, like his Maker's, to Mankind.
With such a Soul that (had he Mines in store)
He'd ne'er be Rich while any Man was Poor ;
A Heart so great, that, had he but a Purse,
'Twould have supplied the Poor o' th' Universe.
Now he's above the Praises of my Pen,
The Best of Ministers and best of Men !

Then speak not of him with a mournful Voice ;
For why should we Repine and he Rejoice?
His Harvest has been full, his Season long,
And long he charmed us with his Heavenly Song,
The same, the very same, which flaming Love,
Fired with celestial Raptures, sings above,
Touched with a Sacred Influence, that's given
From that Eternal Harmony in Heaven.
How much Celestial Vision comprehends,
Whether to Human Actions it extends,
Whether he's now informed of things below,
Is needless as impossible to know :
For sight of Spirits is unprescribed by Space—
What see they not who see the Eternal Face ?

   .     .     .     .     .

And could he now, in his exalted state,
His thoughts by Sympathy communicate,
Or some superior way—for Spirits converse
Without the helps of Voice,—could he rehearse
To our Conception what is heaven above,
'Twould be concisely thus—All Heaven is Love."

These passages are taken from one of the first pieces ascribed to Defoe, of which we know certainly that he was the writer. By his father's wish and the advice of Dr. Annesley, young Daniel Foe was to be trained for the Nonconformist ministry, and he was sent at the age of fourteen to the academy of the Reverend Charles Morton at Newington Green. In the sixth volume of his " Review," Defoe referred to this intention on his behalf, saying, " It is not often that I trouble you with any of my divinity; the pulpit is none of my office. It was my disaster first to be set apart for, and then to be set apart from, the honour of that sacred employ." He looked back always with great regard to Charles Morton, but he objected to the usual training of Dissenting ministers in these academies. Many, he argued, of the poor youths, who were sent by help of a fund for their support to receive in the academy three years of training, were, for want of free access to libraries or to cultivated society, not well able to take their stand in life as cultivated Christian gentlemen. " At Newington," he said, in another of his writings, published in 1712, on " The Present State of Parties in Great Britain," which dealt specially with the state of the Dissenters, " the master or tutor read all his lectures, gave all his systems, whether of Philosophy or Divinity, in English, and had all his declaimings and dissertations in the same tongue. And though the scholars from that place were not destitute in the languages, yet it is observed of them, they were by this made masters of the English tongue, and more of them excelled in that particular than of any school at that time." Among the ministers whom Charles Morton had taught, Defoe then named Samuel Wesley, who married Dr. Annesley's daughter Anne.

Charles Morton, about ten years after Daniel Foe first came to him, left Newington Green for New England, where he was chosen pastor of a church at Charlestown, near Boston, and lived until he was almost eighty years old. He took with him those of his pupils who shared his dread of what might follow upon the revocation in France of the Edict of Nantes, and the accession in England of a Roman Catholic king, and who were willing to seek larger freedom of worship on the other side of the Atlantic.

Training at Newington, and in after years, enabled Defoe to write as well as read Latin, to read Greek, to speak French fluently, and to translate and speak Italian and Spanish. He obtained also some knowledge of Dutch. He had connections in Spain, and it may even be that his family had Spanish origins, and at some former time had anglicised the name of Foà into Foe.

The design of education for the Nonconformist pulpit having been abandoned, Daniel Foe, when he had left the Newington Academy, was trained for business in the City until the time of the accession of James II. He then shared that dread for the future of England which caused Charles Morton to leave the country, and, with some other young men who had been students under Morton, he rode west to join the force of James, Duke of Monmouth, who landed at Lyme on the 11th June 1685, was proclaimed king at Taunton nine days afterwards, was defeated at Sedgmoor, near Bridgewater, on the 6th of July, and after another nine days was beheaded upon Tower Hill. After a few more days, in August, Judge Jeffries began in the West Country the Bloody Assizes, at which more than three hundred were executed after short trials, many more were whipped, imprisoned, or fined, and more than a thousand were sent to the American plantations. Defoe names friends from his old school who were among the victims, "two or three of your Western martyrs, that, had they lived, would have been extraordinary men of their kind, viz., Kitt, Battersby, young Jenkyns, Hewling." Happily their comrade Foe was not included in the list. Later in the year he began business as a factor in the hosiery trade in Freeman's Court, Cornhill, where he remained engaged in the same business for the next eight or nine years, until 1694.

In 1687 appeared "A Letter containing some Reflections on His Majesty's Declaration for Liberty of Conscience, dated the 4th of April 1687." It was issued without date or printer's name or place of publication on the title-page, and was probably the

B

first piece printed by Defoe, who was then twenty-six years old.
The King, by his own sole will, suspended all the penal laws
that were directed against Roman Catholics and Nonconformists.
Many Nonconformists, feeling the relief, expressed their gratitude.
Ralph Thoresby, who had gone several miles to hear his minister
in secret, now heard him preach in public, and wrote in his diary,
for himself and for his fellow-worshippers, that the Declaration
of Indulgence "gave us ease in this case, and though we dreaded
a snake in the grass, we accepted it with due thankfulness."
Daniel Foe's pamphlet disclosed the snake in the grass. It also
warned the Dissenters against addresses of thanks to a king for
setting himself above the law. "I will take," he said, "the
boldness to add one thing, that the King's suspending of laws
strikes at the root of this whole Government, and subverts it
quite. The Lords and Commons have such a share in it, that no
law can be either made, repealed, or, which is all one, suspended
but by their consent."

The next year was 1688. The King issued in April a second
Letter of Indulgence. By an Order of Council on the 4th of
May, he required that it be read by the ministers of all persua-
sions in all churches and chapels throughout the kingdom,—on
the 20th of May in London ; in the country on the 3rd of June.
The Archbishop of Canterbury and six Bishops signed a Letter
of Protest to the King, prompted, they said, not by want of loyalty,
or want of tenderness to the Dissenters, but by the consideration
that His Majesty's Declaration was "founded upon such a Dispensing Power as hath often been declared illegal in Parliament."

The seven prelates were committed to the Tower, tried, and
acquitted. The soldiers in the camp at Hounslow shared the
rejoicing of the people. The birth of a son to King James quickened the revolutionary movement. On the 5th of November
1688, William of Orange landed at Brixham, near Torbay, where
a block of stone records that "On this stone, and near this spot,
William, Prince of Orange, first set foot on landing in England."
During the advance to London, Daniel Foe was among those
who poured out to welcome the deliverer. He joined at Henley

William's army, and in the next year, 1689, on the 29th of October—he being married to his first wife Mary, and with a home
at Tooting in Surrey—he rode as a trooper in a volunteer regiment that escorted William and Mary to a banquet at Guildhall.
"Their Majesties," says Oldmixon, "attended by their Royal
Highnesses and a numerous train of nobility and gentry, went first
to a balcony prepared for them at the Angel in Cheapside, to see
the show; which, for the great number of livery-men, the full
appearance of the militia and artillery company, the rich adorn-
ments of the pageants, and the splendour and good order of the
whole proceeding, outdid all that had been seen before on that
occasion; and what deserved to be particularly mentioned, was a
royal regiment of volunteer horse, made up of the chief citizens,
who, being gallantly mounted and richly accoutred, were led by
the Earl of Monmouth, now Earl of Peterborough, and attended
their Majesties from Whitehall.  Among these troopers, who were
for the most part Dissenters, was Daniel Foe, at that time a hosier
in Freeman's Yard, Cornhill."

## CHAPTER II.

### (1689–1697.)

DANIEL FOE was adventurous. He had tried ventures in foreign trade that kept him for some time in Spain ; he had been also to France. He made ventures with ships' cargoes, and in 1692 suffered losses that made him a bankrupt heavily in debt. Those were days of imprisonment for debt, by which a bankrupt might be deprived of the power of recovering himself. " He who is unable to pay his debts at once," wrote Foe, " may yet be able to pay them at leisure ; and you should not meanwhile murder him by law, for such is perpetual imprisonment." To avoid an obdurate creditor until a composition had been made, Defoe went to Bristol, where he was known as " the Sunday gentleman," for being abroad only on the day when he was free from arrest. He lodged at the Red Lion in Castle Street, and it was at this time that he wrote his " Essay on Projects," which was first printed in 1697. In this volume, the first of his earlier works which is a bound book, the writer's genius pours out suggestion after suggestion for the common good. There is in it a quickness of invention that again and again runs in advance of the day when it is written, to walk abreast with men of the generations yet unborn.

His debts having been at last reduced, by composition with his creditors, to five thousand pounds, Daniel Foe in 1694 was free again to earn, and turned all that was outside the composition into debt of honour. In 1705 he told a noble lord, who reproached him with being mercenary, that "with a numerous family, and no help but his own industry, he had forced his way with undiscouraged diligence through a sea of misfortunes, and reduced his debts, exclusive of composition, from seventeen thousand to less than five thousand pounds." We have evidence to the same effect from an adversary, John Tutchin, who said in "A Dialogue between a Dissenter and the Observator," published in 1702, "I must do one piece of justice to the man, though I love him no better than you do : it is this—that meeting a gentleman in a coffee-house, when I and everybody else were railing at him, the gentleman took us up with this short speech, 'Gentlemen,' said he, 'I know this De Foe as well as any of you, for I was one of his creditors, compounded with him, and discharged him fully. Several years afterwards he sent for me, and though he was clearly discharged, he paid me all the remainder of his debt, voluntarily and of his own accord ; and he told me that, as far as God should enable him, he intended to do so with everybody. When he had done, he desired me to set my hand to a paper to acknowledge it, which I readily did, and found a great many names to the paper before me ; and I think myself bound to own it, though I am no friend to the book he wrote no more than you.'" The book here referred to was his famous " Shortest Way with the Dissenters," which will be found in later pages of the present volume.

In 1694, when Daniel Foe began the world again, he did not return to Freeman's Court, and he did not accept friendly offers that were made to him of very good commissions from foreign merchants with whom he had corresponded, if he would settle at Cadiz. He attached himself to works at Tilbury for the manufacture of Dutch tiles. The accession of William III. had brought the use of Dutch tiles into fashion, and it was a profitable speculation to provide a supply of them within easy reach of the London builders, who would otherwise have gone to Holland for them. Defoe became sole owner of these Pantile Works, and their success enabled him to proceed, as he did, towards the full payment of his creditors.

His strong interest in the maintenance of the settlement of the Revolution caused Daniel Foe also "to be concerned," as he said afterwards, "with some eminent persons at home in proposing ways and means to the Government for raising money to supply the occasions of the war," then newly begun. He published a tract in 1694, called "The Englishman's Choice and True Interest: in the Vigorous Prosecution of the War against France, and serving King William and Queen Mary, and Acknowledging their Right."

When an excise duty was put upon glass as a way of raising money for the war, Daniel Foe, who had advised it, was, as he says, "without the least application of mine, and being then seventy miles from London, sent for to be accountant to the Commissioners of the Glass Duty, in which service I continued to the determination of their Commission." The first imposition of this duty was in 1605; the Commission came to an end by the repeal of the duty by Acts passed in 1688 and 1699, after which it was not re-established until 1745, from which date it remained in force till 1845.

In 1697, when thus in service of the Government, and owner of the prosperous Pantile Works at Tilbury, Defoe published his first actual book—not pamphlet—the "Essay on Projects," which he had written in the days of his trouble, when he was the "Sunday gentleman" at Bristol. Here the book is:—

A N

# E S S A Y

U P O N

## Projects.

*L O N D O N:*

Printed by *R. R.* for *Tho. Cockerill,* at
the Corner of *Warwick-Lane,* near
*Pater-noster-Row.* MDCXCVII.

# PREFACE

## DALBY THOMAS, Esq.,

*One of the Commissioners for Managing His Majesty's
Duties on Glass. &c.*[1]

SIR,

THIS preface comes directed to you, not as Commissioner,
&c., under whom I have the honour to serve His Majesty;
nor as a friend, though I have great obligations of that sort also;
but as the most proper judge of the subjects treated of, and more
capable than the greatest part of mankind to distinguish and
understand them.

Books are useful only to such whose genius are suitable to the
subject of them; and to dedicate a book of projects to a person
who had never concerned himself to think that way, would be
like music to one that has no ear.

And yet your having a capacity to judge of these things no way
brings you under the despicable title of a projector, any more than
knowing the practices and subtleties of wicked men makes a man
guilty of their crimes.

The several chapters of this book are the results of particular
thoughts, occasioned by conversing with the public affairs during
the present war with France. The losses and casualties which
attend all trading nations in the world, when involved in so cruel
a war as this, have reached us all, and I am none of the least
sufferers. If this has put me, as well as others, on inventions and
projects, so much the subject of this book, it is no more than a
proof of the reason I give for the general projecting humour of
the nation.

[1] He was a great West India merchant.

One unhappiness I lie under in the following book, viz., that having kept the greatest part of it by me for near five years, several of the thoughts seem to be hit by other hands, and some by the public; which turns the tables upon me, as if I had borrowed from them.

As particularly that of the seamen, which you know well I had contrived long before the Act for registering seamen was proposed; and that of educating women, which I think myself bound to declare was formed long before the book called "Advice to the Ladies" was made public. And yet I do not write this to magnify my own invention, but to acquit myself from grafting on other people's thoughts. If I have trespassed upon any person in the world, it is upon yourself, from whom I had some of the notions about county banks and factories for goods, in the chapter of Banks; and yet I do not think that my proposal for the women or the seamen clashes at all either with that book or the public method of registering seamen.

I have been told since this was done, that my proposal for a Commission of Inquiries into Bankrupt Estates is borrowed from the Dutch. If there is anything like it among the Dutch, it is more than ever I knew, or know yet; but if so, I hope it is no objection against our having the same here, especially if it be true that it would be so publicly beneficial as is expressed.

What is said of friendly societies I think no man will dispute with me, since one has met with so much success already in the practice of it, I mean, the Friendly Society for Widows, of which you have been pleased to be a governor.

Friendly societies are very extensive, and, as I have hinted, might be carried on to many particulars. I have omitted one which was mentioned in discourse with yourself, where a hundred tradesmen, all of several trades, agree together to buy whatever they want of one another, and nowhere else, prices and payments to be settled among themselves; whereby every man is sure to have ninety-nine customers, and can never want a trade: and I could have filled up the book with instances of like nature, but I never designed to tire the reader with particulars.

The proposal of the pension-office you will soon see offered to the public, as an attempt for the relief of the poor; which, if it meets with encouragement, will every way answer all the great things I have said of it.

I had wrote a great many sheets about the coin, about bringing in plate to the Mint, and about our standard; but so many great heads being upon it, with some of whom my opinion does not agree, I would not venture to appear in print upon that subject.

Ways and Means also I have laid by on the same score; only adhering to this one point, that be it by taxing the wares they sell, be it by taxing them in stock, be it by composition, which, by the way, I believe is the best; be it by what way soever the Parliament please, the retailers are the men who seem to call upon us to be taxed, if not by their own extraordinary good circumstances, though that might bear it, yet by the contrary in all other degrees of the kingdom.

Besides, the retailers are the only men who could pay it with least damage, because it is in their power to levy it again upon their customers in the prices of their goods, and is no more than paying a higher rent for their shops.

The retailers of manufactures, especially so far as relates to the inland trade, have never been taxed yet, and their wealth or number is not easily calculated; trade and land has been handled roughly enough; and these are the men who now lie as a reserve to carry on the burden of the war.

These are the men who, were the land-tax collected as it should be, ought to pay the King more than that whole bill ever produced; and yet these are the men who, I think I may venture to say, do not pay a twentieth part in that bill.

Should the King appoint a survey over the assessors, and indict all those who were found faulty, allowing a reward to any discoverer of an assessment made lower than the literal sense of the Act implies, what a register of frauds and connivances would be found out!

In a general tax, if any should be excused, it should be the poor, who are not able to pay, or at least are pinched in the necessary parts of life by paying; and yet here a poor labourer, who works for twelve-pence or eighteen-pence a day, does not drink a pot of beer but pays the King a tenth part for excise; and really pays more to the King's taxes in a year than a country shop-keeper, who is alderman of the town, worth perhaps two or three thousand pounds, brews his own beer, pays no excise, and in the land-tax is rated it may be at £100, and pays £1, 4s. per annum, but ought, if the Act were put in due execution, to pay £36 per annum to the King.

If I were to be asked how I would remedy? I would answer, It should be by some method in which every man may be taxed in due proportion to his estate, and the Act put in execution according to the true intent and meaning of it; in order to which a Commission of Assessment should be granted to twelve men, such as His Majesty should be well satisfied of, who should go through the whole kingdom, three in a body, and should make a new assessment of personal estates, not to meddle with land.

To these assessors should all the old rates, parish-books, poor-rates, and highway rates also be delivered; and upon due inquiry to be made into the manner of living and reputed wealth of the people, the stock or personal estate of every man should be assessed, without connivance; and he who is reputed to be worth a thousand pounds, should be taxed at a thousand pounds, and so on; and he who was an overgrown rich tradesman of twenty or thirty thousand pounds estate, should be taxed so, and plain English and plain dealing be practised indifferently throughout the kingdom. Tradesmen and landed men should have neigh-bours' fare, as we call it; and a rich man should not be passed by when a poor man pays.

We read of the inhabitants of Constantinople that they suf-fered their city to be lost for want of contributing in time for its defence, and pleaded poverty to their generous Emperor when he went from house to house to persuade them; and yet when the Turks took it, the prodigious, immense wealth they found in it made them wonder at the sordid temper of the citizens.

England (with due exceptions to the Parliament and the freedom wherewith they have given to the public charge) is much like Constantinople. We are involved in a dangerous, a chargeable, but withal a most just and necessary war, and the richest and moneyed men in the kingdom plead poverty, and the French, or King James, or the devil may come, for them, if they can but conceal their estates from the public notice, and get the assessors to tax them at an under-rate.

These are the men this Commission would discover, and here they should find men taxed at £500 stock who are worth £20,000. Here they should find a certain rich man, near Hackney, rated to-day in the tax-book at £1000 stock, and to-morrow offering £27,000 for an estate.

Here they should find Sir Josiah Child perhaps taxed to the King at £5000 stock, perhaps not so much, whose cash no man can guess at. And multitudes of instances I could give by name without wrong to the gentlemen.

And not to run on in particulars, I affirm that in the land-tax ten certain gentlemen in London put together did not pay for half so much personal estate called stock as the poorest of them is reputed really to possess.

I do not inquire at whose door this fraud must lie; it is none of my business. I wish they would search into it whose power can punish it. But this with submission I presume to say: the King is thereby defrauded and horribly abused, the true intent and meaning of Acts of Parliament evaded, the nation involved in debt by fatal deficiencies and interests, fellow-subjects abused, and new inventions for taxes occasioned.

The last chapter in this book is a proposal about entering all the seamen in England into the King's pay, a subject which deserves to be enlarged into a book itself, and I have a little volume of calculations and particulars by me on that head, but I thought them too long to publish. In short, I am persuaded were that method proposed to those gentlemen to whom such things belong, the greatest sum of money might be raised by it with the least injury to those who pay it that ever was or will be during the war.

Projectors, they say, are generally to be taken with allowance of one half at least; they always have their mouths full of millions, and talk big of their own proposals, and therefore I have not exposed the vast sums my calculations amount to; but I venture to say I could procure a farm on such a proposal as this at three millions per annum, and give very good security for payment. Such an opinion I have of the value of such a method, and when that is done the nation would get three more by paying it, which is very strange, but might easily be made out.

In the chapter of Academies I have ventured to reprove the vicious custom of swearing. I shall make no apology for the fact, for no man ought to be ashamed of exposing what all men ought to be ashamed of practising. But methinks I stand corrected by my own laws a little in forcing the reader to repeat some of the worst of our vulgar imprecations in reading my thoughts against it, to which, however, I have this to reply :—

First, I did not find it easy to express what I mean without putting down the very words, at least not so as to be very intelligible.

Secondly, why should words repeated only to expose the vice taint the reader more than a sermon preached against lewdness should the assembly? for of necessity it leads the hearer to the thoughts of the fact ; but the morality of every action lies in the end, and if the reader by ill use renders himself guilty of the fact in reading which I designed to expose by writing, the fault is his, not mine.

I have endeavoured everywhere in this book to be as concise as possible, except where calculations obliged me to be particular, and having avoided impertinence in the book, I would avoid it too in the preface, and therefore shall break off with subscribing myself,

> Sir,
>
> > Your most obliged humble Servant,
> >
> > > D. F.

# INTRODUCTION.

NECESSITY, which is allowed to be the mother of invention, has so violently agitated the wits of men at this time, that it seems not at all improper, by way of distinction, to call it the Projecting Age. For though in times of war and public confusions the like humour of invention has seemed to stir, yet, without being partial to the present, it is, I think, no injury to say the past ages have never come up to the degree of projecting and inventing, as it refers to matters of negoce and methods of civil polity, which we see this age arrived to.

Nor is it a hard matter to assign probable causes of the perfection in this modern art. I am not of their melancholy opinion who ascribe it to the general poverty of the nation, since I believe it is easy to prove the nation itself, taking it as one general stock, is not at all diminished or impoverished by this long, this chargeable war, but, on the contrary, was never richer since it was inhabited.

Nor am I absolutely of the opinion that we are so happy as to be wiser in this age than our forefathers, though at the same time, I must own, some parts of knowledge in science as well as art have received improvements in this age altogether concealed from the former.

The art of war, which I take to be the highest perfection of human knowledge, is a sufficient proof of what I say, especially in conducting armies and in offensive engines. Witness the new ways of mines, fougades, entrenchments, attacks, lodgments, and a long *et cetera* of new inventions which want names, practised in sieges and encampments; witness the new sorts of bombs and

unheard-of mortars of seven to ten ton weight, with which our
fleets, standing two or three miles off at sea, can imitate God
Almighty Himself, and rain fire and brimstone out of heaven,
as it were, upon towns built on the firm land; witness also our
new-invented Child of Hell, the machine which carries thunder,
lightning, and earthquakes in its bowels, and tears up the most
impregnable fortifications.

But if I would search for a cause from whence it comes to
pass that this age swarms with such a multitude of projectors
more than usual, who, besides the innumerable conceptions which
die in the bringing forth, and (like abortions of the brain) only
come into the air and dissolve, do really every day produce new
contrivances, engines, and projects to get money, never before
thought of,—if, I say, I would exar      whence this comes to pass,
it must be thus :—

The losses and depredations which this war brought with it at
first were exceeding many, suffered chiefly by the ill conduct of
merchants themselves, who did not apprehend the danger to be
really what it was; for before our Admiralty could possibly settle
convoys, cruisers, and stations for men-of-war all over the world,
the French covered the sea with their privateers, and took an
incredible number of our ships.   I have heard the loss computed
by those who pretended they were able to guess, at about fifteen
millions of pounds sterling, in ships and goods, in the first two
or three years of the war, a sum which, if put into French, would
make such a rumbling sound of great numbers as would fright a
weak accomptant out of his belief, being no less than one hundred
and ninety millions of livres.   The weight of this loss fell chiefly
on the trading part of the nation, and amongst them, on the
merchants; and amongst them, again, upon the most refined
capacities, as the insurers, &c. ; and an incredible number of the
best merchants in the kingdom sunk under the load, as may
appear a little by a bill which once passed the House of Commons for the relief of merchant insurers who had suffered by the
war with France.  If a great many fell, much greater were the
number of those who felt a sensible ebb of their fortunes, and

with difficulty bore up under the loss of great part of their estates. These, prompted by necessity, rack their wits for new contrivances, new inventions, new trades, stocks, projects, and anything to retrieve the desperate credit of their fortunes. That this is probable to be the cause will appear further thus :—France, though I do not believe all the great outcries we make of their misery and distress, if one half of which be true, they are certainly the best subjects in the world, yet, without question, has felt its share of the losses and damages of the war ; but the poverty there falling chiefly on the poorer sort of people, they have not been so fruitful in inventions and practices of this nature, their genius being quite of another strain. As for the gentry and more capable sort, the first thing a Frenchman flies to in his distress is the army ; and he seldom cc·  ·back from thence to get an estate by painful industry, but either has his brains knocked out or makes his fortune there.

If industry be in any business rewarded with success, it is in the merchandising part of the world, who, indeed, may more truly be said to live by their wits than any people whatsoever. All foreign negoce, though to some it is a plain road by the help of custom, yet it is in its beginning all project, contrivance, and invention. Every new voyage the merchant contrives is a project, and ships are sent from port to port, as markets and merchandises differ, by the help of strange and universal intelligence, wherein some are so exquisite, so swift, and so exact, that a merchant sitting at home in his counting-house at once converses with all parts of the known world. This, and travel, make a true-bred merchant the most intelligent man in the world, and consequently the most capable when urged by necessity to contrive new ways to live ; and from hence, I humbly conceive, may very properly be derived the projects so much the subject of the present discourse. And to this sort of men it is easy to trace the original of banks, stocks, stock-jobbing, assurances, friendly societies, lotteries, and the like.

To this may be added the long annual inquiry of the House of Commons for Ways and Means, which has been a particular movement to set all the heads of the nation at work, and I appeal with submission to the gentlemen of that Honourable House if the greatest part of all the Ways and Means, out of the common road of land-taxes, polls, and the like, have not been handed to them from the merchant, and in a great measure paid by them too.

However, I offer this but as an essay at the original of this prevailing humour of the people; and as it is probable, so it is also possible to be otherwise, which I submit to future demonstration.

Of the several ways this faculty of projecting has exerted itself, and of the various methods, as the genius of the authors has inclined, I have been a diligent observer, and in most an unconcerned spectator; and perhaps have some advantage from thence more easily to discover the *faux pas* of the actors. If I have given an essay towards anything new, or made discovery to advantage of any contrivance now on foot, all men are at the liberty to make use of the improvement: if any fraud is discovered, as now practised, it is without any particular reflection upon parties or persons.

Projects of the nature I treat about are, doubtless, in general of public advantage, as they tend to improvement of trade, and employment of the poor, and the circulation and increase of the public stock of the kingdom; but this is supposed of such as are built on the honest basis of ingenuity and improvement, in which, though I will allow the author to aim primarily at his own advantage, yet with the circumstances of public benefit added.

Wherefore it is necessary to distinguish among the projects of the present times between the honest and the dishonest.

There are, and that too many, fair pretences of fine discoveries, new inventions, engines, and I know not what, which, being advanced in notion, and talked up to great things to be performed when such and such sums of money shall be advanced and such and such engines are made, have raised the fancies of credulous people to such a height, that merely on the shadow of expectation they have formed companies, chose committees, appointed officers, shares, and books, raised great stocks, and cried up an empty notion to that degree that people have been betrayed to part with their money for shares in a new-nothing; and when the inventors have carried on the jest till they have sold all their own interest, they leave the cloud to vanish of itself, and the poor purchasers to quarrel with one another, and go to law about settlements, transferrings, and some bone or other thrown among them by the subtlety of the author, to lay the blame of the miscarriage upon themselves. Thus the shares at first begin to fall by degrees, and happy is he that sells in time, till like brass money it will go at last for nothing at all. So have I seen shares in joint-stocks, patents, engines, and undertakings blown up by the air of great words, and the name of some man of credit concerned, to £100 for a 500th part or share, some more, and at last dwindle away till it has been stock-jobbed down to £12, £10, £9, £8, a share, and at last no buyer; that is, in short, the fine new word for nothing-worth, and many families ruined by the purchase. If I should name linen manufactures, saltpetreworks, copper-mines, diving-engines, dipping, and the like, for instances of this, I should, I believe, do no wrong to truth, or to some persons too visibly guilty.

I might go on upon this subject to expose the frauds and tricks of stockbrokers, engineers, patentees, committees, with those Exchange mountebanks we very properly call brokers; but I have not gall enough for such a work; but as a general rule of caution to those who would not be tricked out of their estates by such pretenders to new inventions, let them observe that all such people who may be suspected of design have assuredly this in their proposal, your money to the author must go before the experiment. And here I could give a very diverting history of a patent-monger whose cully was nobody but myself, but I refer it to another occasion.

But this is no reason why invention upon honest foundations and to fair purposes should not be encouraged; no, nor why the author of any such fair contrivances should not reap the harvest of his own ingenuity. Our Acts of Parliament for granting patents to first inventors for fourteen years is a sufficient acknowledgment of the due regard which ought to be had to such as find out anything which may be of public advantage. New discoveries in trade, in arts and mysteries, of manufacturing goods, or improvement of land are, without question, of as great benefit as any discoveries made in the works of Nature by all the Academies and Royal Societies in the world.

There is, it is true, a great difference between new inventions and projects, between improvement of manufactures or lands, which tend to the immediate benefit of the public and employing of the poor, and projects framed by subtle heads, with a sort a *deceptio visus* and legerdemain, to bring people to run needless and unusual hazards. I grant it, and give a due preference to the first, and yet success has so sanctified some of those other sorts of projects, that it would be a kind of blasphemy against fortune to disallow them: witness Sir William Phipps' voyage to the wreck; it was a mere project, a lottery of a hundred thousand to one odds; a hazard which, if it had failed, everybody would have been ashamed to have owned themselves concerned in, a voyage that would have been as much ridiculed as Don Quixote's adventure upon the windmill. Bless us! that folks should go three thousand miles to angle in the open sea for pieces of eight! Why, they would have made ballads of it, and the merchants would have said of every unlikely adventure, "It was like Phipps's wreck-voyage." But it had success, and who reflects upon the project?

> Nothing is so partial as the laws of fate,
> Erecting blockheads to suppress the great.
> Sir Francis Drake the Spanish plate-fleet won,
> He had been a pirate if he had got none.
> Sir Walter Raleigh strove, but missed the plate,
> And therefore died a traitor to the state.
>
> Endeavour bears a value more or less,
> Just as 'tis recommended by success:
> The lucky coxcomb every man will prize,
> And prosperous actions always pass for wise.

However, this sort of projects comes under no reflection as to their honesty, save that there is a kind of honesty a man owes to himself and to his family that prohibits him throwing away his estate in impracticable, improbable adventures. But still some hit, even of the most unlikely, of which this was one of Sir William Phipps, who brought home a cargo of silver of near £200,000 sterling in pieces of eight, fished up out of the open sea, remote from any shore, from an old Spanish ship which had been sunk above forty years.

# THE
# HISTORY OF PROJECTS.

—⊷—

WHEN I speak of writing a history of projects, I do not mean either of the introduction of, or continuing necessary inventions, or the improvement of arts and sciences before known; but a short account of projects and projecting, as the word is allowed in the general acceptation at this present time, and I need not go far back for the original of the practice.

Invention of arts with engines and handicraft instruments for their improvement requires a chronology as far back as the eldest son of Adam, and has to this day afforded some new discovery in every age.

The building of the ark by Noah, so far as you will allow it a human work, was the first project I read of; and no question seemed so ridiculous to the graver heads of that wise though wicked age, that poor Noah was sufficiently bantered for it; and had he not been set on work by a very peculiar direction from Heaven, the good old man would certainly have been laughed out of it, as a most senseless, ridiculous project.

The building of Babel was a right project; for indeed the true definition of a project, according to modern acceptation, is, as is said before, a vast undertaking too big to be managed, and therefore likely enough to come to nothing; and yet, as great as they are, it is certainly true of them all, even as the projectors propose, that, according to the old tale, if so many eggs are hatched, there will be so many chickens, and those chickens may lay so many eggs more, and those eggs produce so many chickens more, and so on. Thus it was most certainly true that if the people of the old world could have built a house up to heaven, they should never be drowned again on earth, and they only had forgot to measure the height; that is, as in other projects, it only miscarried, or else it would have succeeded.

And yet, when all is done, that very building, and the incredible height it was carried, is a demonstration of the vast knowledge of that infant age of the world, who had no advantage of the experiments or invention of any before themselves.

> Thus when our fathers, touched with guilt,
> That huge stupendous staircase built,
> We mock indeed the fruitless enterprise,
> For fruitless actions seldom pass for wise;
> But were the mighty ruins left, they'd show
> To what degree that untaught age did know.

I believe a very diverting account might be given of this, but I shall not attempt it. Some are apt to say with Solomon, "No new thing happens under the sun; but what is, has been;" yet I make no question but some considerable discovery has been made in these latter ages, and inventions of human original produced, which the world was ever without before, either in whole or in part; and I refer only to two cardinal points—the use of the loadstone at sea and the use of gunpowder and guns; both which, as to the inventing part, I believe the world owes as absolutely to those particular ages as it does the working in brass and iron to Tubal Cain, or the inventing of music to Jubal, his brother. As to engines and instruments for handicraft men, this age, I dare say, can show such as never were so much as thought of, much less imitated, before; for I do not call that a real invention which has something before done like it: I account that more properly an improvement. For handicraft instruments I know none owes more to true genuine contrivance, without borrowing from any further use, than a mechanic engine contrived in our time called a knitting-frame, which, built with admirable symmetry, works really with a very happy success, and may be observed by the curious to have a more than ordinary composition; for which I refer to the engine itself, to be seen in every stocking-weaver's garret.

I shall trace the original of the projecting humour that now reigns no farther back than the year 1680, dating its birth as a monster then, though by times it had indeed something of life in the time of the late civil war. I allow no age has been altogether without something of this nature, and some very happy projects are left to us as a taste of their success, as the water-houses for supplying of the City of London with water, and since that the New River, both very considerable undertakings and perfect projects, adventured on the risk of success. In the reign of King Charles the First infinite projects were set on foot for raising money without a Parliament, oppressing by monopolies and Privy Seals; but these are excluded our scheme as irregularities, for thus the French are as fruitful in projects as we, and these are rather stratagems than projects. After the Fire of London, the contrivance of an engine to quench fires was a project the author was said to get well by, and we have found to be very useful. But about the year 1680 began the art and mystery of projecting to creep into the world. Prince Rupert,[1] uncle to King Charles the Second, gave great encouragement to that part of it that respects engines and mechanical motions, and Bishop Wilkins[2] added as much of the theory to it as writing a

---

[1] Prince Rupert of Bavaria, grandson of James I. by his daughter Elizabeth, who married Frederick the Elector Palatine, came to England in 1642 and served in the Civil War till his dismissal after the surrender of Bristol to General Fairfax. He served at sea after the Restoration; and after the close of war with the Dutch devoted himself wholly to science until his death in 1682. He was one of the first Fellows of the Royal Society and an active member of the Board of Trade. He was one of the first who engraved in mezzotint, and his old interest in munitions of war caused him to improve the making of gunpowder and to invent the gun-metal referred to in the text. It was named after its inventor " Prince's Metal."

[2] John Wilkins, who was born in 1614, and died in 1672, four years after he had been made Bishop of Chester, was the son of Walter Wilkins, citizen and gold-smith. He was Warden of Wadham College when he married Oliver Cromwell's sister Robina. He was one of the most ingenious men of the time. His house was like a museum from the front door to the top. John Evelyn spoke of him as

book could do. The Prince has left us a metal called by his name; and the first project upon that was, as I remember, casting of guns of that metal, and boring them, done both by a peculiar method of his own, and which died with him, to the great loss of the undertaker, who to that purpose had, with no small charge, erected a water-mill at Hackney Marsh, known by the name of the Temple Mill, which mill very happily performed all parts of the work; and I have seen of those guns on board the *Royal Charles*, a first-rate ship, being of a reddish colour, different either from brass or copper. I have heard some reasons of state assigned why that project was not permitted to go forward, but I omit them, because I have no good authority for it. After this we saw a floating machine, to be wrought with horses, for the towing of great ships both against wind and tide; and another for the raising of ballast, which, as unperforming engines, had the honour of being made, exposed, tried, and laid by before the Prince died.

If thus we introduce it into the world under the conduct of that Prince, when he died it was left a hopeless brat, and had hardly any hand to own it, till the wreck-voyage before noted, performed so happily by Captain Phipps, afterwards Sir William, whose strange performance set a great many heads at work to

that most obliging and universally curious Dr. Wilkins, who had wonderful trans-parent apiaries; a hollow statue which spoke through a concealed tube; also "a variety of shadows, dials, perspectives, and many other artificial, mathematical, and magical curiosities." As a young man Wilkins wrote, in 1638, a "Discourse tend-ing to prove that 'tis probable there may be another Habitable World in the Moon," and he was not afraid to suggest that "'tis possible for some of our pos-terity to find out a conveyance to this other world; and if there be inhabitants there to have commerce with them." He published in 1641 a book called "Mer-cury, or the Secret and Swift Messenger: shewing how a man may with Privacy and Speed Communicate his Thoughts to a Friend at any Distance." His most famous book is a folio in which he set forward his Project for a Universal Lan-guage; this was published in 1668 as "An Essay towards a Real Character and and a Philosophical Character." The projects of his to which Defoe is here refer-ring will be found in a volume which he entitled "Mathematical Magick," first printed while he was at Oxford, and republished in 1680. It abounds in sugges-tions of what may be achieved by applied mathematics in the way of mechanical motion, including a sailing chariot to be driven by the wind, and a submarine vessel to make voyages under water, exempt from storms that vex the surface.

contrive something for themselves. He was immediately followed by my Lord Mordant, Sir John Narborough, and others from several parts, whose success made them soon weary of the work.

The project of the penny-post, so well known and still prac-tised, I cannot omit, nor the contriver, Mr. Dockwray,[1] who has had the honour to have the injury done him in that affair repaired in some measure by the public justice of the Parliament. And the experiment proving it to be a noble and useful design, the author must be remembered wherever mention is made of that affair, to his very great reputation.

It was no question a great hardship for a man to be master of so fine a thought, that had both the essential ends of a project in it—public good and private advantage—and that the public should reap the benefit and the author be left out, the injustice of which, no doubt, discouraged many a good design; but since an alteration in public circumstances has recovered the lost attri-bute of justice, the like is not to be feared. And Mr. Dockwray has had the satisfaction to see the former injury disowned, and an honourable return made even by them who did not the injury, in bare respect to his ingenuity.

A while before this several people, under the patronage of some great persons, had engaged in planting of foreign colonies, as William Penn, the Lord Shaftesbury, Dr. Cox, and others, in Penn-sylvania, Carolina, East and West Jersey, and the like places, which I do not call projects, because it was only prosecuting what had been formerly begun. But here begins the forming of public

---

[1] This penny-post was a private speculation for the conveyance of letters and parcels, not above one pound in weight, between different parts of the city for a penny, and of the suburbs for twopence within a ten mile radius. Then, as now, the postal service at large was in the hands of the Government. The projector of this penny-post was Robert Murray, an upholsterer, who made over the right of working it to Mr. William Dockwray. It was started in 1683, with six large offices in the city and a receiving house in each of the principal streets; but as the revenues of the Post-Office were settled on the Duke of York, a suit in the Court of King's Bench deprived Mr. Dockwray of the benefit of his enterprise. It was annexed to the crown, and became the foundation of the London District Post. Amends were made to Dockwray in 1690 by a pension of £500 a year for seven years, renewed by a new patent in 1697, when he was also appointed Comptroller of the Penny-Post. So matters stood when Defoe's Essay appeared.

joint-stocks, which, together, with the East India, African, and Hudson Bay Companies, before established, begot a new trade, which we call by a new name, stock-jobbing, which was at first only the simple occasional transferring of interest and shares from one to another, as persons alienated their estates; but by the industry of the Exchange brokers, who got the business into their hands, it became a trade, and one, perhaps, managed with the greatest intrigue, artifice, and trick that ever anything that appeared with a face of honesty could be handled with; for while the brokers held the box, they made the whole Exchange the gamesters, and raised and lowered the prices of stocks as they pleased, and always had both buyers and sellers who stood ready innocently to commit their money to the mercy of their mercenary tongues. This upstart of a trade having tasted the sweetness of success which generally attends a novel proposal, introduces the illegitimate wandering object I speak of as a proper engine to find work for the brokers. Thus stock-jobbing nursed projecting, and projecting in return has very diligently pimped for its foster-parent, till both are arrived to be public grievances, and indeed are now almost grown scandalous.

AN

# ESSAY ON PROJECTS.

— ᛭ —

## OF PROJECTORS.

MAN is the worst of all God's creatures to shift for himself. No other animal is ever starved to death. Nature without has provided them both food and clothes, and Nature within has placed an instinct that never fails to direct them to proper means for a supply; but man must either work or starve, slave or die. He has indeed reason given him to direct him, and few who follow the dictates of that reason come to such unhappy exigencies; but when, by the errors of a man's youth, he has reduced himself to such a degree of distress as to be absolutely without three things, money, friends, and health, he dies in a ditch, or in some worse place—an hospital.

Ten thousand ways there are to bring a man to this, and but very few to bring him out again.

Death is the universal deliverer, and therefore some who want courage to bear what they see before them hang themselves for fear; for certainly self-destruction is the effect of cowardice in the highest extreme.

Others break the bounds of laws to satisfy that general law of Nature, and turn open thieves, housebreakers, highwaymen, clippers, coiners, &c., till they run the length of the gallows, and get a deliverance the nearest way at St. Tyburn.

Others, being masters of more cunning than their neighbours, turn their thoughts to private methods of trick and cheat, a modern way of thieving, every jot as criminal, and in some degree worse than the other, by which honest men are gulled with fair pretences to part from their money, and then left to take their course with the author, who skulks behind the curtain of a protection, or in the Mint or Friars, and bids defiance as well to honesty as the law.

Others, yet urged by the same necessity, turn their thoughts to honest invention, founded upon the platform of ingenuity and integrity.

These two last sorts are those we call projectors; and as there are always more geese than swans, the number of the latter are very inconsiderable in comparison of the former; and as the greater number denominates the less, the just contempt we have of the former sort bespatters the other, who, like cuckolds, bear reproach of other people's crimes.

A mere projector, then, is a contemptible thing, driven by his own desperate fortune to such a strait that he must be delivered by a miracle or starve; and when he has beat his brains for some such miracle in vain, he finds no remedy but to paint up some bauble or other, as players make puppets talk big, to show like a strange thing, and then cry it up for a new invention; gets a patent for it, divides it into shares, and they must be sold. Ways and means are not wanting to swell the new whim to a vast magnitude. Thousands and hundreds of thousands are the least of his discourse, and sometimes millions, till the ambition of some honest coxcomb is wheedled to part with his money for it, and then

" . . . nascitur ridiculus mus,"

the adventurer is left to carry on the project, and the projector laughs at him. The diver shall walk at the bottom of the Thames; the saltpetre-maker shall build Tom Turd's Pond into houses; the engineers build models and windmills to draw water, till funds are raised to carry it on by men who have more money than brains, and then good-night patent and invention. The projector has done his business and is gone.

But the honest projector is he who, having by fair and plain principles of sense, honesty, and ingenuity brought any contrivance to a suitable perfection, makes out what he pretends to, picks nobody's pocket, puts his project into execution, and contents himself with the real produce as the profit of his invention.

# OF BANKS.

BANKS, without question, if rightly managed, are, or may be, of great advantage, especially to a trading people, as the English are; and among many others, this is one particular case in which that benefit appears, that they bring down the interest of money, and take from the goldsmiths, scriveners, and others, who have command of running cash, their most delicious trade of taking advantage of the necessities of the merchant in extravagant discounts and premiums for advance of money when either large customs or foreign remittances call for disbursements beyond his common ability; for by the easiness of terms on which the merchant may have money, he is encouraged to venture farther in trade than otherwise he would do. Not but that there are other great advantages a Royal Bank might procure in this kingdom, as has been seen in part by this, as advancing money to the Exchequer upon Parliamentary funds and securities, by which in time of a war our preparation for any expedition need not be in any danger of miscarriage for want of money, though the taxes raised be not speedily paid, nor the Exchequer burdened with the excessive interest paid in former reigns upon anticipations of the revenue. Landed men might be supplied with moneys upon securities on easier terms, which would prevent the loss of multitudes of estates now ruined and devoured by insolent and merciless mortgagees and the like. But now we unhappily see a Royal Bank established by Act of Parliament, and another with a large fund upon the Orphan Stock, and yet these advantages, or others which we expected, not answered, though the pretensions in both have not been wanting at such times as they find it needful to introduce themselves into public esteem, by giving out prints of what they were rather able to do than really intended to practise. So that our having two banks at this time settled, and more erecting, has not yet been able to reduce the interest of money, not because the nature and foundation of their constitution does not tend towards it, but because, finding their hands full of better business, they are wiser than, by being slaves to old obsolete pro- posals, to lose the advantage of the great improvement they can make of their stock.

This, however, does not at all reflect on the nature of a bank, nor of the benefit it would be to the public trading part of the kingdom, whatever it may seem to do on the practice of the present. We find four or five banks now in view to be settled. I confess I expect no more from those to come than we have found from the past; and I think I make no breach on either my charity or good manners in saying so; and I reflect not upon any of the banks that are or shall be established for not doing what I mention, but for making such publications of what they would do. I cannot think any man had expected the Royal Bank should lend money on mortgages at 4 per cent., nor was it much the better for them to make publication they would do so from the beginning of January next after their settlement, since to this day, as I am informed, they have not lent one farthing in that manner.

Our banks are indeed nothing but so many goldsmiths' shops, where the credit being high (and the directors as high), people lodge their money; and they, the directors I mean, make their advantage of it. If you lay it at demand, they allow you nothing; if at time, 3 per cent., and so would any goldsmith in Lombard Street have done before; but the very banks themselves are so awkward in lending, so strict, so tedious, so inquisitive, and withal so public in their taking securities, that men who are anything tender won't go to them; and so the easiness of borrowing money, so much designed, is defeated; for here is a private interest to be made, though it be a public one; and, in short, it is only a great trade carried on for the private gain of a few concerned in the original stock; and though we are to hope for great things because they have promised them, yet they are all future that we know of.

And yet all this while a bank might be very beneficial to this kingdom; and this might be so if either their own ingenuity or public authority would oblige them to take the public good into equal concern with their private interest.

To explain what I mean :—Banks being established by public authority, ought also, as all public things are, to be under limitations and restrictions from that authority; and those limitations being regulated with a proper regard to the ease of trade in general, and the improvement of the stock in particular, would make a bank a useful, profitable thing indeed.

First, a bank ought to be of a magnitude proportioned to the trade of the country it is in; which this bank is so far from, that it is no more to the whole than the least goldsmith's cash in Lombard Street is to the bank. From whence it comes to pass, that already more banks are contriving; and I question not but banks in London will erelong be as frequent as lotteries. The consequence of which, in all probability, will be the diminishing their reputation, or a civil war with one another. It is true the Bank of England has a capital stock; but yet, were that stock wholly clear of the public concern of the Government, it is not above a fifth part of what would be necessary to manage the whole business of the town; which it ought, though not to do, at least to be able to do. And I suppose I may venture to say above one half of the stock of the present bank is taken up in the affairs of the Exchequer.

I suppose nobody will take this discourse for an invective against the Bank of England. I believe it is a very good fund, a very useful one, and a very profitable one. It has been useful to the Government, and it is profitable to the proprietors; and the establishing it at such a juncture,[1] when our enemies were

---

[1] The Bank of England was first established in 1694, between the date of the first writing and the date of the publication of this " Essay on Projects." Its projector was William Paterson; its charter was dated July 27, 1694; its first capital was £1,200,000, and this was invested in the war as loan at interest to the Government of William and Mary.

making great boasts of our poverty and want of money, was a particular glory to our nation, and the City in particular. That when the *Paris Gazette* informed the world that the Parliament had indeed given the King grants for raising money in funds to be paid in remote years; but money was so scarce that no anticipations could be procured : that just then, besides three millions paid into the Exchequer that spring on other taxes by way of advance, there was an overplus stock to be found of £1,200,000 sterling, or (to make it speak French) of above fifteen millions, which was all paid voluntarily into the Exchequer in less than             Besides this, I believe, the present Bank of England has been very useful to the Exchequer, and to supply the King with remittances for the payment of the army in Flanders; which has also, by the way, been very profitable to itself. But still this bank is not of that bulk that the business done here requires; nor is it able with all the stock it has to procure the great proposed benefit, the lowering the interest of money; whereas all foreign banks absolutely govern the interest, both at Amsterdam, Genoa, and other places. And this defect, I conceive, the multiplicity of banks cannot supply, unless a perfect understanding could be secured between them.

To remedy this defect several methods might be proposed. Some I shall take the freedom to hint at.

First, that the present bank increase their stock to at least five millions sterling, to be settled as they are already, with some small limitations to make the methods more beneficial.

Five millions sterling is an immense sum; to which add the credit of their cash, which would supply them with all the overplus money in the town, and probably might amount to half as much more; and then the credit of running bills, which by circulating would no question be an equivalent to the other half; so that in stock, credit, and bank bills, the balance of their cash would be always ten millions sterling, a sum that everybody who can talk of does not understand.

But then to find business for all this stock, which, though it be a strange thing to think of, is nevertheless easy when it comes to be examined. And first for the business. This bank should enlarge the number of their directors as they do of their stock, and should then establish several sub-committees, composed of their own members, who should have the directing of several offices relating to the distinct sorts of business they referred to ; to be overruled and governed by the Governor and Directors in a body, but to have a conclusive power as to contracts. Of these there should be—

One office for loan of money for customs of goods, which by a plain method might be so ordered that the merchant might with ease pay the highest customs down, and so by allowing the bank 4 per cent. advance, be first sure to secure the £10 per cent. which the King allows for prompt payment at the Custom-house, and be also freed from the troublesome work of finding bondsmen and securities for the money, which has exposed many a man to the tyranny of extents either for himself or his friend, to his utter ruin, who under a more moderate prosecution had been able to pay all his debts, and by this method has been torn to pieces and disabled from making any tolerable proposal to his creditors. This is a scene of large business, and would in proportion employ a large cash. And it is the easiest thing in the world to make the bank the paymaster of all the large customs, and yet the merchant have so honourable a possession of his goods as may be neither any diminution to his reputation or any hindrance to their sale.

As, for example, suppose I have 100 hogsheads of tobacco to import, whose customs by several duties come to £1000, and want cash to clear them. I go with my bill of loading to the bank, who appoint their officer to enter the goods and pay the duties, which goods so entered by the bank shall give them title enough to any part or the whole, without the trouble of bills of sale, or conveyances, defeasances, and the like. The goods are carried to a warehouse at the waterside, where the merchant has a free and public access to them as if in his own warehouse, and an honourable liberty to sell and deliver either the whole (paying their disburse), or a part without it, leaving but sufficient for the payment; and out of that part delivered, either by notes under the hand of the purchaser, or any other way, he may clear the same, without any exactions but of £4 per cent., and the rest are his own.

The ease this would bring to trade, the deliverance it would bring to the merchants from the insults of goldsmiths, &c., and the honour it would give to our management of public imposts, with the advantages to the Custom-house itself and the utter destruction of extortion, would be such as would give a due value to the bank and make all mankind acknowledge it to be a public good. The grievance of exactions upon merchants in this case is very great; and when I lay the blame on the gold-smiths, because they are the principal people made use of on such occasions, I include a great many other sorts of brokers and money-jobbing artists, who all get a snip out of the merchant. I myself have known a goldsmith in Lombard Street lend a man £700 to pay the customs of a hundred pipes of Spanish wines. The wines were made over to him for security by bill of sale, and put into a cellar, of which the goldsmith kept the key; the merchant was to pay £6 per cent. interest on the bond, and to allow £10 per cent. premium for advancing the money. When he had the wines in possession, the owner could not send his cooper to look after them, but the goldsmith's man must attend all the while, for which he would be paid five shillings a day. If he brought a customer to see them, the goldsmith's man must show them. The money was lent for two months; he could not be admitted to sell or deliver a pipe of wine out single, or two or three at a time as he might have sold them; but on a word or two spoken amiss to the goldsmith, or which he was pleased to take so, he would have none sold but the whole parcel together. By this usage the goods lay on hand, and every month the money remained the goldsmith demanded a guinea per cent. forbearance besides the interest, till at last, by leakage, decay, and other accidents, the wines begin to lessen. Then the goldsmith begins to tell the merchant he is afraid the wines are not worth the money he has lent, and demands further security; and in a little while, growing higher and rougher, he tells him he must have his money. The merchant, too much at his mercy because he cannot provide the money, is forced to consent to the sale, and the goods—being reduced to seventy pipes sound wine and four unsound (the rest being sunk for filling up)—were sold for £13 per pipe the sound and £3 the unsound, which amounted to £922 together :—

| | | | |
|---|---|---|---|
| The cooper's bill came to . . . . . | £30 | 0 | 0 |
| The cellarage, a year and a half, to . . . | 18 | 0 | 0 |
| Interest on the bond, to . . . . . | 63 | 0 | 0 |
| The goldsmith's men for attendance. , . | 8 | 0 | 0 |
| Allowance for advance of the money, and forbearance . . . . . . | 74 | 0 | 0 |
| | £193 | 0 | 0 |
| Principal money borrowed . . . | 700 | 0 | 0 |
| | £893 | 0 | 0 |
| Due to the merchant . . . . . . | 29 | 0 | 0 |
| | £922 | 0 | 0 |

By the moderatest computation that can be, these wines cost the merchant as follows :—

### First Cost, with Charges on Board.

| | | | |
|---|---|---|---|
| In Lisbon 15 mille reis per pipe is 1500 mille reis exchange, at 6s. 4d. per mille rei . . | £475 | 0 | 0 |
| Freight to London, then at £3 per ton . . | 150 | 0 | 0 |
| Assurance on £500, at 2 per cent. . . | 10 | 0 | 0 |
| Petty charges . . . . . . . | 5 | 0 | 0 |
| | £640 | 0 | 0 |

So that it is manifest by the extortion of this banker the poor man lost the whole capital, with freight and charges, and made but £29 produce of a hundred pipes of wine.

One other office of this bank, and which would take up a considerable branch of the stock, is for lending money upon pledges, which should have annexed to it a warehouse and factory, where all sorts of goods might publicly be sold by the consent of the owners, to the great advantage of the owner, the bank receiving £4 per cent. interest, and 2 per cent. commission for sale of the goods.

A third office should be appointed for discounting bills, tallies, and notes, by which all tallies of the Exchequer, and any part of the revenue, should at stated allowances be ready money to any person, to the great advantage of the Government, and ease of all such as are any ways concerned in public undertakings.

A fourth office for lending money upon land securities at 4 per cent. interest, by which the cruelty and injustice of mortgagees would be wholly restrained, and a register of mortgages might be very well kept, to prevent frauds.

A fifth office for exchanges and foreign correspondence.

A sixth for inland exchanges, where a very large field of business lies before them.

Under this head it will not be improper to consider that this method will most effectually answer all the notions and proposals of county banks; for by this office they would be all rendered useless and unprofitable, since one bank, of the magnitude I mention, with a branch of its office set apart for that business, might with ease manage all the inland exchange of the kingdom.

By which such a correspondence with all the trading towns in England might be maintained as that the whole kingdom should trade with the bank. Under the direction of this office a public cashier should be appointed in every county, to reside in the capital town as to trade, and in some counties more, through whose hands all the cash of the revenue of the gentry and of trade should be returned on the bank in London, and from the bank again on their cashier in every respective county or town, at the small exchange of ½ per cent., by which means all loss of money carried upon the road, to the encouragement of robbers and ruining of the country, who are sued for those robberies, would be more effectually prevented, than by all the statutes against highwaymen that are or can be made.

As to public advancings of money to the Government, they

may be left to the directors in a body, as all other disputes and contingent cases are; and whoever examines these heads of business apart, and has any judgment in the particulars, will, I suppose, allow that a stock of ten millions may find employment in them, though it be indeed a very great sum.

I could offer some very good reasons why this way of management by particular offices for every particular sort of business is not only the easiest, but the safest way of executing an affair of such variety and consequence; also I could state a method for the proceedings of those private offices, their conjunction with and dependence on the general Court of the Directors, and how the various accounts should centre in one general capital account of stock, with regulations and appeals; but I believe them to be needless, at least in this place.

If it be objected here that it is impossible for one joint-stock to go through the whole business of the kingdom, I answer, I believe it is not either impossible or impracticable, particularly on this one account, that almost all the country business would be managed by running bills, and those the longest abroad of any, their distance keeping them out, to the increasing the credit, and consequently the stock, of the bank.

## OF THE MULTIPLICITY OF BANKS.

What is touched at in the foregoing part of this chapter refers to one Bank Royal, to preside, as it were, over the whole cash of the kingdom. But because some people do suppose this work fitter for many banks than for one, I must a little consider that head. And first, allowing those many banks could without clashing maintain a constant correspondence with one another in passing each other's bills as current from one to another, I know not but it might be better performed by many than by one, for as harmony makes music in sound, so it produces success in business.

A civil war among merchants is always the ruin of trade. I cannot think a multitude of banks could so consist with one another in England as to join interests and uphold one another's credit without joining stocks too. I confess if it could be done, the convenience to trade would be visible.

If I were to propose which way these banks should be established, I answer: Allowing a due regard to some gentlemen who have had thoughts of the same, whose methods I shall not so much as touch upon, much less discover, my thoughts run upon quite different methods, both for the fund and the establishment.

Every principal town in England is a corporation upon which the fund may be settled, which will sufficiently answer the difficult and chargeable work of suing for a corporation by patent or Act of Parliament.

A general subscription of stock being made, and by deeds of settlement placed in the mayor and aldermen of the city or corporation for the time being, in trust, to be declared by deeds of uses, some of the directors being always made members of the said corporation and joined in the trust, the bank hereby becomes the public stock of the town, something like what they call the rents of the town-house in France, and is managed in the name of the said corporation, to whom the directors are accountable, and they back again to the general court. For example:—

Suppose the gentlemen or tradesmen of the county of Norfolk, by a subscription of cash, design to establish a bank. The subscriptions being made, the stock is paid into the chamber of the city of Norwich, and managed by a court of directors, as all banks are, and chosen out of the subscribers, the mayor only of the city to be always one; to be managed in the name of the corporation of the city of Norwich, but for the uses in a deed of trust to be made by the subscribers and mayor and aldermen at large mentioned. I make no question, but a bank thus settled would have as firm a foundation as any bank need to have, and every way answer the ends of a corporation.

Of these sorts of banks England might very well establish fifteen at the several towns hereafter mentioned, some of which, though they are not the capital towns of the counties, yet are more the centre of trade, which in England runs in veins, like mines of metal in the earth :—

| | |
|---|---|
| Canterbury. | Leeds, or Halifax, or York. |
| Salisbury. | Nottingham. |
| Exeter. | Warwick or Birmingham. |
| Bristol. | Oxford or Reading. |
| Worcester. | Bedford. |
| Shrewsbury. | Norwich. |
| Manchester. | Colchester. |
| Newcastle-upon-Tyne. | |

Every one of these banks to have a cashier in London, unless they could all have a general correspondence and credit with the Bank Royal.

These banks in their respective counties should be a general staple and factory for the manufactures of the said county, where every man that had goods made might have money at a small interest for advance, the goods in the meantime being sent forward to market to a warehouse for that purpose erected in London, where they should be disposed of to all the advantages the owner could expect, paying only 1 per cent. commission. Or if the maker wanted credit in London, either for Spanish wool, cotton, oil, or any goods while his goods were in the warehouse of the said bank, his bill should be paid by the bank to the full value of his goods, or at least within a small matter. These banks, either by correspondence with each other or an order to their cashier in London, might with ease so pass each other's bills that a man who has cash at Plymouth, and wants money at Berwick, may transfer his cash at Plymouth to Newcastle in half an hour's time, without either hazard, or charge, or time, allowing only $\frac{1}{2}$ per cent. exchange ; and so of all the most distant parts of the kingdom. Or if he wants money at Newcastle, and has goods at Worcester or at any other clothing town, sending his goods to be sold by the factory of the Bank of Worcester, he may remit by the bank to Newcastle, or anywhere else, as readily as if his goods were sold and paid for, and no exactions made upon him for the convenience he enjoys.

This discourse of banks the reader is to understand to have no relation to the present posture of affairs with respect to the scarcity of current money, which seems to have put a stop to that part of a stock we call credit, which always is, and indeed must be, the most essential part of a bank, and without which no bank can pretend to subsist, at least to advantage.

A bank is only a great stock of money put together, to be employed by some of the subscribers in the name of the rest, for the benefit of the whole. This stock of money subsists not barely on the profits of its own stock, for that would be inconsiderable, but upon the contingencies and accidents which multiplicity of business occasions ; as, for instance, a man that comes for money, and knows he may have it to-morrow. Perhaps he is in haste, and will not take it to-day. Only that he may be sure of it to-morrow, he takes a memorandum under the hand of the officer that he shall have it whenever he calls for it, and this memorandum we call a bill. To-morrow, when he intended to fetch his money, comes a man to him for money ; and to save himself the labour of telling, he gives him the memorandum or bill aforesaid for his money. This second man does as the first, and a third does as he did, and so the bill runs about a month, two, or three ; and this is what we call credit; for by the circulation of a quantity of these bills the bank enjoys the full benefit of as much stock in real value as the supposititious value of the bills amounts to, and wherever this credit fails this advantage fails ; for immediately all men come for their money, and the bank must die of itself; for I am sure no bank by the simple improvement of their single stock can ever make any considerable advantage.

I confess a bank who can lay a fund for the security of their bills, which shall produce, first, an annual profit to the owner, and yet make good the passant bill, may stand, and be advantageous too, because there is a real and a supposititious value both, and the real always ready to make good the supposititious ; and this I know no way to bring to pass but by land, which at the same time that it lies transferred, to secure the value of every bill given out, brings in a separate profit to the owner; and this way no question but the whole kingdom might be a bank to itself, though no ready money were to be found in it.

I had gone on in some sheets with my notion of land being the best bottom for public banks, and the easiness of bringing it to answer all the ends of money deposited, with double advantage; but I find myself happily prevented by a gentleman who has published the very same, though since this was written; and I was always master of so much wit as to hold my tongue while they spoke who understood the thing better than myself.

Mr. John Asgill of Lincoln's Inn, in a small tract entituled "Several Assertions Proved in Order to Create another Species of Money than Gold and Silver," has so distinctly handled this very case, with such strength of argument, such clearness of reason, such a judgment, and such a style, as all the ingenious part of the world must acknowledge themselves extremely obliged to him for that piece.

At the sight of which book I laid by all that had been written by me on that subject; for I had much rather confess myself incapable of handling that point like him, than have convinced the world of it by my impertinence.

# OF THE HIGHWAYS.

IT is a prodigious charge the whole nation groans under for the repair of highways, which, after all, lie in a very ill posture too. I make no question but if it was taken into consideration by those who have the power to direct it, the kingdom might be wholly eased of that burden, and the highways be kept in good condition, which now lie in a most shameful manner in most parts of the kingdom, and in many places wholly impassable ; from whence arise tolls and impositions upon passengers and travellers, and, on the other hand, trespasses and encroachments upon lands adjacent, to the great damage of the owners.

The rate for the highways is the most arbitrary and unequal tax in the kingdom ; in some places two or three rates of sixpence per pound in the year ; in others, the whole parish cannot raise wherewith to defray the charge, either by the very bad condition of the road or distance of materials ; in others, the surveyors raise what they never expend, and the abuses, exactions, connivances, frauds, and embezzlements are innumerable.

The Romans, while they governed this island, made it one of their principal cares to make and repair the highways of the kingdom, and the chief roads we now use are of their marking out ; the consequence of maintaining them was such, or at least so seemed, that they thought it not below them to employ their legionary troops in the work, and it was sometimes the business of whole armies, either when in winter quarters, or in the intervals of truce or peace with the natives. Nor have the Romans left us any greater tokens of their grandeur and magnificence than the ruins of those causeways and street-ways, which are at this day to be seen in many parts of the kingdom, some of which have by the visible remains been discovered to traverse the whole kingdom, and others for more than a hundred miles are to be traced from colony to colony, as they had particular occasion. The famous highway or street called Watling Street, which some will tell you began at London Stone, and passing that very street in the City which we to this day call by that name, went on west to that spot where Tyburn now stands, and then turned north-west in so straight a line to St. Albans, that it is now the exactest road (in one line for twenty miles) in the kingdom, and though disused now as the chief, yet is as good, and I believe the best road to St. Albans, and is still called the Street-way; from whence it is traced into Shropshire above a hundred and sixty miles, with a multitude of visible antiquities upon it, discovered and described very accurately by Mr. Camden. The Fosse, another Roman work, lies at this day as visible and as plain a high causeway, of above thirty feet broad, ditched on either side, and coped and paved where need is, as exact and every jot as beautiful as the King's new road through Hyde Park, in which figure it now lies from near Marshfield to Cirencester, and again from Cirencester to the hill three miles this side Gloucester, which is not less than twenty-six miles, and is made use of as the great road to those towns, and probably has been so for a thousand years with little repairs.

If we set aside the barbarity and customs of the Romans as heathens, and take them as a civil government, we must allow they were the pattern of the whole world for improvement and increase of arts and learning, civilising and methodising nations and countries conquered by their valour; and if this was one of their great cares, that consideration ought to move something. But to the great example of that generous people I will add three arguments :—

(1.) It is useful, and that as it is convenient for carriages, which in a trading country is a great help to negoce, and promotes universal correspondence, without which our inland trade could not be managed. And under this head I could name a thousand conveniences of a safe, pleasant, well-repaired highway, both to the inhabitant and the traveller, but I think it is needless.

(2.) It is easy. I question not to make it appear it is easy to put all the highroads, especially in England, in a noble figure, large, dry, and clean, well drained and free from floods, impassable sloughs, deep cart-ruts, high ridges, and all the inconveniences they now are full of; and when once done, much easier still to be maintained so.

(3.) It may be cheaper, and the whole assessment for the repairs of highways for ever be dropped, or applied to other uses for the public benefit.

Here I beg the reader's favour for a small digression.

I am not proposing this as an undertaker, or setting a price to the public for which I will perform it, like one of the projectors I speak of, but laying open a project for the performance, which, whenever the public affairs will admit our governors to consider of, will be found so feasible that no question they may find undertakers enough for the performance, and in this undertaking age I do not doubt but it would be easy at any time to procure persons at their own charge to perform it for any single county, as a pattern and an experiment for the whole kingdom.

The proposal is as follows :—

First, that an Act of Parliament be made, with liberty for the undertakers to dig and trench, to cut down hedges and trees, or whatever is needful for ditching, draining, and carrying off water, cleaning, enlarging, and levelling the roads, with power to lay open or enclose lands ; to encroach into lands, dig, raise, and level fences, plant and pull up hedges or trees, for the enlarging, widening, and draining the highways ; with power to turn either the roads, or watercourses, rivers, and brooks, as by the directors of the works shall be found needful, always allowing satisfaction to be first made to the owners of such lands, either by assigning to them equivalent lands or payment in money, the value to be adjusted by two indifferent persons, to be named by the Lord Chancellor or Lord Keeper for the time being; and no watercourse to be turned from any water-mill without satisfaction first made both to the landlord and tenant.

But before I proceed I must say a word or two to this article.

The chief, and almost the only, cause of the deepness and foulness of the roads is occasioned by the standing water, which, for want of due care to draw it off by scouring and opening ditches and drains, and other watercourses, and clearing of passages, soaks into the earth, and softens it to such a degree that it cannot bear the weight of horses and carriages;[1] to prevent which, the power to dig, trench, and cut down, &c., mentioned above will be of absolute necessity. But because the liberty seems very large, and some may think it is too great a power to be granted to any body of men over their neighbours, it is answered :—

(1.) It is absolutely necessary, or the work cannot be done; and the doing of the work is of much greater benefit than the damage can amount to.

(2.) Satisfaction to be made to the owner, and that first, too, before the damage be done, is an unquestionable equivalent; and both together, I think, are a very full answer to any objection in that case.

Besides this Act of Parliament, a Commission must be granted

---

[1] Roads at this time were tracks over the soft earth which usually went along hills to avoid the mud and the frequent flooding of low ground. The track often became worn so deep as to make a hollow-way with banks as high as the head of a horseman. Hence the name of our London district still called Holloway. When a road was trampled into hopeless ruts and pools of mud, the owner of the ground might dig it up and provide another track. Sussex girls were said to be long-legged from the continuous pull on their muscles in getting their feet out of the sticky mud. Forty years after Defoe's "Essay on Projects" appeared, Lord Hervey, at Kensington, complained that "the road between this place and London is grown so infamously bad that we live here in the same solitude as we would do if cast on a rock in the middle of the ocean, and all the Londoners tell us that there is between them and us an impassable gulf of mud." In bad weather it took two hours to drag a royal carriage from St. James's Palace to Kensington. Many ways were impassable in winter. Two or three years after the publication of this "Essay on Projects" the Rev. James Brome, rector of Cheriton, in Kent, began "Three Years' Travels in England, Scotland, and Wales," of which he printed his account in 1726. He had to start in the spring, when roads were becoming passable, use guides to conduct him from one place to another, and go into winter quarters when the roads became unfit for travelling. The first English road-maker, John Metcalf, was not born when Defoe included a plan for the construction of sufficient roads in this "Essay on Projects," and Metcalf's first three miles of well-constructed road were laid down in Yorkshire, between Minskip and Fearnsby, more than thirty years after Defoe was dead.

to fifteen, at least, in the name of the undertakers, to whom every county shall have power to join ten, who are to sit with the said fifteen so often and so long as the said fifteen do sit for affairs relating to that county; which fifteen, or any seven of them, shall be directors of the works, to be advised by the said ten, or any five of them, in matters of right and claim; and the said ten to adjust differences in the countries, and to have right by process to appeal in the name either of lords of manors, or privileges of towns or corporations, who shall be either damaged or encroached upon by the said work: all appeals to be heard and determined immediately by the said Lord Chancellor, or Commission from him, that the work may receive no interruption.

This Commission shall give power to the said fifteen to press waggons, carts, and horses, oxen, and men, and detain them to work a certain limited time, and within certain limited space of miles from their own dwellings, and at a certain rate of payment. No men, horses, or carts, to be pressed against their consent, during the times of haytime or harvest, or upon market-days, if the person aggrieved will make affidavit he is obliged to be with his horses or carts at the said markets.

It is well known to all who have any knowledge of the condition the highways in England now lie in, that in most places there is a convenient distance of land left open for travelling, either for driving of cattle or marching of troops of horse, with perhaps as few lanes or defiles as in any countries. The cross-roads, which are generally narrow, are yet broad enough in most places for two carriages to pass; but, on the other hand, we have on most of the highroads a great deal of waste land thrown in, as it were, for an overplus to the highway; which, though it be used of course by cattle and travellers on occasion, is indeed no benefit at all either to the traveller as a road, or to the poor as a common, or to the lord of the manor as a waste; upon it grows neither timber nor grass in any quantity answerable to the land; but, though to no purpose, is trodden down, poached, and overrun by drifts of cattle in the winter, or spoiled with the dust in the summer. And this I have observed in many parts of England to be as good land as any of the neighbouring enclosures, as capable of improvement, and to as good purpose.

These lands only being enclosed and manured, leaving the roads to dimensions without measure sufficient, are the fund upon which I build the prodigious stock of money that must do this work. These lands, which I shall afterwards make an essay to value, being enclosed, will be either saleable to raise money, or fit to exchange with those gentlemen who must part with some land where the ways are narrow; always reserving a quantity of these lands to be let out to tenants; the rent to be paid into the public stock or bank of the undertakers, and to be reserved for keeping the ways in the same repair; and the said bank to forfeit the lands if they are not so maintained.

Another branch of the stock must be hands, for a stock of men is a stock of money; to which purpose every county, city, town, and parish shall be rated at a set price, equivalent to eight years' payment for the repair of highways, which each county, &c., shall raise, not by assessment in money, but by pressing of men, horses, and carriages for the work, the men, horses, &c., to be employed by the directors; in which case all corporal punishment, as of whippings, stocks, pillories, houses of correction, &c., might be easily transmuted to a certain number of days' work on the highways; and in consideration of this provision of men, the country should for ever after be acquitted of any contribution, either in money or work, for repair of the highways, building of bridges excepted.

There lies some popular objection against this undertaking, and the first is the great controverted point of England—enclosure of the common, which tends to depopulation and injures the poor.

(2.) Who shall be judges or surveyors of the work, to oblige the undertakers to perform to a certain limited degree.

For the first, the enclosure of the common, a clause that runs as far as to an encroachment upon Magna Charta, and a most considerable branch of the property of the poor, I answer it thus :—

(1.) The lands we enclose are not such as from which the poor do indeed reap any benefit, or at least any that is considerable.

(2.) The bank and public stock, who are to manage this great undertaking, will have so many little labours to perform and offices to bestow that are fit only for labouring poor persons to do, as will put them in a condition to provide for the poor who are so injured that can work; and to those who cannot, may allow pensions for overseeing, supervising, and the like, which will be more than equivalent.

(3.) For depopulations, the contrary should be secured, by obliging the undertakers, at such and such certain distances, to erect cottages, two at least in a place, which would be useful to the work and safety of the traveller, to which should be an allotment of land, always sufficient to invite the poor inhabitant, in which the poor should be tenant for life gratis, doing duty upon the highway as should be appointed; by which, and many other methods, the poor should be great gainers by the proposal, instead of being injured.

(4.) By this erecting of cottages at proper distances, a man might travel over all England as through a street, where he could never want either rescue from thieves or directions for his way.

(5.) This very undertaking, once duly settled, might in a few years so order it that there should be no poor for the common; and if so, what need of a common for the poor? Of which in its proper place.

As to the second objection, who should oblige the undertakers to the performance? I answer:—

(1.) Their commission and charter should become void, and all their stock forfeit, and the lands enclosed and unsold remain as a pledge, which would be security sufficient.

(2.) The ten persons chosen out of every county should have power to inspect and complain, and the Lord Chancellor upon such complaint to make a survey, and to determine by a jury, in which case on default they shall be obliged to proceed.

(3.) The lands settled on the banks shall be liable to be extended for the uses mentioned, if the same at any time be not maintained in the condition at first provided, and the bank to be amerced upon complaint of the country.

E

These and other conditions, which, on a legal settlement to be made by wiser heads than mine, might be thought on, I do believe would form a constitution so firm, so fair, and so equally advantageous to the country, to the poor, and to the public, as has not been put in practice in these latter ages of the world. To discourse of this a little in general, and to instance in a place, perhaps, that has not its fellow in the kingdom, the parish of Islington in Middlesex. There lies through this large parish the greatest road in England, and the most frequented, especially by cattle for Smithfield Market. This great road has so many branches, and lies for so long a way through the parish, and withal has the inconvenience of a clayey ground, and no gravel at hand, that, modestly speaking, the parish is not able to keep it in repair, by which means several cross-roads in the parish lie wholly impassable, and carts and horses, and men too, have been almost buried in holes and sloughs, and the main road itself has for many years lain in a very ordinary condition, which occasioned several motions in Parliament to raise a toll at Highgate for the performance of what it was impossible the parish should do, and yet was of so absolute necessity to be done. And is it not very probable the parish of Islington would part with all the waste land upon their roads to be eased of the intolerable assessment for repair of the highway, and answer the poor, who reap but a small benefit from it, some other way? And yet I am free to affirm that for a grant of waste and almost useless land, lying open to the highway, those lands to be improved, as they might easily be, together with the eight years' assessment to be provided in workmen, a noble, magnificent causeway might be erected, with ditches on either side deep enough to receive the water, and drains sufficient to carry it off, which causeway should be four feet high at least, and from thirty to forty feet broad, to reach from London to Barnet, paved in the middle to keep it coped, and so supplied with gravel and other proper materials as should secure it from decay with small repairing.

I hope no man would be so weak now as to imagine that by lands lying open to the road to be assigned to the undertakers, I should mean that all Finchley Common should be enclosed and sold for this work; but lest somebody should start such a preposterous objection, I think it is not improper to mention that wherever a highway is to be carried over a large common, forest, or waste, without a hedge on either hand, for a certain distance, there the several parishes shall allot the directors a certain quantity of the common to lie parallel with the road, at a proportionate number of feet to the length and breadth of the said road; consideration also to be had to the nature of the ground, or else giving them only room for the road directly, shall suffer them to enclose in any one spot so much of the said common as shall be equivalent to the like quantity of land lying by the road; thus where the land is good, and the materials for erecting a causeway near, the less land may serve, and on the contrary the more; but in general, allowing them the quantity of land proportioned to the length of the causeway, and forty rod in breadth, though where the **land** is poor, as on downs and plains, the proportion must be considered to be adjusted by the country.

Another point, for the dimensions of roads, should be adjusted; and the breadth of them, I think, cannot be less than thus :—

From London, every way, 10 miles, the high post-road to be built full 40 feet in breadth and 4 feet high, the ditches 8 feet broad and 6 feet deep, and from thence onward 30 feet, and so in proportion.

Cross-roads to be 20 feet broad, and ditches proportioned; no lanes and passes less than nine feet, without ditches.

The middle of the high causeways to be paved with stone, chalk, or gravel, and kept always two feet higher than the sides, that the water might have a free course into the ditches, and persons kept in constant employment to fill up holes, let out water, open drains, and the like, as there should be occasion—a proper work for highwaymen, and such malefactors as might on those services be exempted from the gallows.

It may here be objected that eight years assessment to be demanded down is too much in reason to expect any of the poorer sort can pay; as, for instance, if a farmer, who keeps a team of horse, be at the common assessment to work a week, it must not be put so hard upon any man as to work eight weeks together. It is easy to answer this objection.

So many as are wanted must be had; if a farmer's team cannot be spared without prejudice to him so long together, he may spare it at sundry times, or agree to be assessed, and pay the assessments at sundry payments, and the bank may make it as easy to them as they please.

Another method, however, might be found to fix this work at once, as suppose a bank be settled for the highways of the county of Middlesex, which, as they are without doubt the most used of any in the kingdom, so also they require the more charge, and in some parts lie in the worst condition of any in the kingdom.

If the Parliament fix the charge of the survey of the highways upon a bank to be appointed for that purpose for a certain term of years, the bank undertaking to do the work or to forfeit the said settlement.

As thus: Suppose the tax on land and tenements for the whole county of Middlesex does or should be so ordered as it might amount to £20,000 per annum, more or less, which it now does, and much more, including the work of the farmer's teams, which must be accounted as money, and is equivalent to it, with some allowance to be rated for the City of London, &c., who do enjoy the benefit and make the most use of the said roads, both for carrying of goods and bringing provisions to the city, and therefore, in reason, ought to contribute towards the highways; for it is a most unequal thing that the road from Highgate to Smithfield Market, by which the whole city is, in a manner, supplied with live cattle, and the road by those cattle horribly spoiled, should lie all upon that one parish of Islington to repair; wherefore I will suppose a rate for the highways to be gathered through the City of London of £10,000 per annum more, which may be appointed to be paid by carriers, drovers, and all such as keep teams, horses, or coaches, and the like, or many ways as is most equal and reasonable. The waste lands in the said county, which by the consent of the parishes, lords of the manors, and proprietors, shall be allowed to the undertakers when enclosed and let out, may (the land in Middlesex generally letting high) amount to £5000 per annum more. If then an Act of Parliament be procured to settle the tax of £30,000 per annum for eight years, most of which will be levied in workmen, and not in money, and the waste lands for ever, I dare be bold to offer that the highways for the whole county of Middlesex should be put into the following form, and the £5000 per annum land be bound to remain as a security to maintain them so, and the county be never burdened with any further tax for the repair of the highways.

And that I may not propose a matter in general, like begging the question, without demonstration, I shall enter into the particulars how it may be performed, and that under these following heads of articles :—

1. *What I propose to do to the highways.*
2. *What the charge will be.*
3. *How to be raised.*
4. *What security for performance.*
5. *What profit to the undertaker.*

1. What I propose to do to the highways.

I answer, first, not repair them, and yet, secondly, not alter them, that is, not alter the course they run, but perfectly build them as a fabric. And to descend to the particulars, it is first necessary to note which are the roads I mean, and their dimensions.

First, the high post-roads, and they are for the county of Middlesex as follows :—

| | | | Miles. |
|---|---|---|---|
| From London to Staines, which is . . . . | 15 |
| ,, ,, Colebrook is from Hounslow . | 5 |
| ,, ,, Uxbridge . . . . . | 15 |
| ,, ,, Busby, the old street-way . .· | 10 |
| ,, ,, Barnet, or near it . . . . | 9 |
| ,, ,, Waltham Cross in Ware Road . | 10 |
| ,, ,, Bow . . . . . . . | 2 |

——
66

Besides these, there are cross-roads, bye-roads, and lanes, which must also be looked after, and that some of them may be put into condition, others may be wholly slighted and shut up, or made drift-ways, bridle-ways, or foot-ways, as may be thought convenient by the countries.

The cross-roads of most repute are as follows :—

|  |  | Miles. |
|---|---|---:|
| From London to Hackney, Old Ford, and Bow . . . | | 5 |
| „ Hackney to Dalston and Islington . . . . | | 2 |
| „ „ Hornsey, Muswell Hill, to Whetston . . | | 8 |
| „ Tottenham to The Chase, South Gate, &c., called Green-lanes . . . . . . . . . | | 6 |
| „ Enfield-Wash to Enfiel Town, Whetston, Totteridge, to Edgworth . . . . . . . . | | 10 |
| „ London to Hampstead, Hendon, and Edgworth . . | | 8 |
| „ Edgworth to Stanmore, to Pinner, to Uxbridge . . | | 8 |
| „ London to Harrow and Pinner Green . . . . | | 11 |
| „ „ Chelsea, Fulham . . . . . . | | 4 |
| „ Brantford to Thistleworth, Twickenham, and Kingston . | | 6 |
| „ Kingston to Staines, Colebrook, and Uxbridge . . . | | 17 |
| „ „ Chertsey Bridge . . . . . | | 5 |
|  |  | 90 |
| Overplus miles . . . . . . . . . | | 50 |
|  |  | 140 |

And because there may be many parts of the cross-roads which cannot be accounted in the number above-mentioned, or may slip my knowledge or memory, I allow an overplus of 50 miles to be added to the 90 miles above, which together makes the cross-roads of Middlesex to be 140 miles.

For the bye-lanes, such as may be slighted, need nothing but to be ditched up, such as are for private use of lands, for carrying off corn ; and driving cattle, are to be looked after by private hands.

But of the last sort, not to be accounted by particulars in the small county of Middlesex, we cannot allow less in cross bye-lanes, from village to village, and from dwelling-houses which stand out of the way to the roads, than 1000 miles.

So in the whole county I reckon up :—

|  | Miles. |
|---|---|
| Of the high post-road . . . . . . | 67 |
| Of cross-roads less public . . . . . | 140 |
| Of bye-lanes and passes . . . . . | 1000 |
|  | 1207 |

These are the roads I mean, and thus divided under their several denominations.

To the question, What I would do to them? I answer :—

(1.) For the 67 miles of high post-road I propose to throw up a firm strong causeway, well bottomed, 6 feet high in the middle and 4 feet on the side, faced with brick or stone, and crowned with gravel, chalk, or stone, as the several countries they are made through will afford, being 44 feet in breadth, with ditches on either side 8 feet broad and 4 feet deep, so the whole breadth will be 60 feet, if the ground will permit.

At the end of every two miles, or such-like convenient distances, shall be a cottage erected, with half an acre of ground allowed, which shall be given gratis, with 1s. per week wages, to such poor man of the parish as shall be approved, who shall once at least every day view his walk, to open passages for the water to run into the ditches, to fill up holes or soft places.

Two riders shall be allowed to be always moving the rounds to view everything out of repair, and make report to the directors, and to see that the cottagers do their duty.

(2.) For the 140 miles of cross-road, a like causeway to be made, but of different dimensions, the breadth 20 feet, if the ground will allow it, the ditches 4 feet broad, 3 feet deep, the height in the middle 3 feet, and on the sides 1 foot, or 2 where it may be needful, to be also crowned with gravel, and 1s. per week to be allowed to the poor of every parish ; the constables to be bound to find a man to walk on the highway every division, for the same purpose as the cottagers do on the greater roads.

Posts to be set up at every turning to note whither it goes, for the direction of strangers, and how many miles distant.

(3.) For 1000 miles bye-lanes, only good and sufficient care to keep them in repair as they are, and to carry the water off by clearing and cutting the ditches, and laying materials where it is wanted.

This is what I propose to do to them, and what, if once performed, I suppose all people would own to be an undertaking both useful and honourable.

(2.) The second question I propose to give an account of, is what the charge will be ; which I account thus :—

The work of the great causeway I propose shall not cost less than 10s. per foot, supposing materials to be bought, carriage and men's labour to be all hired, which for 67 miles in length is no less than the sum of £176,880 ; as thus—

Every mile, accounted at 1760 yards, and three feet to the yard, is 5280 feet, which at 10s. per foot is £2640 per mile, and that again multiplied by 67 makes the sum of £176,880, into which I include the charge of watercourses, mills to throw off water where needful, drains, &c.

To this charge must be added ditching to enclose land for thirty cottages, and building thirty cottages at £40 each, which is £1200.

The work of the smaller causeway I propose to finish at the rate of 12d. per foot, which being for 140 miles in length, at 5280 feet per mile, amounts to £36,960.

Ditching, draining, and repairing 1000 miles, supposed at 3s. per rod, as for 320,000 rods, is £48,000, which added to the two former accounts, is thus—

| | |
|---|---:|
| The high post-roads or the great causeway . | £178,080 |
| The small causeway . . . . . . | 36,960 |
| Bye-lanes, &c. . . . . . . . | 48,000 |
| | £263,040 |

If I were to propose some measures for the easing this charge, I could, perhaps, lay a scheme down how it may be performed for less than one half of this charge.

As first, by a grant of the court at the Old Bailey, whereby all such criminals as are condemned to die for smaller crimes may, instead of transportation, be ordered a year's work on the highways ; others, instead of whipping, a proportionate time, and the like, which would, by a moderate computation, provide us generally a supply of two hundred workmen, and coming in as fast as they go off, and let the overseers alone to make them work.

Secondly, by an agreement with the Guinea Company to furnish two hundred negroes, who are generally persons that do a great deal of work ; and all these are subsisted very reasonably out of a public storehouse.

Thirdly, by carts and horses, to be bought, not hired, with a few able carters ; and to the other a few workmen that have judgment to direct the rest ; and thus I question not the great causeway shall be done for 4s. per foot charge ; but of this by the bye.

Fourthly, a liberty to ask charities and benevolences to the work.

(3.) To the question, How this money shall be raised ? I think, if the Parliament settle the tax on the country for eight years, at £30,000 per annum, no man need ask how it shall be raised. It will be easy enough to raise the money ; and no parish can grudge to pay a little larger rate for such a term, on condition never to be taxed for the highways any more.

Eight years' assessment at £30,000 per annum is enough to afford to borrow the money by way of anticipation, if need be, the fund being secured by Parliament, and appropriated to that use and no other.

(4.) As to what security for performance.

The lands which are enclosed may be appropriated by the same Act of Parliament to the bank and undertakers, upon condition of performance, and to forfeit to the use of the several parishes to which they belong, in case, upon presentation by the grand juries, and reasonable time given, any part of the roads in such and such parishes be not kept and maintained in that posture they are proposed to be. Now the lands thus settled are an eternal security to the country for the keeping the roads in repair, because they will always be of so much value over the needful charge as will make it worth while to the undertakers to preserve their title to them ; and the tenure of them being so precarious as to be liable to forfeiture or default, they will always be careful to uphold the causeways.

Lastly, What profit to the undertakers? for we must allow them to gain, and that considerably, or no man would undertake such a work.

To this I propose, first :—

During the work, allow them out of the stock £3000 per annum for management.

After the work is finished, so much of the £5000 per annum as can be saved, and the roads kept in good repair, let be their own ; and if the lands secured be not of the value of £5000 a year, let so much of the eight years' tax be set apart as may purchase land to make them up; if they come to more, let the benefit be to the adventurers.

It may be objected here that a tax of £30,000 for eight years will come in as fast as it can well be laid out, and so no anticipations will be requisite, for the whole work proposed cannot be probably finished in less time ; and if so—

| | | |
|---|---|---|
| The charge of the country amounts to | . . | £240,000 |
| The lands saved eight years' revenue | . . | 40,000 |
| | | £280,000 |

which is £13,000 more than the charge ; and if the work be done so much cheaper, as is mentioned, the profit to the undertaker will be unreasonable.

To this I say : I would have the undertakers bound to accept the salary of £3000 per annum for management, and if a whole year's tax can be spared, either leave it unraised upon the country, or put it in bank to be improved against any occasion of building, perhaps, a great bridge ; or some very wet season or frost may so damnify the works as to make them require more than ordinary repair. But the undertakers should make no private advantage of such an overplus ; there might be ways enough found for it.

Another objection lies against the possibility of enclosing the lands upon the waste, which generally belong to some manor, whose different tenures may be so cross, and so otherwise encumbered, that even the lords of those manors, though they were willing, could not convey them.

This may be answered, in general, that an Act of Parliament is omnipotent with respect of titles and tenures of land, and can empower lords and tenants to consent to what else they could not. As to particulars, they cannot be answered till they are proposed, but there is no doubt but an Act of Parliament may adjust it all in one head.

What a kingdom would England be if this were performed in all the counties of it! and yet I believe it is feasible, even in the worst. I have narrowly observed all the considerable ways in that impassable county of Sussex, which, especially in some parts in the Wild, as they very properly call it, of the county, hardly admits the country-people to travel to markets in winter, and makes corn dear at market because it cannot be brought, and cheap at the farmer's house because he cannot carry it to market; yet even in that county would I undertake to carry on this proposal, and that to great advantage, if backed with the authority of an Act of Parliament.

I have seen in that horrible country the road, 60 to 100 yards broad, lie from side to side all poached with cattle, the land of no manner of benefit, and yet no going with a horse but at every step up to the shoulders, full of sloughs and holes, and covered with standing water. It costs them incredible sums of money to repair them, and the very places that are mended would fright a young traveller to go over them. The Romans mastered this work, and by a firm causeway made a highway quite through this deep country, through Darkin in Surrey to Stansted, and thence to Okeley, and so on to Arundel. Its name tells us what it was made of, for it was called Stone Street, and many visible parts of it remain to this day.

Now, would any lord of a manor refuse to allow forty yards in breadth out of that road I mention to have the other twenty made into a firm, fair, and pleasant causeway over that wilderness of a country?

Or would not any man acknowledge that putting this country into a condition for carriages and travellers to pass would be a great work? The gentlemen would find the benefit of it in the rent of their lands and price of their timber; the country people would find the difference in the sale of their goods, which now they cannot carry beyond the first market-town, and hardly thither; and the whole county would reap an advantage a hundred to one greater than the charge of it. And since the want we feel of any convenience is generally the first motive to contrivance for a remedy, I wonder no man ever thought of some expedient for so considerable a defect.

# OF ASSURANCES.

ASSURANCES among merchants I believe may plead prescription, and has been of use time out of mind in trade, though perhaps never so much a trade as now.

It is a compact among merchants; its beginning being an accident to trade, and arose from the disease of men's tempers, who having run larger adventures in a single bottom than afterwards they found convenient, grew fearful and uneasy, and discovering their uneasiness to others, who, perhaps, had no effects in the same vessel, they offer to bear part of the hazard for part of the profit. Convenience made this a custom, and custom brought it into a method, till at last it becomes a trade.

I cannot question the lawfulness of it, since all risk in trade is for gain; and when I am necessitated to have a greater cargo of goods in such or such a bottom than my stock can afford to lose, another may surely offer to go a part with me; and as it is just, if I give another part of the gain, he should run part of the risk, so it is as just that if he runs part of my risk, he should have part of the gain. Some object the disparity of the premium to the hazard, when the insurer runs the risk of £100 on the seas from Jamaica to London for 40s., which, say they, is preposterous and unequal. Though this objection is hardly worth answering to men of business, yet it looks something fair to them that know no better, and for the information of such I trouble the reader with a few heads.

First, they must consider the insurer is out no stock.

Secondly, it is but one risk the insurer runs, whereas the assured has had a risk out, a risk of debts abroad, a risk of a market, and a risk of his factor, and has a risk of a market to come, and therefore ought to have an answerable profit.

Thirdly, if it has been a trading voyage, perhaps the adventurer has paid three or four such premiums, which sometimes make the insurer clear more by a voyage than the merchant. I myself have paid £100 insurances in those small premiums on a voyage I have not gotten £50 by, and I suppose I am not the first that has done so neither.

This way of assuring has also, as other arts of trade have, suffered some improvement (if I may be allowed that term) in our age, and the first step upon it was an insurance office for houses, to insure them from fire. Common fame gives the project to Dr. Barebone, a man, I suppose, better known as a builder than a physician. Whether it were his, or whose it was, I do not inquire; it was settled on a fund of ground-rents, to answer in case of loss, and met with very good acceptance.

But it was soon followed by another by way of friendly society, where all who subscribe pay their quota to build up any man's house who is a contributor, if it shall happen to be burnt. I will not decide which is the best, or which succeeded best, but I believe the latter brings in most money to the contriver.

Only one benefit I cannot omit which they reap from these two societies who are not concerned in either, that if any fire happen, whether in houses insured or not insured, they have each of them a set of lusty fellows, generally watermen, who, being immediately called up, wherever they live, by watchmen appointed, are, it must be confessed, very active and diligent in helping to put out the fire.

As to any further improvement to be made upon assurances in trade, no question there may, and I doubt not but, on payment of a small duty to the Government, the King might be made the general insurer of all foreign trade; of which more under another head.

I am of the opinion also that an office of insurance, erected to insure the titles of lands in an age where they are so precarious as now, might be a project not unlikely to succeed, if established on a good fund. But I shall say no more to that, because it seems to be a design in hand by some persons in town, and is indeed no thought of my own.

Insuring of life I cannot admire.[1]  I shall say nothing to it, but that in Italy, where stabbing and poisoning is so much in vogue, something may be said for it, and on contingent annuities, and yet I never knew the thing much approved of on any account.

[1] It is remarkable that Defoe, in so many respects before his time, did not recognise as we now do the great value of life insurance.  It had been expressly forbidden in France by an ordinance of 1681, setting forth a code of marine insurance, and by regulations concerning insurance issued long before in 1612, at Amsterdam. Its practice had not been ventured upon in England when Defoe wrote at Bristol the first draft of the "Essay on Projects."  The first life insurance company—the "Amicable," afterwards called the "Hand in Hand"—was founded only in 1696, about a year before Defoe's Essay was published, and did not obtain its charter until 1706.  The first insurances were against risks to which a man was liable in his own life and work, the first to be so guarded against being the common and great risk at sea.  The earliest known record of a practice of marine insurance is an ordinance issued in 1435 by the magistrates of Barcelona.  The earliest Italian law on the subject is dated 1523.  About the same time the practice was introduced among us by the Lombards settled in London ; and about eighty years later, near the close of Elizabeth's reign, there is reference to it as an immemorial usage among merchants, both English and foreign, who have great ventures at sea.  Fire insurance followed, but was only beginning when Defoe wrote.  It is nearly of the same date as life insurance, and has developed more in England than in other countries. Friendly societies are a form of insurance that was provided in the Middle Ages by the trades guilds, that paid from a common fund for the misfortunes of each out of the well-being of all.  Adapted to modern conditions of life, not without frequent mistakes, they have been developed among us in various ways since Defoe's time.

## OF FRIENDLY SOCIETIES.

ANOTHER branch of insurance is by contribution or (to borrow the term from that before mentioned) friendly societies, which is, in short, a number of people entering into a mutual compact to help one another in case any disaster or distress fall upon them.

If mankind could agree, as these might be regulated, all things which have casualty in them might be secured. But one thing is particularly required in this way of assurances; none can be admitted but such whose circumstances are at least in some degree alike, and so mankind must be sorted into classes; and as their contingencies differ, every different sort may be a society upon even terms; for the circumstances of people as to life differ extremely by the age and constitution of their bodies and difference of employment; as he that lives on shore against him that goes to sea, or a young man against an old man, or a shopkeeper against a soldier, are unequal. I don't pretend to determine the controverted point of predestination, the fore-knowledge and decrees of Providence. Perhaps, if a man be decreed to be killed in the trenches, the same fore-knowledge ordered him to list himself a soldier that it might come to pass, and the like of a seaman; but this I am sure, speaking of second causes, a seaman or a soldier is subject to more contingent hazards than other men, and therefore is not upon equal terms to form such a society, nor is an annuity on the life of such a man worth so much as it is upon other men. Therefore, if a society should agree together to pay the executor of every member so much after the decease of the said member, the seamen's executors would most certainly have an advantage, and receive more than they pay. So that it is necessary to sort the world into parcels, seamen with seamen, soldiers with soldiers, and the like.

Nor is this a new thing. The friendly society must not pretend to assume to themselves the contrivance of the method, or think us guilty of borrowing from them when we draw this into other branches; for I know nothing is taken from them but the bare word Friendly Society, which they cannot pretend to be any considerable piece of invention neither.

I can refer them to the very individual practice in other things, which claims prescription beyond the beginning of the last age, and that is in our marshes and fens in Essex, Kent, and the Isle of Ely, where great quantities of land being with much pains and a vast charge recovered out of the seas and rivers, and maintained with banks (which they call walls), the owners of those lands agree to contribute to the keeping up those walls and keeping out the sea, which is all one with a friendly society; and if I have a piece of land in any level or marsh, though it bounds nowhere on the sea or river, yet I pay my proportion to the maintenance of the said wall or bank; and if at any time the sea breaks in, the damage is not laid upon the man in whose land the breach happened, unless it was by his neglect, but it lies on the whole land, and is called a level lot.

Again, I have known it practised in troops of horse, especially when it was so ordered that the troopers mounted themselves, where every private trooper has agreed to pay perhaps twopence per diem out of his pay into a public stock, which stock was employed to remount any of the troop who by accident should lose his horse.

Again, the sailors' contribution to the chest at Chatham is another friendly society; and more might be named.

To argue against the lawfulness of this, would be to cry down common equity as well as charity; for as it is kind that my neighbour should relieve me if I fall into distress or decay, so it is but equal he should do so if I agreed to have done the same for him; and if God Almighty has commanded us to relieve and help one another in distress, sure it must be commendable to bind ourselves by agreement to obey that command; nay, it seems to be a project that we are led to by the Divine rule, and has such a latitude in it that, for aught I know, as I said, all the disasters in the world might be prevented by it, and mankind be secured from all the miseries, indigences, and distresses that happen in the world. In which I crave leave to be a little particular.

First, general peace might be secured all over the world by it, if all the Powers agreed to suppress him that usurped or encroached upon his neighbour. All the contingencies of life might be fenced against by this method (as fire is already), as thieves, floods by land, storms by sea, losses of all sorts, and death itself, in a manner, by making it up to the survivor.

I shall begin with the seamen; for as their lives are subject to more hazards than others, they seem to come first in view.

## I.—OF SEAMEN.[1]

Sailors are *les enfans perdus*, the forlorn hope of the world; they are fellows that bid defiance to terror, and maintain a constant war with the elements, who, by the magic of their art, trade in the very confines of death, and are always posted within shot, as I may say, of the grave. It is true their familiarity with danger makes them despise it, for which, I hope, nobody will say they are the wiser; and custom has so hardened them, that we find them the worst of men, though always in view of their last moment.

I have observed one great error in the custom of England relating to these sort of people, and which this way of friendly society would be a remedy for.

If a seaman who enters himself or is pressed into the King's

---

[1] The foundation-stone of Greenwich Hospital, the first attempt to provide a home for seamen disabled in the service of the country, was laid by John Evelyn on the 30th of June 1696. The Hospital was not opened till six or seven years after the publication of Defoe's "Essay on Projects," and then was ready only for forty-two inmates. It was not until 1746 that there was attached to this Hospital an establishment for the relief and support of disabled seamen, and the widows and children of such as should be killed, slain, or drowned in the merchant service.

service be by any accident wounded or disabled, to recompense him for the loss he receives a pension during life, which the sailors call smart-money, and is proportioned to their hurt, as for the loss of an eye, arm, leg, or finger, and the like; and as it is a very honourable thing, so it is but reasonable that a poor man who loses his limbs (which are his estate) in the service of the Government, and is thereby disabled from his labour to get his bread, should be provided for, and not suffered to beg or starve for want of those limbs he lost in the service of his country.

But if you come to the seamen in the merchant service, not the least provision is made, which has been the loss of many a good ship, with many a rich cargo, which would otherwise have been saved.

And the sailors are in the right of it, too. For instance, a merchant-ship coming home from the Indies, perhaps very rich, meets with a privateer (not so strong but that she might fight him and perhaps get off); the captain calls up his crew, tells them, "Gentlemen, you see how it is; I don't question but we may clear ourselves of this caper if you will stand by me." One of the crew, as willing to fight as the rest, and as far from a coward as the captain, but endowed with a little more wit than his fellows, replies, "Noble captain, we are all willing to fight, and don't question but to beat him off. But here is the case, if we are taken, we shall be set on shore, and then sent home, and lose perhaps our clothes and a little pay; but if we fight and beat the privateer, perhaps half a score of us may be wounded and lose our limbs, and then we are undone and our families. If you will sign an obligation to us that the owners or merchants shall allow a pension to such as are maimed, that we may not fight for the ship and go a-begging ourselves, we will bring off the ship or sink by her side; otherwise I am not willing to fight for my part." The captain cannot do this; so they strike, and the ship and cargo is lost.

If I should turn this supposed example into a real history, and name the ship and the captain that did so, it would be too plain to be contradicted.

Wherefore, for the encouragement of sailors in the service of the merchant, I would have a friendly society erected for seamen, wherein all sailors or seafaring men entering their names, places of abode, and the voyages they go upon, at an office of insurance for seamen, and paying there a certain small quarterage of 1s. per quarter, should have a sealed certificate from the governors of the said office for the articles hereafter mentioned.

1. If any such seaman, either in fight or by any other accident at sea, come to be disabled, he should receive from the said office the following sums of money, either in pension for life or ready money, as he pleased :—

| For the loss of an eye | | | £ 25, | or | £2 | per annum for life. |
|---|---|---|---|---|---|---|
| ,, | ,, | both eyes . | 100 | ,, | 8 | ,, | ,, |
| ,, | ,, | one leg | 50 | ,, | 4 | ,, | ,, |
| ,, | ,, | both legs . | 80 | ,, | 6 | ,, | ,, |
| ,, | ,, | right hand | 80 | ,, | 6 | ,, | ,, |
| ,, | ,, | left hand . | 50 | ,, | 4 | ,, | ,, |
| ,, | ,, | right arm . | 100 | ,, | 8 | ,, | ,, |
| ,, | ,, | left arm . | 80 | ,, | 6 | ,, | ,, |
| ,, | ,, | both hands | 160 | ,, | 12 | ,, | ,, |
| ,, | ,, | both arms . | 200 | ,, | 16 | ,, | ,, |

Any broken arm, or leg, or thigh, towards the cure, £10.

If taken by the Turks, £50 towards his ransom.

If he become infirm, and unable to go to sea or maintain himself, by age or sickness, £6 per annum.

To their wives, if they are killed or drowned, £50.

In consideration of this, every seaman subscribing to the society shall agree to pay to the receipt of the said office his quota of the sum to be paid whenever and as often as such claims are made, the claims to be entered into the office, and upon sufficient proof made, the governors to regulate the division, and publish it in print.

For example : suppose 4000 seamen subscribe to this society, and after six months—for no man should claim sooner than six months—a merchant-ship having engaged a privateer, there come several claims together, as thus :—

| | |
|---|---:|
| A was wounded and lost one leg . . . . | £50 |
| B blown up with powder, and has lost an eye . . | 25 |
| C had a great shot took off his arm . . . . | 100 |
| D with a splinter had an eye struck out . . . | 25 |
| | £200 |
| E was killed with a great shot, to be paid to his wife . | 50 |
| | £250 |

The governors hereupon settle the claims of these persons, and make publication, that whereas such and such seamen, members of the society, have in an engagement with a French privateer been so and so hurt, their claim upon the office, by the rules and agreements of the said office, being adjusted by the governors, amounts to £250, which being equally divided among the subscribers, comes to 1s. 3d. each, which all persons that are subscribers to the said office are desired to pay in for their respective subscriptions, that the said wounded persons may be relieved accordingly, as they expect to be relieved, if the same or the like casualty should befall them.

It is but a small matter for a man to contribute if he gave 1s. 3d. out of his wages to relieve five wounded men of his own fraternity, but at the same time to be assured that if he is hurt or maimed he shall have the same relief, it is a thing so rational that hardly any one but a harebrained fellow that thinks of nothing would omit entering himself into such an office.

I shall not enter further into this affair, because perhaps I may give the proposal to some persons who may set it on foot; and then the world may see the benefit of it by the execution.

## II.—For Widows.

The same method of friendly society, I conceive, would be a very proper proposal for widows.

We have abundance of women who have been bred well and lived well, ruined in a few years, and perhaps left young with a house full of children and nothing to support them, which falls generally upon the wives of the inferior clergy, or of shopkeepers and artificers.

They marry wives with perhaps £300 to £1000 portion, and can settle no jointure upon them. Either they are extravagant and idle and waste it, or trade decays, or losses, or a thousand contingencies happen to bring a tradesman to poverty, and he breaks. The poor young woman, it may be, has three or four children, and is driven to a thousand shifts, while he lies in the Mint or Friars under the dilemma of a statute of bankruptcy; but if he dies, then she is absolutely undone, unless she has friends to go to.

Suppose an office to be erected, to be called "An Office of Insurance for Widows," upon the following conditions :—

Two thousand women, or their husbands for them, enter their names into a register to be kept for that purpose, with the names, age, and trade of their husbands, with the place of their abode, paying at the time of their entering 5s. down, with 1s. 4d. per quarter, which is to the setting up and support of an office, with clerks and all proper officers for the same, for there is no maintaining such without charge. They receive every one of them a certificate, sealed by the secretary of the office and signed by the governors, for the articles hereafter mentioned.

If any one of the women become a widow at any time after six months from the date of her subscription, upon due notice being given and claim made at the office in form as shall be directed, she shall receive within six months after such claim made the sum of £500 in money, without any deduction, saving some small fees to the officers, which the trustees must settle, that they may be known.

In consideration of this, every woman so subscribing obliges herself to pay, as often as any member of the society becomes a widow, the due proportion or share allotted to her to pay towards the £500 for the said widow, provided her share does not exceed the sum of 5s.

No seamen's or soldiers' wives to be accepted into such a proposal as this, on the account before mentioned, because the contingencies of their lives are not equal to others, unless they will admit this general exception, supposing they do not die out of the kingdom.

It might also be an exception, that if the widow that claimed had really, *bonâ fide*, left her by her husband, to her own use, clear of all debts and legacies, £2000, she should have no claim ; the intent being to aid the poor, not add to the rich. But there lie a great many objections against such an article ; as—

(1.) It may tempt some to forswear themselves.

(2.) People will order their wills so as to defraud the exception.

One exception must be made, and that is, either very unequal matches, as when a woman of nineteen marries an old man of seventy, or women who have infirm husbands,—I mean known and publicly so. To remedy which, two things are to be done :—

(1.) The office must have moving officers without-doors, who shall inform themselves of such matters, and if any such circumstances appear, the office should have fourteen days' time to return their money and declare their subscriptions void.

(2.) No woman whose husband had any visible distemper should claim under a year after her subscription.

One grand objection against this proposal is, how you will oblige people to pay either their subscription or their quarterage.

To this I answer : By no compulsion (though that might be performed too), but altogether voluntary ; only with this argument to move it, that if they do not continue their payments, they lose the benefit of their past contributions.

I know it lies as a fair objection against such a project as this, that the number of claims are so uncertain, that nobody knows what they engage in when they subscribe, for so many may die annually out of two thousand as may make my payment £20 or £25 per annum ; and if a woman happen to pay that for twenty years, though she receives the £500 at last, she is a great loser ; but if she dies before her husband, she has lessened his estate considerably, and brought a great loss upon him.

First, I say to this, that I would have such a proposal as this be so fair and so easy, that if any person who had subscribed found the payments too high and the claims fall too often, it should be at their liberty at any time, upon notice given, to be released and stand obliged no longer; and if so, *volenti non fit injuria,*—every one knows best what their own circumstances will bear.

In the next place, because death is a contingency no man can directly calculate, and all that subscribe must take the hazard; yet that a prejudice against this notion may not be built on wrong grounds, let us examine a little the probable hazard, and see how many shall die annually out of 2000 subscribers, accounting by the common proportion of burials to the number of the living.

Sir William Petty, in his "Political Arithmetic,"[1] by a very ingenious calculation, brings the account of burials in London to be one in forty annually, and proves it by all the proper rules of proportioned computation, and I will take my scheme from thence.

If, then, one in forty of all the people in England die, that supposes fifty to die every year out of our two thousand subscribers; and for a woman to contribute 5s. to every one would certainly be to agree to pay £12, 10s. per annum upon her husband's life, to receive £500 when he died, and lose it if she died first; and yet this would not be a hazard beyond reason too great for the gain.

But I shall offer some reasons to prove this to be impossible in our case. First, Sir William Petty allows the City of London to contain about a million of people, and our yearly bill of mortality never yet amounted to 25,000 in the most sickly years we have had, Plague years excepted; sometimes but to 20,000, which is but one in fifty. Now, it is to be considered here that children and ancient people make up, one time with another, at least one-third of our bills of mortality, and our assurances lie upon none but the middle age of the people, which is the only age wherein life is anything steady; and if that be allowed, there cannot die,

---

[1] Sir William Petty died in 1687. His "Essays on Political Arithmetic" were being published during the last five years of his life. I have reprinted them in a threepenny book, No. 142 of the National Library.

by his computation, above one in eighty of such people every year; but because I would be sure to leave room for casualty, I will allow one in fifty shall die out of our number subscribed.

Secondly, it must be allowed that our payments falling due only on the death of husbands, this one in fifty must not be reckoned upon the two thousand; for it is to be supposed at least as many women shall die as men, and then there is nothing to pay, so that one in fifty upon one thousand is the most that I can suppose shall claim the contribution in a year, which is twenty claims a year at 5s. each, and is £5 per annum, and if a woman pays this for twenty years, and claims at last, she is gainer enough, and no extraordinary loser if she never claims at all. And I verily believe any office might undertake to demand, at all ventures, not above £6 per annum, and secure the subscriber £500 in case she come to claim as a widow.

I forbear being more particular on this thought, having occasion to be larger in other prints, the experiment being resolved upon by some friends, who are pleased to think this too useful a project not to be put in execution; and therefore I refer the reader to the public practice of it.

I have named these two cases as special experiments of what might be done by assurance in way of friendly society; and I believe I might without arrogance affirm that the same thought might be improved into methods that should prevent the general misery and poverty of mankind, and at once secure us against beggars, parish poor, almshouses, and hospitals; and by which not a creature so miserable or so poor but should claim subsistence as their due, and not ask it of charity.

I cannot believe any creature so wretchedly base as to beg of mere choice, but either it must proceed from want or sordid prodigious covetousness; and thence I affirm there can be no beggar but he ought to be either relieved or punished, or both. If a man begs for mere covetousness, without want, it is a baseness of soul so extremely sordid, as ought to be used with the utmost contempt, and punished with the correction due to a dog. If he begs for want, that want is procured by slothfulness and idleness, or by accident; if the latter, he ought to be relieved, if the former, he ought to be punished for the cause, but at the same time relieved also; for no man ought to starve, let his crime be what it will.

I shall proceed, therefore, to a scheme by which all mankind, be he never so mean, so poor, so unable, shall gain for himself a just claim to a comfortable subsistence whensoever age or casualty shall reduce him to a necessity of making use of it. There is a poverty so far from being despicable, that it is honourable, when a man by direct casualty, sudden providence, and without any procuring of his own, is reduced to want relief from others, as by fire, shipwreck, loss of limbs, and the like.

These are sometimes so apparent, that they command the charity of others; but there are also many families reduced to decay, whose conditions are not so public, and yet their necessities as great. Innumerable circumstances reduce men to want, and pressing poverty obliges some people to make their cases public or starve; and from thence came the custom of begging, which sloth and idleness has improved into a trade. But the method I propose, thoroughly put in practice, would remove the cause, and the effect would cease of course.

Want of consideration is the great reason why people do not provide in their youth and strength for old age and sickness, and the ensuing proposal is, in short, only this: That all persons in the time of their health and youth, while they are able to work and spare it, should lay up some small inconsiderable part of their gettings as a deposit in safe hands, to lie as a store in bank to relieve them, if by age or accident they come to be disabled or incapable to provide for themselves, and that if God so bless them that they nor theirs never come to need it, the overplus may be employed to relieve such as shall.

If an office in the same nature with this were appointed in every county in England, I doubt not but poverty might easily be prevented, and begging wholly suppressed.

# A PENSION-OFFICE.

THAT an office be erected in some convenient place, where shall be a secretary, a clerk, and a searcher, always attending. That all sorts of people, who are labouring people and of honest repute, of what calling or condition soever, men or women —beggars and soldiers excepted—who being sound of their limbs and under fifty years of age, shall come to the said office and enter their names, trades, and places of abode into a register to be kept for that purpose, and shall pay down at the time of the said entering the sum of sixpence, and from thence one shilling per quarter, shall every one have an assurance under the seal of the said office for these following conditions :—

(1.) Every such subscriber, if by any casualty (drunkenness and quarrels excepted) they break their limbs, dislocate joints, or are dangerously maimed or bruised, able surgeons appointed for that purpose shall take them into their care and endeavour their cure gratis.

(2.) If they are at any time dangerously sick, on notice given to the said office, able physicians shall be appointed to visit them and give their prescriptions gratis.

(3.) If by sickness or accident, as aforesaid, they lose their limbs or eyes, so as to be visibly disabled to work, and are otherwise poor and unable to provide for themselves, they shall either be cured at the charge of the office, or be allowed a pension for subsistence during life.

(4.) If they become lame, aged, bedrid, or by real infirmity of body (the pox excepted) are unable to work, and otherwise incapable to provide for themselves, on proof made that it is really and honestly so, they shall be taken into a college or hospital provided for that purpose, and be decently maintained during life.

(5.) If they are seamen, and die abroad on board the merchants' ships they were employed in, or are cast away and drowned, or taken and die in slavery, their widows shall receive a pension during their widowhood.

(6.) If they were tradesmen, and paid the parish rates, if by decay and failure of trade they break and are put in prison for debt, they shall receive a pension for subsistence during close imprisonment.

(7.) If by sickness or accidents they are reduced to extremities of poverty for a season, on a true representation to the office they shall be relieved as the governors shall see cause.

It is to be noted that in the 4th article such as by sickness and age are disabled from work and poor shall be taken into the house and provided for, whereas in the 3rd article they who are blind or have lost limbs, &c., shall have pensions allowed them.

The reason of this difference is this :—A poor man or woman that has lost his hand, or leg, or sight, is visibly disabled, and we cannot be deceived, whereas other infirmities are not so easily judged of, and everybody would be claiming a pension, when but few will demand being taken into an hospital but such as are really in want.

And that this might be managed with such care and candour as a design which carries so good a face ought to be, I propose the following method for putting it in practice.

I suppose every undertaking of such a magnitude must have some principal agent to push it forward, who must manage and direct everything, always with direction of the governors.

And first, I will suppose one general office erected for the great parishes of Stepney and Whitechapel; and as I will lay down afterwards some methods to oblige all people to come in and subscribe, so I may be allowed to suppose here that all the inhabitants of those two large parishes (the meaner labouring sort I mean) should enter their names, and that the number of them should be 100,000, as I believe they would be at least.

First, there should be named fifty of the principal inhabitants of the said parishes (of which the churchwardens for the time being, and all the justices of the peace dwelling in the bounds of the said parish, and the ministers resident for the time being, to be part) to be governors of the said office.

The said fifty to be first nominated by the Lord Mayor of London for the time being, and every vacancy to be supplied in ten days at farthest by the majority of voices of the rest.

The fifty to choose a committee of eleven, to sit twice a week, of whom three to be a quorum, with a chief governor, a deputy-governor, and a treasurer.

In the office, a secretary with clerks of his own, a registrar and two clerks, four searchers, a messenger—one in daily attendance under salary—a physician, a surgeon, and four visitors.

In the hospital, more or less, according to the number of people entertained, a housekeeper, a steward, nurses, a porter, and a chaplain.

For the support of this office, and that the deposit money might go to none but the persons and uses for whom it is paid, and that it might not be said officers and salaries was the chief end of the undertaking, as in many a project it has been, I propose that the manager or undertaker, whom I mentioned before, be the secretary, who shall have a clerk allowed him, whose business it shall be to keep the register, take the entries, and give out the tickets sealed by the governors and signed by himself, and to enter always the payment of quarterage of every subscriber. And that there may be no fraud or connivance, and too great trust be not reposed in the said secretary, every subscriber who brings his quarterage is to put it into a great chest, locked up with eleven locks, every member of the committee to keep a key, so that it cannot be opened but in the presence of them all; and every time a subscriber pays his quarterage, the secretary shall give him a sealed

ticket, thus—

| CHRISTMAS, 1796. |
| --- |

which shall be allowed as the receipt of quarterage for that quarter.

*Note.*—The reason why every subscriber shall take a receipt or ticket for his quarterage, is, because this must be the standing law of the office, that if any subscriber fail to pay their quarterage, they shall never claim after it until double so much be paid, nor not at all that quarter, whatever befalls them.

The secretary should be allowed to have twopence for every ticket of entry he gives out, and a penny for every receipt he gives for quarterage, to be accounted for as follows :—

One-third to himself in lieu of salary, he being to pay three clerks out of it ;

One-third to the clerks and other officers among them ;

And one-third to defray the incident charges of the office. Thus calculated :—

One hundred thousand subscribers paying a penny each every quarter is . . . . . £1,666 3 4

One-third—

To the secretary and three clerks (per annum) . £555 7 9

One-third—

| | | | | | |
|---|---|---|---|---|---|
| To a registrar . | . | . | . | £100 0 0 | |
| To a clerk | . | . | . | . 50 0 0 | |
| To four searchers | . | . | . | . 100 0 0 | |
| To a physician . | . | . | . | . 100 0 0 | |
| To a surgeon . | . | . | . | . 100 0 0 | |
| To four visitors | . | . | . | . 100 0 0 | |
| | | | | | 550 0 0 |

One-third to incident charges, such as—

| | | | | | |
|---|---|---|---|---|---|
| To ten committee-men, 5s. each sitting twice per week, is . | . | £260 0 0 | |
| To a clerk of committees . | . | . 50 0 0 | |
| To a messenger | . | . | . | . 40 0 0 | |
| A house for the office | . | . | . 40 0 0 | |
| A house for the hospital . | . | . 100 0 0 | |
| Contingencies . | . | . | . | . 70 15 7 | |
| | | | | | 560 15 7 |

£1,666 3 4

All the charge being thus paid out of such a trifle as a penny per quarter, the next consideration is to examine what the incomes of this subscription may be, and in time what may be the demands upon it.

| | | | |
|---|---|---|---|
| If 100,000 persons subscribe, they pay down at their entering 6d. each, which is . . . . . | £2,500 | 0 | 0 |
| And the first year's payment is in stock at 1s. per quarter . . . . . . . . . | 20,000 | 0 | 0 |
| It must be allowed that under three months the subscriptions will not be well complete; so the payment of quarterage shall not begin but from the day after the books are full, or shut up; and from thence one year is to pass before any claim can be made; and the money coming in at separate times, I suppose no improvement upon it for the first year, except of the £2500, which, lent to the King on some good fund at 7 per cent. interest, advances the first year . . . . . . | 175 | 0 | 0 |
| The quarterage of the second year, abating for a thousand claims . . . . . . . | 19,800 | 0 | 0 |
| And the interest of the first year's money at the end of the second year, lent to the King, as aforesaid, at 7 per cent. interest, is . . . . . | 1,774 | 10 | 0 |
| The quarterage of the third year, abating for claims . | 19,400 | 0 | 0 |
| The interest of former cash to the end of the third year . . . . . . . . . | 3,284 | 8 | 0 |
| Income of three years . . . . . . . | £66,933 | 18 | 0 |

*Note.*—Any person may pay 2s. up to 5s. quarterly if they please, and upon a claim will be allowed in proportion.

To assign what shall be the charge upon this, where contingency has so great a share, is not to be done; but by way of political arithmetic a probable guess may be made.

It is to be noted that the pensions I propose to be paid to persons claiming by the third, fifth, and sixth articles are thus: Every person who paid 1s. quarterly shall receive 12d. weekly, and so in proportion; every 12d. paid quarterly by any one person to receive so many shillings weekly if they come to claim a pension.

The first year no claim is allowed; so the bank has in stock completely £22,500. From thence we are to consider the number of claims.

Sir William Petty in his "Political Arithmetic" supposes not above one in forty to die per annum out of the whole number of people; and I can by no means allow that the circumstances of our claims will be as frequent as death; for these reasons :—

(1.) Our subscriptions respect all persons grown and in the prime of their age; past the first, and providing against the last part of danger. Sir William's account including children and old people, who always make up one-third of the bills of mortality.

(2.) Our claims will fall thin at first for several years; and let but the money increase for ten years, as it does in the account for three years, it would be almost sufficient to maintain the whole number.

(3.) Allow that casualty and poverty are our debtor-side, health, prosperity, and death are the creditor-side of the account, and in all probable accounts those three articles will carry off three-fourth parts of the number, as follows :—If one in forty shall die annually, as no doubt they shall, and more, that is 2500 a year, which in twenty years is 50,000 of the number. I hope I may be allowed one-third to be out of condition to claim, apparently living without the help of charity, and one-third in health of body and able to work, which put together makes 83,332, so it leaves 16,668 to make claims of charity and pensions in the first twenty years, and one half of them must, according to Sir William Petty, die on our hands in twenty years, so there remains but 8334.

But to put it out of doubt, beyond the proportion to be guessed at, I will allow they shall fall thus :—

The first year, we are to note, none can claim, and the second year the number must be very few, but increasing; wherefore I suppose—

| | | | | | | |
|---|---|---|---|---|---|---|
| One in every 500 shall claim the second year, which is 200, the charge whereof is | . | . | . | . | £500 | 0 | 0 |
| One in every 100 the third year is 1000, the charge | . | 2500 | 0 | 0 |
| Together with the former 200 | . | . | . | . | 500 | 0 | 0 |

£3000 0 0

To carry on the calculation :—

| | | | |
|---|---:|---:|---:|
| We find the stock at the end of the third year . | £66,933 | 18 | 0 |
| The quarterage of the fourth year, abating as before . . . . . . . | 19,000 | 0 | 0 |
| Interest of the stock . . . . . | 4,882 | 17 | 6 |
| The quarterage of the fifth year . . . | 18,600 | 0 | 0 |
| Interest of the stock . . . . . | 6,473 | 0 | 0 |
| | £115,879 | 15 | 6 |

| | | | |
|---|---:|---:|---:|
| The charge . . . . . . | £3,000 | 0 | 0 |
| Two thousand to fall the fourth year . | 5,000 | 0 | 0 |
| And the old continued . . . . | 3,000 | 0 | 0 |
| Two thousand the fifth year . . | 5,000 | 0 | 0 |
| The old continued . . . . . | 11,000 | 0 | 0 |
| | £27,000 | 0 | 0 |

By this computation the stock is increased above the charge in five years £89,379, 15s. 6d., and yet here are sundry articles to be considered on both sides of the account that will necessarily increase the stock and diminish the charge.

| | | | |
|---|---:|---:|---:|
| First, in the five years' time 6200 having claimed charity, the number being abated for in the reckoning above for stock, it may be allowed new subscriptions will be taken in to keep the number full, which in five years amounts to . . . . . . | £3,400 | 0 | 0 |
| Their sixpences is . . . . . . | 155 | 0 | 0 |
| | £3,555 | 0 | 0 |

| | | | |
|---|---:|---:|---:|
| Which added to £115,879, 15s. 6d. augments the stock to . . . . . . | £119,434 | 15 | 6 |

| | | | |
|---|---:|---:|---:|
| Six thousand two hundred persons claiming help, which falls, to be sure, on the aged and infirm, I think, at a modest computation, in five years' time 500 of them may be dead, which, without allowing annually, we take at an abatement of £4000 out of the charge . | £4,000 | 0 | 0 |
| Which reduces the charge to . . . . | £23,000 | 0 | 0 |

Besides this, the interest of the quarterage, which is supposed in the former account to lie dead till the year is out, which, cast up from quarter to quarter, allowing it to be put out quarterly, as it may well be, amounts to, by computation for five years, £5250.

From the fifth year, as near as can be computed, the number of pensioners being so great, I make no doubt but they shall die off of the hands of the undertaker as fast as they shall fall in, excepting so much difference as the payment of every year, which the interest of the stock shall supply.

For example :—

| | | | |
|---|---:|---:|---:|
| At the end of the fifth year the stock in hand | £94,629 | 15 | 6 |
| The payment of the sixth year . . . . | 20,000 | 0 | 0 |
| Interest of the stock . . . . . | 5,408 | 4 | 0 |
| | £120,037 | 19 | 6 |
| Allow an overplus charge for keeping in the house, which will be dearer than pensions, £10,000 per annum . . . . . | 10,000 | 0 | 0 |
| Charge of the sixth year . . . . . | 22,500 | 0 | 0 |
| Balance in cash . . . . . . | 87,537 | 19 | 6 |
| | £120,037 | 19 | 6 |

This also is to be allowed, that all those persons who are kept by the office in the house shall have employment provided for them, whereby no person shall be kept idle, the works to be suited to every one's capacity without rigour, only some distinction to those who are most willing to work, the profits of the said work to the stock of the house.

Besides this, there may great and very profitable methods be found out to improve the stock beyond the settled interest of 7 per cent., which perhaps may not always be to be had, for the Exchequer is not always borrowing money; but a bank of £80,000 employed by faithful hands need not want opportunities of great and very considerable improvement.

Also, it would be a very good object for persons who die rich to leave legacies to, which in time might be very well supposed to raise a standing revenue to it.

I will not say but various contingencies may alter the charge of this undertaking, and swell the claims beyond proportion further than I extend it; but all that, and much more, is sufficiently answered in the calculations by above £80,000 in stock to provide for it.

As to the calculation being made on a vast number of subscribers, and more than, perhaps, will be allowed likely to subscribe, I think the proportion may hold good in a few as well as in a great many; and perhaps if twenty thousand subscribed, it might be as effectual. I am indeed willing to think all men should have sense enough to see the usefulness of such a design, and be persuaded by their interest to engage in it: but some men have less prudence than brutes, and will make no provision against age till it comes; and to deal with such, two ways might be used by authority to compel them :—

(1.) The churchwardens and justices of peace should send the beadle of the parish, with an officer belonging to this office, about to the poorer parishioners, to tell them that since such honourable provision is made for them to secure themselves in old age from poverty and distress, they should expect no relief from the parish if they refused to enter themselves, and by sparing so small a part of their earnings to prevent future misery.

(2.) The churchwardens of every parish might refuse the removal of persons and families into their parish but upon their having entered into this office.

(3.) All persons should be publicly desired to forbear giving anything to beggars, and all common beggars suppressed after a certain time, for this would effectually suppress beggary at last.

And to oblige the parishes to do this on behalf of such a project, the governor of the house should secure the parish against all charges coming upon them from any person who did subscribe and pay the quarterage, and that would most certainly oblige any parish to endeavour that all the labouring meaner people in the parish should enter their names; for in time it would most certainly take all the poor in the parish off their hands.

I know that by law no parish can refuse to relieve any person or family fallen into distress, and therefore to send them word they must expect no relief would seem a vain threatening; but thus far the parish may do, they shall be esteemed as persons who deserve no relief, and shall be used accordingly ; for who, indeed, would ever pity that man in his distress who, at the expense of two pots of beer a month, might have prevented it and would not spare it ?

As to my calculations, on which I do not depend neither, I say this : If they are probable, and that in five years' time a subscription of a hundred thousand persons would have £87,537, 19s. 6d. in cash, all charges paid, I desire any one but to reflect what will not such a sum do. For instance, were it laid out in the million lottery tickets, which are now sold at £6 each, and bring in £1 per annum for fifteen years, every £1000 so laid out pays back in time £2500, and that time would be as fast as it would be wanted, and therefore be as good as money ; or if laid out in improving rents, as ground-rents with buildings to devolve in time, there is no question but a revenue would be raised in time to maintain one third part of the number of subscribers, if they should come to claim charity.

And I desire any man to consider the present state of this kingdom, and tell me if all the people of England, old and young, rich and poor, were to pay into one common bank 4s. per annum a head, and that 4s. duly and honestly managed, whether the overplus paid by those who die off, and by those who never come to want, would not in all probability maintain all that should be poor, and for ever banish beggary and poverty out of the kingdom ?

# OF WAGERING.

WAGERING, as now practised by policies and contracts, is become a branch of assurance; it was before more properly a part of gaming, and, as it deserved, had but a very low esteem, but shifting sides, and the war providing proper subjects, as the contingencies of sieges, battles, treaties, and campaigns, it increased to an extraordinary reputation, and offices were erected on purpose, which managed it to a strange degree and with great advantage, especially to the office-keepers, so that, as has been computed, there was not less gaged on one side and other upon the second siege of Limerick than two hundred thousand pounds.

How it is managed, and by what trick and artifice it became a trade, and how insensibly men were drawn into it, an easy account may be given.

I believe novelty was the first wheel that set it on work, and I need make no reflection upon the power of that charm. It was wholly a new thing, at least upon the Exchange of London; and the first occasion that gave it room among public discourse was some persons forming wagers on the return and success of King James, for which the Government took occasion to use them as they deserved.

I have heard a bookseller in King James's time say, "That if he would have a book sell, he would have it burnt by the hand of the common hangman." The man no doubt valued his profit above his reputation; but people are so addicted to prosecute a thing that seems forbid, that this very practice seemed to be encouraged by its being contraband.

The trade increased, and first on the Exchange, and then in coffee-houses, it got life, till the brokers, those vermin of trade, got hold of it, and then particular offices were set apart for it, and an incredible resort thither was to be seen every day.

These offices had not been long in being, but they were thronged with sharpers and setters as much as the Groom-Porters or any gaming ordinary in town, where a man had nothing to do but make a good figure and prepare the keeper of the office to give him credit as a good man, and though he had not a groat to pay, he should take guineas and sign policies till he had received perhaps £300 or £400 in money on condition to pay great odds, and then success tries the man.  If he wins, his fortune is made ; if not, he is a better man than he was before by just so much money; for as to the debt, he is your humble servant in the Temple or Whitehall.

But besides those who are but the thieves of the trade, there is a method as effectual to get money as possible, managed with more appearing honesty but no less art, by which the wagerer, in confederacy with the office-keeper, shall lay vast sums, great odds, and yet be always sure to win.

For example :—A town in Flanders, or elsewhere, during the war is besieged; perhaps at the beginning of the siege the defence is vigorous and relief probable, and it is the opinion of most people the town will hold out so long, or perhaps not be taken at all.  The wagerer has two or three more of his sort in con-junction, of which always the office-keeper is one, and they run down all discourse of the taking the town, and offer great odds it shall not be taken by such a day.  Perhaps this goes on a week, and then the scale turns ; and though they seem to hold the same opinion still, yet underhand the office-keeper has orders to take all the odds, which by their example was before given, against the taking the town ; and so all their first given odds are easily secured, and yet the people brought into a vein of betting against the siege of the town too.  Then they order all the odds to be taken as long as they will run, while they themselves openly give odds, and sign policies and oftentimes take their own money, till they have received perhaps double what they at first laid. Then they turn the scale at once, and cry down the town, and lay that it shall be taken till the length of the first odds is fully run; and by this manœuvre, if the town be taken, they win perhaps two or three thousand pounds, and if it be not taken, they are no losers neither.

It is visible by experience, not one town in ten is besieged but it is taken. The art of war is so improved, and our generals are so wary, that an army seldom attempts a siege but when they are almost sure to go on with it, and no town can hold out if a relief cannot be had from abroad.

Now if I can, by first laying £500 to £200 with A, that the town shall not be taken, wheedle in B to lay me £5000 to £2000 of the same; and after that, by bringing down the vogue of the siege, reduce the wagers to even hand, and lay £2000 with C that the town shall not be taken; by this method it is plain—

If the town be not taken, I win £2200 and lose £2000.
If the town be taken, I win £5000 and lose £2500.

This is gaming by rule, and in such a knot it is impossible to lose; for if it is in any man's, or company of men's power, by any artifice to alter the odds, it is in their power to command the money out of every man's pocket who has no more wit than to venture.

# OF FOOLS.

OF all persons who are objects of our charity, none move my compassion like those whom it has pleased God to leave in a full state of health and strength, but deprived of reason to act for themselves. And it is, in my opinion, one of the greatest scandals upon the understanding of others to mock at those who want it. Upon this account, I think the hospital we call Bedlam to be a noble foundation, a visible instance of the sense our ancestors had of the greatest unhappiness which can befall human kind.[1] Since as the soul in man distinguishes him from

[1] Bedlam was then the only Hospital for the Insane. St. Luke's, the second, was not established until 1751. In the year 1247 a priory was founded in Bishopsgate Street for the Order of St. Mary of Bethlehem, or of the Star of Bethlehem. It was founded by a grant of houses and land from Simon Fitz Mary, Alderman and Sheriff of London, to be under the Bishop of Bethlehem, in the Holy Land, and to give him entertainment when he came to England. The site of the original priory is now partly covered by Liverpool Street and the adjoining railway stations. In 1347 the property in Bethlem was seized by the Crown. A commission of inquiry into the conduct of the porter of the house leads to knowledge of the fact that in 1403 it made provision for six lunatics, who required "six chains of iron with six locks; four pairs of manacles of iron, and two pair of stocks." This care of lunatics appears to have been transferred to Bethlem from a house at the corner of St. Martin's Lane by Charing Cross, on a site within the present area of Trafalgar Square, where a king thought they were too near his palace. Thus by Henry the Eighth's time Bedlam was a recognised name for a lunatic. In 1546 the City obtained from the King the government of Bedlam on condition that new buildings were erected. In September 1557 the management of Bedlam was transferred to the governors of Bridewell, subject to the jurisdiction of the citizens; it was under their charge in Defoe's time, and the hospitals remain united. In 1632 the buildings were enlarged, and there is note of expenditure upon fetters and straw. In 1657, Evelyn records in his Diary that he visited Bedlam: "I stepped into Bedlam, where I saw several poor miserable creatures in chains; one of them mad with making verses." Lunatics discharged to make room for others were the Bedlam beggars, 'Tom o' Bedlams, who blew ox-horns when they came to ask for alms, and displayed brass badges on their arms in evidence that they were Bed-

a brute, so where the soul is dead (for so it is as to acting), no brute so much a beast as a man. But since never to have it, and to have lost it, are synonymous in the effect, I wonder how it came to pass that in the settlement of that hospital they made no provisions for persons born without the use of their reason, such as we call fools, or more properly naturals.

We use such in England with the last contempt, which I think is a strange error, since though they are useless to the commonwealth, they are only so by God's direct providence, and no previous fault.

I think it would very well become this wise age to take care of such, and perhaps they are a particular rent-charge on the great family of mankind left by the Maker of us all, like a younger brother, who, though the estate be given from him, yet his father expected the heir should take some care of him.

If I were to be asked who ought in particular to be charged with this work, I would answer in general, those who have a portion of understanding extraordinary; not that I would lay a tax on any man's brains, or discourage wit by appointing wise men to maintain fools, but some tribute is due to God's goodness for bestowing extraordinary gifts, and who can it be better paid to than such as suffer for want of the same bounty?

For the providing, therefore, some subsistence for such, that natural defects may not be exposed :—

It is proposed that a fool-house be erected, either by public authority, or by the City, or by an Act of Parliament, into which all that are naturals or born fools, without respect or distinction, should be admitted and maintained.

For the maintenance of this a small stated contribution, settled

lamites. In 1675 the governors published a caution to the public that no such badges were then given, "and that the same is a false pretence to colour their wandering and begging, and to deceive the people, to the dishonour of the government of that Hospital." At that time the old order was passing away ; a new site, corresponding with what is now the south side of Finsbury Circus, was occupied in 1678 with a new building large enough to contain a hundred and twenty patients or more, the first large asylum specially built for the insane. That was the Bedlam of 1697.

by the authority of an Act of Parliament, without any damage to the persons paying the same, might be very easily raised by a tax upon learning, to be paid by the authors of books.

| | | |
|---|---|---|
| Every book that shall be printed in folio, from forty sheets and upwards, to pay at the licensing (for the whole impression) . . . . . £5 | 0 | 0 |
| Under forty sheets . . . . . . . 2 | 0 | 0 |
| Every quarto . . . . . . . . 1 | 0 | 0 |
| Every octavo of ten sheets and upward . . . . 1 | 0 | 0 |
| Every octavo under ten sheets, and every book bound in twelves . . . . . . . . 0 | 10 | 0 |
| Every stitched pamphlet . . . . . . 0 | 2 | 0 |

Reprinted copies the same rates.

This tax, to be paid into the Chamber of London for the space of twenty years, would without question raise a fund sufficient to build and purchase a settlement for this house.

I suppose this little tax, being to be raised at so few places as the printing-presses or the licensers of books, and consequently the charge but very small in gathering, might bring in about £1500 per annum for the term of twenty years, which would perform the work to the degree following.

The house should be plain and decent (for I do not think the ostentation of buildings necessary or suitable to works of charity), and be built somewhere out of town for the sake of the air.

The building to cost about £1000, or, if the revenue exceed, to cost £2000 at most, and the salaries mean in proportion.

*In the House.*

| | | |
|---|---|---|
| A steward . . . . . £30 | per ann. |
| A purveyor . . . . . 20 | ,, |
| A cook . . . . . . 20 | ,, |
| A butler . . . . . . 20 | ,, |
| Six women to assist the cook and clean the house, at £4 each . . . . . . 24 | ,, |
| Six nurses to tend the people, £3 each . . 18 | ,, |
| A chaplain . . . . . . 20 | ,, |
| £152 | ,, |

A hundred alms-people at £8 per annum, diet, &c.    800 per ann.
                                                    ————
                                              £952    ,,
The table for the officers, and contingencies and
   clothes for the alms-people and firing, put
   together  .    .    .    .    .    .    .    500    ,,
An auditor of the accounts, a committee of the
   governors, and two clerks.

Here I suppose £1500 per annum revenue to be settled upon the house, which it is very probable might be raised from the tax aforesaid.   But since an Act of Parliament is necessary to be had for the collecting this duty, and that taxes for keeping of fools would be difficultly obtained while they are so much wanted for wise men, I would propose to raise the money by voluntary charity, which would be a work would leave more honour to the undertakers than feasts and great shows, which our public bodies too much diminish their stocks with.

But to pass all supposititious ways, which are easily thought of but hardly procured, I propose to maintain fools out of our own folly.   And whereas a great deal of money has been thrown about in lotteries, the following proposal would very easily perfect our work.

### A CHARITY LOTTERY.

That a lottery be set up by the authority of the Lord Mayor and Court of Aldermen for a hundred thousand tickets at twenty shillings each, to be drawn by the known way and method of drawing lotteries, as the million-lottery was drawn, in which no allowance to be made to anybody, but the fortunate to receive the full sum of one hundred thousand pounds put in, without discount, and yet this double advantage to follow :—

(1.) That an immediate sum of one hundred thousand pounds shall be raised and paid into the Exchequer for the public use.

(2.) A sum of above twenty thousand pounds be gained to be put into the hands of known trustees, to be laid out in a charity for the maintenance of the poor.

That as soon as the money shall be come in, it shall be paid into the Exchequer, either on some good fund, if any suitable, or on the credit of the Exchequer, and that when the lottery is drawn, the fortunate to receive tallies or bills from the Exchequer for their money, payable at four years.

The Exchequer receives this money, and gives out tallies according to the prizes when it is drawn, all payable at four years, and the interest of this money for four years is struck in tallies proportioned to the time, and given to the trustees, which is the profit I propose for the work.

Thus the fortunate have an immediate title to their prizes at four years without interest, and the hospital will have also an immediate title to £6000 per annum for four years, which is the interest at 6 per cent. annum.

If any should object against the time of staying for their prizes, it should be answered thus : That whoever did not like to stay the time for their money, upon discounting four years at 8 per cent. should have their money down.

I think this specimen will inform anybody what might be done by lotteries were they not hackneyed about in private hands, who by fraud and ill management put them out of repute, and so neither gain themselves nor suffer any useful handsome design to succeed.

It would be needless, I suppose, to mention that such a proposal as this ought to be set on foot by public approbation, and by men of known integrity and estate, that there may be no room left for a suspicion of private advantage.

If this or any equivalent proposal succeeded to raise the money, I would have the house established as aforesaid, with larger or smaller revenues, as necessity obliged; then the persons to be received should be without distinction or respect, but principally such as were really poor and friendless; and any that were kept already by any parish collection, the said parish should allow forty shillings yearly towards their maintenance, which no parish would refuse that subsisted them wholly before.

I make no question but that if such an hospital was erected within a mile or two of the City, one great circumstance would happen, viz., that the common sort of people, who are very much addicted to rambling in the fields, would make this house the customary walk, to divert themselves with the objects to be seen there, and to make what they call sport with the calamity of others, as is now shamefully allowed in Bedlam.

To prevent this, and that the condition of such, which deserves pity, not contempt, might not be the more exposed by this charity, it should be ordered that the steward of the house be in commission of the peace within the precincts of the house only, and authorised to punish by limited fines or otherwise any person that shall offer any abuse to the poor alms-people, or shall offer to make sport at their condition.

If any person at reading of this should be so impertinent as to ask, to what purpose I would appoint a chaplain in an hospital of fools, I could answer him very well by saying : for the use of the other persons, officers, and attendants in the house.

But besides that, pray, why not a chaplain for fools as well as for knaves, since both, though in a different manner, are incapable of reaping any benefit by religion, unless by some invisible influence they are made docile? and since the same secret Power can restore these to their reason as must make the other sensible, pray, why not a chaplain? Idiots indeed were denied the communion in the primitive churches, but I never read they were not to be prayed for, or were not admitted to hear.

If we allow any religion, and a Divine Supreme Power, whose influence works invisibly on the hearts of men (as he must be worse than the people we talk of who denies it), we must allow at the same time that Power can restore the reasoning faculty to an idiot, and it is our part to use the proper means of supplicating Heaven to that end, leaving the disposing part to the issue of unalterable Providence.

The wisdom of Providence has not left us without examples of some of the most stupid natural idiots in the world who have been restored to their reason, or, as one would think, had reason infused after a long life of idiotism—perhaps, among other wise ends, to confute that sordid supposition that idiots have no souls.

# OF BANKRUPTS.

THIS chapter has some right to stand next to that of fools, for besides the common acceptation of late, which makes every unfortunate man a fool, I think no man so much made a fool of as a bankrupt.[1]

If I may be allowed so much liberty with our laws, which are generally good, and above all things are tempered with mercy, leniency, and freedom, this has something in it of barbarity. It gives a loose to the malice and revenge of the creditor, as well as a power to right himself, while it leaves the debtor no way to show himself honest. It contrives all the ways possible to drive the debtor to despair, and encourages no new industry, for it makes him perfectly incapable of anything but starving.

This law, especially as it is now frequently executed, tends wholly to the destruction of the debtor, and yet very little to the advantage of the creditor.

1. The severities to the debtor are unreasonable, and, if I may say so, a little inhuman, for it not only strips him of all in a moment, but renders him for ever incapable of helping himself or relieving his family by future industry, if he escapes from prison, which is hardly done too. If he has nothing left, he must starve or live on charity. If he goes to work, no man dare pay him his wages, but he shall pay it again to the creditors. If he has any private stock left for a subsistence, he can put it

---

[1] It has been held that the old Roman Law of the Twelve Tables gave power to creditors to cut the body of a bankrupt debtor into as many pieces as would give each creditor a proportionate share. In England, by an Act of the year 1624, a bankrupt might be set for two hours in the pillory with one of his ears first nailed to it, and then cut off. All debtors in Defoe's time, honest or dishonest, might be sent to prison.

nowhere; every man is bound to be a thief and take it from him. If he trusts it in the hands of a friend, he must receive it again as a great courtesy, for that friend is liable to account for it. I have known a poor man prosecuted by a statute to that degree that all he had left was a little money which he knew not where to hide. At last, that he might not starve, he gives it to his brother, who had entertained him. The brother, after he had his money, quarrels with him to get him out of his house; and when he desires him to let him have the money lent him, gives him this for answer, "I cannot pay you safely, for there is a statute against you;" which run the poor man to such extremities that he destroyed himself. Nothing is more frequent than for men who are reduced by miscarriage in trade to compound and set up again and get good estates, but a statute, as we call it, for ever shuts up all doors to the debtor's recovery, as if breaking were a crime so capital that he ought to be cast out of human society and exposed to extremities worse than death. And, which will further expose the fruitless severity of this law, it is easy to make it appear that all this cruelty to the debtor is so far (generally speaking) from advantaging the creditors, that it destroys the estate, consumes it in extravagant charges, and unless the debtor be consenting, seldom makes any considerable dividends. And I am bold to say there is no advantage made by the prosecuting of a statute with severity but what might be doubly made by methods more merciful. And though I am not to prescribe to the legislators of the nation, yet by way of essay I take leave to give my opinion and my experience in the methods, consequences, and remedies of this law.

All people know, who remember anything of the times when that law was made, that the evil it was pointed at was grown very rank, and breaking to defraud creditors so much a trade that the Parliament had good reason to set up a Fury to deal with it; and I am far from reflecting on the makers of that law, who, no question, saw it was necessary at that time. But as laws, though in themselves good, are more or less so as they are more or less seasonable, squared, and adapted to the circumstances and time of the evil they are made against, so it were worth while (with submission) for the same authority to examine :—

(1.) Whether the length of time since that Act was made has not given opportunity to debtors—

(*a.*) To evade the force of the Act by ways and shifts, to avoid the power of it, and secure their estates out of the reach of it?

(*b.*) To turn the point of it against those whom it was made to relieve? Since we see frequently now that bankrupts desire statutes, and procure them to be taken out against themselves.

(2.) Whether the extremities of this law are not often carried on beyond the true intent and meaning of the Act itself by persons who, besides being creditors, are also malicious, and gratify their private revenge by prosecuting the offender, to the ruin of his family.

If these two points are to be proved, then I am sure it will follow that this Act is now a public grievance to the nation ; and I doubt not but will be one time or other repealed by the same wise authority that made it.

(1.) Time and experience has furnished the debtors with ways and means to evade the force of this statute, and to secure their estate against the reach of it, which renders it often insignificant, and consequently the knave, against whom the law was particularly bent, gets off; while he only who fails of mere necessity, and whose honest principle will not permit him to practise those methods, is exposed to the fury of this Act. And as things are now ordered, nothing is more easy than for a man to order his estate so that a statute shall have no power over it, or at least but a little.

If the bankrupt be a merchant, no statute can reach his effects beyond the seas, so that he has nothing to secure but his books, and away he goes into the Friars. If a shopkeeper, he has more difficulty ; but that is made easy, for there are men (and carts) to be had whose trade it is, and who in one night shall remove the greatest warehouse of goods or cellar of wines in the town, and carry them off into those nurseries of rogues, the Mint and Friars ; and our constables and watch, who are the allowed magistrates of the night, and who shall stop a poor little lurking thief, that, it may be, has stole a bundle of old clothes worth 5s., shall let them all pass without any disturbance, and see a hundred honest men robbed of their estates before their faces, to the eternal infamy of the justice of the nation.

And were a man but to hear the discourse among the inhabitants of those dens of thieves, when they first swarm about a newcomer to comfort him, for they are not all hardened to a like degree at once: "Well," says the first, "come, don't be concerned; you have got a good parcel of goods away, I promise you; you need not value all the world." "Ah! would I had done so," says another; "I'd have laughed at all my creditors." "Ay!" says the young proficient in the hardened trade, "but my creditors!" "Damn the creditors," says a third; "why, there's such a one and such a one, they have creditors too, and they won't agree with them; and here they live like gentlemen, and care not a farthing for them. Offer your creditors half a crown in the pound, and pay it them in old debts; and if they won't take it, let them alone; they'll come after you, never fear it." "Oh, but a statute!" says he again. "Oh, but the devil!" cries the Minter. "Why, 'tis the statutes we live by," say they; "why, if 'twere not for statutes, creditors would comply, and debtors would compound, and we honest fellows here of the Mint would be starved. Prithee, what need you care for a statute? A thousand statutes can't reach you here." This is the language of the country, and the newcomer soon learns to speak it (for I think I may say, without wronging any man, I have known many a man go in among them honest, that is, without ill design, but I never knew one come away so again). Then comes a graver sort among this black crew (for here, as in hell, are fiends of degrees and different magnitude), and he falls into discourse with the newcomer and gives him more solid advice: "Look you, sir, I am concerned to see you melancholy; I am in your circumstance too, and if you'll accept of it, I'll give you the best advice I can," and so begins the grave discourse.

The man is in too much trouble not to want counsel, so he

H

thanks him, and he goes on: "Send a summons to your creditors and offer them what you can propose in the pound (always reserving a good stock to begin the world again), which, if they will take, you are a free man, and better than you were before; if they won't take it, you know the worst of it; you are on the better side of the hedge with them. If they will not take it, but will proceed to a statute, you have nothing to do but to oppose force with force, for the laws of Nature tell you you must not starve; and a statute is so barbarous, so unjust, so malicious a way of proceeding against a man, that I do not think any debtor obliged to consider anything but his own preservation when once they go on with that. For why," says the old studied wretch, "should the creditors spend your estate in the Commission, and then demand the debt of you too? Do you owe anything to the Commission of the statute?" "No," says he. "Why, then," says he, "I warrant their charges will come to £200 out of your estate, and they must have 10s. a day for starving you and your family. I cannot see why any man should think I am bound in conscience to pay the extravagance of other men. If my creditors spend £500 in getting in my estate by a statute, which I offered to surrender without it, I'll reckon that £500 paid them; let them take it among them, for equity is due to a bankrupt as well as to any man, and if the laws do not give it us, we must take it."

This is too rational discourse not to please him, and he proceeds by this advice. The creditors cannot agree, but take out a statute, and the man that offered at first, it may be, 10s. in the pound, is kept in that cursed place till he has spent it all and can offer nothing, and then gets away beyond sea, or after a long consumption gets off by an Act of relief to poor debtors, and all the charges of the statute fall among the creditors. Thus I knew a statute taken out against a shopkeeper in the country, and a considerable parcel of goods too seized; and yet the creditors, what with charges and two or three suits at law, lost their whole debts and 8s. per pound contribution-money for charges; and the poor debtor, like a man under the surgeon's hand, died in the operation.

(2.) Another evil that time and experience has brought to light from this Act is when the debtor himself shall confederate with some particular creditor to take out a statute, and this is a masterpiece of plot and intrigue; for perhaps some creditor honestly received, in the way of trade, a large sum of money of the debtor for goods sold him when he was *sui juris*, and he by consent shall own himself a bankrupt before that time, and the statute shall reach back to bring in an honest man's estate to help pay a rogue's debt. Or a man shall go and borrow a sum of money upon a parcel of goods, and lay them to pledge; he keeps the money, and the statute shall fetch away the goods to help forward the composition. These are tricks I can give too good an account of, having more than once suffered by the experiment. I could give a scheme of more ways, but I think it is needless to prove the necessity of laying aside that law, which is pernicious to both debtor and creditor, and chiefly hurtful to the honest man whom it was made to preserve.

The next inquiry is, whether the extremities of this law are not often carried on beyond the true intent and meaning of the Act itself, for malicious and private ends, to gratify passion and revenge?

I remember the answer a person gave me who had taken out statutes against several persons, and some his near relations, who had failed in his debt; and when I was one time dissuading him from prosecuting a man who owed me money as well as him, I used this argument with him:—" You know the man has nothing left to pay." "That's true," says he, "I know that well enough." "To what purpose, then," said I, "will you prosecute him?" "Why, revenge is sweet," said he. Now a man that will prosecute a debtor, not as a debtor, but by way of revenge, such a man is, I think, not intentionally within the benefit of our law.

In order to state the case right, there are four sorts of people to be considered in this discourse, and the true case is how to distinguish them.

(1.) There is the honest debtor, who fails by visible necessity, losses, sickness, decay of trade, or the like.

(2.) The knavish, designing, or idle, extravagant debtor, who fails because either he has run out his estate in excesses, or on purpose to cheat and abuse his creditors.

(3.) There is the moderate creditor, who seeks but his own, but will omit no lawful means to gain it, and yet will hear reasonable and just arguments and proposals.

(4.) There is the rigorous severe creditor, that values not whether the debtor be honest man or knave, able or unable, but will have his debt whether it be to be had or no, without mercy, without compassion, full of ill language, passion, and revenge.

How to make a law to suit to all these is the case: that a necessary favour might be shown to the first, in pity and compassion to the unfortunate, in commiseration of casualty and poverty, which no man is exempt from the danger of: that a due rigour and restraint be laid upon the second, that villainy and knavery might not be encouraged by a law: that a due care be taken of the third, that men's estates may, as far as can, be secured to them; and due limits set to the last, that no man may have an unlimited power over his fellow-subjects, to the ruin of both life and estate.

All which I humbly conceive might be brought to pass by the following method, to which I give the title of

## A COURT OF INQUIRIES.

This court should consist of a select number of persons, to be chosen yearly out of the several Wards of the City by the Lord Mayor and Court of Aldermen, and out of the several Inns-of-Court by the Lord Chancellor or Lord Keeper, for the time being, and to consist of a president, a secretary, and a treasurer, to be chosen by the rest, and named every year also; a judge of causes for the proof of debts; fifty-two citizens out of every Ward, too, of which number to be twelve merchants; two lawyers (barristers at least) out of each of the Inns-of-Court.

That a Commission of Inquiry into bankrupt estates be given to these, confirmed and settled by Act of Parliament, with power to hear, try, and determine causes as to proof of debts, and disputes in accounts between debtor and creditor, without appeal.

The office for this court to be at Guildhall, where clerks should be always attending, and a quorum of the Commissioners to sit *de die in diem* from three to six o'clock in the afternoon.

To this court every man who finds himself pressed by his affairs, so that he cannot carry on his business, shall apply himself as follows :—

He shall go to the secretary's office and give in his name, with this short petition :—

To the Honourable the President and Commissioners of His Majesty's Court of Inquiries. The humble petition of A. B., of the parish of      in the      . haberdasher.

*Sheweth,*

That your petitioner, being unable to carry on his business by reason of great losses and decay of trade, and being ready and willing to make a full and entire discovery of his whole estate, and to deliver up the same to your honours upon oath, as the law directs, for the satisfaction of his creditors, and having to that purpose entered his name into the books of your office on the      of this instant,

Your petitioner humbly prays the protection of this Honourable Court.

And shall ever pray, &c.

The secretary is to lay this petition before the Commissioners, who shall sign it of course; and the petitioner shall have an officer sent home with him immediately, who shall take possession of his house and goods, and an exact inventory of everything therein shall be taken at his entrance by other officers also, appointed by the court; according to which inventory the first officer and the bankrupt also shall be accountable.

This officer shall supersede even the Sheriff in possession, excepting by an extent for the King; only with this provision :—
That if the Sheriff be in possession by warrant on judgment,

obtained by due course of law, and without fraud or deceit, and *bona fide* in possession before the debtor entered his name in the office, in such case the plaintiff to have a double dividend allotted to his debt, for it was the fault of the debtor to let execution come upon his goods before he sought for protection; but this not to be allowed upon judgment confessed.

If the Sheriff be in possession by *fieri facias* for debt immediately due to the King, the officer shall quit his possession to the Commissioners, and they shall see the King's debt fully satisfied before any division be made to the creditors.

The officers in this case to take no fee from the bankrupt, nor to use any indecent or uncivil behaviour to the family (which is a most notorious abuse now permitted to the Sheriff's officers), whose fees I have known, on small executions, on pretence of civility, amount to as much as the debt, and yet behave themselves with unsufferable insolence all the while.

This officer being in possession, the goods may be removed or not removed, the shop shut up or not shut up, as the bankrupt upon his reasons given to the Commissioners may desire.

The inventory being taken, the bankrupt shall have fourteen days' time, and more if desired, upon showing good reasons to the Commissioners, to settle his books and draw up his accounts, and then shall deliver up all his books, together with a full and true account of his whole estate, real and personal, to which account he shall make oath, and afterwards to any particular of it, if the Commissioners require.

After this account given in, the Commissioners shall have power to examine upon oath all his servants, or any other person, and if it appears that he has concealed anything, in breach of his oath, to punish him as is hereafter specified.

Upon a fair and just surrender of all his estate and effects, *bona fide*, according to the true intent and meaning of the Act, the Commissioners shall return to him in money, or such of his goods as he shall choose, at a value by a just appraisement, £5 per cent. of all the estate he surrendered to him, together with a full and free discharge from all his creditors.

The remainder of the estate of the debtor to be fairly and equally divided among the creditors, who are to apply themselves to the Commissioners. The Commissioners to make a necessary inquiry into the nature and circumstances of the debts demanded, that no pretended debt be claimed for the private account of the debtor, in order to which inquiry they shall administer the following oath to the creditor for the proof of the debt:—

I, A. B., do solemnly swear and attest that the account hereto annexed is true and right, and every article therein rightly and truly stated, and charged in the names of the persons to whom they belong; and that there is no person or name named, concealed, or altered in the said account by me, or by my knowledge, order, or consent; and that the said          does really and *bonâ fide* owe and stand indebted to me for my own proper account the full sum of          mentioned in the said account, and that for a fair and just value made good to him, as by the said account expressed; and also that I have not made or known of any private contract, promise, or agreement between him, the said          (or anybody for him) and me, or any person whatsoever. So help me God.

Upon this oath, and no circumstances to render the person suspected, the creditor shall have an unquestioned right to his dividend, which shall be made without the delays and charges that attend the commissions of bankrupts. For—

(1.) The goods of the debtor shall upon the first meeting of the creditors be either sold in parcels, as they shall agree, or divided among them in due proportion to their debts.

(2.) What debts are standing out, the debtors shall receive summonses from the Commissioners to pay by a certain time limited; and in the meantime the secretary is to transmit accounts to the persons owing it, appointing them a reasonable time to consent or disprove the account.

And every six months a just dividend shall be made among the creditors of the money received; and so if the effects lie abroad, authentic procurations shall be signed by the bankrupt to the Commissioners, who thereupon correspond with the persons abroad in whose hands such effects are, who are to remit the same as the Commissioners order; the dividend to be made, as before, every six months, or oftener if the court see cause.

If any man thinks the bankrupt has so much favour by these articles, that those who can dispense with an oath have an opportunity to cheat their creditors, and that hereby too much encouragement is given to men to turn bankrupt, let them consider the easiness of the discovery, the difficulty of a concealment, and the penalty on the offender.

(1.) I would have a reward of 30 per cent. be provided, to be paid to any person who should make discovery of any part of the bankrupt's estate concealed by him, which would make discoveries easy and frequent.

(2.) Any person who should claim any debt among the creditors, for the account of the bankrupt, or his wife or children, or with design to relieve them out of it, other or more than is *bona fide* due to him for value received and to be made out; or any person who shall receive in trust or by deed of gift any part of the goods or other estate of the bankrupt, with design to preserve them for the use of said bankrupt, or his wife or children, or with design to conceal them from the creditors, shall forfeit for every such act £500, and have his name published as a cheat, and a person not fit to be credited by any man. This would make it very difficult for the bankrupt to conceal anything.

(3.) The bankrupt having given his name, and put the officer into possession, shall not remove out of the house any of his books; but during the fourteen days' time which he shall have to settle the accounts, shall every night deliver the books into the hands of the officer; and the Commissioners shall have liberty, if they please, to take the books the first day and cause duplicates to be made, and then to give them back to the bankrupt to settle the accounts.

(4.) If it shall appear that the bankrupt has given in a false account, has concealed any part of his goods or debts, in breach of his oath, he shall be set in the pillory at his own door, and be imprisoned during life without bail.

(5.) To prevent the bankrupt concealing any debts abroad, it should be enacted that the name of the bankrupt being entered at the office, where every man might search gratis, should be publication enough ; and that after such entry, no discharge from the bankrupt should be allowed in account to any man, but whoever would adventure to pay any money to the said bankrupt or his order, should be still debtor to the estate, and pay it again to the Commissioners.

And whereas wiser heads than mine must be employed to compose this law, if ever it be made, they will have time to consider of more ways to secure the estate for the creditors, and, if possible, to tie the hands of the bankrupt yet faster.

This law, if ever such a happiness should arise to this kingdom, would be a present remedy for a multitude of evils which now we feel, and which are a sensible detriment to the trade of this nation.

(1.) With submission, I question not but it would prevent a great number of bankrupts, which now fall by divers causes ; for—

(a.) It would effectually remove all crafty designed breakings, by which many honest men are ruined ; and

(b.) Of course it would prevent the fall of those tradesmen who are forced to break by the knavery of such.

(2.) It would effectually suppress all those sanctuaries and refuges of thieves, the Mint, Friars, Savoy, Rules, and the like ; and that these two ways :—

(a.) Honest men would have no need of it, here being a more safe, easy, and more honourable way to get out of trouble.

(b.) Knaves should have no protection from those places, and the Act be fortified against those places by the following clauses, which I have on purpose reserved to this head.

Since the provision this Court of Inquiries makes for the ease and deliverance of every debtor who is honest is so considerable, it is most certain that no man but he who has a design to cheat his creditors will refuse to accept of the favour ; and therefore it should be enacted :—

That if any man who is a tradesman or merchant shall break

or fail, or shut up shop, or leave off trade, and shall not either pay or secure to his creditors their full and whole debts, twenty shillings in the pound, without abatement or deduction, or shall convey away their books or goods in order to bring their creditors to any composition, or shall not apply to this office as aforesaid, shall be guilty of felony, and upon conviction of the same shall suffer as a felon, without benefit of clergy.

And if any such person shall take sanctuary either in the Mint, Friars, or other pretended privilege place, or shall convey thither any of their goods as aforesaid to secure them from their creditors, upon complaint thereof made to any of His Majesty's justices of the peace, they shall immediately grant warrants to the constable, &c., to search for the said persons and goods, who shall be aided and assisted by the trained-bands, if need be, without any charge to the creditors, to search for and discover the said persons and goods; and whoever were aiding in the carrying in the said goods, or whoever knowingly received either the goods or the person, should be also guilty of felony.

For as the indigent debtor is a branch of the commonwealth which deserves its care, so the wilful bankrupt is one of the worst sort of thieves. And it seems a little unequal that a poor fellow, who for mere want steals from his neighbour some trifle, shall be sent out of the kingdom, and sometimes out of the world, while a sort of people who defy justice and violently resist the law shall be suffered to carry men's estates away before their faces, and no officers to be found who dare execute the law upon them.

Any man would be concerned to hear with what scandal and reproach foreigners do speak of the impotence of our constitution in this point; that in a civilised government, as ours is, the strangest contempt of authority is shown that can be instanced in the world.

I may be a little the warmer on this head on account that I have been a larger sufferer by such means than ordinary; but I appeal to all the world as to the equity of the case; what the difference is between having my house broken up in the night to be robbed, and a man coming in good credit and with a proffer of ready money in the middle of the day, and buying £500 of goods, and carry them directly from my warehouse into the Mint, and the next day laugh at me and bid me defiance; yet this I have seen done. I think it is the justest thing in the world that the last should be esteemed the greater thief, and deserves most to be hanged.

I have seen a creditor come with his wife and children and beg of the debtor only to let him have part of his own goods again, which he had bought knowing and designing to break. I have seen him with tears and entreaties petition for his own, or but some of it, and be taunted and sworn at and denied by a saucy insolent bankrupt, that the poor man has been wholly ruined by the cheat. It is by the villainy of such, many an honest man is undone, families starved and sent a-begging, and yet no punishment prescribed by our laws for it.

By the aforesaid Commission of Inquiry all this might be most effectually prevented, an honest, indigent tradesman preserved, knavery detected and punished, Mints, Friars, and privilege places suppressed,[1] and without doubt a great number of insolences avoided and prevented, of which many more particulars might be insisted upon; but I think these may be sufficient to lead anybody into the thought; and for the method, I leave it to the wise heads of the nation, who know better than I how to state the law to the circumstances of the crime.

[1] The parts of London in which there was this freedom from arrest were the Mint, Whitefriars, Salisbury Court, Mitre Court, the Savoy, Clink, Deadman's Place, Montague Close, Fulwood's Rents, Baldwin's Gardens, and the Minories. The privilege was abolished in 1696, the year before the printing of this "Essay on Projects," but it was maintained by custom till the reign of George the Second.

# OF ACADEMIES.

WE have in England fewer of these than in any part of the world, at least where learning is in so much esteem. But to make amends, the two great seminaries we have are, without comparison, the greatest—I won't say the best—in the world; and though much might be said here concerning universities in general, and foreign academies in particular, I content myself with noting that part in which we seem defective. The French, who justly value themselves upon erecting the most celebrated Academy of Europe, owe the lustre of it very much to the great encouragement the kings of France have given to it. And one of the members, making a speech at his entrance, tells you, "That it is not the least of the glories of their invincible monarch to have engrossed all the learning of the world in that sublime body."

The peculiar study of the Academy of Paris has been to refine and correct their own language, which they have done to that happy degree that we see it now spoken in all the courts of Christendom as the language allowed to be most universal.[1]

I had the honour once to be a member of a small society, who seemed to offer at this noble design in England; but the greatness of the work and the modesty of the gentlemen concerned

---

[1] The Project of the French Academy in 1634, as expressed by Chapelain at the second meeting of its founders, was "To attempt the purifying of our language, and the rendering it capable of the highest eloquence." To this end the Academicians were "in the first place to regulate the terms and phrases by a large Dictionary and a very exact Grammar, which might give it a part of those ornaments it wants, and that afterwards it might acquire the rest by a Rhetorique and a Poetique which should be composed to serve as a rule to them that would write in verse and prose."

prevailed with them to desist an enterprise which appeared too great for private hands to undertake. We want indeed a Richelieu to commence such a work; for I am persuaded were there such a genius in our kingdom to lead the way, there would not want capacities who could carry on the work to a glory equal to all that has gone before them. The English tongue is a subject not at all less worthy the labour of such a society than the French, and capable of a much greater perfection. The learned among the French will own that the comprehensiveness of expression is a glory in which the English tongue not only equals, but excels its neighbours. Rapin, St. Evremont, and the most eminent French authors have acknowledged it; and my Lord Roscommon, who is allowed to be a good judge of English, because he wrote it as exactly as any ever did, expresses what I mean in these lines :—

> " For who did ever in French authors see
>     The comprehensive English energy?
>     The weighty bullion of one sterling line,
>         Drawn to French wire, would through whole pages shine."

" And if our neighbours will yield us, as their greatest critic has done, the preference for sublimity and nobleness of style, we will willingly quit all pretensions to their insignificant gaiety."

It is a great pity that a subject so noble should not have some as noble to attempt it; and for a method, what greater can be set before us than the Academy of Paris, which, to give the French their due, stands foremost among all the great attempts in the learned part of the world.

The present King of England, of whom we have seen the whole world writing panegyrics and encomiums, and whom his enemies, when their interest does not silence them, are apt to say more of than ourselves; as in the war he has given surprising instances of a greatness of spirit more than common, so in peace, I dare say with submission, he shall never have an opportunity to illustrate his memory more than by such a foundation; by which he shall have opportunity to darken the glory of the French King in peace, as he has by his daring attempts in the war.

Nothing but pride loves to be flattered, and that only it is as a vice which blinds us to our own imperfections. I think princes are particularly unhappy in having their good actions magnified, as their evil actions covered. But King William, who has already won praise by the steps of dangerous virtue, seems reserved for some actions which are above the touch of flattery, whose praise is in themselves.

And such would this be; and because I am speaking of a work which seems to be proper only for the hand of the King himself, I shall not presume to carry on this chapter to the model as I have done in other subjects. Only thus far :—

That a society be erected by the King himself, if His Majesty thought fit, and composed of none but persons of the first figure in learning; and it were to be wished our gentry were so much lovers of learning that birth might always be joined with capacity.

The work of this society should be to encourage polite learning, to polish and refine the English tongue, and advance the so much neglected faculty of correct language, to establish purity and propriety of style, and to purge it from all the irregular additions that ignorance and affectation have introduced; and all those innovations in speech, if I may call them such, which some dogmatic writers have the confidence to foster upon their native language, as if their authority were sufficient to make their own fancy legitimate.

By such a society I dare say the true glory of our English style would appear, and among all the learned part of the world be esteemed, as it really is, the noblest and most comprehensive of all the vulgar languages in the world.

Into this society should be admitted none but persons eminent for learning, and yet none, or but very few, whose business or trade was learning. For I may be allowed, I suppose, to say we have seen many great scholars, mere learned men, and graduates in the last degree of study, whose English has been far from polite, full of stiffness and affectation, hard words, and long unusual coupling of syllables and sentences, which sound harsh and untunable to the ear, and shock the reader both in expression and understanding.

In short, there should be room in this society for neither clergyman, physician, or lawyer. Not that I would put an affront upon the learning of any of those honourable employments, much less upon their persons. But if I do think that their several professions do naturally and severally prescribe habits of speech to them peculiar to their practice, and prejudicial to the study I speak of, I believe I do them no wrong. Nor do I deny but there may be, and now are, among some of all those professions men of style and language, great masters of English, whom few men will undertake to correct ; and where such do at any time appear, their extraordinary merit should find them a place in this society ; but it should be rare, and upon very extraordinary occasions, that such be admitted.

I would therefore have this society wholly composed of gentlemen, whereof twelve to be of the nobility, if possible, and twelve private gentlemen, and a class of twelve to be left open for mere merit, let it be found in who or what sort it would, which should lie as the crown of their study, who have done something eminent to deserve it. The voice of this society should be sufficient authority for the usage of words, and sufficient also to expose the innovations of other men's fancies ; they should preside with a sort of judicature over the learning of the age, and have liberty to correct and censure the exorbitance of writers, especially of translators. The reputation of this society would be enough to make them the allowed judges of style and language ; and no author would have the impudence to coin without their authority. Custom, which is now our best authority for words, would always have its original here, and not be allowed without it. There should be no more occasion to search for derivations and constructions, and it would be as criminal then to coin words as money.

The exercises of this society would be lectures on the English tongue, essays on the nature, origin, usage, authorities, and differences of words, on the propriety, purity, and cadence of style, and of the politeness and manner in writing, reflections upon irregular usages, and corrections of erroneous customs in words; and, in short, everything that would appear necessary to the bringing our English tongue to a due perfection, and our gentlemen to a capacity of writing like themselves; to banish pride and pedantry, and silence the impudence and impertinence of young authors, whose ambition is to be known, though it be by their folly.

I ask leave here for a thought or two about that inundation custom has made upon our language and discourse by familiar swearing, and I place it here because custom has so far prevailed in this foolish vice, that a man's discourse is hardly agreeable without it, and some have taken upon them to say it is pity it should not be lawful, it is such a grace in a man's speech, and adds so much vigour to his language.

I desire to be understood right, and that by swearing I mean all those cursory oaths, curses, execrations, imprecations, asseverations, and by whatsoever other names they are distinguished, which are used in vehemence of discourse in the mouths almost of all men, more or less, of what sort soever.

I am not about to argue anything of their being sinful and unlawful, as forbid by divine rules; let the parson alone tell you that, who has, no question, said as much to as little purpose in this case as any other; but I am of the opinion that there is nothing so impertinent, so insignificant, so senseless and foolish as our vulgar way of discourse when mixed with oaths and curses; and I would only recommend a little consideration to our gentlemen, who have sense and wit enough, and would be ashamed to speak nonsense in other things, but value themselves upon their parts, I would but ask them to put into writing the commonplaces of their discourse, and read them over again, and examine the English, the cadence, the grammar of them, then let them turn them into Latin, or translate them into any other language, and but see what a jargon and confusion of speech they make together.

Swearing, that lewdness of the tongue, that scum and excrement of the mouth, is of all vices the most foolish and senseless; it makes a man's conversation unpleasant, his discourse fruitless, and his language nonsense.

It makes conversation unpleasant, at least to those who do not use the same foolish way of discourse, and indeed is an affront to all the company who swear not as he does; for if I swear and curse in company, I either presume all the company likes it, or affront them who do not.

Then it is fruitless, for no man is believed a jot the more for all the asseverations, damnings, and swearings he makes. Those who are used to it themselves do not believe a man the more, because they know they are so customary that they signify little to bind a man's intention; and they who practise them not have so mean an opinion of those that do, as makes them think they deserve no belief.

Then they are the spoilers and destroyers of a man's discourse, and turn it into perfect nonsense; and to make it out, I must descend a little to particulars, and desire the reader a little to foul his mouth with the brutish, sordid, senseless expressions which some gentlemen call polite English and speaking with a grace.

Some part of them, indeed, though they are foolish enough, as effects of a mad, inconsiderate rage, are yet English; as when a man swears he will do this or that, and it may be adds "God damn him, he will," that is, "God damn him if he don't." This, though it be horrid in another sense, yet may be read in writing, and is English. But what language is this?—

"Jack, God damn me, Jack, how do'st do, thou little dear son of a whore? How hast thou done this long time, by God?" and then they kiss; and the other, as lewd as himself, goes on :—

"Dear Tom, I am glad to see thee, with all my heart; let me die. Come, let us go take a bottle; we must not part so; prithee let's go and be drunk, by God."

This is some of our new florid language, and the graces and delicacies of style, which, if it were put into Latin, I would fain know which is the principal verb.

But for a little further remembrance of this impertinence, go

I

among the gamesters, and there nothing is more frequent than "God damn the dice," or "God damn the bowls."

Among the sportsmen it is "God damn the hounds," when they are at a fault, or "God damn the horse," if he baulks a leap. They call men "sons of bitches and dogs," "sons of whores;" and innumerable instances may be given of the like gallantry of language, grown now so much a custom.

It is true custom is allowed to be our best authority for words, and it is fit it should be so; but reason must be the judge of sense in language, and custom can never prevail over it. Words, indeed, like ceremonies in religion, may be submitted to the magistrate; but sense, like the essentials, is positive, unalterable, and cannot be submitted to any jurisdiction: it is a law to itself; it is ever the same; even an Act of Parliament cannot alter it.

Words and even usages in style may be altered by custom, and proprieties in speech differ according to the several dialects of the country, and according to the different manner in which several languages do severally express themselves.

But there is a direct signification of words, or a cadence in expression, which we call speaking sense; this, like truth, is sullen and the same, ever was and will be so, in what manner and in what language soever it is expressed. Words without it are only noise, which any brute can make as well as we, and birds much better; for words without sense make but dull music. Thus a man may speak in words, but perfectly unintelligible as to meaning; he may talk a great deal, but say nothing. But it is the proper position of words adapted to their significations which makes them intelligible, and conveys the meaning of the speaker to the understanding of the hearer, the contrary to which we call nonsense; and there is a superfluous crowding in of insignificant words more than are needful to express the thing intended, and this is impertinence; and that again, carried to an extreme, is ridiculous.

Thus when our discourse is interlined with needless oaths, curses, and long parentheses of imprecations, and with some of very indirect signification, they become very impertinent, and these being run to the extravagant degree instanced in before, become perfectly ridiculous and nonsense; and without forming it into an argument, it appears to be nonsense by the contradictoriness, and it appears impertinent by the insignificancy of the expression.

After all, how little it becomes a gentleman to debauch his mouth with foul language, I refer to themselves in a few particulars.

This vicious custom has prevailed upon good manners too far, but yet there are some degrees to which it has not yet arrived.

As first, the worst slaves to this folly will neither teach it to nor approve of it in their children. Some of the most careless will indeed negatively teach it, by not reproving them for it, but sure no man ever ordered his children to be taught to curse or swear.

2. The grace of swearing has not obtained to be a mode yet among the women. "God damn you" does not fit well upon a female tongue; it seems to be a masculine vice, which the women are not arrived to yet; and I would only desire those gentlemen who practise it themselves to hear a woman swear. It has no music at all there, I am sure; and just as little does it become any gentleman, if he would suffer himself to be judged by all the laws of sense or good manners in the world.

It is a senseless, foolish, ridiculous practice; it is a mean to no manner of end; it is words spoken which signify nothing; it is folly acted for the sake of folly, which is a thing even the devil himself does not practise. The devil does evil, we say, but it is for some design, either to seduce others, or, as some divines say, from a principle of enmity to his Maker. Men steal for gain, and murder to gratify their avarice or revenge; whoredoms and ravishments, adulteries and sodomy, are committed to please a vicious appetite, and have always alluring objects; and generally all vices have some previous cause and some visible tendency; but this, of all vicious practices, seems the most nonsensical and ridiculous; there is neither pleasure nor profit, no design pursued, no lust gratified, but it is a mere frenzy of the tongue, a vomit of the brain, which works by putting a contrary upon the course of nature.

Again, other vices men find some reason or other to give for or excuses to palliate; men plead want to extenuate theft, and strong provocations to excuse murders, and many a lame excuse they will bring for whoring; but this sordid habit, even those that practise it will own to be a crime, and make no excuse for it; and the most I could ever hear a man say for it was, that he could not help it.

Besides, as it is an inexcusable impertinence, so it is a breach upon good manners and conversation for a man to impose the clamour of his oaths upon the company he converses with. If there be any one person in the company that does not approve the way, it is an imposing upon him with a freedom beyond civility; as if a man should fart before a justice, or talk bawdy before the Queen, or the like.

To suppress this, laws, Acts of Parliament, and proclamations are baubles and banters, the laughter of the lewd party, and never had, as I could perceive, any influence upon the practice; nor are any of our magistrates fond or forward of putting them in execution.

It must be example, not penalties, must sink this crime, and if the gentlemen of England would once drop it as a mode, the vice is so foolish and ridiculous in itself, it would soon grow odious and out of fashion.

This work such an Academy might begin, and I believe nothing would so soon explode the practice as the public discouragement of it by such a society, where all our customs and habits both in speech and behaviour should receive an authority. All the disputes about precedency of wit, with the manners, customs, and usages of the theatre, would be decided here. Plays should pass here before they were acted, and the critics might give their censures and damn at their pleasure; nothing would ever die which once received life at this original. The two theatres might end their jangle and dispute for priority no more; wit and real worth should decide the controversy, and here should be the infallible judge.

The strife would then be only to do well,
And he alone be crowned who did excel.
Ye call them Whigs who from the Church withdrew,
But now we have our stage-dissenters too,
Who scruple ceremonies of pit and box,
And very few are sound and orthodox,
But love disorder so, and are so nice,
They hate conformity, though 'tis in vice.
Some are for patent hierarchy, and some,
Like the old Gauls, seek out for elbow-room;
Their arbitrary governors disown,
And build a conventicle-stage of their own.
Fanatic beaus make up the gaudy show,
And Wit alone appears incognito.
Wit and Religion suffer equal fate;
Neglect of both attends the warm debate;
For while the parties strive and countermine,
Wit will as well as Piety decline.

Next to this, which I esteem as the most noble and most use-ful proposal in this book, I proceed to academies for military studies; and because I design rather to express my meaning than make a large book, I bring them all into one chapter.

I allow that war is the best academy in the world, where men study by necessity and practise by force, and both to some pur-pose, with duty in the action and a reward in the end; and it is evident to any man who knows the world, or has made any observations on things, what an improvement the English nation has made during this Seven Years' War.

But should you ask how dear it first cost, and what a condition England was in for a war at first on this account, how almost all our engineers and great officers were foreigners, it may put us in mind how necessary it is to have our people so practised in the arts of war that they may not be novices when they come to the experiment.

I have heard some who were no great friends to the Govern-ment take advantage to reflect upon the King in the beginning of his wars in Ireland, that he did not care to trust the English, but all his great officers, his generals, and engineers, were foreigners.

And though the case was so plain as to need no answer, and the persons such as deserved none, yet this must be observed, though it was very strange, that when the present King took possession of this kingdom, and seeing himself entering upon the bloodiest war this age has known, began to regulate his army, he found but very few among the whole martial part of the nation fit to make use of for general officers, and was forced to employ strangers and make them Englishmen, as the Counts Schomberg, Ginkel, Solms, Ruvigny, and others. And yet it is to be observed also, that all the encouragement imaginable was given to the English gentlemen to qualify themselves, by giving no less than sixteen regiments to gentlemen of good families, who had never been in any service and knew but very little how to command them. Of these, several are now in the army, and have the rewards suitable to their merit, being major-generals, brigadiers, and the like.

If, then, a long peace had so reduced us to a degree of ignorance that might have been dangerous to us had we not a King who is always followed by the greatest masters in the world, who knows what peace and different governors may bring us to again?

The manner of making war differs perhaps as much as anything in the world; and if we look no farther back than our civil wars, it is plain a general then would hardly be fit to be a colonel now, saving his capacity of improvement. The defensive art always follows the offensive; and though the latter has extremely got the start of the former in this age, yet the other is mightily improving also.

We saw in England a bloody civil war, where, according to the old temper of the English, fighting was the business. To have an army lying in such a post as not to be able to come at them was a thing never heard of in that war; even the weakest party would always come out and fight—Dunbar fight, for instance; and they that were beaten to-day would fight again to-morrow, and seek one another out with such eagerness, as if they had been in haste to have their brains knocked out. Encampments, intrenchments, batteries, counter-marchings, fortifying of camps, and cannonadings were strange and almost unknown things, and whole campaigns were passed over and hardly any tents made use of. Battles, surprises, storming of towns, skirmishes, sieges, ambuscades, and beating up quarters was the news of every day. Now it is frequent to have armies of fifty thousand men of a side stand at bay within view of one another, and spend a whole campaign in dodging, or, as it is genteelly called, observing one another, and then march off into winter quarters. The difference is in the maxims of war, which now differ as much from what they were formerly as long perukes do from piqued beards, or as the habits of the people do now from what they then were. The present maxims of the war are—

> Never fight without a manifest advantage,
> And always encamp so as not to be forced to it.

And if two opposite generals nicely observe both these rules, it is impossible they should ever come to fight.

I grant that this way of making war spends generally more money and less blood than former wars did ; but then it spins wars out to a greater length, and I almost question whether, if this had been the way of fighting of old, our civil war had not lasted till this day. Their maxim was—

> Wherever you meet your enemy, fight him.

But the case is quite different now, and I think it is plain in the present war that it is not he who has the longest sword, so much as he who has the longest purse, will hold the war out best. Europe is all engaged in the war, and the men will never be exhausted while either party can find money, but he who finds himself poorest must give out first ; and this is evident in the French King, who now inclines to peace, and owns it, while at the same time his armies are numerous and whole ; but the sinews fail ; he finds his exchequer fail, his kingdom drained, and money hard to come at : not that I believe half the reports we have had of the misery and poverty of the French are true, but it is manifest the King of France finds, whatever his armies may do, his money will not hold out so long as the confederates, and therefore he uses all the means possible to procure a peace, while he may do it with the most advantage.

There is no question but the French may hold the war out several years longer, but their King is too wise to let things run to extremity; he will rather condescend to peace upon hard terms now than stay longer, if he finds himself in danger to be forced to worse.

This being the only digression I design to be guilty of, I hope I shall be excused it.

The sum of all is this, that since it is so necessary to be in a condition for war in a time of peace, our people should be inured to it. It is strange that everything should be ready but the soldier: ships are ready, and our trade keeps the seamen always taught, and breeds up more; but soldiers, horsemen, engineers, gunners, and the like, must be bred and taught. Men are not born with muskets on their shoulders nor fortifications in their heads; it is not natural to shoot bombs and undermine towns: for which purpose I propose—

## A ROYAL ACADEMY FOR MILITARY EXERCISES.

The founder the King himself, the charge to be paid by the public, and settled by a revenue from the Crown, to be paid yearly.

I propose this to consist of four parts :—

(1.) A college for breeding up of artists in the useful practice of all military exercises, the scholars to be taken in young and be maintained, and afterwards under the King's care for preferment, as their merit and His Majesty's favour shall recommend them, from whence His Majesty would at all times be furnished with able engineers, gunners, firemasters, bombardiers, miners, and the like.

The second college for voluntary students in the same exercises, who should all, upon certain limited conditions, be entertained, and have all the advantages of the lectures, experiments, and learning of the college, and be also capable of several titles, profits, and settlements in the said college, answerable to the fellows in the universities.

The third college for temporary study, into which any person who is a gentleman and an Englishman entering his name and conforming to the orders of the house, shall be entertained like a gentleman for one whole year gratis, and taught by masters appointed out of the second college.

The fourth college, of schools only, where all persons whatsoever, for a small allowance, shall be taught and entered in all the particular exercises they desire; and this to be supplied by the proficients of the first college.

I could lay out the dimensions and necessary incidents of all this work, but since the method of such a foundation is easy and regular from the model of other colleges, I shall only state the economy of the house.

The building must be very large, and should rather be stately and magnificent in figure than gay and costly in ornament; and I think such a house as Chelsea College, only about four times as big, would answer it, and yet I believe might be finished for as little charge as has been laid out in that palace-like hospital.

The first college should consist of one general, five colonels, twenty captains, being such as graduates by preferment, at first named by the founder, and after the first settlement to be chosen out of the first or second college, with apartments in the college and salaries :—

| | | | | |
|---|---|---|---|---|
| The general | . | . | . | £300 per annum. |
| The colonels | . | . | . | 100 ,, |
| The captains | . | . | . | 60 ,, |

Two thousand scholars, among whom shall be the following degrees :—

| | | | |
|---|---|---|---|
| 100 governors | . | . | allowed £10 per annum. |
| 200 directors | . | ,, | 5 ,, |
| 200 exempts | . | ,, | 5 ,, |
| 500 proficients. | | | |
| 1000 juniors. | | | |

The general to be named by the founder out of the colonels,

the colonels to be named by the general out of the captains, the captains out of the governors, the governors from the directors, and the directors from the exempts, and so on.

The juniors to be divided into ten schools; the schools to be thus governed:—Every school has 100 juniors in ten classes. Every class to have two directors.

| | |
|---|---:|
| 100 classes of juniors is  .    .    .    . | 1000 |
| Each class two directors  .    .    .    . | 200 |
| | ———— |
| | 1200 |

The proficients to be divided into five schools. Every school to have ten classes of ten each; every class two governors.

| | |
|---|---:|
| Fifty classes of proficients is .    .    . | 500 |
| Each class two governors is  .    .    . | 100 |
| | ———— |
| | 600 |

The exempts to be supernumerary, having a small allowance, and maintained in the college till preferment offer.

The second college to consist of voluntary students, to be taken in, after a certain degree of learning, from among the proficients of the first, or from any other schools, after such and such limitations of learning, who study at their own charge, being allowed certain privileges, as chambers rent-free, on condition of residence; commons gratis, for certain fixed terms; preferment, on condition of a term of years' residence; use of libraries, instruments, and lectures of the college.

This college should have the following preferments, with salaries :—

| | |
|---|---|
| A governor  .    .    .    . | £200 per annum. |
| A president  .    .    .    . | 100  ,, |
| Fifty college-majors .    .    . | 50  ,, |
| 200 proficients  .    .    . | 10  ,, |
| 500 voluntary students, without allowance. | |

The third and fourth colleges, consisting only of schools for temporary study, may be thus :—

The third, being for gentlemen to learn the necessary arts and exercises to qualify them for the service of their country, and entertaining them one whole year at the public charge, may be supposed to have always one thousand persons on its hands, and cannot have less than a hundred teachers, whom I would thus order :—

Every teacher shall continue at least one year, but by allowance two years at most; shall have twenty pounds per annum extraordinary allowance; shall be bound to give their constant attendance, and shall have always five college-majors of the second college to supervise them, who shall command a month, and then be succeeded by five others, and so on. Ten pounds per annum extraordinary to be paid them for their attendance.

The gentlemen who practise to be put to no manner of charge, but to be obliged strictly to the following articles :—

(1.) To constant residence, not to lie out of the house without leave of the college-major.

(2.) To perform all the college exercises as appointed by the masters, without dispute.

(3.) To submit to the orders of the house.

To quarrel or give ill language should be a crime to be punished by way of fine only, the college-major to be judge, and the offender be put into custody till he ask pardon of the person wronged, by which means every gentleman who has been affronted has sufficient satisfaction.

But to strike, challenge, draw, or fight should be more severely punished; the offender to be declared no gentleman, his name posted up at the college gate, his person expelled the house, and to be pumped as a rake if ever he is taken within the college walls.

The teachers of this college to be chosen, one half out of the exempts of the first college, and the other out of the proficients of the second.

The fourth college being only of schools, will be neither chargeable nor troublesome, but may consist of as many as shall offer themselves to be taught, and supplied with teachers from the other schools.

The proposal being of so large an extent, must have a proportionable settlement for its maintenance, and the benefit being to the whole kingdom, the charge will naturally lie upon the public, and cannot well be less, considering the number of persons to be maintained, than as follows :—

### First College.

|  | Per Annum. |
|---|---|
| The general | £300 |
| 5 colonels at £100 per annum each | 500 |
| 20 captains ,, 60 ,, ,, | 1,200 |
| 100 governors ,, 10 ,, ,, | 1,000 |
| 200 directors ,, 5 ,, ,, | 1,000 |
| 200 exempts ,, 5 ,, ,, | 1,000 |
| 2000 heads for subsistence at £20 per head per annum, including provision, and all the officers' salaries in the house, as butlers, cooks, purveyors, nurses, maids, laundresses, stewards, clerks, servants, chaplains, porters, and attendants, which are numerous | 40,000 |

### Second College.

|  |  |
|---|---|
| A governor | 200 |
| A president | 100 |
| Fifty college-majors at £50 per annum | 2,500 |
| 200 proficients at £10 per annum | 2,000 |
| Commons for 500 students during times of exercise at £5 per annum each | 2,500 |
| 200 proficients' subsistence, reckoning as above | 4,000 |

### Third College.

|  |  |
|---|---|
| The gentlemen here are maintained as gentlemen, and are to have good tables, who shall therefore have an allowance at the rate of £25 per head, all officers to be maintained out of it, which is | 25,000 |
| 100 teachers, salary and subsistence, ditto | 4,500 |
| Fifty college-majors at £10 per annum is | 500 |

|  |  |
|---|---|
| Annual charge | £86,300 |
| The building to cost | 50,000 |
| Furniture, beds, tables, chairs, linen, &c. | 10,000 |
| Books, implements, and utensils for experiments | 2,000 |
| So the immediate charge would be | £62,000 |

The annual charge  .  .  .  .  .  .  . £86,300
To which add the charges of exercises and experiments  .  3,700
                                                          ————
                                                          £90,000

The King's magazines to furnish them with 500 barrels of gunpowder per annum for the public uses of exercises and experiments.

In the first of these colleges should remain the governing part, and all the preferments be made from thence, to be supplied in course from the other; the general of the first to give orders to the other, and be subject only to the founder.

The government should be all military, with a constitution for the same regulated for that purpose, and a council to hear and determine the differences and trespasses by the college laws.

The public exercises likewise military, and all the schools be disciplined under proper officers, who are so in turn, or by order of the general, and continue but for the day.

The several classes to perform several studies, and but one study to a distinct class, and the persons as they remove from one study to another to change their classes, but so as that in the general exercises all the scholars may be qualified to act all the several parts, as they may be ordered.

The proper studies of this college should be the following :—

| | |
|---|---|
| Geometry. | Bombarding. |
| Astronomy. | Gunnery. |
| History. | Fortification. |
| Navigation. | Encamping. |
| Decimal arithmetic. | Entrenching. |
| Trigonometry. | Approaching. |
| Dialling. | Attacking. |
| Gauging. | Delineation. |
| Mining. | Architecture. |
| Fireworking. | Surveying. |

And all arts or sciences appendixes to such as these.

With exercises for the body, to which all should be obliged, as their genius and capacities led them ; as—

(1.) Swimming, which no soldier, and indeed no man whatever, ought to be without.

(2.) Handling all sorts of firearms.

(3.) Marching and countermarching in form.

(4.) Fencing and the long staff.

(5.) Riding and managing or horsemanship.

(6.) Running, leaping, and wrestling.

And herewith should also be preserved and carefully taught all the customs, usages, terms of war, and terms of art used in sieges, marches of armies, and encampment, that so a gentleman taught in this college should be no novice when he comes into the King's armies, though he have seen no service abroad. I remember the story of an English gentleman, an officer at the siege of Limerick in Ireland, who, though he was brave enough upon action, yet for the only matter of being ignorant of the terms of art, and knowing not how to talk camp language, was exposed to be laughed at by the whole army for mistaking the openings of the trenches, which he thought had been a mine against the town.

The experiments of these colleges would be as well worth publishing as the acts of the Royal Society. To which purpose the house must be built where they may have ground to cast bombs, to raise regular works, as batteries, bastions, half moons, redoubts, hornworks, forts, and the like, with the convenience of water to draw round such works, to exercise the engineers in all the necessary experiments of draining and mining under ditches. There must be room to fire great shot a distance, to cannonade a camp, to throw all sorts of fireworks and machines that are or shall be invented, to open trenches, form camps, &c.

Their public exercises will be also very diverting, and more worth while for any gentleman to see than the sights or shows which our people in England are so fond of.

I believe, as a constitution might be formed from these generals, this would be the greatest, the gallantest, and the most useful foundation in the world. The English gentry would be the best qualified, and consequently best accepted abroad, and most useful at home of any people in the world, and His Majesty should never more be exposed to the necessity of employing foreigners in the posts of trust and service in his armies.

And that the whole kingdom might in some degree be better qualified for service, I think the following project would be very useful.

When our military weapon was the long-bow, at which our English nation in some measure excelled the whole world, the meanest countryman was a good archer, and that which qualified them so much for service in the war was their diversion in times of peace, which also had this good effect, that when an army was to be raised they needed no disciplining, and for the encouragement of the people to an exercise so publicly profitable an Act of Parliament was made to oblige every parish to maintain butts for the youth in the country to shoot at.

Since our way of fighting is now altered, and this destructive engine, the musket, is the proper arms for the soldier, I could wish the diversion also of the English would change too, that our pleasures and profit might correspond. It is a great hindrance to this nation, especially where standing armies are a grievance, that if ever a war commence, men must have at least a year before they are thought fit to face an enemy, to instruct them how to handle their arms, and new-raised men are called raw soldiers. To help this, at least in some measure, I would propose that the public exercises of our youth should by some public encouragement (for penalties will not do it) be drawn off from the foolish boyish sports of cocking and cricketing, and from tippling, to shooting with a firelock, an exercise as pleasant as it is manly and generous; and swimming, which is a thing so many ways profitable, besides its being a great preservative of health, that methinks no man ought to be without it.

For shooting; the colleges I have mentioned above, having provided for the instructing the gentry at the King's charge, the gentry in return of that favour should introduce it among the country people, which might easily be done thus :—

If every country gentleman, according to his degree, would contribute to set up a prize to be shot for by the town he lives in, or the neighbourhood, about once a year, or twice a year, or oftener, as they think fit; which prize not single only to him who shoots nearest, but according to the custom of shooting.

This would certainly set all the young men in England a shooting, and make them marksmen, for they would be always practising and making matches among themselves too, and the advantage would be found in a war; for no doubt if all the soldiers in a battalion took a true level at their enemy, there would be much more execution done at a distance than there is; whereas, it has been known now that a battalion of men has received the fire of another battalion, and not lost above thirty or forty men; and I suppose it will not easily be forgot how at the battle of Aughrim a battalion of the English army received the whole fire of an Irish regiment of dragoons, but never knew to this day whether they had any bullets or no; and I need appeal no further than to any officer that served in the Irish war what advantages the English armies made of the Irish being such wonderful marksmen.

Under this head of Academies I might bring in a project for—

### An Academy for Women.

I have often thought of it as one of the most barbarous customs in the world, considering us as a civilised and a Christian country, that we deny the advantages of learning to women. We reproach the sex every day with folly and impertinence, while I am confident, had they the advantages of education equal to us, they would be guilty of less than ourselves.

One would wonder, indeed, how it should happen that women are conversible at all, since they are only beholden to natural parts for all their knowledge. Their youth is spent to teach them to stitch and sew or make baubles. They are taught to read indeed, and perhaps to write their names or so, and that is the height of a woman's education. And I would but ask any who slight the sex for their understanding, what is a man (a gentleman, I mean) good for that is taught no more?

I need not give instances, or examine the character of a gentleman with a good estate and of a good family and with tolerable parts, and examine what figure he makes for want of education.

The soul is placed in the body like a rough diamond, and must be polished, or the lustre of it will never appear: and it is manifest that as the rational soul distinguishes us from brutes, so education carries on the distinction and makes some less brutish than others. This is too evident to need any demonstration. But why then should women be denied the benefit of instruction? If knowledge and understanding had been useless additions to the sex, God Almighty would never have given them capacities, for He made nothing needless. Besides, I would ask such what they can see in ignorance that they should think it a necessary ornament to a woman? or how much worse is a wise woman than a fool? or what has the woman done to forfeit the privilege of being taught? Does she plague us with her pride and impertinence? Why did we not let her learn, that she might have had more wit? Shall we upbraid women with folly, when it is only the error of this inhuman custom that hindered them being made wiser?

The capacities of women are supposed to be greater and their senses quicker than those of the men; and what they might be capable of being bred to is plain from some instances of female wit, which this age is not without; which upbraids us with injustice, and looks as if we denied women the advantages of education for fear they should vie with the men in their improvements.

To remove this objection, and that women might have at least a needful opportunity of education in all sorts of useful learning, I propose the draught of an Academy for that purpose.

I know it is dangerous to make public appearances of the sex. They are not either to be confined or exposed; the first will disagree with their inclinations and the last with their reputations, and therefore it is somewhat difficult; and I doubt a method proposed by an ingenious lady in a little book called "Advice to

K

the Ladies " would be found impracticable, for, saving my respect to the sex, the levity, which perhaps is a little peculiar to them, at least in their youth, will not bear the restraint; and I am satisfied nothing but the height of bigotry can keep up a nunnery. Women are extravagantly desirous of going to heaven, and will punish their pretty bodies to get thither; but nothing else will do it, and even in that case sometimes it falls out that nature will prevail.

When I talk, therefore, of an academy for women, I mean both the model, the teaching, and the government different from what is proposed by that ingenious lady, for whose proposal I have a very great esteem, and also great opinion of her wit; different, too, from all sorts of religious confinement, and, above all, from vows of celibacy.

Wherefore the academy I propose should differ but little from public schools, wherein such ladies as were willing to study should have all the advantages of learning suitable to their genius.

But since some severities of discipline more than ordinary would be absolutely necessary to preserve the reputation of the house, that persons of quality and fortune might not be afraid to venture their children thither, I shall venture to make a small scheme by way of essay.

The house I would have built in a form by itself, as well as in a place by itself. The building should be of three plain fronts, without any jettings or bearing-work, that the eye might at a glance see from one coin to the other; the gardens walled in the same triangular figure, with a large moat, and but one entrance.

When thus every part of the situation was contrived as well as might be for discovery, and to render intriguing dangerous, I would have no guards, no eyes, no spies set over the ladies, but shall expect them to be tried by the principles of honour and strict virtue.

And if I am asked why, I must ask pardon of my own sex for giving this reason for it :—

I am so much in charity with women, and so well acquainted with men, that it is my opinion there needs no other care to prevent intriguing than to keep the men effectually away; for though inclination, which we prettily call love, does sometimes move a little too visibly in the sex, and frailty often follows, yet I think, verily, custom, which we miscall modesty, has so far the ascendant over the sex, that solicitation always goes before it.

> Custom with women 'stead of virtue rules ;
> It leads the wisest and commands the fools ;
> For this alone, when inclinations reign,
> Though virtue's fled, will acts of vice restrain.
> Only by custom 'tis that virtue lives,
> And love requires to be asked before it gives ;
> For that which we call modesty is pride ;
> They scorn to ask, and hate to be denied.
> 'Tis custom thus prevails upon their want ;
> They'll never beg what asked they easily grant ;
> And when the needless ceremony is over,
> Themselves the weakness of the sex discover.
> If then desires are strong and nature free,
> Keep from her men and opportunity ;
> Else 'twill be vain to curb her by restraint,
> But keep the question off, you keep the saint.

In short, let a woman have never such a coming principle, she will let you ask before she complies, at least if she be a woman of any honour.

Upon this ground I am persuaded such measures might be taken that the ladies might have all the freedom in the world within their own walls, and yet no intriguing, no indecencies, nor scandalous affairs happen ; and in order to this the following customs and laws should be observed in the colleges, of which I would propose one at least in every county in England, and about ten for the City of London.

After the regulation of the form of the building as before :—

(1.) All the ladies who enter into the house should set their hands to the orders of the house, to signify their consent to submit to them.

(2.) As no woman should be received but who declared herself willing, and that it was the act of her choice to enter herself, so no person should be confined to continue there a moment longer than the same voluntary choice inclined her.

(3.) The charges of the house being to be paid by the ladies, every one that entered should have only this encumbrance, that she should pay for the whole year, though her mind should change as to her continuance.

(4.) An Act of Parliament should make it felony without clergy for any man to enter by force or fraud into the house, or to solicit any woman, though it were to marry, while she was in the house. And this law would by no means be severe, because any woman who was willing to receive the addresses of a man might discharge herself of the house when she pleased ; and, on the contrary, any woman who had occasion, might discharge herself of the impertinent addresses of any person she had an aversion to by entering into the house.

In this house, the persons who enter should be taught all sorts of breeding suitable to both their genius and their quality, and in particular music and dancing, which it would be cruelty to bar the sex of, because they are their darlings ; but besides this, they should be taught languages, as particularly French and Italian ; and I would venture the injury of giving a woman more tongues than one.

They should, as a particular study, be taught all the graces of speech and all the necessary air of conversation, which our common education is so defective in that I need not expose it. They should be brought to read books, and especially history, and so to read as to make them understand the world, and be able to know and judge of things when they hear of them.

To such whose genius would lead them to it I would deny no sort of learning ; but the chief thing in general is to cultivate the understandings of the sex, that they may be capable of all sorts of conversation ; that their parts and judgments being improved, they may be as profitable in their conversation as they are pleasant.

Women, in my observation, have little or no difference in them, but as they are or are not distinguished by education. Tempers indeed may in some degree influence them, but the main distinguishing part is their breeding.

The whole sex are generally quick and sharp. I believe I may be allowed to say generally so, for you rarely see them lumpish and heavy when they are children, as boys will often be. If a woman be well-bred, and taught the proper management of her natural wit, she proves generally very sensible and retentive; and without partiality, a woman of sense and manners is the finest and most delicate part of God's creation; the glory of her Maker, and the great instance of His singular regard to man, His darling creature, to whom He gave the best gift either God could bestow or man receive. And it is the sordidest piece of folly and ingratitude in the world to withhold from the sex the due lustre which the advantages of education gives to the natural beauty of their minds.

A woman well bred and well taught, furnished with the additional accomplishments of knowledge and behaviour, is a creature without comparison; her society is the emblem of sublimer enjoyments; her person is angelic and her conversation heavenly; she is all softness and sweetness, peace, love, wit, and delight. She is every way suitable to the sublimest wish, and the man that has such a one to his portion has nothing to do but to rejoice in her and be thankful.

On the other hand, suppose her to be the very same woman, and rob her of the benefit of education, and it follows thus :—

If her temper be good, want of education makes her soft and easy. Her wit, for want of teaching, makes her impertinent and talkative. Her knowledge, for want of judgment and experience, makes her fanciful and whimsical. If her temper be bad, want of breeding makes her worse, and she grows haughty, insolent, and loud. If she be passionate, want of manners makes her termagant and a scold, which is much at one with lunatic. If she be proud, want of discretion (which still is breeding) makes her conceited, fantastic, and ridiculous. And from these she degenerates to be turbulent, clamorous, noisy, nasty, and the devil.

Methinks mankind for their own sakes, since, say what we will of the women, we all think fit one time or other to be concerned with them, should take some care to breed them up to be suitable and serviceable, if they expected no such thing as delight from them. Bless us! what care do we take to breed up a good horse and to break him well, and what a value do we put upon him when it is done, and all because he should be fit for our use; and why not a woman? Since all her ornaments and beauty without suitable behaviour is a cheat in nature, like the false tradesman, who puts the best of his goods uppermost, that the buyer may think the rest are of the same goodness.

Beauty of the body, which is the woman's glory, seems to be now unequally bestowed, and Nature, or rather Providence, to lie under some scandal about it, as if it was given a woman for a snare to men, and so make a kind of a she-devil of her; because, they say, exquisite beauty is rarely given with wit, more rarely with goodness of temper, and never at all with modesty. And some, pretending to justify the equity of such a distribution, will tell us it is the effect of the justice of Providence in dividing particular excellences among all His creatures, share and share alike, as it were, that all might for something or other be acceptable to one another, else some would be despised.

I think both these notions false, and yet the last, which has the show of respect to Providence, is the worst, for it supposes Providence to be indigent and empty, as if it had not wherewith to furnish all the creatures it had made, but was fain to be parsimonious in its gifts, and distribute them by piecemeal for fear of being exhausted.

If I might venture my opinion against an almost universal notion, I would say most men mistake the proceedings of Providence in this case, and all the world at this day are mistaken in their practice about it. And because the assertion is very bold, I desire to explain myself.

That Almighty First Cause which made us all is certainly the fountain of excellence, as it is of being, and by an invisible influence could have diffused equal qualities and perfections to all the creatures it has made, as the sun does its light, without the least ebb or diminution to Himself, and has given indeed to every individual sufficient to the figure His providence had designed him in the world.

I believe it might be defended if I should say that I do suppose God has given to all mankind equal gifts and capacities in
that He has given them all souls equally capable, and that the
whole difference in mankind proceeds either from accidental
difference in the make of their bodies or from the foolish difference of education.

1. From accidental difference in bodies. I would avoid discoursing here of the philosophical position of the soul in the
body. But if it be true, as philosophers do affirm, that the
understanding and memory is dilated or contracted according
to the accidental dimensions of the organ through which it is
conveyed, then, though God has given a soul as capable to me as
another, yet if I have any natural defect in those parts of the
body by which the soul should act, I may have the same soul
infused as another man, and yet he be a wise man and I a very
fool. For example, if a child naturally have a defect in the
organ of hearing, so that he could never distinguish any sound,
that child shall never be able to speak or read, though it have a
soul capable of all the accomplishments in the world. The brain
is the centre of the soul's actings, where all the distinguishing
faculties of it reside; and it is observable a man who has a
narrow contracted head, in which there is not room for the due
and necessary operations of nature by the brain, is never a man
of very great judgment; and that proverb, "A great head and
little wit," is not meant by nature, but is a reproof upon sloth, as
if one should, by way of wonder, say, "Fie, fie! you that have a
great head have but little wit; that's strange! that must certainly
be your own fault." From this notion I do believe there is a
great matter in the breed of men and women—not that wise men
shall always get wise children, but I believe strong and healthy
bodies have the wisest children, and sickly, weakly bodies affect
the wits as well as the bodies of their children. We are easily
persuaded to believe this in the breeds of horses, cocks, dogs, and
other creatures, and I believe it is as visible in men.

But to come closer to the business, the great distinguishing
difference which is seen in the world between men and women is

in their education, and this is manifested by comparing it with the difference between one man or woman and another.

And herein it is that I take upon me to make such a bold assertion that all the world are mistaken in their practice about women; for I cannot think that God Almighty ever made them so delicate, so glorious creatures, and furnished them with such charms, so agreeable and so delightful to mankind, with souls capable of the same accomplishments with men, and all to be only stewards of our houses, cooks, and slaves.

Not that I am for exalting the female government in the least; but, in short, I would have men take women for companions, and educate them to be fit for it. A woman of sense and breeding will scorn as much to encroach upon the prerogative of the man as a man of sense will scorn to oppress the weakness of the woman. But if the women's souls were refined and improved by teaching, that word would be lost; to say, the weakness of the sex as to judgment, would be nonsense, for ignorance and folly would be no more to be found among women than men. I remember a passage which I heard from a very fine woman; she had wit and capacity enough, an extraordinary shape and face, and a great fortune, but had been cloistered up all her time, and for fear of being stolen, had not had the liberty of being taught the common necessary knowledge of women's affairs; and when she came to converse in the world, her natural wit made her so sensible of the want of education, that she gave this short reflection on herself:—"I am ashamed to talk with my very maids," says she, "for I don't know when they do right or wrong. I had more need go to school than be married."

I need not enlarge on the loss the defect of education is to the sex, nor argue the benefit of the contrary practice; it is a thing will be more easily granted than remedied. This chapter is but an essay at the thing, and I refer the practice to those happy days, if ever they shall be, when men shall be wise enough to mend it.

# OF A COURT MERCHANT.

I ASK pardon of the learned gentlemen of the long robe if I do them any wrong in this chapter, having no design to affront them when I say that, in matters of debate among merchants, when they come to be argued by lawyers at the bar, they are strangely handled. I myself have heard very famous lawyers make sorry work of a cause between the merchant and his factor; and when they come to argue about exchanges, discounts, protests, demurrages, charter-parties, freights, port-charges, assurances, barratries, bottomries, accounts current, accounts in commission, and accounts in company, and the like, the solicitor has not been able to draw a brief, nor the counsel to understand it. Never was young parson more put to it to make out his text when he has got into the pulpit without his notes, than I have seen a counsel at the bar when he would make out a cause between two merchants; and I remember a pretty history of a particular case, by way of instance, when two merchants contending about a long factorage account that had all the niceties of merchandising in it, and labouring on both sides to instruct their counsel and to put them in when they were out, at last they found them make such ridiculous stuff of it that they both threw up the cause and agreed to a reference; which reference in one week, without any charge, ended all the dispute, which they had spent a great deal of money in before to no purpose.

Nay, the very judges themselves (no reflection upon their learning) have been very much at a loss in giving instructions to a jury, and juries much more to understand them; for when all is done, juries, which are not always, nor often indeed, of the wisest men, are, to be sure, ill umpires in causes so nice that the very lawyer and judge can hardly understand them.

The affairs of merchants are accompanied with such variety of circumstances, such new and unusual contingencies, which change and differ in every age, with a multitude of niceties and punctilios, and those again altering as the customs and usages of countries and states do alter, that it has been found impracticable to make any laws that could extend to all cases; and our law itself does tacitly acknowledge its own imperfection in this case by allowing the custom of merchants to pass as a kind of law in cases of difficulty.

Wherefore it seems to me a most natural proceeding that such affairs should be heard before and judged by such as by known experience and long practice in the customs and usages of foreign negoce are, of course, the most capable to determine the same.

Besides the reasonableness of the argument, there are some cases in our laws in which it is impossible for a plaintiff to make out his case or a defendant to make out his plea; as, in particular, when his proofs are beyond seas; for no protests, certifications, or procurations are allowed in our courts as evidence; and the damages are infinite and irretrievable by any of the proceedings of our laws.

For the answering all these circumstances, a court might be erected by authority of Parliament, to be composed of six Judge Commissioners, who should have power to hear and decide as a Court of Equity, under the title of a Court Merchant.

The proceedings of this court should be short, the trials speedy, the fees easy, that every man might have immediate remedy where wrong is done. For in trials at law about merchants' affairs, the circumstances of the case are often such, that the long proceedings of Courts of Equity are more pernicious than in other cases, because the matters to which they are generally relating are under greater contingencies than in other cases, as effects in hands abroad which want orders, ships and seamen lying at demurrage, and in pay, and the like.

These six judges should be chosen of the most eminent

merchants of the kingdom, to reside in London, and to have power by commission to summon a council of merchants, who should decide all cases on the hearing of both parties, with appeal to the said judges.

Also to delegate by commission petty councils of merchants in the most considerable ports of the kingdom for the same purpose. The six judges themselves to be only judges of appeal; all trials to be heard before the council of merchants, by methods and proceedings singular and concise. The council to be sworn to do justice, and to be chosen annually out of the principal merchants of the City.

The proceedings here should be without delay, the plaintiff to exhibit his grievance by way of brief, and the defendant to give in his answer, and a time of hearing to be appointed immediately. The defendant by motion shall have liberty to put off hearing upon showing good cause, not otherwise. At hearing, every man to argue his own cause if he pleases, or introduce any person to do it for him.

Attestations and protests from foreign parts regularly procured and authentically signified in due form to pass in evidence; affidavits in due form, likewise attested and done before proper magistrates within the King's dominions, to be allowed as evidence.

The party aggrieved may appeal to the six judges, before whom they shall plead by counsel, and from their judgment to have no appeal.

By this method infinite controversies would be avoided and disputes amicably ended, a multitude of present inconveniences avoided, and merchandising matters would in a merchant-like manner be decided by the known customs and methods of trade.

# OF SEAMEN.

IT is observable that whenever this kingdom is engaged in a war with any of its neighbours, two great inconveniences constantly follow, one to the King and one to the Trade.

1. That to the King is, that he is forced to press seamen for the manning of his navy, and force them involuntarily into the service; which way of violently dragging men into the fleet is attended with sundry ill circumstances, as—

(1.) Our naval preparations are retarded and our fleets always late for want of men, which has exposed them not a little, and been the ruin of many a good and well-laid expedition.

(2.) Several irregularities follow, as the officers taking money to dismiss able seamen, and filling up their complement with raw and improper persons.

(3.) Oppressions, quarrellings, and oftentimes murders, by the rashness of press-masters and the obstinacy of some unwilling to go.

(4.) A secret aversion to the service, from a natural principle, common to the English nation, to hate compulsion.

(5.) Kidnapping people out of the kingdom, robbing houses, and picking pockets, frequently practised under pretence of pressing, as has been very much used of late.

With various abuses of the like nature, some to the King, and some to the subject.

2. To Trade by the extravagant price set on wages for seamen, which they impose on the merchant with a sort of authority, and he is obliged to give by reason of the scarcity of men; and that not from a real want of men; for in the height of a press, if a merchant-man wanted men, and could get a protection for them, he might have any number immediately, and none without it, so shy were they of the public service.

The first of these things has cost the King above three millions sterling since the war, in these three particulars :—

1. Charge of pressing on sea and on shore, and in small craft employed for that purpose.

2. Ships lying in harbour for want of men at a vast charge of pay and victuals for those they had.

3. Keeping the whole navy in constant pay and provisions all the winter, for fear of losing the men against summer, which has now been done several years, besides bounty-money and other expenses to court and oblige the seamen.

The second of these, viz., the great wages paid by the merchant, has cost trade since the war above twenty millions sterling. The coal trade gives a specimen of it, who for the first three years of the war gave £9 a voyage to common seamen, who before sailed for 36s., which, computing the number of ships and men used in the coal trade and of voyages made, at eight hands to a vessel, does, modestly accounting, make £89,600 difference in one year in wages to seamen in the coal trade only.

For other voyages the difference of sailors' wages is 50s. per month, and 55s. per month to foremastmen, who before went for 26s. per month, besides subjecting the merchant to the insolence of the seamen, who are not now to be pleased with any provisions, will admit no half pay, and command of the captains even what they please ; nay, the King himself can hardly please them.

For cure of these inconveniences the following project is proposed, with which the seamen can have no reason to be dissatisfied nor are at all injured, and yet the damage sustained will be prevented, and an immense sum of money spared which is now squandered away by the profuseness and luxury of the seamen ; for if prodigality weakens the public wealth of the kingdom in general, then are the seamen but ill commonwealths-men, who are not visibly the richer for the prodigious sums of money paid them either by the King or the merchant.

The project is this :—

That by an Act of Parliament an office or court be erected, within the jurisdiction of the Court of Admiralty, and subject to the Lord High Admiral, or otherwise independent, and subject only to a Parliamentary authority, as the Commission for taking and stating the public accounts.

In this court or office, or the several branches of it (which to that end shall be subdivided and placed in every seaport in the kingdom), shall be listed and entered into immediate pay all the seamen in the kingdom, who shall be divided into colleges or chambers of sundry degrees, suitable to their several capacities, with pay in proportion to their qualities, as boys, youths, servants, men able, and raw midshipmen, officers, pilots, old men, and pensioners.

The circumstantials of this :—

1. No captain or master of any ship or vessel should dare to hire or carry to sea with him any seaman but such as he shall receive from the office aforesaid.

2. No man whatsoever, seaman or other, but applying himself to the said office to be employed as a sailor, should immediately enter into pay, and receive for every able seaman 24s. per month, and juniors in proportion ; to receive half pay while unemployed, and liberty to work for themselves, only to be at call of the office, and leave an account where to be found.

3. No sailor could desert, because no employment would be to be had elsewhere.

4. All ships at their clearing at the custom-house should receive a ticket to the office for men, where would be always choice rather than scarcity ; who should be delivered over by the office to the captain or master without any trouble or delay ; all liberty of choice to be allowed both to masters and men, only so as to give up all disputes to the officers appointed to decide.

*Note.*—By this would be avoided the great charge captains and owners are at to keep men on board before they are ready to go ; whereas now the care of getting men will be over, and all come on board in one day ; for the captain carrying the ticket to the office, he may go and choose his men if he will ; otherwise they will be sent on board her, by tickets sent to their dwellings, to repair on board such a ship.

5. For all these men that the captain or master of the ship takes he shall pay the office, not the seamen, 28s. per month (which 4s. per month overplus of wages will be employed to pay the half pay to the men out of employ), and so in proportion of wages for juniors.

6. All disputes concerning the mutinying of mariners, or other matters of debate between the captains and men, to be tried by way of appeal in a court for that purpose, to be erected as aforesaid.

7. All discounting of wages and time, all damages of goods, averages, stopping of pay, and the like, to be adjusted by stated and public rules and laws in print, established by the same Act of Parliament; by which means all litigious suits in the Court of Admiralty (which are infinite) would be prevented.

8. No ship that is permitted to enter at the custom house and take in goods should ever be refused men, or delayed in delivering them above five days after a demand made and a ticket from the custom-house delivered; general cases, as arrests and embargoes, excepted.

### The Consequences of this Method.

1. By this means the public would have no want of seamen, and all the charges and other inconveniences of pressing men would be prevented.

2. The intolerable oppression upon trade from the exorbitance of wages and insolence of mariners would be taken off.

3. The following sums of money should be paid to the office, to lie in bank as a public fund for the service of the nation, to be disposed of by order of Parliament, and not otherwise; a committee being always substituted in the intervals of the session to audit the accounts, and a treasury for the money, to be composed of members of the House, and to be changed every session of Parliament :—

1. Four shillings per month wages advanced by the merchants to the office for the men, more than the office pays them.

2. In consideration of the reducing men's wages, and consequently freights, to the former prices, or near them, the owners of

ships or merchants shall pay at the importation of all goods 40s. per ton freight, to be stated upon all goods and ports in proportion, reckoning it on wine tonnage from Canaries as the standard, and on special freights in proportion to the freight formerly paid, and half the said price in times of peace.

*Note.*—This may well be done, and no burden; for if freights are reduced to their former prices (or near it), as they will be if wages are so too, then the merchant may well pay it.  As for instance: Freight from Jamaica to London, formerly at £6, 10s. per ton, now at £18 and £20; from Virginia, at £5 to £6, 10s., now at £14, £16, and £17; from Barbadoes, at £6, now at £16; from Oporto, at £2, now at £6, and the like.

The payment of the aforesaid sums being a large bank for a fund, and it being supposed to be in fair hands and currently managed, the merchants shall further pay upon all goods shipped out, and shipped on board from abroad, for and from any port of this kingdom, £4 per cent. on the real value *bona fide*, to be sworn to, if demanded.   In consideration whereof, the said office shall be obliged to pay and make good all losses, damages, averages, and casualties whatsoever, as fully as by the custom of assurances now is done, without any discounts, rebates, or delays whatsoever; the said £4 per cent. to be stated on the voyage to the Barbadoes, and enlarged or taken off in proportion to the voyage, by rules and laws to be printed and publicly known.

Reserving only that then, as reason good, the said office shall have power to direct ships of all sorts how, and in what manner, and how long they shall sail with or wait for convoys; and shall have power (with limitations) to lay embargoes on ships in order to compose fleets for the benefit of convoys.

These rules formerly noted to extend to all trading by sea, the coasting and home-fishing trade excepted; and for them it should be ordered :—

First, for coals, the colliers being provided with men at 28s. per month, and convoys in sufficient number, and proper stations from Tynemouth Bar to the river, so as they need not go in fleets but, as wind and weather presents, run all the way under the protection of the men-of-war, who should be continually cruising from station to station; they would be able to perform their voyage in as short a time as formerly, and at as cheap pay, and consequently could afford to sell their coals at 17s. per chaldron, as well as formerly at 15s.

Wherefore, there should be paid into the treasury appointed at Newcastle, by bond to be paid where they deliver, 10s. per chaldron, Newcastle measure, and the stated price at London to be 27s. per chaldron in the Pool, which is 30s. at the buyer's house; and is so far from being dear, in time of war especially, as it is cheaper than ever was known in a war; and the officers should by proclamation confine the seller to that price.

In consideration also of the charge of convoys, the ships bringing coals shall all pay £1 per cent. on the value of the ship, to be agreed on at the office, and all convoy money exacted by commanders of ships shall be relinquished, and the office to make good all losses of ships, not goods, that shall be lost by enemies only.

These heads indeed are such as would need some explication, if the experiment were to be made, and, with submission, would reduce the seamen to better circumstances; at least it would have them in readiness for any public service much easier than by all the late methods of encouragement by registering seamen, &c.

For by this method all the seamen in the kingdom should be the King's hired servants, and receive their wages from him, whoever employed them; and no man could hire or employ them but from him: the merchant should hire them of the King, and pay the King for them; nor would there be a seaman in England out of employ, which, by the way, would prevent their seeking service abroad: if they were not actually at sea, they would receive half-pay, and might be employed in works about the yards, stores, and navy, to keep all things in repair.

If a fleet or squadron was to be fitted out, they would be manned in a week's time, for all the seamen in England would be ready; nor would they be shy of the service; for it is not an aversion to the King's service, nor it is not that the duty is harder

L

in the men-of-war than the merchant-men; nor it is not fear of danger which makes our seamen lurk, and hide, and hang back in time of war; but it is wages is the matter; 24s. per month in the King's service, and 40s. to 50s. per month from the merchant, is the true cause; and the seaman is in the right of it, too; for who would serve their king and country, and fight, and be knocked on the head at 24s. per month, that have 50s. without that hazard? And till this be remedied in vain are all the encouragements which can be given to seamen; for they tend but to make them insolent and encourage their extravagance.

Nor would this proceeding be any damage to the seamen in general; for 24s. per month wages, and to be kept in constant service, or half pay when idle, is really better to the seamen than 45s. per month, as they now take it, considering how long they often lie idle on shore out of pay. For the extravagant price of seamen's wages, though it has been an intolerable burden to trade, has not visibly enriched the sailors; and they may as well be content with 24s. per month now as formerly.

On the other hand, trade would be sensibly revived by it, the intolerable price of freights would be reduced, and the public would reap an immense benefit by the payments mentioned in the proposal; as—

(1.) Four shillings per month upon the wages of all the seamen employed by the merchant, which, if we allow 200,000 seamen always in employ, as there cannot be less in all the ships belonging to England, is £40,000 per month.

(2.) Forty shillings per ton freight upon all goods imported.

(3.) Four per cent. on the value of all goods exported or imported.

(4.) Ten shillings per chaldron upon all the coals shipped at Newcastle, and 1 per cent. on the ships which carry them.

What these four articles would pay to the Exchequer yearly it would be very difficult to calculate, and I am too near the end of this book to attempt it. But I believe no tax ever given since this war has come near it.

It is true out of this the public would be to pay half pay to the seamen who shall be out of employ, and all the losses and damages on goods and ships, which, though it might be considerable, would be small compared to the payment aforesaid; for, as the premium of 4 per cent. is but small, so the safety lies upon all men being bound to insure. For I believe any one will grant me this, it is not the smallness of a premium ruins the insurer, but it is the smallness of the quantity he insures; and I am not at all ashamed to affirm that let but a premium of £4 per cent. be paid into one man's hand for all goods imported and exported, and any man may be the general insurer of the kingdom, and yet that premium can never hurt the merchant neither.

So that the vast revenue this would raise would be felt nowhere; neither poor nor rich would pay the more for coals; foreign goods would be brought home cheaper, and our own goods carried to market cheaper; owners would get more by ships, merchants by goods, and losses by sea would be no loss at all to anybody, because repaid by the public stock.

Another unseen advantage would arise by it; we should be able to outwork all our neighbours, even the Dutch themselves, by sailing as cheap and carrying goods as cheap in time of war as in peace; an advantage which has more in it than is easily thought of, and would have a noble influence upon all our foreign trade. For what could the Dutch do in trade if we could carry our goods to Cadiz at 50s. per ton freight, and they give £8 or £10 and the like in other places? Whereby we could be able to sell cheaper or get more than our neighbours.

There are several considerable clauses might be added to this proposal, some of great advantage to the general trade of the kingdom, some to particular trades, and more to the public; but I avoid being too particular in things which are but the product of my own private opinion.

If the Government should ever proceed to the experiment, no question but much more than has been hinted at would appear, nor do I see any great difficulty in the attempt, or who would be aggrieved at it, and there I leave it, rather wishing than expecting to see it undertaken.

## THE CONCLUSION.

UPON a review of the several chapters of this book, I find that instead of being able to go further, some things may have suffered for want of being fully expressed, which if any person object against, I only say I cannot now avoid it. I have endeavoured to keep to my title, and offered but at an Essay, which any one is at liberty to go on with as they please, for I can promise no supplement. As to errors of opinion, though I am not yet convinced of any, yet I nowhere pretend to infallibility. However, I do not willingly assert anything which I have not good grounds for. If I am mistaken, let him that finds the error inform the world better, and never trouble himself to animadvert upon this, since I assure him I shall not enter into any pen-and-ink contest on the matter.

As to objections which may lie against any of the proposals made in this book, I have in some places mentioned such as occurred to my thoughts. I shall never assume that arrogance to pretend no other or further objections may be raised, but I do really believe no such objection can be raised as will overthrow any scheme here laid down so as to render the thing impracticable. Neither do I think but that all men will acknowledge most of the proposals in this book would be of as great, and perhaps greater, advantage to the public than I have pretended to.

As for such who read books only to find out the author's *faux pas*, who will quarrel at the meanness of style, errors of pointing, dulness of expression, or the like, I have but little to say to them. I thought I had corrected it very carefully, and yet some mispointings and small errors have slipt me, which it is too late to help. As to language, I have been rather careful to make it speak English suitable to the manner of the story than to dress it up with exactness of style, choosing rather to have it free and familiar, according to the nature of essays, than to strain at a perfection of language which I rather wish for than pretend to be master of.

---—*—---

## CHAPTER III.

### (1697-1702.)

THE "Poor Man's Plea" was another work of Defoe's that appeared a few weeks after the "Essay upon Projects." Its full title was "The Poor Man's Plea in Relation to all the Proclamations, Declarations, Acts of Parliament, &c., which have been, or shall be, made or published for a Reformation of Manners, and Suppressing Immorality in the Nation;" and it was published in the year 1698. Physicians, Defoe reasoned, try first to remove the cause of a distemper, and if that will not work the cure, they proceed then to apply remedies to the disease itself. The reigning distemper of the nation was then, he said, without doubt, immorality. The King and Parliament, its proper physicians, were well inclined to undertake its cure. "'Tis a great Work, well worthy their utmost Pains : The Honour of it, were it once perfected, would add more trophies to the Crown than all the Victories of the Bloody War, or the glory of this Honourable Peace." The honourable peace was that made by the Treaty of Ryswick, signed by England, France, Spain, and Holland in September 1697, and by Germany at the end of the next following month.

But the patient, Defoe said, must be willing to use the prescriptions of the physician he calls in. Wickedness is an ancient inhabitant of this country. Reformation of manners partly came with the stricter morality of a reformed religion in the days of Edward VI. and Queen Elizabeth. "In King James the First's time, the Court affecting something more of gallantry and gaiety, luxury got footing; and twenty years' peace, together with no extraordinary examples from the Court, gave too great encouragement to licentiousness. If it took footing in King James the First's time, it took a deep root in the reign of his son, and the liberty given the soldiers in the Civil War dispersed all manner of profaneness throughout the kingdom. That prince, though very pious in his own person and practice, had the misfortune to be the first King of England, and perhaps in the world, that ever established wickedness by a law. By what unhappy counsel or secret ill fate he was guided to it, it is hard to determine; but 'The Book of Sports,' as it was called, tended more to the vitiating the practice of this kingdom as to keeping the Lord's Day, than all the Acts of Parliament, Proclamations, and endeavours of future princes have done, or ever will do, to reform it. . . . In the time of King Charles the Second, lewdness and all manner of debauchery arrived to its meridian. The encouragement it had from the practice and allowance of the Court is an invincible demonstration how far the influence of our Government extends in the practice of the people.

"The present King and his late Queen"—Queen Mary had died of small-pox on the 28th of December 1694—"whose glorious memory will be dear to the nation as long as the world stands, have had all this wicked knot to unravel. This was the first thing the Queen set upon while the King was engaged in his wars abroad. She first gave all sorts of vice a general discouragement, and on the contrary, raised the value of virtue and sobriety by her royal example. The King having brought the war to a glorious conclusion and settled an honourable peace, in his very first speech to his Parliament proclaims a new war against profaneness and immorality." The Parliament enacts laws, but we of the Plebeii, said Defoe, are aggrieved by a reforming rigour that makes the real work impossible; "wherefore we find ourselves forced to seek redress of our grievances in the old honest way of petitioning Heaven to relieve us; and in the meantime we solemnly enter our protestation against the vicious part of the nobility and gentry of the nation; as follows:"—and then follows the Poor Man's Plea, that, firstly, the rich are as bad as the poor; that, secondly, the laws made by the rich punish the poor and let themselves go free; or if the laws themselves do not so, that is the effect of their administration. "Wherefore, till the nobility, gentry, justices of the peace, and clergy will be pleased either to reform their own manners and suppress their own immoralities, or find out some method and power impartially to punish themselves when guilty, we humbly crave leave to object against setting any poor man in the stocks, or sending him to the House of Correction for immoralities, as the most unequal and unjust way of proceeding in the world." "The man with a gold ring and gay clothes may swear before the justice or at the justice, may reel home through the open streets, and no man take any notice of it; but if a poor man get drunk or swears an oath, he must to the stocks without remedy." Defoe then called on the rich, in the name of the poor, to set an example of right life by putting away drunkenness, swearing, and licentiousness. For drunkenness he said: "To this day it is added to the character of a man as an additional title when you would speak well of him, 'He is an honest drunken fellow;' as if his drunkenness was a recommendation to his honesty. From the practice of this nasty faculty our gentlemen have arrived to the teaching of it, and that it might be effectually preserved to the next age, have very early instructed the youth in it. Nay, so far has custom prevailed, that the top of a gentleman's entertainment has been to make his friend drunk, and the friend is so much reconciled to it, that he takes that for the effect of his kindness which he ought as much to be affronted at as if he had kicked him down-stairs. . . . If there were any reason why a Rich Man should be permitted in the public exercise of open immoralities, and not the Poor Man, something might be said; but if there be any difference, it lies the other way.  For the vices of a poor man affect only himself; but the rich man's wickedness affects all the neighbourhood, gives offence to the sober, encourages and hardens the lewd, and quite overthrows the weak resolutions of such as are but indifferently fixed in their virtue and morality.  If my own watch goes false, it deceives me and none else; but if the town-clock goes false, it deceives the whole parish."  If it was said that a justice is passive and can only act on information, while informers are discredited, "it might be answered," said Defoe, "that in the time of executing the laws against Dissenters a great many gentlemen were found very vigorous in prosecuting their neighbours.  They did not stick to appear in person to disturb meetings and demolish the meeting-houses, and rather than fail, be informers themselves; the reason was because they had also a dislike of the thing.  But we never found a Dissenting gentleman or justice of the peace forward to do this because they approved of it.  Now, were our gentlemen and magistrates real enemies to the immoralities of this age, did they really hate drunkenness as a vice, they would be forward and zealous to root the practice of it out of the neighbourhood; they would not be backward or ashamed to detect vice or to disturb drunken assemblies."  And the gist of the whole pamphlet was that there would be little need of laws against immorality and profaneness if the example of all men of influence were such as to put vice out of fashion.

The corruption of society was not exaggerated by Defoe.  Ten or eleven years after the publication of the " Poor Man's Plea," Jonathan Swift was led by like considerations to the printing of his Argument upon the Inconvenience of Abolishing Christianity and of his Project for the Advancement of Religion.  Such questionings, indeed, are at the beginning of a chapter in the " History of Europe " which ends with the outbreak of the great French Revolution.

Defoe's " Pacificator" was published as a verse-pamphlet on the 20th of February 1700, a plea for peace in Literature between the Men of Sense and the Men of Wit.

> " That each may choose the part he can do well,
> And let the strife be only to excel."

The part he modestly assigns to " Foe" among the writers is lampoon. He had signed the Introduction to his " Essay upon Projects," D. F., Daniel Foe, and as D. F. he was now reasoning upon the question of Occasional Conformity. The law closed civic offices against all who did not qualify for them by taking sacrament according to the ordinances of the Church of England. Some Nonconformists reasoned that if the law required a particular act of conformity as a ceremony precedent to the appointment to a mayoralty or other public office, they might obey the law by conforming upon that particular occasion. Sir Thomas Abney, who had so conformed to qualify himself for office as Lord Mayor of London, was one of the congregation of the famous Puritan divine John Howe, who had been chaplain to Cromwell, had been driven by the Act of Uniformity in 1662 from his living at Torrington in Devonshire, and was then, about seventy years old, preaching in London. He died in April 1705. Defoe, in reprinting his former " Enquiry into the Occasional Conformity of Dissenters," addressed a new preface respectfully to Howe, asking for a word from him upon the morality of the practice, and suggesting that if he had no answer, " the world must believe that Dissenters do allow themselves to practise what they cannot defend."

The death of Charles II. of Spain, on the 1st of November 1700, put an end to the peace established at Ryswick in 1697, by giving rise to the War of the Spanish Succession. Of the two sisters of Charles II. of Spain, the elder, Maria Theresa, had become the wife of Louis XIV. She had renounced upon her marriage her own claim to the Spanish throne. Her son's claim, it was urged on the part of France, she had not power to renounce. Her younger sister, Margaret Theresa, had married, without any such renunciation, the Emperor Leopold I., and their daughter, with such renunciation, had become the wife of the Electoral Prince of Bavaria, who claimed the Spanish throne in her right, and denied her power of renouncing. But the Emperor Leopold himself was a third claimant, because his mother was a daughter of Philip III. of Spain. He claimed Spain, therefore, for his son by a second marriage, the Archduke Charles, who called himself Charles III. of Spain. In this respect Louis XIV. had as good a claim as the Emperor Leopold; the mothers of both were daughters of Philip III., while the dead King of Spain had been son of his son. That the strength of Spain should be added to the strength of France, when the influence of France in English politics was for support of the lost cause of absolute monarchy and another restoration of the Stuarts, contented no friend of the English Revolution. There had been two treaties of partition before the death of the King of Spain, and while his death was being looked for month by month; the second treaty, signed at London on the 21st February 1700, was caused by the death in 1699 of Margaret Theresa's grandchild, the Electoral Prince of Bavaria, who was to have inherited Spain, the Netherlands, and the Indies, while the Dauphin was to have all that was Spanish on the French side of the Pyrenees and of the mountains of Navarre, Alava, and Biscay; also Naples, Sicily, the ports of Tuscany, and the marquisate of Final; but Milan was to go to the Archduke Charles. By the second treaty of partition the Prince of Bavaria's claim to the Spanish throne was transferred to the Archduke Charles, who gave up Milan to be joined to all Spain held in Italy that was the share of France. King Charles of Spain, insulted by the much-partitioning of his dominions before he was dead, followed a suggestion of the French ambassador, and bequeathed his dominions to Philip, Duke of Anjou, second son of the Dauphin, and to the Archduke Charles if they were refused on behalf of the Duke of Anjou. But Louis XIV. did not refuse, and to men of Defoe's mind, in the latter part of the reign of William III. and the earlier years of Queen Anne, Louis XIV. seemed to be a Geryon the Second,

threatening liberty as Geryon the First had done when Philip the
Second prepared his Armada to subdue the England of Elizabeth.
William III. at first accepted the French claim. The Emperor
Leopold levied war upon France in Italy upon his own behalf.
On the 7th of September 1701 King William signed a treaty with
the Emperor and the States of Holland for the recovery from
France of Flanders as a barrier to Holland, and of the Milanese
as a barrier to the Empire. This treaty was known afterwards
as the Grand Alliance. Nine days after it had been signed, King
James the Second, late of England, died at St. Germain's, and
Louis XIV. openly acknowledged James's son, born in 1688, James
Francis Edward Stuart, afterwards known as the Chevalier St.
George and the Old Pretender, to be King of England. He
was then only a boy in his thirteenth year. William III. dismissed the French Ambassador from London and recalled the
English Ambassador from Paris. The peace signed at Ryswick in
September 1697 was at an end, and a new war was to begin on
the 4th of May 1702, and last until the Peace of Utrecht on the
13th of March 1713. Technically it was the War of the Spanish
Succession ; actually it was a struggle, very welcome to the Whigs,
against a power that might grow strong enough to secure the victory for those who would recall the Stuart family, and set aside
the limitation of the power of the Crown.

On the 15th November 1701, Defoe published a pamphlet on
the relations between England and France, which he called "The
Two Great Questions Considered : I. What the French King will
do with respect to the Spanish Monarchy; II. What Measures
the English ought to take." A preface to this pamphlet an-
nounced that, while it was being printed, letters from France
advised that the King of France had saluted his grandson, the
Duke of Anjou, as King of Spain. There followed upon this a
reply to an adversary, and then another pamphlet, "The Danger
of the Protestant Religion Considered, from the Present Prospect
of a Religious War in Europe." Defoe's counsel was in the direction of King William's action. In another way also he supported
the King.

The principle of authority, as understood by the friends of the Stuarts, had many supporters in England, who looked upon King William as a foreigner, and were willing enough to spread a like opinion. Large grants of forfeited lands in Ireland had been given to Keppels, Bentincks, and other of William's trusted friends and countrymen. The House of Commons had resolved on a resumption of the forfeitures. There were angry conferences with the House of Lords, and the Commons resolved to address the King against admission of any foreigners except Prince George of Denmark to the Royal Councils.

To defend the King against this form of attack, especially as it had been formulated by John Tutchin in a doggrel poem called "The Foreigners," Defoe wrote in his own masterly doggrel his famous satire called "The True-Born Englishman." The poem of "The Foreigners" was by the same John Tutchin who in the following year bore frank witness that, however little he liked Defoe's opinions, he knew him to have dealt most honestly with his creditors.

"The True-Born Englishman" was the most popular piece published in King William's reign. It was called by its author afterwards, in the preface to the second volume of his collected writings, "a remarkable example, by which the author, though he eyed in it no profit, had he been to enjoy the profit of his own labour, had gained above £1000. A book that, besides nine editions of the author, has been twelve times printed by other hands, some of which have been sold for one penny, others two-pence, and others sixpence, the author's edition being fairly printed and on good paper, and could not be sold under a shilling. Eighty thousand of the small ones have been sold in the streets for twopence or at a penny, and the author, thus abased and discouraged, had no remedy but patience." The poem was the occasion of Defoe's personal introduction to the King, who had received from it very substantial help. It abso-lutely put an end to the use of the phrase "True-Born English-man" as a political missile.

Defoe wrote pamphlets also in 1701, teaching purity of election upon the question of the succession to the Crown, raised by the death, in July 1700, of the Princess of Anne's son, the Duke of Gloucester. When the House of Commons was in conflict with the House of Lords, and a Committee of the Commons was preparing articles of impeachment against the Earls of Portland and Oxford and Lords Somers and Halifax—a state of things reflected in Swift's first pamphlet, his "Discourse of the Contests and Dissensions between the Nobles and Commons in Athens and Rome"—Defoe went to the House of Commons, guarded by sixteen gentlemen of quality, and presented in aid of the Kentish petitioners, who called on the House of Commons to support the King, his "Legion's Memorial." It ended with a warning to the Commons that if they continued to neglect their duty they might "expect to be treated according to the resentments of an injured nation ; for Englishmen are no more to be slaves to Parliaments than to a king. Our name is Legion, and we are many." Supplies were voted. Parliament rose. The five Kentish petitioners, who had been given into the custody of the Serjeant-at-Arms, were set free, and feasted publicly in Mercers' Hall. This was at the end of June 1701. The death of James II. on the 16th of September, and the action thereupon of Louis XIV., raised the war spirit in England. Defoe wrote pamphlets following the course of these events, arguing that there was not a *casus belli* against Louis XIV. for words giving mere empty titles to the Stuart family. The King of France was bound by the Treaty of Ryswick not to assist any enemy of King William. On the other hand, England was bound to the Emperor by treaty that required her to join in war against the Duke of Anjou as claimant of the Spanish crown; but this was no case for war against the King of France, unless he actively supported the claim of his grandson. As the world went, this was but a temperate way of showing that there would soon come to be good technical reason for a war with France. While it was addressed against mere fury of opinion, it was in perfect agreement with the counsels of the King.

Thus matters stood, when a fall from his horse on the 21st of February caused the death of William III. on the 8th of March

1702, and the actual declaration of war on the 4th of May was one of the first acts of the reign of Queen Anne.

While Defoe was thus putting his heart into the great questions that seemed to him to concern the maintenance of the position that had been won by the English Revolution, he was, in the last years of William III., busy with the management of the Dutch Pantile Works at Tilbury, where there were a hundred men employed. He was bettering his fortunes and supporting wife and children by the brickworks, while he wrote more pieces than are here recorded in aid of the cause that he supported with his " True-Born Englishman."

A true

# COLLECTION

OF THE

# WRITINGS

OF THE

# AUTHOR

OF THE

True Born *English-man*.

---

Corrected by himself.

---

*L O N D O N:*

Printed, and are to be Sold by most Booksellers in
*London* and *Westminster.*  M DCC III.

# AN EXPLANATORY PREFACE.

—⊷—

IT is not that I see any reason to alter my opinion in anything
I have written which occasions this epistle, but I find it
necessary, for the satisfaction of some persons of honour as well
as wit, to pass a short explication upon it, and tell the world what
I mean, or rather what I do not mean, in some things wherein I
find I am liable to be misunderstood.

I confess myself something surprised to hear that I am taxed
with bewraying my own nest and abusing our nation by discovering the meanness of our original, in order to make the English
contemptible abroad and at home ; in which I think they are mistaken. For why should not our neighbours be as good as we to
derive from ? And I must add that, had we been an unmixed
nation, I am of opinion it had been to our disadvantage. For,
to go no further, we have three nations about us as clear from
mixtures of blood as any in the world, and I know not which of
them I could wish ourselves to be like—I mean the Scots, the
Welsh, and Irish ; and if I were to write a reverse to the satire, I
would examine all the nations of Europe, and prove that those
nations which are most mixed are the best, and have least of bar-
barism and brutality among them ; and abundance of reasons
might be given for it, too long to bring into a preface.

But I give this hint to let the world know that I am far from
thinking it is a satire upon the English nation to tell them they
are derived from all the nations under heaven—that is, from
several nations. Nor is it meant to undervalue the original of
the English, for we see no reason to like them the worse, being
the relics of Romans, Danes, Saxons, and Normans, than we

M

should have done if they had remained Britons; that is, than if
they had been all Welshmen.

But the intent of the satire is pointed at the vanity of those who
talk of their antiquity and value themselves upon their pedigree,
their ancient families, and being true-born; whereas it is impossible we should be true-born, and if we could, should have lost by
the bargain.

Those sort of people who call themselves true-born and tell
long stories of their families, and, like a nobleman of Venice,
think a foreigner ought not to walk on the same side of the street
with them, are owned to be meant in this satire. What they
would infer from their own original I know not, nor is it easy to
make out whether they are the better or the worse for their ancestors. Our English nation may value themselves for their wit,
wealth, and courage, and I believe few will dispute it with them;
but for long originals and ancient true-born families of English,
I would advise them to waive the discourse. A true Englishman
is one that deserves a character, and I have nowhere lessened
him that I know of; but as for a true-born Englishman, I confess I do not understand him.

From hence I only infer that an Englishman, of all men, ought
not to despise foreigners as such, and I think the inference is
just, since what they are to-day we were yesterday, and to-morrow
they will be like us. If foreigners misbehave in their several
stations and employments, I have nothing to do with that; the
laws are open to punish them equally with natives, and let them
have no favour.

But when I see the town full of lampoons and invectives against
Dutchmen only because they are foreigners, and the King reproached and insulted by insolent pedants and ballad-making
poets for employing foreigners, and for being a foreigner himself,
I confess myself moved by it to remind our nation of their own
original, thereby to let them see what a banter is put upon ourselves in it, since, speaking of Englishmen *ab origine*, we are really
foreigners ourselves.

I could go on to prove it is also impolitic in us to discourage foreigners, since it is easy to make it appear that the multitudes of foreign nations who have taken sanctuary here have been the greatest additions to the wealth and strength of the nation, the great essential whereof is the number of its inhabitants. Nor would this nation have ever arrived to the degree of wealth and glory it now boasts of if the addition of foreign nations, both as to manufactures and arms, had not been helpful to it. This is so plain that he who is ignorant of it is too dull to be talked with.

The satire, therefore, I must allow to be just till I am otherwise convinced, because nothing can be more ridiculous than to hear our people boast of that antiquity which, if it had been true, would have left us in so much worse a condition than we are in now; whereas we ought rather to boast among our neighbours that we are a part of themselves, or the same original as they, but bettered by our climate, and, like our language and manufactures, derived from them and improved by us to a perfection greater than they can pretend to.

This we might have valued ourselves upon without vanity; but to disown our descent from them, talking big of our ancient families and long originals, and stand at a distance from foreigners, like the enthusiast in religion, with a " Stand off; I am more holy than thou !"—this is a thing so ridiculous in a nation, derived from foreigners as we are, that I could not but attack them as I have done.

And whereas I am threatened to be called to a public account for this freedom, and the publisher of this has been new-papered in gaol already for it, though I see nothing in it for which the Government can be displeased, yet if at the same time those people who, with an unlimited arrogance in print, every day affront the King, prescribe the Parliament, and lampoon the Government may be either punished or restrained, I am content to stand and fall with the public justice of my native country which I am not sensible I have anywhere injured.

Nor would I be misunderstood concerning the clergy, with whom, if I have taken any license more than becomes a satire, I question not but those gentlemen, who are men of letters, are also men of so much candour as to allow me a loose at the crimes of the guilty without thinking the whole profession lashed, who are innocent. I profess to have very mean thoughts of those gentlemen who have deserted their own principles, and exposed even their morals as well as loyalty, but not at all to think it affects any but such as are concerned in the fact.

Nor would I be misrepresented as to the ingratitude of the English to the King and his friends, as if I meant the English as a nation are so. The contrary is so apparent, that I would hope it should not be suggested of me; and, therefore, when I have brought in Britannia speaking of the King, I suppose her to be the representative or mouth of the nation as a body. But if I say we are full of such who daily affront the King and abuse his friends, who print scurrilous pamphlets, virulent lampoons, and reproachful public banter against both the King's person and Government, I say nothing but what is too true. And that the satire is directed at such I freely own, and cannot say but I should think it very hard to be censured for this satire while such remain unquestioned and tacitly approved. That I can mean none but such is plain from these few lines :—

> " Ye Heavens, regard ! Almighty Jove, look down,
> And view thy injured monarch on the throne.
> On their ungrateful heads due vengeance take
> Who sought his aid and then his part forsake."

If I have fallen upon our vices, I hope none but the vicious will be angry. As for writing for interest, I disown it. I have neither place, nor pension, nor prospect; nor seek none, nor will have none. If matter of fact justifies the truth of the crimes, the satire is just. As to the poetic liberties, I hope the crime is pardonable. I am content to be stoned provided none will attack me but the innocent.

If my countrymen would take the hint and grow better-natured from my ill-natured poem, as some call it, I would say this of it, that though it is far from the best satire that ever was written, it would do the most good that ever satire did.

And yet I am ready to ask pardon of some gentlemen too, who, though they are Englishmen, have good-nature enough to see themselves reproved, and can bear it. Those are gentlemen in a true sense that can bear to be told of their *faux pas* and not abuse the reprover. To such I must say this is no satire ; they are exceptions to the general rule ; and I value my performance from their generous approbation more than I can from any opinion I have of its worth.

The hasty errors of my verse I made my excuse for before ; and since the time I have been upon it has been but little, and my leisure less, I have all along strove rather to make the thoughts explicit than the poem correct. However, I have mended some faults in this edition, and the rest must be placed to my account.

As to answers, banters, true English Billingsgate, I expect them till nobody will buy, and then the shop will be shut. Had I wrote it for the gain of the press, I should have been concerned at its being printed again and again by pirates, as they call them, and paragraph-men ; but would they but do it justice and print it true according to the copy, they are welcome to sell it for a penny if they please.

The pence indeed is the end of their works. I will engage, if nobody will buy, nobody will write. And not a patriot-poet of them all now will, in defence of his native country—which I have abused, they say—print an answer to it, and give it about for God's sake.

# THE PREFACE.

THE end of satire is reformation; and the author, though he doubts the work of conversion is at a general stop, has put his hand to the plough.

I expect a storm of ill language from the fury of the town, and especially from those whose English talent it is to rail. And without being taken for a conjuror, I may venture to foretell that I shall be cavilled at about my mean style, rough verse, and incorrect language; things I might indeed have taken more care in, but the book is printed; and though I see some faults, it is too late to mend them. And this is all I think needful to say to them.

Possibly somebody may take me for a Dutchman, in which they are mistaken. But I am one that would be glad to see Englishmen behave themselves better to strangers and to governors also, that one might not be reproached in foreign countries for belonging to a nation that wants manners.

I assure you, gentlemen, strangers use us better abroad; and we can give no reason but our ill-nature for the contrary here.

Methinks an Englishman, who is so proud of being called a good fellow, should be civil; and it cannot be denied but we are in many cases, and particularly to strangers, the churlishest people alive.

As to vices, who can dispute our intemperance, while an honest drunken fellow is a character in a man's praise? All our reformations are banters, and will be so till our magistrates and gentry reform themselves by way of example. Then, and not till then, they may be expected to punish others without blushing.

As to our ingratitude, I desire to be understood of that particular people who, pretending to be Protestants, have all along endeavoured to reduce the liberties and religion of this nation into the hands of King James and his Popish Powers; together with such who enjoy the peace and protection of the present Government, and yet abuse and affront the King, who procured it, and openly profess their uneasiness under him. These, by whatsoever names or titles they are dignified or distinguished, are the people aimed at; nor do I disown but that it is so much the temper of an Englishman to abuse his benefactor that I could be glad to see it rectified.

Those who think I have been guilty of any error in exposing the crimes of my own countrymen to themselves, may, among many honest instances of the like nature, find the same thing in Mr. Cowley, in his imitation of the second Olympic ode of Pindar. His words are these—

> " But in this thankless world the givers
> Are envied even by the receivers :
> 'Tis now the cheap and frugal fashion
> Rather to hide than pay an obligation.
> Nay, 'tis much worse than so ;
> It now an artifice doth grow
> Wrongs and outrages to do,
> Lest men should think we owe."

# THE INTRODUCTION.

SPEAK, Satire; for there's none can tell like thee
    Whether 'tis folly, pride, or knavery
That makes this discontented land appear
Less happy now in times of peace than war?
Why civil feuds disturb the nation more
Than all our bloody wars have done before?
    Fools out of favour grudge at knaves in place,
And men are always honest in disgrace:
The Court preferments make men knaves in course;
But they which would be in them would be worse.
'Tis not at foreigners that we repine,
Would foreigners their perquisites resign:
The grand contention's plainly to be seen,
To get some men put out, and some put in.
For this our Senators make long harangues,
And florid Members whet their polished tongues.
Statesmen are always sick of one disease,
And a good pension gives them present ease:
That's the specific makes them all content
With any King and any Government.
Good patriots at Court abuses rail,
And all the nation's grievances bewail;
But when the sovereign balsam's once applied,
The zealot never fails to change his side;
And when he must the golden key resign,
The railing spirit comes about again.
    Who shall this bubbled nation disabuse,

While they their own felicities refuse,
Who at the wars have made such mighty pother,
And now are falling out with one another:
With needless fears the jealous nation fill,
And always have been saved against their will:
Who fifty millions sterling have disbursed,
To be with peace and too much plenty cursed:
Who their old monarch eagerly undo,
And yet uneasily obey the new?
Search, Satire, search: a deep incision make;
The poison's strong, the antidote's too weak.
'Tis pointed Truth must manage this dispute,
And downright English, Englishmen confute.

Whet thy just anger at the nation's pride,
And with keen phrase repel the vicious tide;
To Englishmen their own beginnings show,
And ask them why they slight their neighbours so.
Go back to elder times and ages past,
And nations into long oblivion cast;
To old Britannia's youthful days retire,
And there for true-born Englishmen inquire.
Britannia freely will disown the name,
And hardly knows herself from whence they came:
Wonders that they of all men should pretend
To birth and blood, and for a name contend.
Go back to causes where our follies dwell,
And fetch the dark original from hell:
Speak, Satire, for there's none like thee can tell.

THE

# TRUE-BORN ENGLISHMAN.

—⊢—

## PART I.

WHEREVER God erects a house of prayer,
⠀⠀⠀⠀The Devil always builds a chapel there :[1]
And 'twill be found upon examination,
The latter has the largest congregation :
For ever since he first debauched the mind,
He made a perfect conquest of mankind.
With uniformity of service, he
Reigns with a general aristocracy.
No non-conforming sects disturb his reign,
For of his yoke there's very few complain.
He knows the genius and the inclination,
And matches proper sins for every nation,
He needs no standing-army government ;
He always rules us by our own consent :
His laws are easy, and his gentle sway
Makes it exceeding pleasant to obey :
The list of his vicegerents and commanders,
Outdoes your Cæsars or your Alexanders.

---

[1] This old proverb was quoted by Robert Burton in his "Anatomy of Melancholy" (1621), "Where God hath a temple the Devil hath a chapel" (Part III. sc. iv. subs. 1). It was also No. 670 in George Herbert's "Jacula Prudentium," first published in 1640, where it ran, "No sooner is a temple built to God but the Devil builds a chapel hard by." Defoe was the first rhymer of the proverb, and the rider to it is his own.

They never fail of his infernal aid,
And he's as certain ne'er to be betrayed.
Through all the world they spread his vast command,
And Death's eternal empire is maintained.
They rule so politicly and so well,
As if they were Lords Justices of Hell,
Duly divided to debauch mankind,
And plant infernal dictates in his mind.

 Pride, the first peer, and president of Hell,
To his share Spain, the largest province, fell.
The subtile Prince thought fittest to bestow
On these the golden mines of Mexico,
With all the silver mountains of Peru,
Wealth which would in wise hands the world undo :
Because he knew their genius was such,
Too lazy and too haughty to be rich.
So proud a people, so above their fate,
That if reduced to beg, they'll beg in state ;
Lavish of money to be counted brave,
And proudly starve because they scorn to save.
Never was nation in the world before
So very rich and yet so very poor.

 Lust chose the torrid zone of Italy,
Where blood ferments in rapes and sodomy :
Where swelling veins o'erflow with liquid streams,
With heat impregnate from Vesuvian flames :
Whose flowing sulphur forms infernal lakes,
And human body of the soil partakes.
There nature ever burns with hot desires,
Fanned with luxuriant air from subterranean fires ;
Here, undisturbed in floods of scalding lust,
The Infernal King reigns with infernal gust.

 Drunkenness, the darling favourite of Hell,
Chose Germany to rule ; and rules so well,
No subjects more obsequiously obey,
None please so well or are so pleased as they.

The cunning artist manages so well,
He lets them bow to Heaven and drink to Hell.
If but to wine and him they homage pay,
He cares not to what deity they pray,
What god they worship most, or in what way.
Whether by Luther, Calvin, or by Rome
They sail for Heaven, by Wine he steers them home.

Ungoverned Passion settled first in France, ✓
Where mankind lives in haste and thrives by chance;
A dancing nation, fickle and untrue,
Have oft undone themselves and others too;
Prompt the infernal dictates to obey,
And in Hell's favour none more great than they.

The Pagan world he blindly leads away,
And personally rules with arbitrary sway;
The mask thrown off, plain Devil his title stands,
And what elsewhere he tempts he there commands.
There with full gust the ambition of his mind
Governs, as he of old in Heaven designed.
Worshipped as God, his Paynim altars smoke,
Embrued with blood of those that him invoke.

The rest by Deputies he rules as well,
And plants the distant colonies of Hell.
By them his secret power he maintains,
And binds the world in his infernal chains.

By Zeal the Irish, and the Russ by Folly
Fury the Dane, the Swede by Melancholy;
By stupid Ignorance the Muscovite;
The Chinese by a child of Hell called Wit.
Wealth makes the Persian too effeminate,
And Poverty the Tartars desperate;
The Turks and Moors by Mah'met he subdues,
And God has given him leave to rule the Jews.
Rage rules the Portuguese and Fraud the Scotch,
Revenge the Pole and Avarice the Dutch.

Satire, be kind, and draw a silent veil

Thy native England's vices to conceal;
Or, if that task's impossible to do,
At least be just and show her virtues too—
Too great the first; alas, the last too few!

England, unknown as yet, unpeopled lay;
Happy had she remained so to this day,
And not to every nation been a prey.
Her open harbours and her fertile plains
(The merchant's glory those, and these the swain's)
To every barbarous nation have betrayed her,
Who conquer her as oft as they invade her;
So beauty's guarded but by innocence,
That ruins her, which should be her defence.

Ingratitude, a devil of black renown,
Possessed her very early for his own.
An ugly, surly, sullen, selfish spirit,
Who Satan's worst perfections does inherit;
Second to him in malice and in force,
All devil without, and all within him worse.
He made her first-born race to be so rude,
And suffered her so oft to be subdued;
By several crowds of wandering thieves o'errun,
Often unpeopled, and as oft undone;
While every nation that her powers reduced
Their languages and manners introduced.
From whose mixed relics our compounded breed
By spurious generation does succeed,
Making a race uncertain and uneven,
Derived from all the nations under Heaven.

The Romans first with Julius Cæsar came,
Including all the nations of that name,
Gauls, Greeks, and Lombards, and, by computation
Auxiliaries or slaves of every nation.
With Hengist, Saxons; Danes with Sueno came,
In search of plunder, not in search of fame.

Scots, Picts, and Irish from the Hibernian shore,
And conquering William brought the Normans o'er.
  All these their barbarous offspring left behind,
The dregs of armies, they of all mankind;
Blended with Britons, who before were here,
Of whom the Welsh ha' blessed the character.
  From this amphibious ill-born mob began
That vain ill-natured thing, an Englishman.
The customs, surnames, languages, and manners
Of all these nations are their own explainers:
Whose relics are so lasting and so strong,
They ha' left a shibboleth upon our tongue,
By which with easy search you may distinguish
Your Roman-Saxon-Danish Norman English.
The great invading Norman [1] let us know
What conquerors in after-times might do.
To every musketeer [2] he brought to town,
He gave the lands which never were his own.
When first the English crown he did obtain,
He did not send his Dutchmen back again.
No reassumptions in his reign were known,
D'Avenant might there ha' let his book alone.
No Parliament his army could disband;
He raised no money, for he paid in land.
He gave his legions their eternal station,
And made them all freeholders of the nation.
He cantoned out the country to his men,
And every soldier was a denizen.
The rascals thus enriched, he called them lords,
To please their upstart pride with new-made words,
And Doomsday Book his tyranny records.
  And here begins our ancient pedigree,
That so exalts our poor nobility:
'Tis that from some French trooper they derive,
Who with the Norman bastard did arrive;

---

[1] William the Conqueror. [D.F.]          [2] Or archer. [D.F.]

The trophies of the families appear,
Some show the sword, the bow, and some the spear, }
Which their great ancestor, forsooth, did wear.
These in the herald's register remain,
Their noble mean extraction to explain,
Yet who the hero was, no man can tell,
Whether a drummer or a colonel :
The silent record blushes to reveal
Their undescended dark original.          ·

But grant the best, how came the change to pass,
A true-born Englishman of Norman race?
A Turkish horse can show more history
To prove his well-descended family.
Conquest, as by the moderns [1] 'tis expressed,
May give a title to the lands possessed :
But that the longest sword should be so civil
To make a Frenchman English, that's the devil.

These are the heroes that despise the Dutch,
And rail at new-come foreigners so much,
Forgetting that themselves are all derived
From the most scoundrel race that ever lived ;
A horrid crowd of rambling thieves and drones,
Who ransacked kingdoms and dispeopled towns,
The Pict and painted Briton, treacherous Scot,
By hunger, theft, and rapine hither brought ;
Norwegian pirates, buccaneering Danes,
Whose red-haired offspring everywhere remains,
Who, joined with Norman-French, compound the breed
From whence your true-born Englishmen proceed.

And lest by length of time it be pretended
The climate may this modern breed ha' mended,
Wise Providence, to keep us where we are,
Mixes us daily with exceeding care.
We have been Europe's sink, the jakes where she
Voids all her offal outcast progeny.

----

[1] Dr. Sherlock, *de facto.* [D.F.]

From the eighth Henry's time, the strolling bands
Of banished fugitives from neighbouring lands
Have here a certain sanctuary found :
The eternal refuge of the vagabond,
Where, in but half a common age of time,
Borrowing new blood and manners from the clime,
Proudly they learn all mankind to contemn,
And all their race are true-born Englishmen.

    Dutch, Walloons, Flemings, Irishmen, and Scots,
Vaudois and Valtelins, and Hugonots,
In good Queen Bess's charitable reign,
Supplied us with three hundred thousand men.
Religion—God, we thank Thee !—sent them hither,
Priests, Protestants, the Devil and all together :
Of all professions and of every trade,
All that were persecuted or afraid ;
Whether for debt or other crimes they fled,
David at Hachilah was still their head.

    The offspring of this miscellaneous crowd
Had not their new plantations long enjoyed,
But they grew Englishmen, and raised their votes
At foreign shoals for interloping Scots.
The royal branch[1] from Pictland did succeed,
With troops of Scots and Scabs from North-by-Tweed.
The seven first years of his pacific reign
Made him and half his nation Englishmen.
Scots from the northern frozen banks of Tay,
With packs and plods came whigging all away :
Thick as the locusts which in Egypt swarmed,
With pride and hungry hopes completely armed ;
With native truth, diseases, and no money,
Plundered our Canaan of the milk and honey.
Here they grew quickly lords and gentlemen,
And all their race are true-born Englishmen.

    The civil wars, the common purgative,

           [1] K. J. I.  [D.F.]

Which always use to make the nation thrive,
Made way for all that strolling congregation
Which thronged in Pious Charles's restoration.[1]
The royal refugee our breed restores,
With foreign courtiers and with foreign whores,
And carefully repeopled us again,
Throughout his lazy, long, lascivious reign,
With such a blest and true-born English fry,
As much illustrates our nobility.
A gratitude which will so black appear,
As future ages must abhor to hear,
When they look back on all that crimson flood,
Which streamed in Lindsay's and Carnarvon's blood,
Bold Strafford, Cambridge, Capel, Lucas, Lisle,
Who crowned in death his father's funeral pile.
The loss of whom, in order to supply,
With true-born English nationality,
Six bastard Dukes survive his luscious reign,
The labours of Italian Castlemaine,[2]
French Portsmouth,[3] Tabby Scot, and Cambrian.
Besides the numerous bright and virgin throng,
Whose female glories shade them from my song.
  This offspring, if one age they multiply,
May half the house with English peers supply;

---

[1] K. C. II. [D.F.]

[2] Lady Castlemaine, of the Italian-French family of Villars, was first known to Charles II. as Mrs. Palmer. Afterwards her husband was made Earl of Castlemaine, and in 1668 she was made Duchess of Cleveland. Of the cost of this woman Andrew Marvell wrote :—" They have signed and sealed ten thousand pounds a year more to the Duchess of Cleveland ; who has likewise near ten thousand pounds a year out of the new farm of the country excise of beer and ale ; five thousand pounds a year out of the Post Office ; and, they say, the reversion of all the King's leases, the reversion of all places in the Custom House, the green-wax, and, indeed, what not? All promotions, spiritual and temporal, pass under her cognisance," &c. Charles II. had by her five children.

[3] Louise Renée de Puencovet de Queroualle came over to Dover as a maid of honour, and was created Duchess of Portsmouth in August 1673. She cost as much as Lady Castlemaine. Her son, Charles Lennox, was made Duke of Richmond. The Duchess of Portsmouth was living when this satire appeared. She died in 1734.

N

There with true English pride they may contemn
Schomberg and Portland,[1] new made noblemen.
   French cooks, Scotch pedlars, and Italian whores,
Were all made lords or lords' progenitors.
Beggars and bastards by his new creation
Much multiplied the peerage of the nation;
Who will be all, ere one short age runs o'er,
As true-born lords as those we had before.
   Then to recruit the Commons he prepares
And heal the latent breaches of the wars;
The pious purpose better to advance,
He invites the banished Protestants of France:
Hither for God's sake and their own they fled,
Some for religion came, and some for bread;
Two hundred thousand pairs of wooden shoes,
Who, God be thanked, had nothing left to lose,
To Heaven's great praise did for religion fly,
To make us starve our poor in charity.
In every port they plant their fruitful train,
To get a race of true-born Englishmen;
Whose children will, when riper years they see,
Be as ill-natured and as proud as we;
Call themselves English, foreigners despise,
Be surly like us all, and just as wise.
   Thus from a mixture of all kinds began
That heterogeneous thing an Englishman;
In eager rapes and furious lust begot,
Betwixt a painted Briton and a Scot;
Whose gendering offspring quickly learned to bow,
And yoke their heifers to the Roman plough;
From whence a mongrel half-bred race there came,
With neither name nor nation, speech nor fame;

---

[1] Frederick de Schomberg, an old favourite of King William's, was made Duke of Schomberg on the 10th of April 1689. Another friend of the King's, William Bentinck, was created Earl of Portland on the 9th of April 1689. His son and heir was raised to a dukedom in 1716.

In whose hot veins new mixtures quickly ran,
Infused betwixt a Saxon and a Dane ;
While their rank daughters, to their parents just,
Received all nations with promiscuous lust.
This nauseous brood directly did contain
The well-extracted brood of Englishmen.
 Which medley cantoned in a Heptarchy,
A rhapsody of nations to supply,
Among themselves maintained eternal wars,
And still the ladies loved the conquerors.
The Western Angles all the rest subdued,
A bloody nation, barbarous and rude,
Who by the tenure of the sword possessed
One part of Britain, and subdued the rest.
And as great things denominate the small,
The conquering part gave title to the whole ;
The Scot, Pict, Briton, Roman, Dane, submit,
And with the English-Saxon all unite ;
And these the mixtures have so close pursued,
The very name and memory's subdued.
No Roman now, no Briton does remain ;
Wales strove to separate, but strove in vain ;
The silent nations undistinguished fall,
And Englishman's the common name of all.
Fate jumbled them together, God knows how ;
Whate'er they were, they're true-born English now.
 The wonder which remains is at our pride,
To value that which all men else deride.
For Englishmen to boast of generation
Cancels their knowledge and lampoons the nation.
A true-born Englishman's a contradiction,
In speech an irony, in fact a fiction ;
A banter made to be a test to fools,
Which those that use it justly ridicules ;
A metaphor invented to express
A man akin to all the universe.

For, as the Scots, as learned men have said,
Throughout the world their wandering seed have spread;
So open-handed England, 'tis believed,
Has all the gleanings of the world received.
    Some think of England 'twas our Saviour meant,
The Gospel should to all the world be sent,
Since, when the blessed sound did hither reacn,
They to all nations might be said to preach.
    'Tis well that virtue gives nobility,
How shall we else the want of birth and blood supply?
Since scarce one family is left alive
Which does not from some foreigner derive.
Of sixty thousand English gentlemen,
Whose name and arms in registers remain,
We challenge all our heralds to declare
Ten families which English-Saxons are.
    France justly owns the ancient noble line
Of Bourbon, Montmorency, and Lorraine,
The Germans too their House of Austria show
And Holland their invincible Nassau,
Lines which in heraldry were ancient grown
Before the name of Englishman was known.
Even Scotland, too, her elder glory shows,
Her Gordons, Hamiltons, and her Monros,
Douglas, Mackays, and Grahams, names well.known
Long before ancient England knew her own.
    But England, modern to the last degree,
Borrows or makes her own nobility,
And yet she boldly boasts of pedigree;
Repines that foreigners are put upon her,
And talks of her antiquity and honour;
Her Sackvilles, Saviles, Capels, De la Meres,
Mohuns, and Montagues, Darcys, and Veres,
Not one have English names, yet all are English peers.
Your Hermans, Papillons, and Lavalliers,
Pass now for true-born English knights and squires,
And make good senate members or Lord Mayors.

Wealth, howsoever got, in England makes
Lords of mechanics, gentlemen of rakes :
Antiquity and birth are needless here ;
'Tis impudence and money makes a peer.
  Innumerable City knights, we know,
From Bluecoat Hospital and Bridewell flow ;
Draymen and porters fill the city Chair,
And footboys magisterial purple wear.
Fate has but very small distinction set
Betwixt the counter and the coronet.
Tarpaulin lords, pages of high renown,
Rise up by poor men's valour, not their own.
Great families of yesterday we show,
And lords whose parents were the Lord knows who.

---

## PART II.

THE breed's described : Now, Satire, if you can,
Their temper show, for manners make the man.
Fierce, as the Briton ; as the Roman, brave ;
And less inclined to conquer than to save ;
Eager to fight, and lavish of their blood,
And equally of fear and forecast void.
The Pict has made 'em sour, the Dane morose ;
False from the Scot, and from the Norman worse.
What honesty they have, the Saxons gave them,
And that, now they grow old, begins to leave them.
The climate makes them terrible and bold,
And English beef their courage does uphold ;
No danger can their daring spirit pall,
Always provided that their belly's full.
  In close intrigues their faculty's but weak,
For generally whate'er they know they speak,
And often their own counsels undermine
By their infirmity, and not design ;

From whence the learned say it does proceed,
That English treasons never can succeed ;
For they're so open-hearted, you may know
Their own most secret thoughts, and others too.

The lab'ring poor, in spite of double pay,
Are saucy, mutinous, and beggarly,
So lavish of their money and their time,
That want of forecast is the nation's crime.
Good drunken company is their delight,
And what they get by day they spend by night.
Dull thinking seldom does their heads engage,
But drink their youth away, and hurry on old age.
Empty of all good husbandry and sense,
And void of manners most when void of pence,
Their strong aversion to behaviour's such,
They always talk too little or too much ;
So dull, they never take the pains to think,
And seldom are good-natured, but in drink.

In English ale their dear enjoyment lies,
For which they'll starve themselves and families.
An Englishman will fairly drink as much
As will maintain two families of Dutch :
Subjecting all their labour to their pots ;
The greatest artists are the greatest sots.

The country poor do by example live ;
The gentry lead them, and the clergy drive :
What may we not from such examples hope ?
The landlord is their god, the priest their pope.
A drunken clergy and a swearing bench
Has given the Reformation such a drench,
As wise men think there is some cause to doubt
Will purge good manners and religion out.

Nor do the poor alone their liquor prize ;
The sages join in this great sacrifice ;
The learned men who study Aristotle,
Correct him with an explanation bottle ;

Praise Epicurus rather than Lysander,
And Aristippus [1] more than Alexander.
The doctors, too, their Galen here resign,
And generally prescribe specific wine ;
The graduate's 'study's grown an easier task,
While for the urinal they toss the flask ;
The surgeon's art grows plainer every hour,
And wine's the balm which into wounds they pour
Poets long since Parnassus have forsaken,
And say the ancient bards were all mistaken.
Apollo's lately abdicate and fled,
And good King Bacchus governs in his stead
He does the chaos of the head refine,
And atom-thoughts jump into words by wine :
The inspirations of a finer nature,
As wine must needs excel Parnassus' water.

    Statesmen their weighty politics refine,
And soldiers raise their courages by wine ;
Cecilia gives her choristers their choice,
And lets them all drink wine to clear their voice.

    Some think the clergy first found out the way,
And wine's the only spirit by which they pray ;
But others, less profane than so, agree
It clears the lungs and helps the memory ;
And therefore all of them divinely think,
Instead of study, 'tis as well to drink.

    And here I would be very glad to know
Whether our Asgilites may drink or no ;
Th' enlight'ning fumes of wine would certainly
Assist them much when they begin to fly ;
Or if a fiery chariot should appear,
Inflamed by wine, they'd have the less to fear.
Even the gods themselves, as mortals say,
Were they on earth, would be as drunk as they ;

---

[1] The drunkard's name for Canary.  [D.F.]

Nectar would be no more celestial drink,
They'd all take wine, to teach them how to think.
But English drunkards gods and men outdo,
Drink their estates away, and money too.
Colon's in debt, and if his friends should fail
To help him out, must die at last in gaol;
His wealthy uncle sent a hundred nobles
To pay his trifles off, and rid him of his troubles;
But Colon, like a true-born Englishman,
Drank all the money out in bright champagne,
And Colon does in custody remain.
Drunk'ness has been the darling of this realm
E'er since a drunken pilot had the helm.

In their religion they are so uneven,
That each man goes his own by-way to Heaven,
Tenacious of mistakes to that degree
That ev'ry man pursues it sep'rately,
And fancies none can find the way but he:
So shy of one another they are grown,
As if they strove to get to Heaven alone.
Rigid and zealous, positive and grave,
And evr'y grace but Charity they have.
This makes them so ill-natured and uncivil,
That all men think an Englishman the devil.

Surly to strangers, froward to their friend;
Submit to love with a reluctant mind.
Resolved to be ungrateful and unkind,
If by necessity reduced to ask,
The giver has the difficultest task;
For what's bestowed they awkwardly receive,
And always take less freely than they give.
The obligation is their highest grief,
And never love where they accept relief.
So sullen in their sorrow, that 'tis known
They'll rather die than their afflictions own;
And if relieved, it is too often true

That they'll abuse their benefactors too ;
For in distress, their haughty stomach's such,
They hate to see themselves obliged too much.
Seldom contented, often in the wrong,
Hard to be pleased at all, and never long.

   If your mistakes their ill opinion gain,
No merit can their favour re-obtain ;
And if they're not vindictive in their fury,
'Tis their unconstant temper does secure ye.
Their brain's so cool, their passion seldom burns,
For all's condensed before the flame returns ;
The fermentation's of so weak a matter,
The humid damps the fume, and runs it all to water.
So, though the inclination may be strong,
They're pleased by fits, and never angry long.

   Then, if good-nature shows some slender proof,
They never think they have reward enough,
But, like our modern Quakers of the town,
Expect your manners, and return you none.

   Friendship, th' abstracted union of the mind,
Which all men seek, but very few can find :
Of all the nations in the universe,
None talk on't more, or understand it less ;
For if it does their property annoy,
Their property their friendship will destroy.

   As you discourse them, you shall hear them tell
All things in which they think they do excel.
No panegyric needs their praise record ;
An Englishman ne'er wants his own good word.
His long discourses gen'rally appear
Prologued with his own wond'rous character.
But first to illustrate his own good name,
He never fails his neighbour to defame ;
And yet he really designs no wrong—
His malice goes no further than his tongue.

But pleased to tattle, he delights to rail,
To satisfy the lech'ry of a tale.
His own dear praises close the ample speech ;
Tells you how wise he is—that is, how rich :
For wealth is wisdom ; he that's rich is wise ;
And all men learnéd poverty despise.
His generosity comes next, and then
Concludes that he's a true-born Englishman ;
And they, 'tis known, are generous and free,
Forgetting and forgiving injury :
Which may be true, thus rightly understood,
Forgiving ill turns, and forgetting good.

   Cheerful in labour when they've undertook it,
But out of humour when they're out of pocket.
But if their belly and their pocket's full,
They may be phlegmatic, but never dull :
And if a bottle does their brains refine,
It makes their wit as sparkling as their wine.

   As for the general vices which we find
They're guilty of, in common with mankind,
Satire, forbear, and silently endure ;
We must conceal the crimes we cannot cure.
Nor shall my verse the brighter sex defame,
For English beauty will preserve her name,
Beyond dispute, agreeable and fair,
And modester than other nations are :
For where the vice prevails, the great temptation
Is want of money more than inclination.
In general, this only is allowed,
They're something noisy, and a little proud.

   An Englishman is gentlest in command,
Obedience is a stranger in the land :
Hardly subjected to the magistrate,
For Englishmen do all subjection hate ;
Humblest when rich, but peevish when they're poor,
And think, whate'er they have, they merit more.

The meanest English ploughman studies law,
And keeps thereby the magistrates in awe ;
Will boldly tell them what they have to do,
And sometimes punish their omissions too.
　Their liberty and property's so dear,
They scorn their laws or governors to fear :
So bugbeared with the name of slavery,
They can't submit to their own liberty.
Restraint from ill is freedom to the wise ;
But Englishmen do all restraint despise.
Slaves to their liquor, drudges to the pots,
The mob are statesmen and their statesmen sots.
　Their governors they count such dangerous things,
That 'tis their custom to affront their kings :
So jealous of the power their kings possest,
They suffer neither power nor king to rest.
The bad with force they easily subdue :
The good with constant clamours they pursue ;
And did King Jesus reign, they'd murmur too.
A discontented nation, and by far
Harder to rule in times of peace than war :
Easily set together by the ears,
And full of causeless jealousies and fears :
Apt to revolt, and willing to rebel,
And never are contented when they're well.
No Government could ever please them long,
Could tie their hands, or rectify their tongue :
In this to ancient Israel well compared,
Eternal murmurs are among them heard.
　It was but lately that they were oppressed,
Their rights invaded, and their laws suppressed :
When nicely tender of their liberty,
Lord ! what a noise they made of slavery.
In daily tumult showed their discontent,
Lampooned the King, and mocked his Government.

And if in arms they did not first appear,
'Twas want of force, and not for want of fear.
In humbler tone than English used to do,
At foreign hands for foreign aid they sue.

    William, the great successor of Nassau,
Their prayers heard and their oppressions saw :
He saw and saved them ; God and him they praised,
To this their thanks, to that their trophies raised.
But, glutted with their own felicities,
They soon their new deliverer despise ;
Say all their prayers back, their joy disown,
Unsing their thanks, and pull their trophies down ;
Their harps of praise are on the willows hung,
For Englishmen are ne'er contented long.

    The reverend clergy, too ! Who would have thought
That they, who had such non-resistance taught,
Should e'er to arms against their prince be brought,
Who up to Heaven did regal power advance,
Subjecting English laws to modes of France,
Twisting religion so with loyalty,
As one could never live and t'other die.
And yet no sooner did their prince design
Their glebes and perquisites to undermine,
But, all their passive doctrines laid aside,
The clergy their own principles denied ;
Unpreached their non-resisting cant, and prayed
To Heaven for help and to the Dutch for aid.
The Church chimed all her doctrines back again,
And pulpit champions did the cause maintain ;
Flew in the face of all their former zeal,
And non-resistance did at once repeal.

    The Rabbis say it would be too prolix
To tie religion up to politics :
The Church's safety is *suprema lex*.
And so, by a new figure of their own,
Their former doctrines all at once disown ;

As laws *post facto* in the Parliament
In urgent cases have obtained assent,
But are as dangerous precedents laid by,
Made lawful only by necessity.
    The reverend fathers then in arms appear,
And men of God become the men of war.
The nation, fired by them, to arms apply,
Assault their Antichristian monarchy ;
To their due channel all our laws restore,
And made things what they should have been before.
But when they came to fill the vacant throne,
And the pale priests looked back on what they'd done ;
How English liberty began to thrive,
And Church of England loyalty outlive ;
How all their persecuting days were done,
And their deliverer placed upon the throne :
The priests, as priests are wont to do, turned tail ;
They're Englishmen, and nature will prevail.
Now they deplore the ruins they have made,
And murmur for the master they betrayed,
Excuse those crimes they could not make him mend,
And suffer for the cause they can't defend.
Pretend they'd not have carried things so high,
And proto-martyrs make for Popery.
Had the prince done as they designed the thing,
Have set the clergy up to rule the King,
Taken a donative for coming hither,
And so have left their King and them together,
We had, say they, been now a happy nation.
No doubt we had seen a blessed reformation :
For wise men say 't's as dangerous a thing,
A ruling priesthood as a priest-rid king ;
And of all plagues with which mankind are curst,
Ecclesiastic tyranny's the worst.
    If all our former grievances were feigned,
King James has been abused and we trepanned ;

Bugbeared with Popery and power despotic,
Tyrannic government and leagues exotic:
The Revolution's a fanatic plot,
William a tyrant, Sunderland a sot:
A factious army and a poisoned nation
Unjustly forced King James's abdication.

But if he did the subjects' rights invade,
Then he was punished only, not betrayed;
And punishing of kings is no such crime,
But Englishmen have done it many a time.

When kings the sword of justice first lay down,
They are no kings, though they possess the crown:
Titles are shadows, crowns are empty things:
The good of subjects is the end of kings;
To guide in war and to protect in peace;
Where tyrants once commence the kings do cease;
For arbitrary power's so strange a thing,
It makes the tyrant and unmakes the king.

If kings by foreign priests and armies reign,
And lawless power against their oaths maintain,
Then subjects must have reason to complain.

If oaths must bind us when our kings do ill,
To call in foreign aid is to rebel.
By force to circumscribe our lawful prince
Is wilful treason in the largest sense;
And they who once rebel, most certainly
Their God, and king, and former oaths defy.
If we allow no mal-administration
Could cancel the allegiance of the nation,
Let all our learned sons of Levi try
This ecclesiastic riddle to untie:
How they could make a step to call the prince,
And yet pretend to oaths and innocence?

By the first address they made beyond the seas,
They're perjured in the most intense degrees;
And without scruple for the time to come

May swear to all the kings in Christendom.
And truly did our kings consider all,
They'd never let the clergy swear at all;
Their politic allegiance they'd refuse,
For whores and priests do never want excuse.
But if the mutual contract were dissolved,
The doubts explained, the difficulties solved,
That kings, when they descend to tyranny,
Dissolve the bond and leave the subject free,
The government's ungirt when justice dies,
And constitutions are non-entities;
The nation's all a mob; there's no such thing
As Lords or Commons, Parliament or King.
A great promiscuous crowd the hydra lies
Till laws revive and mutual contract ties;
A chaos free to choose for their own share
What case of government they please to wear.
If to a king they do the reins commit,
All men are bound in conscience to submit;
But then that king must by his oath assent
To *postulatas* of the government,
Which if he breaks, he cuts off the entail,
And power retreats to its original.
    This doctrine has the sanction of assent
From Nature's universal Parliament.
The voice of Nature and the course of things
Allow that laws superior are to kings.
None but delinquents would have justice cease;
Knaves rail at laws as soldiers rail at peace;
For justice is the end of government,
As reason is the test of argument.
No man was ever yet so void of sense
As to debate the right of self-defence,
A principle so grafted in the mind,
With Nature born, and does like Nature bind;

Twisted with reason and with Nature too,
As neither one or other can undo.

    Nor can this right be less when national;
Reason, which governs one, should govern all.
Whate'er the dialects of courts may tell,
He that his right demands can ne'er rebel,
Which right, if 'tis by governors denied,
May be procured by force or foreign aid;
For tyranny's a nation's term of grief,
As folks cry " Fire " to hasten in relief;
And when the hated word is heard about,
All men should come to help the people out.

    Thus England groaned—Britannia's voice was heard,
And great Nassau to rescue her appeared,
Called by the universal voice of Fate—
God and the people's legal magistrate.
Ye Heavens regard! Almighty Jove look down,
And view thy injured monarch on the throne.
On their ungrateful heads due vengeance take,
Who sought his aid and then his part forsake.
Witness, ye Powers! It was our call alone,
Which now our pride makes us ashamed to own.
Britannia's troubles fetched him from afar
To court the dreadful casualties of war;
But where requital never can be made,
Acknowledgment's a tribute seldom paid.

    He dwelt in bright Maria's circling arms,
Defended by the magic of her charms
From foreign fears and from domestic harms.
Ambition found no fuel to her fire;
He had what God could give or man desire.
Till pity roused him from his soft repose,
His life to unseen hazards to expose;
Till pity moved him in our cause t' appear;
Pity! that word which now we hate to hear.
But English gratitude is always such,

To hate the hand which doth oblige too much.
   Britannia's cries gave birth to his intent,
And hardly gained his unforeseen assent;
His boding thoughts foretold him he should find
The people fickle, selfish, and unkind.
Which thought did to his royal heart appear
More dreadful than the dangers of the war;
For nothing grates a generous mind so soon
As base returns for hearty service done.
   Satire, be silent! awfully prepare
Britannia's song and William's praise to hear.
Stand by, and let her cheerfully rehearse
Her grateful vows in her immortal verse.
Loud Fame's eternal trumpet let her sound;
Listen, ye distant Poles and endless round.
May the strong blast the welcome news convey
As far as sound can reach or spirit can fly.
To neighb'ring worlds, if such there be, relate
Our hero's fame, for theirs to imitate.
To distant worlds of spirits let her rehearse:
For spirits, without the help of voice, converse.
May angels hear the gladsome news on high,
Mixed with their everlasting symphony.
And Hell itself stand in suspense to know
Whether it be the fatal blast or no.

----

## BRITANNIA.

   The fame of virtue 'tis for which I sound,
And heroes with immortal triumphs crowned.
Fame, built on solid virtue, swifter flies
Than morning light can spread my eastern skies.
The gath'ring air returns the doubling sound,
And loud repeating thunders force it round;
Echoes return from caverns of the deep;
Old Chaos dreamt on't in eternal sleep;

Time hands it forward to its latest urn,
From whence it never, never shall return;
Nothing is heard so far or lasts so long;
'Tis heard by every ear and spoke by every tongue.

    My hero, with the sails of honour furled,
Rises like the great genius of the world.
By Fate and Fame wisely prepared to be
The soul of war and life of victory;
He spreads the wings of virtue on the throne,
And every wind of glory fans them on.
Immortal trophies dwell upon his brow,
Fresh as the garlands he has won but now.

    By different steps the high ascent he gains,
And differently that high ascent maintains.
Princes for pride and lust of rule make war,
And struggle for the name of conqueror.
Some fight for fame, and some for victory;
He fights to save, and conquers to set free.

    Then seek no phrase his titles to conceal,
And hide with words what actions must reveal.
No parallel from Hebrew stories take
Of god-like kings my similes to make;
No borrowed names conceal my living theme,
But names and things directly I proclaim.
'Tis honest merit does his glory raise,
Whom that exalts let no man fear to praise:
Of such a subject no man need be shy,
Virtue's above the reach of flattery.
He needs no character but his own fame,
Nor any flattering titles but his name:
William's the name that's spoke by every tongue,
William's the darling subject of my song.
Listen, ye virgins to the charming sound,
And in eternal dances hand it round:
Your early offerings to this altar bring,
Make him at once a lover and a king.

May he submit to none but to your arms,
Nor ever be subdued but by your charms.
May your soft thoughts for him be all sublime,
And every tender vow be made for him.
May he be first in every morning thought,
And Heaven ne'er hear a prayer when he's left out.
May every omen, every boding dream,
Be fortunate by mentioning his name ;
May this one charm infernal power affright,
And guard you from the terrors of the night ;
May every cheerful glass, as it goes down
To William's health, be cordials to your own.
Let every song be chorused with his name,
And music pay a tribute to his fame ;
Let every poet tune his artful verse,
And in immortal strains his deeds rehearse.
And may Apollo never more inspire
The disobedient bard with his seraphic fire ;
May all my sons their graceful homage pay,
His praises sing, and for his safety pray.

Satire, return to our unthankful isle,
Secured by Heaven's regard and William's toil ;
To both ungrateful and to both untrue,
Rebels to God, and to good-nature too.
If e'er this nation be distressed again,
To whomsoe'er they cry, they'll cry in vain ;
To Heaven they cannot have the face to look,
Or, if they should, it would but Heaven provoke.
To hope for help from man would be too much,
Mankind would always tell them of the Dutch ;
How they came here our freedoms to obtain,
Were paid and cursed, and hurried home again ;
How by their aid we first dissolved our fears,
And then our helpers damned for foreigners.
'Tis not our English temper to do better,
For Englishmen think every man their debtor.

'Tis worth observing that we ne'er complained
Of foreigners, nor of the wealth they gained,
Till all their services were at an end.
Wise men affirm it is the English way
Never to grumble till they come to pay,
And then they always think, their temper's such,
The work too little and the pay too much.
As frightened patients, when they want a cure,
Bid any price, and any pain endure;
But when the doctor's remedies appear,
The cure's too easy and the price too dear.

Great Portland ne'er was bantered when he strove
For us his master's kindest thoughts to move;
We ne'er lampooned his conduct when employed
King James's secret counsels to divide:
Then we caressed him as the only man
Which could the doubtful oracle explain;
The only Hushai able to repel
The dark designs of our Achitopel;
Compared his master's courage to his sense,
The ablest statesman and the bravest prince.
On his wise conduct we depended much,
And liked him ne'er the worse for being Dutch.
Nor was he valued more than he deserved,
Freely he ventured, faithfully he served.
In all King William's dangers he has shared;
In England's quarrels always he appeared:
The Revolution first, and then the Boyne,
In both his counsels and his conduct shine;
His martial valour Flanders will confess,
And France regrets his managing the peace.
Faithful to England's interest and her king;
The greatest reason of our murmuring.
Ten years in English service he appeared,
And gained his master's and the world's regard:
But 'tis not England's custom to reward.

The wars are over, England needs him not;
Now he's a Dutchman, and the Lord knows what.
  Schomberg, the ablest soldier of his age,
With great Nassau did in our cause engage :
Both joined for England's rescue and defence,
The greatest captain and the greatest prince.
With what applause his stories did we tell !
Stories which Europe's volumes largely swell.
We counted him an army in our aid :
Where he commanded, no man was afraid.
His actions with a constant conquest shine,
From Villa-Viciosa to the Rhine.
France, Flanders, Germany, his fame confess,
And all the world was fond of him, but us.
Our turn first served, we grudged him the command :
Witness the grateful temper of the land.
  We blame the King that he relies too much
On strangers, Germans, Hugonots, and Dutch,
And seldom does his great affairs of state
To English counsellors communicate.
The fact might very well be answered thus :
He has so often been betrayed by us,
He must have been a madman to rely
On English Godolphin's fidelity.
For, laying other arguments aside,
This thought might mortify our English pride,
That foreigners have faithfully obeyed him,
And none but Englishmen have e'er betrayed him.
They have our ships and merchants bought and sold,
And bartered English blood for foreign gold.
First to the French they sold our Turkey fleet,
And injured Talmarsh next at Camaret.
The King himself is sheltered from their snares,
Not by his merit, but the crown he wears.
Experience tells us 'tis the English way
Their benefactors always to betray.

And lest examples should be too remote,
A modern magistrate of famous note
Shall give you his own character by rote.
I'll make it out, deny it he that can,
His worship is a true-born Englishman,
In all the latitude of that empty word,
By modern acceptations understood.
The parish books his great descent record,
And now he hopes ere long to be a lord.
And truly, as things go, it would be pity
But such as he should represent the City :
While robbery for burnt-offering he brings,
And gives to God what he has stole from kings :
Great monuments of charity he raises,
And good St. Magnus whistles out his praises.
To City gaols he grants a jubilee.
And hires huzzas from his own Mobilee.[1]

Lately he wore the golden chain and gown,
With which equipped, he thus harangued the town.

---

### His Fine Speech, Etc.

With clouted iron shoes and sheep-skin breeches,
More rags than manners, and more dirt than riches ;
From driving cows and calves to Leyton Market,
While of my greatness there appeared no spark yet,
Behold I come, to let you see the pride
With which exalted beggars always ride.
Born to the needful labours of the plough,
The cart-whip graced me, as the chain does now.
Nature and Fate, in doubt what course to take,
Whether I should a lord or plough-boy make,
Kindly at last resolved they would promote me,
And first a knave, and then a knight, they vote me.

---

[1] " Mobile," applied to the moveable, unstable populace, was first abridged to
" mob " in Charles the Second's time.

What Fate appointed, Nature did prepare,
And furnished me with an exceeding care,
To fit me for what they designed to have me ;
And every gift, but honesty, they gave me.

And thus equipped, to this proud town I came,
In quest of bread, and not in quest of fame.
Blind to my future fate, a humble boy,
Free from the guilt and glory I enjoy,
The hopes which my ambition entertained
Were in the name of foot-boy all contained.
The greatest heights from small beginnings rise ;
The gods were great on earth before they reached the skies.

B——well, the generous temper of whose mind
Was ever to be bountiful inclined,
Whether by his ill-fate or fancy led,
First took me up, and furnished me with bread.
The little services he put me to
Seemed labours, rather than were truly so.
But always my advancement he designed,
For 'twas his very nature to be kind.
Large was his soul, his temper ever free ;
The best of masters and of men to me.
And I, who was before decreed by Fate
To be made infamous as well as great,
With an obsequious diligence obeyed him,
Till trusted with his all, and then betrayed him.

All his past kindnesses I trampled on,
Ruined his fortunes to erect my own.
So vipers in the bosom bred, begin
To hiss at that hand first which took them in.
With eager treachery I his fall pursued,
And my first trophies were Ingratitude.

Ingratitude, the worst of human wit,
The basest action mankind can commit ;
Which, like the sin against the Holy Ghost,
Has least of honour, and of guilt the most ;

Distinguished from all other crimes by this,
That 'tis a crime which no man will confess.
That sin alone, which should not be forgiven
On earth, although perhaps it may in Heaven.
    Thus my first benefactor I o'erthrew;
And how should I be to a second true?
The public trusts came next into my care,
And I to use them scurvily prepare.
My needy sovereign lord I played upon,
And lent him many a thousand of his own;
For which great interests I took care to charge,
And so my ill-got wealth became so large.
    My predecessor, Judas, was a fool,
Fitter to have been whipped and sent to school
Than sell a Saviour.   Had I been at hand,
His Master had not been so cheap trepanned;
I would have made the eager Jews have found,
For forty pieces, thirty thousand pound.
    My cousin, Ziba, of immortal fame
(Ziba and I shall never want a name),
First-born of treason, nobly did advance
His master's fall for his inheritance,
By whose keen arts old David first began
To break his sacred oath with Jonathan:
The good old king, 'tis thought, was very loth
To break his word, and therefore broke his oath.
Ziba's a traitor of some quality,
Yet Ziba might have been informed by me:
Had I been there, he ne'er had been content
With half the estate, nor have the government.
    In our late revolution 'twas thought strange
That I, of all mankind, should like the change;
But they who wondered at it never knew
That in it I did my old game pursue;
Nor had they heard of twenty thousand pound,
Which never yet was lost, nor ne'er was found.

Thus all things in their turn to sale I bring,
God and my master first, and then the King;
Till, by successful villanies made bold,
I thought to turn the nation into gold;
And so to forgery my hand I bent,
Not doubting I could gull the Government;
But there was ruffled by the Parliament.
And if I 'scaped the unhappy tree to climb,
'Twas want of law, and not for want of crime.

But my old friend,[1] who printed in my face
A needful competence of English brass,
Having more business yet for me to do,
And loth to lose his trusty servant so,
Managed the matter with such art and skill
As saved his hero and threw down the bill.

And now I'm graced with unexpected honours,
For which I'll certainly abuse the donors.
Knighted, and made a tribune of the people,
Whose laws and properties I'm like to keep well;
The *custos rotulorum* of the City,
And captain of the guards of their banditti.
Surrounded by my catchpoles, I declare
Against the needy debtor open war;
I hang poor thieves for stealing of your pelf,
And suffer none to rob you but myself.

The King commanded me to help reform ye,
And how I'll do it, Miss shall inform ye.
I keep the best seraglio in the nation,
And hope in time to bring it into fashion.
For this my praise is sung by every bard,
For which Bridewell would be a just reward.
In print my panegyrics fill the streets,
And hired gaol-birds their huzzas repeat.
Some charities contrived to make a show,
Have taught the needy rabble to do so,

[1] The Devil.—[D.F.]

Whose empty noise is a mechanic fame,
Since for Sir Belzebub they'd do the same.

---

### The Conclusion.

Then let us boast of ancestors no more,
Or deeds of heroes done in days of yore,
In latent records of the ages past,
Behind the rear of time, in long oblivion placed.
For if our virtues must in lines descend,
The merit with the families would end,
And intermixtures would most fatal grow;
For vice would be hereditary too;
The tainted blood would of necessity
Involuntary wickedness convey.

Vice, like ill-nature, for an age or two
May seem a generation to pursue;
But virtue seldom does regard the breed;
Fools do the wise, and wise men fools succeed.
What is't to us what ancestors we had?
If good, what better? or what worse, if bad?
Examples are for imitation set,
Yet all men follow virtue with regret.

Could but our ancestors retrieve the fate,
And see their offspring thus degenerate;
How we contend for birth and names unknown,
And build on their past actions, not our own;
They'd cancel records, and their tombs deface,
And openly disown the vile degenerate race:
For fame of families is all a cheat,
'Tis personal virtue only makes us great.

—-+-—

## CHAPTER IV.

### (1702–1703.)

DEFOE, at the end of the reign of William III., was living at
Hackney, where the parish register has record of the
baptism on the 24th of December 1701 of "Sophia, daughter of
Daniel Defoe, by Mary his wife." The name Defoe has now
taken the place of Foe, and Daniel Defoe is still managing the
brick and pantile works at Tilbury.

Queen Anne came to the throne in the thirty-eighth year of
her age, and was crowned on the 23rd of April 1702. She looked
upon the Tories as her friends, and she was a faithful and well-
meaning daughter of the Church. She maintained the alliance
against France, and declared war on the 4th of May. Parliament
was dissolved, and a new House returned. In the new House
the Tories were double the number of the Whigs. The memory
of King William was deliberately slighted in the Address to the
Queen, which said that by her wise and happy conduct she had
retrieved the honour of the nation. Objection was made to the
word "retrieved," but it was retained by the vote of a large
majority.

Action was then taken against the Dissenters by a bill against

Occasional Conformity. All office-holders who had taken the Sacrament as required by the Act passed in 1673, and who went afterwards to any Dissenters' meeting, or any meeting for religious worship that was not according to the liturgy of the Church of England, where five persons were present more than the family, were by this new bill to be disabled from holding their employments, and each was to be fined £100, besides £5 for every day in which he continued to hold his office after having been at such a meeting. They were also to be made incapable of holding any other public office until after a whole year's conformity to the Church had been proved on their behalf at Quarter Sessions. If they relapsed again, these penalties were to be all doubled against them. Inferior officers and freemen were now included in the bill, together with the magistrates in corporations, for whom alone the test—satisfied by a single act of communion—had been formerly established.

There was high debate. The mob was stirred to zeal, and showed its zeal by breaking chapel windows. But the greater number of the bishops showed by their temperance in counsel a religious spirit, and some were charged with betrayal of the Church because they did not go with the stream of party feeling. The zeal of the ignorant was quickened by a sermon preached before the University of Oxford on the 2nd of June. Dr. Sacheverell was the preacher, who hung out "the bloody flag and banner of defiance" against all Dissenters. The bill passed the Commons by a great majority, but was lost by disagreement of the Lords. It was upon this occasion, at the end of the year 1702, that Defoe wrote his pamphlet on "The Shortest Way with the Dissenters." In this piece, by ironical adoption of the desire to trample out Dissent, and do it effectually, he reduced the argument of the intolerant to an absurdity.

Defoe had in the course of the year written five or six other pamphlets. Two of these were in verse, and one of these again dwelt on the need of reformation in the manners of society. One of the prose pamphlets was of like intention—advice to ladies not to marry rakes. The failure of Sir George Rooke's attack on

Cadiz in 1702, retrieved by the subsequent destruction of Spanish galleons that were under convoy of thirty French men-of-war in the harbour of Vigo on the 12th of August in that year, was the subject of another piece of Defoe's effective doggrel, which opened with satire and was closed with a triumphant strain. Two pamphlets had dealt with the question of Church and Dissent; and Defoe, who held it mockery of sacred things to take the Sacrament as a political formality for purposes of worldly gain, argued in one of these that occasional conformity was not dissent.

Opposed to all intolerance, Defoe's opening of his pamphlet on the "Shortest Way with the Dissenters" was with a fable of the cock among the horses, that went home to those who had been ready to tyrannise in their own day of power. Intemperance on one side bred intemperance upon the other side; "for what can war but endless war still breed?" The fine irony was, as it usually is, at first misread.[1] The Dissenters thought themselves attacked; and though they were, in fact, defended, in the opening parable they felt a just rebuke. The piece also was not without a passing glance at the condition of occasional conformity. In that matter the notice taken by John Howe of Defoe's appeal to him for a clear utterance was hardly satisfying. In Dr. Edmund Calamy's "Memoirs of the Life of the late Mr. John Howe," the arguments by which he justified occasional conformity, which he avoided giving to Defoe, are fully stated. The chief of them was that a bad man, being a Churchman, though he seldom went to church, might obtain the desired worldly advantages. Was it, then, Christian charity to object to a good man's getting them by an occasional attendance at church service? Why should Defoe find fault with the good rich man of Howe's congregation, Sir Thomas Abney? The Dissenters found Defoe only in occasional conformity with their methods of proceeding. He was one with them in the higher questions of right, not always in the lower questions of policy; and with a wholesome purpose he

---

[1] Not very long ago, a leading article in the *Standard* treated with clever irony our way of seeing Shakespeare at the theatre. Its argument was taken seriously, and even pilloried in *Punch.*

spoke unpalatable truths.    Conscience, they said, had caused
Nonconformists to refuse to worship in the Church; but the
wearing of a mayor's gold chain was not to be foregone by some
of them.    Dissent in their cases, like France in " King John,"—

> " Whose armour conscience buckled on,
> Whom zeal and charity brought to the field
> As God's own soldier, rounded in the ear
> With that same purpose-change, that sly devil,
>
> .    .    .    .    .    .
>
> That smooth-faced gentleman, tickling commodity,
> Commodity, the bias of the world "—

was drawn off from its own determined aim.

A Fellow of a Cambridge College, believing that the author of
" The Shortest Way with the Dissenters" was a thoroughgoing
Churchman, who meant business and had the courage of his con-
victions, wrote thus to his bookseller :—" I received yours, and
with it that pamphlet which makes so much noise, called ' The
Shortest Way with the Dissenters,' for which I thank you.    I join
with that author in all he says, and have such a value for the
book, that, next to the Holy Bible and the Sacred Comments, I
take it for the most valuable piece I have.    I pray God put it into
her Majesty's heart to put what is there proposed in execution."
What was there proposed was " that whoever was found at a
conventicle should be banished the nation and the preacher be
hanged."    That was the " shortest way" with the Dissenters.
" The spirit of martyrdom is over," said Defoe ; " they that will
go to church to be chosen sheriffs and mayors would go to forty
churches rather than be hanged."

When the Tory Government found that this drastic remedy
was the suggestion of a whimsical Dissenter, who was making the
language of intolerance look almost as absurd as it was,—only the
absurdity belonged as fairly to that stage of our slow growth
towards civilisation as other absurdities belong to the stage we
have now reached, and our full civilisation is even yet a long way
off,—this official advertisement was inserted in the *London Gazette*
of the 10th of January 1703 :—

"**Whereas**, Daniel De Foe, alias De Fooe, is charged with writing a scandalous and seditious pamphlet, entitled 'The Shortest Way with the Dissenters.' He is a middle-sized, spare man, about forty years old, of a brown complexion and dark-brown coloured hair, but wears a wig; a hooked nose, a sharp chin, grey eyes, and a large mole near his mouth: was born in London, and for many years was a hose-factor in Freeman's Yard, in Cornhill; and now is owner of the brick and pantile works near Tilbury Fort in Essex: whoever shall discover the said Daniel De Foe to one of her Majesty's principal Secretaries of State, or any of her Majesty's justices of the peace, so he may be apprehended, shall have a reward of £50, which her Majesty has ordered immediately to be paid on such discovery."

On the 25th of February the House of Commons ordered Defoe's pamphlet, which follows in this volume next after the present chapter, to be burnt by the common hangman. After this, the printer and bookseller having been arrested, Defoe gave himself up " rather than others should be ruined by his mistake." He published before his surrender "A Brief Explanation of a late Pamphlet, entitled 'The Shortest Way with the Dissenters;'" but while driven to explain his wit, he retracted no part of his wisdom. He was indicted at the Old Bailey on the 24th of February 1703, and his trial was fixed for the following July. In the interval he wrote a vindication of King William—" King William's Affection to the Church of England Examined "—which passed in a few weeks through four editions. He prepared also a volume which he called " A True Collection of the Writings of the Author of the 'True-Born Englishman.' Corrected by Himself." It included, among twenty-two different pieces, the pamphlet for which at the sessions of the Old Bailey, on the 7th, 8th, and 9th of July, Defoe was sentenced to stand thrice in the pillory with a paper of his crime, to pay a fine of two hundred marks to the Queen, to find sureties of his good behaviour for seven years, and to lie in prison till all be performed.

There was an interval of about three weeks between the sentence and Defoe's first standing in the pillory. He spent the time in finishing a pamphlet on "The Shortest Way to Peace and Union," which he showed to be the way of mutual forbearance and common charity. Dissenters, he argued, should concede to the Church of England its great use and service in association of religion with the State, the Church in its turn conceding to Dissenters a full toleration. This was the shortest way to peace among all Christians in the land. This pamphlet was published on the 29th of July, at the same time with a satirical "Hymn to the Pillory." The 29th of July was also the day on which Defoe appeared first in the pillory, his place of exposure being on that day before the Royal Exchange in Cornhill. On the next day, the 30th, he was pilloried near the Conduit in Cheapside; and on the 31st at Temple Bar. Defoe's "Hymn to the Pillory" was largely sold among the crowd; scraps of its vigorous doggrel passed from lip to lip. Flower-girls supplied their stores to the people to adorn the scaffold of Defoe; the mob itself protected him from insult, drank his health, and followed him with acclamations when he was removed. He had won the battle by his pluck, and had transferred all the disgrace of his pillory to those who placed him in it,

# THE SHORTEST WAY

WITH

# THE DISSENTERS;

OR,

## PROPOSALS FOR THE ESTABLISHMENT

OF

# THE CHURCH.

P

# THE SHORTEST WAY

# THE DISSENTERS.

———◆———

SIR ROGER L'ESTRANGE tells us a story in his collection of fables, of the cock and the horses. The cock was gotten to roost in the stable among the horses, and there being no racks or other conveniences for him, it seems he was forced to roost upon the ground. The horses jostling about for room, and putting the cock in danger of his life, he gives them this grave advice, "Pray, gentlefolks, let us stand still, for fear we should tread upon one another."

There are some people in the world, who now they are un-perched, and reduced to an equality with other people, and under strong and very just apprehensions of being further treated as they deserve, begin, with Æsop's cock, to preach up peace and union, and the Christian duties of moderation, forgetting that, when they had the power in their hands, these graces were strangers in their gates.

It is now near fourteen years[1] that the glory and peace of the purest and most flourishing Church in the world has been eclipsed, buffeted, and disturbed by a sort of men whom God in His providence has suffered to insult over her and bring her down. These have been the days of her humiliation and tribulation. She has borne with invincible patience the reproach of the wicked, and

---

[1] Dating from 1688-89, the Revolution and accession of King William III.

God has at last heard her prayers, and delivered her from the oppression of the stranger.

And now they find their day is over, their power gone, and the throne of this nation possessed by a royal, English, true, and ever-constant member of, and friend to, the Church of England. Now they find that they are in danger of the Church of England's just resentments; now they cry out peace, union, forbearance, and charity, as if the Church had not too long harboured her enemies under her wing, and nourished the viperous brood till they hiss and fly in the face of the mother that cherished them.

No, gentlemen, the time of mercy is past, your day of grace is over; you should have practised peace, and moderation, and charity, if you expected any yourselves.

We have heard none of this lesson for fourteen years past. We have been huffed and bullied with your Act of Toleration; you have told us that you are the Church established by law, as well as others; have set up your canting synagogues at our church doors, and the Church and members have been loaded with reproaches, with oaths, associations, abjurations, and what not. Where has been the mercy, the forbearance, the charity, you have shown to tender consciences of the Church of England, that could not take oaths as fast you made them; that having sworn allegiance to their lawful and rightful King, could not dispense with that oath, their King being still alive, and swear to your new hodge-podge of a Dutch Government? These have been turned out of their livings, and they and their families left to starve; their estates double taxed to carry on a war they had no hand in, and you got nothing by. What account can you give of the multitudes you have forced to comply, against their consciences, with your new sophistical politics, who, like new converts in France, sin because they cannot starve? And now the tables are turned upon you; you must not be persecuted; it is not a Christian spirit.

You have butchered one king, deposed another king, and made a mock king of a third,[1] and yet you could have the face to expect

---

[1] Charles I., James II., William III.

to be employed and trusted by the fourth. Anybody that did not know the temper of your party would stand amazed at the impudence, as well as folly, to think of it.

Your management of your Dutch monarch, whom you reduced to a mere King of Clouts, is enough to give any future princes such an idea of your principles as to warn them sufficiently from coming into your clutches ; and God be thanked the Queen is out of your hands, knows you, and will have a care of you.

There is no doubt but the supreme authority of a nation has in itself a power, and a right to that power, to execute the laws upon any part of that nation it governs. The execution of the known laws of the land, and that with a weak and gentle hand neither, was all this fanatical party of this land have ever called persecution ; this they have magnified to a height, that the sufferings of the Huguenots in France were not to be compared with. Now, to execute the known laws of a nation upon those who transgress them, after voluntarily consenting to the making those laws, can never be called persecution, but justice. But justice is always violence to the party offending, for every man is innocent in his own eyes. The first execution of the laws against Dissenters in England was in the days of King James the First ;[1] and what did it amount to truly? The worst they suffered was at their own request : to let them go to New England and erect a new colony, and give them great privileges, grants, and suitable powers, keep them under protection, and defend them against all invaders, and receive no taxes or revenue from them. This was the cruelty of the Church of England. Fatal leniency ! It was the ruin of that excellent prince, King Charles the First. Had King James sent all the Puritans in England away to the West

---

[1] On the 16th of July, 1604, the Puritan clergy within the Church were required to conform on or before the 30th of November on pain of expulsion. On the 4th of December Whitgift's successor, Richard Bancroft, was consecrated Archbishop of Canterbury. He strictly carried out this order, and declared every man, cleric or lay, to be excommunicated who questioned the complete accordance of the Prayer Book with the Word of God. On the 6th of September, 1620, the *Mayflower* left England with the first freight of English families that sought freedom of worship where they came to be the founders of a New England across the sea.

Indies, we had been a national, unmixed Church; the Church of England had been kept undivided and entire.

To requite the lenity of the father they take up arms against the son; conquer, pursue, take, imprison, and at last put to death the anointed of God, and destroy the very being and nature of government, setting up a sordid impostor, who had neither title to govern nor understanding to manage, but supplied that want with power, bloody and desperate counsels, and craft without conscience.

Had not King James the First withheld the full execution of the laws, had he given them strict justice, he had cleared the nation of them, and the consequences had been plain: his son had never been murdered by them nor the monarchy overwhelmed. It was too much mercy shown them was the ruin of his posterity and the ruin of the nation's peace. One would think the Dissenters should not have the face to believe that we are to be wheedled and canted into peace and toleration when they know that they have once requited us with a civil war, and once with an intolerable and unrighteous persecution for our former civility.

Nay, to encourage us to be easy with them, it is apparent that they never had the upper hand of the Church, but they treated her with all the severity, with all the reproach and contempt that was possible. What peace and what mercy did they show the loyal gentry of the Church of England in the time of their triumphant Commonwealth? How did they put all the gentry of England to ransom, whether they were actually in arms for the King or not, making people compound for their estates and starve their families? How did they treat the clergy of the Church of England, sequestered the ministers, devoured the patrimony of the Church, and divided the spoil by sharing the Church lands among their soldiers, and turning her clergy out to starve? Just such measure as they have meted should be measured them again.

Charity and love is the known doctrine of the Church of England, and it is plain she has put it in practice towards the Dissenters, even beyond what they ought, till she has been wanting to herself, and in effect unkind to her sons, particularly in the too much lenity of King James the First, mentioned before. Had he so rooted the Puritans from the face of the land, which he had an opportunity early to have done, they had not had the power to vex the Church as since they have done.

In the days of King Charles the Second, how did the Church reward their bloody doings with lenity and mercy, except the barbarous regicides of the pretended court of justice? Not a soul suffered for all the blood in an unnatural war. King Charles came in all mercy and love, cherished them, preferred them, employed them, withheld the rigour of the law, and oftentimes, even against the advice of his Parliament, gave them liberty of conscience;[1] and how did they requite him with the villainous contrivance to depose and murder him and his successor at the Rye Plot?[2]

King James, as if mercy was the inherent quality of the family, began his reign with unusual favour to them. Nor could their joining with the Duke of Monmouth against him move him to do himself justice upon them; but that mistaken prince thought to win them by gentleness and love, proclaimed an universal liberty to them, and rather discountenanced the Church of England than them.[3] How they requited him all the world knows.

The late reign is too fresh in the memory of all the world to need a comment; how, under pretence of joining with the Church in redressing some grievances, they pushed things to that extremity, in conjunction with some mistaken gentlemen, as to depose the late King, as if the grievance of the nation could not have been redressed but by the absolute ruin of the prince. Here is an instance of their temper, their peace, and charity. To what height they carried themselves during the reign of a king of their own; how they crept into all places of trust and profit; how they insinuated into the favour of the King, and were at first preferred

---

[1] Charles II. unconstitutionally suspended the penal laws against nonconformists and recusants in 1672.

[2] The story of the Rye House Plot was used for bringing Algernon Sidney and Lord William Russell to the scaffold.

[3] James II. unconstitutionally suspended the penal laws against nonconformists and recusants by Declarations of Indulgence in 1686 and 1688.

to the highest places in the nation; how they engrossed the ministry, and above all, how pitifully they managed, is too plain to need any remarks.

But particularly their mercy and charity, the spirit of union, they tell us so much of, has been remarkable in Scotland. If any man would see the spirit of a Dissenter, let him look into Scotland. There they made entire conquest of the Church, trampled down the sacred orders, and suppressed the Episcopal government with an absolute, and, as they suppose, irretrievable victory, though it is possible they may find themselves mistaken. Now it would be a very proper question to ask their impudent advocate, the Observator, pray how much mercy and favour did the members of the Episcopal Church find in Scotland from the Scotch Presbyterian Government? and I shall undertake for the Church of England that the Dissenters shall still receive as much here, though they deserve but little.

In a small treatise of the sufferings of the Episcopal clergy in Scotland, it will appear what usage they met with; how they not only lost their livings, but in several places were plundered and abused in their persons; the ministers that could not conform turned out with numerous families and no maintenance, and hardly charity enough left to relieve them with a bit of bread. And the cruelties of the parties are innumerable, and not to be attempted in this short piece.

And now to prevent the distant cloud which they perceived to hang over their heads from England. With a true Presbyterian policy, they put in for a union of nations, that England might unite their Church with the Kirk of Scotland, and their Presbyterian members sit in our House of Commons, and their Assembly of Scotch canting long-cloaks in our Convocation. What might have been if our fanatic Whiggish statesmen continued, God only knows; but we hope we are out of fear of that now.

It is alleged by some of the faction—and they began to bully us with it—that if we won't unite with them, they will not settle the crown with us again, but when Her Majesty dies, will choose a king for themselves.

If they won't, we must make them, and it is not the first time we have let them know that we are able. The crowns of these kingdoms have not so far disowned the right of succession, but they may retrieve it again; and if Scotland thinks to come off from a successive to an elective state of government, England has not promised not to assist the right heir and put them into possession without any regard to their ridiculous settlements.[1]

These are the gentlemen, these their ways of treating the Church, both at home and abroad. Now let us examine the reasons they pretend to give why we should be favourable to them, why we should continue and tolerate them among us.

First, they are very numerous, they say; they are a great part of the nation, and we cannot suppress them.

To this may be answered :—

1. They are not so numerous as the Protestants in France, and yet the French King effectually cleared the nation of them at once, and we don't find he misses them at home.[2] But I am not of the opinion they are so numerous as is pretended; their party is more numerous than their persons, and those mistaken people of the Church who are misled and deluded by their wheedling artifices to join with them, make their party the greater; but these will open their eyes when the Government shall set heartily about the work, and come off from them, as some animals which they say always desert a house when it is likely to fall.

---

[1] The oath taken by Tories against the legal right of the Pretender to the crown was said to reserve the question of his divine right of succession. Divine right was unchangeable, but laws were liable to change—and so far as they go, what to-day is treason may be loyalty to-morrow.

[2] The Revocation of the Edict of Nantes was signed on the 17th of October 1685. All Protestant churches were to be demolished, and their ministers who would not be converted were to leave France within a fortnight. Fugitive reformers who did not return within four months would have their property confiscated. Lay Reformers were forbidden to leave France, on pain of the galleys for men and confiscation of body and goods for women. Those who remained were exposed to cruelties of the soldiery. The King thought that his way of conversion by dragoons had reduced a million and a half of French heretics to twelve or fifteen thousand; but between the Revocation and the time when Defoe wrote this pamphlet, it has been estimated that 250,000 French Protestants left France to establish homes in England and elsewhere.

2. The more numerous the more dangerous, and therefore the more need to suppress them; and God has suffered us to bear them as goads in our sides for not utterly extinguishing them long ago.

3. If we are to allow them only because we cannot suppress them, then it ought to be tried whether we can or not; and I am of opinion it is easy to be done, and could prescribe ways and means, if it were proper; but I doubt not the Government will find effectual methods for the rooting the contagion from the face of this land.

Another argument they use, which is this, that it is a time of war, and we have need to unite against the common enemy.

We answer, this common enemy had been no enemy if they had not made him so. He was quiet in peace, and no way disturbed or encroached upon us, and we know no reason we had to quarrel with him.

But further, we make no question but we are able to deal with this common enemy without their help; but why must we unite with them because of the enemy? Will they go over to the enemy if we do not prevent it by a union with them? We are very well contented they should, and make no question we shall be ready to deal with them and the common enemy too, and better without them than with them.

Besides, if we have a common enemy, there is the more need to be secure against our private enemies. If there is one common enemy, we have the less need to have an enemy in our bowels.

It was a great argument some people used against suppressing the old money, that it was a time of war, and it was too great a risk for the nation to run; if we should not master it, we should be undone. And yet the sequel proved the hazard was not so great but it might be mastered, and the success was answerable. The suppressing the Dissenters is not a harder work nor a work of less necessity to the public. We can never enjoy a settled, uninterrupted union and tranquillity in this nation till the spirit of Whiggism, faction, and schism is melted down like the old money.

To talk of the difficulty is to frighten ourselves with chimeras and notions of a powerful party, which are indeed a party without power. Difficulties often appear greater at a distance than when they are searched into with judgment and distinguished from the vapours and shadows that attend them.

We are not to be frightened with it ; this age is wiser than that by all our own experience and theirs too. King Charles the First had early suppressed this party if he had taken more deliberate measures. In short, it is not worth arguing to talk of their arms. Their Monmouths, and Shaftesburys, and Argyles are gone ; their Dutch sanctuary is at an end ; Heaven has made way for their destruction, and if we do not close with the Divine occasion, we are to blame ourselves, and may remember that we had once an opportunity to serve the Church of England by extirpating her implacable enemies, and having let slip the minute that Heaven presented, may experimentally complain, *Post est occasio calva.*

Here are some popular objections in the way :—

As first, the Queen has promised them to continue them in their tolerated liberty, and has told us she will be a religious observer of her word.

What Her Majesty will do we cannot help ; but what, as head of the Church, she ought to do, is another case. Her Majesty has promised to protect and defend the Church of England, and if she cannot effectually do that without the destruction of the Dissenters, she must of course dispense with one promise to comply with another. But to answer this cavil more effectually : Her Majesty did never promise to maintain the toleration to the destruction of the Church ; but it is upon supposition that it may be compatible with the well-being and safety of the Church, which she had declared she would take especial care of. Now if these two interests clash, it is plain Her Majesty's intentions are to uphold, protect, defend, and establish the Church, and this we conceive is impossible.

Perhaps it may be said that the Church is in no immediate danger from the Dissenters, and therefore it is time enough. But this is a weak answer.

For first, if a danger be real, the distance of it is no argument against, but rather a spur to quicken us to prevention, lest it be too late hereafter.

And secondly, here is the opportunity, and the only one perhaps that ever the Church had, to secure herself and destroy her enemies.

The representatives of the nation have now an opportunity; the time is come which all good men have wished for, that the gentlemen of England may serve the Church of England. Now they are protected and encouraged by a Church of England Queen.

What will you do for your sister in the day that she shall be spoken for?

If ever you will establish the best Christian Church in the world; if ever you will suppress the spirit of enthusiasm; if ever you will free the nation from the viperous brood that have so long sucked the blood of their mother; if ever you will leave your posterity free from faction and rebellion, this is the time. This is the time to pull up this heretical weed of sedition that has so long disturbed the peace of our Church and poisoned the good corn.

But, says another hot and cold objector, this is renewing fire and faggot, reviving the act *De Heretico Comburendo;* this will be cruelty in its nature, and barbarous to all the world.

I answer, it is cruelty to kill a snake or a toad in cold blood, but the poison of their nature makes it a charity to our neighbours to destroy those creatures, not for any personal injury received, but for prevention; not for the evil they have done, but the evil they may do.

Serpents, toads, vipers, &c., are noxious to the body, and poison the sensitive life; these poison the soul, corrupt our posterity, ensnare our children, destroy the vitals of our happiness, our future felicity, and contaminate the whole mass.

Shall any law be given to such wild creatures? Some beasts are for sport, and the huntsmen give them advantages of ground; but some are knocked on the head by all possible ways of violence and surprise.

I do not prescribe fire and faggot, but, as Scipio said of Carthage, *Delenda est Carthago.* They are to be rooted out of this nation, if ever we will live in peace, serve God, or enjoy our own. As for the manner, I leave it to those hands who have a right to execute God's justice on the nations and the Church's enemies.

But if we must be frighted from this justice under the specious pretences and odious sense of cruelty, nothing will be effected : it will be more barbarous to our own children and dear posterity when they shall reproach their fathers, as we do ours, and tell us, " You had an opportunity to root out this cursed race from the world under the favour and protection of a true English queen ; and out of your foolish pity you spared them, because, forsooth, you would not be cruel ; and now our Church is suppressed and persecuted, our religion trampled under foot, our estates plundered, our persons imprisoned and dragged to jails, gibbets, and scaffolds : your sparing this Amalekite race is our destruction, your mercy to them proves cruelty to your poor posterity."

How just will such reflections be when our posterity shall fall under the merciless clutches of this uncharitable generation, when our Church shall be swallowed up in schism, faction, enthusiasm, and confusion ; when our Government shall be devolved upon foreigners, and our monarchy dwindled into a republic.

It would be more rational for us, if we must spare this generation, to summon our own to a general massacre, and as we have brought them into the world free, send them out so, and not betray them to destruction by our supine negligence, and then cry, " It is mercy."

Moses was a merciful, meek man, and yet with what fury did he run through the camp, and cut the throats of three-and-thirty thousand of his dear Israelites that were fallen into idolatry. What was the reason ? It was mercy to the rest to make these examples, to prevent the destruction of the whole army.

How many millions of future souls we save from infection and delusion if the present race of poisoned spirits were purged from the face of the land !

It is vain to trifle in this matter, the light, foolish handling of them by mulcts, fines, &c.,—it is their glory and their advantage. If the gallows instead of the Counter, and the galleys instead of the fines, were the reward of going to a conventicle, to preach or hear, there would not be so many sufferers. The spirit of martyrdom is over; they that will go to church to be chosen sheriffs and mayors would go to forty churches rather than be hanged.

If one severe law were made and punctually executed, that whoever was found at a conventicle should be banished the nation and the preacher be hanged, we should soon see an end of the tale. They would all come to church, and one age would make us all one again.

To talk of five shillings a month for not coming to the sacrament, and one shilling per week for not coming to church, this is such a way of converting people as never was known; this is selling them a liberty to transgress for so much money. If it be not a crime, why don't we give them full license? And if it be, no price ought to compound for the committing it, for that is selling a liberty to people to sin against God and the Government.

If it be a crime of the highest consequence both against the peace and welfare of the nation, the glory of God, the good of the Church, and the happiness of the soul, let us rank it among capital offences, and let it receive a punishment in proportion to it.

We hang men for trifles, and banish them for things not worth naming; but an offence against God and the Church, against the welfare of the world and the dignity of religion, shall be bought off for five shillings! This is such a shame to a Christian Government that it is with regret I transmit it to posterity.

If men sin against God, affront His ordinances, rebel against His Church, and disobey the precepts of their superiors, let them suffer as such capital crimes deserve. So will religion flourish, and this divided nation be once again united.

And yet the title of barbarous and cruel will soon be taken off from this law too. I am not supposing that all the Dissenters in

England should be hanged or banished, but, as in cases of rebellions and insurrections, if a few of the ringleaders suffer, the multitude are dismissed; so, a few obstinate people being made examples, there is no doubt but the severity of the law would find a stop in the compliance of the multitude.

To make the reasonableness of this matter out of question, and more unanswerably plain, let us examine for what it is that this nation is divided into parties and factions, and let us see how they can justify a separation, or we of the Church of England can justify our bearing the insults and inconveniences of the party.

One of their leading pastors,[1] and a man of as much learning as most among them, in his answer to a pamphlet, entitled "An Inquiry into the Occasional Conformity," has these words, p. 27, "Do the religion of the Church and the meeting-houses make two religions? Wherein do they differ? The substance of the same religion is common to them both; and the modes and accidents are the things in which only they differ." P. 28: "Thirty-nine articles are given us for the summary of our religion; thirty-six contain the substance of it, wherein we agree; three the additional appendices, about which we have some differences."

Now, if as by their own acknowledgment the Church of England is a true Church, and the difference between them is only in a few modes and accidents, why should we expect that they will suffer galleys, corporeal punishment, and banishment for these trifles? There is no question but they will be wiser; even their own principles will not bear them out in it; they will certainly comply with the laws and with reason; and though at the first severity they may seem hard, the next age will feel nothing of it; the contagion will be rooted out; the disease being cured, there will be no need of the operation; but if they should venture to transgress and fall into the pit, all the world must condemn their obstinacy, as being without ground from their own principles.

Thus the pretence of cruelty will be taken off, and the party

---

[1] John Howe, in his answer to Defoe's request for a statement of opinion from him on Occasional Conformity.

actually suppressed, and the disquiets they have so often brought upon the nation prevented.

Their numbers and their wealth make them haughty, and that is so far from being an argument to persuade us to forbear them, that it is a warning to us, without any delay, to reconcile them to the unity of the Church or remove them from us.

At present, Heaven be praised, they are not so formidable as they have been, and it is our own fault if ever we suffer them to be so. Providence and the Church of England seem to join in this particular, that now the destroyers of the nation's peace may be overturned, and to this end the present opportunity seems to be put into our hands.

To this end her present Majesty seems reserved to enjoy the crown, that the ecclesiastic as well as civil rights of the nation may be restored by her hand. To this end the face of affairs have received such a turn in the process of a few months as never has been before; the leading men of the nation, the universal cry of the people, the unanimous request of the clergy, agree in this, that the deliverance of our Church is at hand. For this end has Providence given us such a Parliament, such a Convocation, such a gentry, and such a Queen as we never had before. And what may be the consequences of a neglect of such opportunities? The succession of the crown has but a dark prospect; another Dutch turn may make the hopes of it ridiculous and the practice impossible. Be the house of our future princes never so well inclined, they will be foreigners, and many years will be spent in suiting the genius of strangers to this crown and the interests of the nation; and how many ages it may be before the English throne be filled with so much zeal and candour, so much tenderness and hearty affection to the Church as we see it now covered with, who can imagine?

It is high time, then, for the friends of the Church of England to think of building up and establishing her in such a manner that she may be no more invaded by foreigners nor divided by factions, schisms, and error.

If this could be done by gentle and easy methods, I should be glad; but the wound is corroded, the vitals begin to mortify, and nothing but amputation of members can complete the cure; all the ways of tenderness and compassion, all persuasive arguments, have been made use of in vain.

The humour of the Dissenters has so increased among the people, that they hold the Church in defiance, and the house of God is an abomination among them; nay, they have brought up their posterity in such prepossessed aversions to our holy religion, that the ignorant mob think we are all idolaters and worshippers of Baal, and account it a sin to come within the walls of our churches.

The primitive Christians were not more shy of a heathen temple or of meat offered to idols, nor the Jews of swine's flesh, than some of our Dissenters are of the Church, and the divine service solemnised therein.

This obstinacy must be rooted out with the profession of it; while the generation are less at liberty daily to affront God Almighty and dishonour His holy worship, we are wanting in our duty to God and our mother, the Church of England.

How can we answer it to God, to the Church, and to our posterity to leave them entangled with fanaticism, error, and obstinacy in the bowels of the nation; to leave them an enemy in their streets, that in time may involve them in the same crimes, and endanger the utter extirpation of religion in the nation?

What is the difference betwixt this and being subjected to the power of the Church of Rome, from whence we have reformed? If one be an extreme on one hand, and one on another, it is equally destructive to the truth to have errors settled among us, let them be of what nature they will.

Both are enemies of our Church and of our peace; and why should it not be as criminal to admit an enthusiast as a Jesuit? Why should the Papist with his seven sacraments be worse than the Quaker with no sacraments at all? Why should religious houses be more intolerable than meeting-houses? Alas, the Church of England! What with Popery on one hand, and schismatics on the other, how has she been crucified between two thieves!

Q

Now let us crucify the thieves. Let her foundations be established upon the destruction of her enemies. The doors of mercy being always open to the returning part of the deluded people, let the obstinate be ruled with the rod of iron.

Let all true sons of so holy and oppressed a mother, exasperated by her afflictions, harden their hearts against those who have oppressed her.

And may God Almighty put it into the hearts of all the friends of truth to lift up a standard against pride and Antichrist, that the posterity of the sons of error may be rooted out from the face of this land for ever.

A

# HYMN TO THE PILLORY.

HAIL hieroglyphic state machine,
 Contrived to punish fancy in :
Men that are men in thee can feel no pain,
And all thy insignificants disdain.
    Contempt, that false new word for shame,
    Is, without crime, an empty name,
    A shadow to amuse mankind,
But never frights the wise or well-fixed mind :
    Virtue despises human scorn,
    And scandals innocence adorn.

    Exalted on thy stool of state,
What prospect do I see of sovereign fate !
    How the inscrutables of Providence
    Differ from our contracted sense !
    Here by the errors of the town
    The fools look out and knaves look on.
Persons or crimes find here the same respect,
    And vice does virtue oft correct,
    The undistinguished fury of the street,
    Which mob and malice mankind greet :
    No bias can the rabble draw,
But dirt throws dirt without respect to merit or to law.

Sometimes, the air of scandal to maintain,
Villains look from thy lofty loops in vain :

But who can judge of crimes by punishment
Where parties rule and Lords subservient?
Justice with change of interest learns to bow,
And what was merit once is murder now:
Actions receive their tincture from the times,
And as they change, are virtues made or crimes.
　　Thou art the state-trap of the law,
But neither can keep knaves nor honest men in awe;
　　　These are too hardened in offence,
　　　And those upheld by innocence.


How have thy opening vacancies received
In every age the criminals of state!
　　And how has mankind been deceived
　　When they distinguish crimes by fate!
Tell us, great engine, how to understand
Or reconcile the justice of the land;
How Bastwick, Prynne, Hunt, Hollingsby, and Pye,
　　　Men of unspotted honesty,
　　　Men that had learning, wit, and sense,
　　　And more than most men have had since,
Could equal title to thee claim
With Oates and Fuller, men of later fame:
　　　Even the learned Selden saw
　　　A prospect of thee through the law:
He had thy lofty pinnacles in view,
But so much honour never was thy due:
Had the great Selden triumphed on thy stage,
　　　Selden, the honour of this age,
　　　No man would ever shun thee more,
Or grudge to stand where Selden stood before.


　　Thou art no shame to truth and honesty,
Nor is the character of such defaced by thee
　　Who suffer by oppressèd injury.

Shame, like the exhalations of the sun,
Falls back where first the motion was begun ;
And they who for no crime shall on thy brows appear,
Bear less reproach than they who placed them there.

But if contempt is on thy face entailed,
   Disgrace itself shall be ashamed ;
Scandal shall blush that it has not prevailed
   To blast the man it has defamed.
Let all that merit equal punishment
Stand there with him, and we are all content.

   There would the famed Sacheverell stand
With trumpet of sedition in his hard,
Sounding the first crusado in the land.
   He from a Church of England pulpit first
   All his Dissenting brethren curst ;
   Doomed them to Satan for a prey,
   And first found out the shortest way.
With him the wise Vice-Chancellor of the press,
Who though our printers licenses defy,
   Willing to show his forwardness,
   Blessed it with his authority.
He gave the Church's sanction to the work,
As Popes bless colours for troops which fight the 'Turk.
   Doctors in scandal these are grown,
For red-hot zeal and furious learning known ;
Professors in reproach, and highly fit
For Juno's académy—Billingsgate.
   Thou, like a true-born English tool,
   Hast from their composition stole,
And now art like to smart for being a fool ;
And as of Englishmen 'twas always meant,
They're better to improve than to invent.
   Upon their model thou hast made
   A monster makes the world afraid.

With them let all the statesmen stand
Who guide us with unsteady hand;
Who armies, fleet, and men betray,
And ruin all the shortest way.
Let all those soldiers stand in sight
Who 're willing to be paid and not to fight;
Agents and colonels who false muster bring
To cheat your country first and then your king.
Bring all your coward captains of the fleet;
Lord! what a crowd will there be when they meet!

They who let Pointis 'scape to Brest,
With all the gods of Carthagena blest;[1]
Those who betrayed our Turkey fleet,
Or injured Talmash sold at Camaret;[2]
Who missed the squadron from Toulon,
And always came too late or else too soon.
All these are heroes whose great actions claim
Immortal honour to their dying fame,
And ought not to have been denied
On thy great counterscarp to have their valour tried.

Why have not these upon thy swelling stage
Tasted the keener justice of the age?

[1] The French Rear-admiral Pointis, commanding an expedition against Carthagena, the rich *entrepôt* between Peru and Spain, took the city by assault after a defence lasting from the 15th to the 30th of April 1697, carried away a rich booty of gold, silver, and precious stones, avoided on his way back one English squadron stronger than his own, fought with another, and came safely into Brest harbour, bringing to his shipowners more than ten millions of livres.

[2] Camaret was a small neck of land in the mouth of the river of Brest which would have commanded the river if the Allies could have become masters of it. Talmash set his heart upon seizing it with a force of 6000 men. The secret purpose became known to the French. The leaders of the expedition found that strong batteries had been set up against them. A council of war decided to abandon the enterprise, but Talmash, believing that the men they saw on shore were but a rabble, landed with 600 brave followers, who were all killed or taken prisoners. Talmash was shot in the thigh, and died a few days afterwards. The fleet returned to Plymouth.

If 'tis because their crimes are too remote
Whom leaden-footed justice has forgot,
    Let's view the modern scenes of fame;
If men and management are not the same,
    When fleets go out with money and with men,
    Just time enough to venture home again;
Navies prepared to guard the insulted coast,
    And convoys settled when our ships are lost.
    Some heroes lately come from sea,
If they were paid their due, should stand with thee.

Papers, too, should their deeds relate,
To prove the justice of their fate,
Their deeds of war at Port Saint Mary's done,[1]
And see the trophies by them which they won;
Let Ormond's declaration there appear,
He'd certainly be pleased to see them there.
    Let some good limner represent
    The ravished nuns, the plundered town,
    The English honour how misspent,
The shameful coming back, and little done.

    The Vigo-men should next appear,
    To triumph on thy theatre;
They who on board the great galoons had been,
Who robbed the Spaniards first, and then the Queen;
Set up their praises to their valour due,
How eighty sail had beaten twenty-two:
    Two troopers so, and one dragoon,
Conquered a Spanish boy, a Pampalone.

---

[1] Port St. Mary's was an open village on the Spanish mainland opposite Cadiz. On the 12th of August 1702, the Duke of Ormond and Sir George Rooke having a fleet in the Bay of Cadiz, and hearing that those on the isle of Cadiz had sent over the best of their property to Port St. Mary's, it was resolved in a council of war, against the strongly-expressed advice of Ormond, not to attack Cadiz, but land for plunder of the unprotected village, which they found deserted but full of riches. They re-embarked with their plunder, and sailed off in such haste that they forgot to take fresh water on board.

Yet let them Ormond's conduct own,
Who beat them first on shore, or little had been done ;
What unknown spoils from thence are come,
How much was brought away, how little home.
If all the thieves should on thy scaffold stand
Who robbed their masters in command,
The multitude would soon outdo
The City crowds of Lord Mayor's show.


Upon thy penitential stools
Some people should be placed for fools,
As some, for instance, who, while they look on,
See others plunder all, and they got none.
Next, the Lieutenant-General,
To get the Devil, lost the De'll and all ;
And he some little badge should bear,
Who ought in justice to have hanged them there.
This had his honour more maintained
Than all the spoils at Vigo gained.


Then clap thy wooden wings for joy,
And greet the men of great employ ;
The authors of the nation's discontent,
And scandal of a Christian government.
Jobbers and brokers of the City stocks,
With forty thousand tallies at their backs,
Who make our banks and companies obey,
Or sink them all the shortest way.
The intrinsic value of our stocks
Is stated in our calculating books.
The imaginary prizes rise and fall
As they command who toss the ball ;
Let them upon thy lofty turrets stand,
With bear-skins on the back, debentures in the hand,
And write in capital upon the post,

That here they should remain
Till this enigma they explain,
How stocks should fall when sails surmount the coast,
And rise again when ships are lost.

Great monster of the law, exalt thy head,
Appear no more in masquerade ;
In homely phrase express thy discontent,
And move it in the approaching Parliament ;
Tell them how papers were instead of coin,
With interest eight per cent., and discount nine ;
Of Irish transport debt unpaid,
Bills false endorsed, and long accounts unmade.
And tell them all the nation hopes to see,
They'll send the guilty down to thee,
Rather than those who write their history.
Then bring those justices upon thy bench
Who vilely break the laws they should defend,
And upon equity entrench
By punishing the crimes they will not mend.
Set every vicious magistrate
Upon thy sumptuous chariot of the state ;
There let them all in triumph ride,
Their purple and their scarlet laid aside.
Let no such Bridewell justices protect
As first debauch the whores which they correct ;
Such who with oaths and drunkenness will sit
And punish far less crimes than they commit.
These certainly deserve to stand
With trophies of authority in each hand.
Upon thy pulpit see the drunken priest,
Who turns the gospel to a daily jest ;
Let the fraternity degrade him there,
Lest they like him appear.
There let him his *Memento Mori* preach,
And by example, not by doctrine, teach.

Next, bring the lewder clergy there,
Who preach those sins down which they can't forbear;
Those sons of God, who every day go in
Both to the daughters and the wives of men;
There let them stand, to be the nation's jest,
And save the reputation of the rest.

Asgill,[1] who for the Gospel left the law,
And deep within the cleft of darkness saw,
   Let him be an example made,
Who durst the parson's province so invade;
   To his new ecclesiastic rules
We owe the knowledge that we all are fools.
Old Charon shall no more dark souls convey,
   Asgill has found the shortest way.
   Vain is your funeral pomp and bells,
   Your gravestones, monuments, and knells;
   Vain are the trophies of the grave,
   Asgill shall all that foppery save,
   And, to the clergy's great reproach,
Shall change the hearse into a fiery coach.
What man the learned riddle can receive
Which none can answer and yet none believe,
Let him recorded on the list remain,
Till he shall Heaven by his own rules obtain.
   If a poor author has embraced thy wood
   Only because he has not understood,
   They punish mankind but by halves
     Till they stand there

---

[1] John Asgill was an eminent lawyer of Lincoln's Inn, who had entered Parliament, and had earned by two pamphlets much credit for wit, when he lost his credit by another pamphlet, published in 1700, arguing that as true believers recovered in Christ all they had lost in Adam, they were exempt from the penalty of death, so that, as Defoe expresses it, going to heaven like Elijah in the flesh, they would "change the hearse into a fiery coach." Asgill had made a fortune in his profession, but this theory of his caused him to be twice expelled from Parliament, and when he died at the age of eighty he had been thirty years a prisoner for debt.

Who against their own principles appear,
And cannot understand themselves.
Those Nimshites, who with furious zeal drive on,
And build up Rome to pull down Babylon,
The real authors of the shortest way,
Who for destruction, not conversion, pray,
    There let those sons of strife remain
    Till this Church riddle they explain ;
How at Dissenters they can raise a storm,
    But would not have them all conform,
For there their certain ruin would come in,
And moderation, which they hate, begin.


Next, bring some lawyers to thy bar,
By innuendo they might all stand there ;
    There let them expiate that guilt,
And pay for all that blood their tongues have spilt.
    These are the mountebanks of state,
Who by the sleight of tongues can crimes create,
And dress up trifles in the robes of fate,
    The mastiffs of a Government,
To worry and run down the innocent.
    There sat a man of mighty fame,
Whose actions speak him plainer than his name ;
In vain he struggled, he harangued in vain,
To bring in whipping sentences again ;
And to debauch a milder Government
With abdicated kinds of punishment.
    No wonder he should law despise
    Who Jesus Christ himself denies ;
    His actions only now direct
    That we when he is made a judge expect.


Let L——ll next, to his disgrace,
With Whitney's horses staring in his face ;

There let his cup of penance be kept full
Till he's less noisy, insolent, and dull.

When all these heroes have passed once thy stage,
And thou hast been the satire of the age,
Wait then a while for all those sons of fame
Whom present power has made too great a name;
Fenced from thy hands, they keep our verse in awe,
Too great for satire and too great for law.
    As they their commands lay down,
They all shall pay their homage to thy cloudy throne;
    And till within thy reach they be,
    Exalt thou them in effigy.

    The martyr of the by-past reign
For whom new oaths have been prepared in vain,[1]
Sherlock's disciple, first by him trepanned,
He for a Knave and they for Fools should stand.
Though some affirm he ought to be excused,
    Since to this day he had refused;
And this was all the frailty of his life,
He damned his conscience to oblige his wife.
But spare that priest whose tottering conscience knew
That if he took but one, he'd perjure two;
Bluntly resolved he would not break them both,
And swore by God he'd never take the oath.
    Hang him, he can't be fit for thee,
    For his unusual honesty.

Thou speaking-trumpet of men s fame,
    Enter in every court thy claim.
Demand them all, for they are all thy own,
Who swear to three kings but are true to none.

---

[1] Sherlock at the beginning of King William's reign incurred suspension as a Nonjuror, but left the Jacobites on finding a passage in a book written eighty years before by Bishop Overall that satisfied his scruples. Sherlock then took the oaths and was made Dean of St. Paul's.

Turncoats of all sides are thy due,
And he who once is false is never true;
To-day can swear, to-morrow can abjure,
For treachery's a crime no man can cure;
Such without scruple for the time to come
May swear to all the kings in Christendom;
    But he's a madman will rely
    Upon their lost fidelity.

    They that in vast employment rob the state,
See them in thy embraces meet their fate.
Let not the millions they by fraud obtain
Protect them from the scandal or the pain.
    They who from mean beginnings grow
    To vast estates, but God knows how;
Who carry untold sums away
From little places, with but little pay;
    Who costly palaces erect,
    The thieves that build them to protect;
The gardens, grottos, fountains, walks, and groves,
Where vice triumphs in pride and lawless loves;
Where mighty luxury and drunkenness reigned,
Profusely spend what they profanely gained.
Tell them there's Mene Tekel on the wall,
Tell them the nation's money paid for all.
    Advance by double front and show,
And let us both the crimes and persons know.
Place them aloft upon thy throne
Who slight the nation's business for their own;
Neglect their posts in spite of double pay,
And run us all in debt the shortest way.

Great pageant, change thy dirty scene,
For on thy steps some ladies may be seen.
When beauty stoops upon thy stage to show,
She laughs at all the humble fools below.

Set Sappho there, whose husband paid for clothes
Two hundred pound a week in furbelows.
There in her silks and scarlets let her shine;
She's beauteous all without, all whore within.
　　Next let gay Urania ride,
Her coach-and-six attending by her side:
　　Long has she waited, but in vain,
　　The City homage to obtain;
The sumptuous harlot longed to insult the chair,
And triumph o'er our City beauties there.
Here let her haughty thoughts be gratified,
　　In triumph let her ride.
　　Let Diadora next appear,
And all that want to know her see her there.


What need of satire to reform the town,
　　Or laws to keep our vices down?
　　Let them to thee due homage pay,
This will reform us all the shortest way.
Let them to thee bring all the knaves and fools,
　　Virtue will guide the rest by rules;
They'll need no treacherous friends, no breach of faith,
No hired evidence with their infecting breath;
　　No servants masters to betray,
　　Or knights o' th' post who swear for pay;
No injured author 'll on thy steps appear,
Nor such as would be rogues, but such as are.
　　The first intent of laws
Was to correct the effect and check the cause,
　　And all the ends of punishment
Were only future mischiefs to prevent.


But justice is inverted when
　　Those engines of the law,
Instead of pinching vicious men,
　　Keep honest ones in awe;

Thy business is, as all men know,
To punish villains, not to make men so.
 Whenever then thou art prepared
To prompt that vice thou should'st reward,
And by the terrors of thy grisly face
 Make men turn rogues to shun disgrace;
The end of thy creation is destroyed,
Justice expires of course, and law's made void.


What are thy terrors, that for fear of thee
 Mankind should dare to sink their honesty?
He's bold to impudence that dare turn knave,
 The scandal of thy company to save:
He that will crimes he never knew confess,
Does more than if he knew those crimes transgress;
 And he that fears thee more than to be base,
 May want a heart, but does not want a face.


Thou like the devil dost appear
Blacker than really thou art by far:
 A wild chimeric notion of reproach,
Too little for a crime, for none too much:
 Let none the indignity resent,
For crime is all the shame of punishment.
Thou bugbear of the law, stand up and speak,
 Thy long misconstrued silence break,
Tell us who 'tis upon thy ridge stands there,
 So full of fault and yet so void of fear;
 And from the paper in his hat,
 Let all mankind be told for what.


Tell them it was because he was too bold,
And told those truths which should not have been told;
 Extol the justice of the land,
Who punish what they will not understand.

Tell them he stands exalted there
For speaking what we would not hear;
 And yet he might have been secure
Had he said less or would he have said more.
 Tell them that this is his reward,
 And worse is yet for him prepared,
Because his foolish virtue was so nice
As not to sell his friends, according to his friends' advice.

And thus he's an example made,
To make men of their honesty afraid,
  That for the time to come they may
  More willingly their friends betray;
Tell them the men that placed him here
Are friends unto the times;
  But at a loss to find his guilt,
  They can't commit his crimes.

# THE EARLIER LIFE

OF

# DANIEL DEFOE.

———

## CHAPTER V.

### (1703–1706.)

A HOSTILE Government could not break Daniel Defoe's spirit, but it broke his fortunes. Mr. George A. Aitken, who is on the point of publishing the first full record of the life of Richard Steele, has given[1] the substance of Defoe's reply to the pleadings of a Paul Whitehurst, who had been in his employment at the brickworks, and had been sued by another person in the same employment on account of drink supplied to the labourers, for which Defoe pleaded his own sole ·liability. The statement made by Defoe in this Chancery suit was signed within a week before the day when he was sentenced to the pillory. He said afterwards, in his *Review* for the 24th of March 1705, that "violence, injury, and barbarous treatment had destroyed him and his undertakings." The Pantile Works were broken up, with a loss to him of three or four thousand pounds, and he now had to depend upon his pen for the support of his wife and six children.

Defoe continued his argument upon Occasional Conformity by replying to a defence of it written by the Rev. James Owen, a dissenting minister at Shrewsbury. Defoe's answer, published

[1] In the *Athenæum* for April 13th, 1889.

R

on the 18th of September 1703, was entitled "The Sincerity of
the Dissenters vindicated from the Scandal of Occasional Conformity." Another pamphlet followed in November; it was another
plea for the full toleration of Dissenters by the Church, and of
the Church Establishment by the Dissenters. He called it "A
Challenge of Peace, addressed to the whole Nation. With an
Enquiry into Ways and Means for bringing it to pass." He had
published earlier in the same month of November, upon a peculiar
view of the survival of the fittest to which he had made allusion
in his "Hymn to the Pillory," "An Enquiry into the Case of Mr.
Asgill's General Translation; showing that 'tis not a nearer way to
Heaven than the Grave."

On the night of Friday the 26th of November 1703, there rose
to its height one of the fiercest storms of which there is a record
in our history. It had begun on the preceding Wednesday, and
it lasted until the following Wednesday, Tuesday's storm being
almost as disastrous as that of Friday. It swept away Eddy-
stone Lighthouse. It wrecked, on the Friday night, twelve of
the Queen's ships. It blew down seven steeples and eight
hundred houses, unrolled the lead and swept away the roofs of
a hundred churches, uprooted in the New Forest alone above
four thousand trees, and, by sea and land, destroyed the lives
of eight thousand people. The loss by rise of the tide in the
Severn alone was estimated at £200,000; in a single level
fifteen thousand sheep were drowned. The records of this
memorable storm Defoe collected into a volume called "The
Storm; or a Collection of the most remarkable Casualties and
Disasters which happened in the Late Dreadful Tempest, both
by Sea and Land."

This volume was published in July 1704, and had for the
motto on its title page, "The Lord hath His way in the Whirlwind and in the Storm, and the Clouds are the Dust of His
Feet," Nahum i. 3. In the preface Defoe argued that God had
spoken in the whirlwind, and held the same opinion that caused
William Langland, in the fourteenth century, in his "Vision of
Piers the Plowman," to connect God's anger against sin with a

"south-west wind on Saturday at even," as well as with the pestilence by which the land was scourged. We do not know, argued Defoe, whence the wind comes or whither it goes; but the storm and the whirlwind have "more of God in their whole appearance than in any other part of operating Nature." Addison, when in his poem of "The Campaign" he celebrated the battle of Blenheim fought in August 1704, while the Great Storm of the preceding November was fresh in every mind, compared Marlborough to the angel of the storm in lines that showed Addison, like Defoe, associating the loud blast of the whirlwind with God's warning against sin :—

> " So when an angel by divine command,
> With rising tempests shakes a guilty land,
> Such as of late o'er pale Britannia past,
> Calm and serene he drives the furious blast ;
> And, pleased the Almighty's orders to perform,
> Rides in the whirlwind and directs the storm."

In the spring of 1704 the Earl of Nottingham, who had pressed hardly on Defoe, was replaced in the Ministry by Robert Harley as Secretary of State. Harley, who understood the worth of a good pen, and showed many kindnesses to writers, sent money from the Treasury to Defoe's wife and family, and to Defoe himself for payment of his fine. In August 1704 Defoe was released from his imprisonment.

But six months before his release there had appeared, on the 17th of February 1704, the first number of Defoe's *Review*, which may be said to have laid the foundation of independent journalism. It was first entitled "A Review of the Affairs of France and of all Europe as influenced by that Nation," and was issued in weekly penny sheets; after the fourth number the paper was reduced to half a sheet, with smaller type and double columns, and the price was raised to twopence. Then, after the eighth number, the *Review* was issued twice a week, on Tuesdays and Saturdays. Five monthly supplements in 1704 contained " Advices from the Scandal Club," which added to the political news and the comment upon it a place for kindly criticism of the faults and follies of the day in aid of the much-needed reformation of society. Out of this supplement to the *Review* came probably to Richard Steele the first suggestion of his *Tatler*, and out of the *Tatler* came the *Spectator*, and out of the *Spectator* came a tribe of essayists who sought to mend the manners of their time. After the eighth number of its second volume, the *Review* appeared three times a week, on Tuesdays, Thursdays, and Saturdays; "and so continued"—wrote John Forster—"without intermission, and written solely by Defoe, for nine years. He wrote it in prison and out of prison; in sickness and in health. It did not cease when circumstances called him from England. No official employment determined it; no politic consideration availed to discontinue it; no personal hostility or party censure weighed with him in the balance against it. 'As to censure,' he exclaimed, 'the writer expects it. He writes to serve the world, not to please it. A few wise, calm, disinterested men, he always had the good help to please and satisfy. By their judgment he desires still to be determined; and if he has any pride, it is that he may be approved by such. To the rest he sedately says their censure deserves no notice.'"

In an "Appeal to Honour and Justice," written after Queen Anne was dead, and when Harley was in the Tower, Defoe wrote thus of his release from prison:—"When Her Majesty came to have the truth of the case laid before her I soon felt the effects of her royal goodness and compassion. And first Her Majesty declared that she had left all that matter to a certain person" [the Earl of Nottingham], "and did not think he would have used me in such a manner. Perhaps these words may seem imaginary to some, and the speaking them to be of no value, and so they would have been if they had not been followed with farther and more convincing proofs of what they imported, which were these, that Her Majesty was pleased particularly to enquire into my circumstances and family, and by my Lord Treasurer Godolphin to send a considerable supply to my wife and family, and to send me to the prison money to pay my fine and the expenses of my discharge. Whether this be a just foundation let my enemies judge. Here is the foundation on which I built my first sense of duty to Her Majesty's person, and the indelible bond of gratitude to my first benefactor" [Harley, whose manner of first approach to him was told in another part of the 'Appeal']. "Gratitude and fidelity are inseparable from an honest man. But to be thus obliged by a stranger, by a man of quality and honour, and after that by the Sovereign under whose administration I was suffering, let any one put himself in my stead, and examine under what principles I could ever act either against such a queen or such a benefactor; and what must my own heart reproach me with; what blushes must have covered my face when I had looked in, and called myself ungrateful to him that saved me thus from distress, or her that fetched me out of the dungeon and gave my family relief?"

Defoe, after his release from prison with broken health, withdrew for a time to Bury St. Edmunds. It was rest to him to use his pen in peace and freedom. He wrote two *Reviews* a week, and produced four pamphlets within a month, following in his own way—aloof from all the crowds of partisans—the chief discussions of the day, and earning his bread with his pen by unremitting service to his country.

Defoe returned to London in October, but was ill till January. During this time a reader of his *Review* sent money for him to distribute to the poor, and in the *Review* for February 20th 1705 he set forth in detail the manner of the distribution. There appeared also, early in 1705, a new edition of the "Collected Writings" of the author of "The True-Born Englishman," with a second volume containing eighteen pieces more.

But the year 1705 was marked by the publication of another book—not pamphlet—" The Consolidator; or, Memoirs of Sundry Transactions from the World in the Moon," which is the next work reprinted in the present volume. Mr. William Lee, whose three volumes on " Daniel Defoe: his Life, and Recently Discovered Writings" (published in 1869) are valued highly by all students of our later literature, speaks thus of " The Consolidator" :—" The book is a prose satire on national and European politics, on the follies of the times ; and also includes criticisms and animadversions upon the poets, men of literature, metaphysicians, and freethinkers of the age.   The work is valuable for its reference to the personal circumstances of the author ; and though wanting the elements of a popular book, in consequence of the enigmatic travestie of proper names into the assumed Lunar language, it abounds with passages of well-pointed satire, such as no other living man—Swift alone excepted—could have approached; and displays an exuberance of imagination, and adaptive fancy, not surpassed in any other of Defoe's productions."   Here the book is, with a few notes to unriddle its not very difficult enigmas.

It is Defoe himself, not a book ; Defoe using the far sight and the clear sight which he makes peculiar to the people in the moon.   He is looking straight into the burning questions of his day.   He is parting wheat from chaff with his own winnowing fan.   Defoe's "Consolidator" appeared in the year after the publication of Swift's "Tale of a Tub," and was also chiefly designed as a protest against irreligious feuds about religion.   It is interesting as a witty study of the English Revolution from the point of view of one who lived through it, and was among its most clear-sighted supporters.   It is a study, also, of Daniel Defoe himself in the year 1705.   His age then was about forty-four, his worldly fortune had just been ruined for the second time, but the close of his earlier life left him in the front still of battle, with unbroken resolution.

# THE

## *CONSOLIDATOR*

O R,

# MEMOIRS

O F

## Sundry Tranſactions

FROM THE

## *World in the Moon.*

## Tranſlated from the Lunar
## LANGUAGE,

By the AUTHOR of
*The True-born Engliſh Man.*

---

*LONDON:*

Printed, and are to be Sold by *Benj. Bragg*
at the *Blue Ball* in *Ave-mary-lane,* 1705.

# THE CONSOLIDATOR, &c.

———⊁———

IT cannot be unknown to any that have travelled into the dominions of the Czar of Muscovy,[1] that this famous rising monarch, having studied all methods for the increase of his power and the enriching as well as polishing his subjects, has travelled through most part of Europe, and visited the Courts of the greatest princes, from whence, by his own observation, as well as by carrying with him artists in most useful knowledge, he has transmitted most of our general practice, especially in war and trade, to his own unpolite people ; and the effects of this curiosity of his are exceeding visible in his present proceedings ; for by the improvements he obtained in his European travels he has modelled his armies, formed new fleets, settled foreign negoce in several remote parts of the world ; and we now see his forces besieging strong towns with regular approaches, and his engineers raising batteries, throwing bombs, &c., like other nations, whereas before they had nothing of order among them, but carried all by onslaught and scalado, wherein they either prevailed by the force of irresistible multitude or were slaughtered by heaps, and left the ditches of their enemies filled with their dead bodies.

We see their armies now formed into regular battalions, and their Strelitz Musqueteers, a people equivalent to the Turk's Janizaries, clothed like our Guards, firing in platoons, and behaving themselves with extraordinary bravery and order.

We see their ships now completely fitted, built, and furnished by the English and Dutch artists, and their men-of-war cruise in

[1] Peter the Great became Czar in 1689, and founded St. Petersburgh in 1703.

the Baltic. Their new city of Petersburgh, built by the present Czar, begins now to look like our Portsmouth, fitted with wet and dry docks, storehouses, and magazines of naval preparations, vast and incredible, which may serve to remind us how we once taught the French to build ships, till they are grown able to teach us how to use them.

As to trade, our large fleets to Archangel may speak for it, where we now send a hundred sail yearly, instead of eight or nine, which were the greatest number we ever sent before; and the importation of tobaccos from England into his dominions would still increase the trade thither, were not the covetousness of our own merchants the obstruction of their advantages. But all this by the bye.

As this great monarch has improved his country by introducing the manners and customs of the politer nations of Europe, so, with indefatigable industry, he has settled a new but constant trade between his country and China by land, where his caravans go twice or thrice a year, as numerous almost and as strong as those from Egypt to Persia. Nor is the way shorter, or the deserts they pass over less wild and uninhabitable, only that they are not so subject to floods of sand, if that term be proper, or to troops of Arabs to destroy them by the way; for this powerful prince, to make this terrible journey feasible to his subjects, has built forts, planted colonies and garrisons at proper distances, where, though they are seated in countries entirely barren, and among uninhabited rocks and sands, yet, by his continual furnishing them from his own stores, the merchants travelling are relieved on good terms, and meet both with convoy and refreshment.

More might be said of the admirable decorations of this journey, and how so prodigious an attempt is made easy, so that now they have an exact correspondence, and drive a prodigious trade between Moscow and Tonquin; but, having a longer voyage in hand, I shall not detain the reader, nor keep him till he grows too big with expectation.

Now, as all men know, the Chinese are an ancient, wise, polite, and most ingenious people, so the Muscovites began to reap the benefit of this open trade, and not only to grow exceeding rich by the bartering for all the wealth of those Eastern countries, but to polish and refine their customs and manners as much on that side as they have from their European improvements on this.

And as the Chinese have many sorts of learning, which these parts of the world never heard of, so all those useful inventions which we admire ourselves so much for are vulgar and common with them, and were in use long before our parts of the world were inhabited. Thus gunpowder, printing, and the use of the magnet and compass, which we call modern inventions, are not only far from being inventions, but fall so far short of the perfection of art they have attained to, that it is hardly credible what wonderful things we are told of from thence; and all the voyages the author has made thither being employed another way, have not yet furnished him with the particulars fully enough to transmit them to view; not but that he is preparing a scheme of all those excellent arts those nations are masters of, for public view, by way of detection of the monstrous ignorance and deficiencies of European science; which may serve as a *lexicon technicum* for this present age, with useful diagrams for that purpose; wherein I shall not fail to acquaint the world with the art of gunnery, as practised in China long before the war of the Giants, and by which those presumptuous animals fired red-hot bullets right up into heaven, and made a breach sufficient to encourage them to a general storm; but, being repulsed with great slaughter, they gave over the siege for that time. This memorable part of history shall be a faithful abridgment of Ibra chizra-le-peglizar, historiographer-royal to the Emperor of China, who wrote *Anno Mundi* 114. His volume is extant in the public library at Tonquin, printed in leaves of vitrified diamond, by an admirable dexterity, struck all at an oblique motion, the engine remaining entire, and still fit for use in the chamber of the Emperor's rarities.

And here I shall give you a draft of the engine itself, and a plan of its operation, and the wonderful dexterity of its performance.

If these labours of mine shall prove successful, I may in my next journey that way take an abstract of their most admirable tracts in navigation and the mysteries of Chinese mathematics, which outdo all modern invention at that rate that it is inconceivable. In this elaborate work I must run through the 365 volumes of Augro-machi-lanquaro-zi, the most ancient mathematician in all China. From thence I shall give a description of a fleet of ships of 100,000 sail, built at the expense of the Emperor Tangro the XV., who having notice of the general deluge, prepared these vessels, to every city and town in his dominions one, and in bulk proportioned to the number of its inhabitants; into which vessels all the people, with such movables as they thought fit to save, and with 120 days' provisions, were received at the time of the Flood; and the rest of their goods being put into great vessels made of chinaware, and fast luted down on the top, were preserved unhurt by the water. These ships they furnished with 600 fathom of chain, instead of cables; which being fastened by wonderful arts to the earth, every vessel rid out the deluge just at the town's end; so that when the waters abated, the people had nothing to do but to open the doors made in the ship's sides and come out, repair their houses, open the great china pots their goods were in, and so put themselves in *statu quo.*

The draft of one of these ships I may perhaps obtain by my interest in the present Emperor's court, as it has been preserved ever since, and constantly repaired, riding at anchor in a great lake about a hundred miles from Tonquin, in which all the people of that city were preserved, amounting, by their computation, to about a million and a half.

And as these things must be very useful in these parts to abate the pride and arrogance of our modern undertakers of great enterprises, authors of strange foreign accounts, philosophical transactions, and the like; if time and opportunity permit, I may let them know how infinitely we are outdone by those refined nations in all manner of mechanic improvements and arts; and in discoursing of this it will necessarily come in my way to speak of a most noble invention, being an engine I would recommend to all people to whom it is necessary to have a good memory, and which I design, if possible, to obtain a draft of, that it may be erected in our Royal Society's laboratory. It has the wonderfullest operations in the world. One part of it furnishes a man of business to dispatch his affairs strangely; for if he be a merchant, he shall write his letters with one hand, and copy them with the other; if he is posting his books, he shall post the debtor side with one hand, and the creditor with the other; if he be a lawyer, he draws his drafts with one hand, and engrosses them with the other.

Another part of it furnishes him with such an expeditious way of writing or transcribing, that a man cannot speak so fast but he that hears shall have it down in writing before it is spoken; and a preacher shall deliver himself to his auditory, and having this engine before him, shall put down everything he says in writing at the same time; and so exactly is this engine squared by lines and rules, that it does not require him that writes to keep his eye upon it.

I am told, in some parts in China they had arrived to such a perfection of knowledge as to understand one another's thoughts, and that it was found to be an excellent preservative to human society against all sorts of frauds, cheats, sharping, and many thousand European inventions of that nature, at which only can we be said to outdo those nations.

I confess I have not yet had leisure to travel those parts, having been diverted by an accidental opportunity of a new voyage I had occasion to make for further discoveries, and the pleasure and usefulness thereof having been very great, I have omitted the other for the present, but shall not fail to make a visit to those parts the first opportunity, and shall give my countrymen the best account I can of those things; for I doubt not in time to bring our nation, so famed for improving other people's discoveries, to be as wise as any of those heathen nations. I wish I had the same prospect of making them half so honest.

I had spent but a few months in this country, but my search after the prodigy of human knowledge the people abounds with led me into acquaintance with some of their principal artists, engineers, and men of letters; and I was astonished at every day's discovery of new and unheard-of worlds of learning; but I improved in the superficial knowledge of their general by nobody so much as by my conversation with the library-keeper of Tonquin, by whom I had admission into the vast collection of books which the emperors of that country have treasured up.

It would be endless to give you a catalogue, and they admit of no strangers to write anything down, but what the memory can retain you are welcome to carry away with you; and amongst the wonderful volumes of ancient and modern learning I could not but take notice of a few, which, besides those I mentioned before, I saw when I looked over this vast collection; and a larger account may be given in our next.

It would be needless to transcribe the Chinese character, or to put their alphabet into our letters, because the words would be both unintelligible and very hard to pronounce; and therefore, to avoid hard words and hieroglyphics, I will translate them as well as I can.

The first class I came to of books was the constitutions of the empire; these are vast great volumes, and have a sort of engine like our Magna Charta to remove them, and with placing them in a frame, by turning a screw opened the leaves, and folded them this way or that, as the reader desires. It was present death for the library-keeper to refuse the meanest Chinese subject to come in and read them, for it is their maxim that all people ought to know the laws by which they are to be governed; and as above all people we find no fools in this country, so the emperors, though they seem to be arbitrary, enjoy the greatest authority in the world, by always observing, with the greatest exactness, the *pacta conventa* of their government. From these principles it is impossible we should ever hear either of the tyranny of princes or rebellion of subjects in all their histories.

At the entrance into this class you find some ancient comments upon the constitution of the empire, written many ages before we pretend the world began; but above all, one I took particular notice of, which might bear this title, "Natural Right proved Superior to Temporal Power," wherein the old author proves the Chinese emperors were originally made so, by Nature's directing the people to place the power of government in the most worthy person they could find ; and the author, giving a most exact history of two thousand emperors, brings them into about thirty-five or thirty-six periods of lines, when the race ended, and when a collective assembly of the nobles, cities, and people nominated a new family to the government.

This being an heretical book as to European politics, and our learned authors having long since exploded this doctrine, and proved that kings and emperors came down from Heaven with crowns on their heads, and all their subjects were born with saddles on their backs, I thought fit to leave it where I found it, lest our excellent tracts of Sir Robert Filmer, Dr. Hammond, Leslie, Sacheverel, and others, who have so learnedly treated of the more useful doctrine of passive obedience, divine right, &c., should be blasphemed by the mob, grow into contempt of the people, and they should take upon them to question their superiors for the blood of Algernon Sidney and Argyle.

For I take the doctrine of passive obedience, &c., among the statesmen to be like the Copernican system of the earth's motion among philosophers, which, though it be contrary to all ancient knowledge, and not capable of demonstration, yet is adhered to in general, because by this they can better solve and give a more rational account of several dark phenomena in Nature than they could before.

Thus our modern statesmen approve of this scheme of government, not that it admits of any rational defence, much less of demonstration, but because by this method they can the better explain, as well as defend, all coercion in cases invasive of natural right than they could do before.

Here I found two famous volumes in chirurgery, being an exact description of the circulation of the blood, discovered long before King Solomon's allegory of the bucket going to the well ; with several curious methods by which the demonstration was

to be made so plain, as would make even the worthy Doctor
B——— himself become a convert to his own eyesight, make him
damn his own elaborate book, and think it worse nonsense than
ever the town had the freedom to imagine.

All our philosophers are fools, and their transactions a parcel
of empty stuff, to the experiments of the Royal Societies in this
country. Here I came to a learned tract of winds, which outdoes even the sacred text, and would make us believe it was not
wrote to those people, for they tell folk whence it comes and
whither it goes. There you have an account how to make '
glasses of hogs' eyes that see the wind, and they give strange
account both of its regular and irregular motions, its composition
and quantities, from whence, by a sort of algebra, they can cast
up its duration, violence, and extent. In these calculations, some
say, those authors have been so exact that they can, as our philosophers say of comets, state their revolutions, and tell us how
many storms there shall happen to any period of time, and when;
and perhaps this may be with much about the same truth.

It was a certain sign Aristotle had never been at China; for
had he seen the 216th volume of the Chinese navigation in the
library I am speaking of, a large book in double folio, wrote by
the famous Mira-cho-cho-lasmo, Vice-Admiral of China, and said
to be printed there about two thousand years before the Deluge,
in the chapter of tides he would have seen the reason of all the
certain and uncertain fluxes and refluxes of that element, how the
exact place is kept between the moon and the tides, with a most
elaborate discourse there of the power of sympathy, and the
manner how the heavenly bodies influence the earthly. Had
he seen this, the Stagyrite would never have drowned himself
because he could not comprehend this mystery.

It is further related of this famous author, that he was no
native of this world, but was born in the moon, and coming
hither to make discoveries, by a strange invention arrived at by
virtuosos of that habitable world, the Emperor of China prevailed upon him to stay and improve his subjects in the most
exquisite accomplishments of those lunar regions; and no won-

der the Chinese are such exquisite artists, and masters of such
sublime knowledge, when this famous author has blest them with
such unaccountable methods of improvement.

There was abundance of vast classes full of the works of this
wonderful philosopher. He gave the how, the modus, of all the
secret operations of nature, and told us how sensation is conveyed to and from the brain, why respiration preserves life, and
how locomotion is directed to, as well as performed by the parts.
There are some anatomical dissections of thought; and a mathematical description of Nature's strong box, the memory, with all
its locks and keys.

There you have that part of the head turned inside outward in
which Nature has placed the materials of reflecting, and, like a
glass beehive, represents to you all the several cells in which are
lodged things past, even back to infancy and conception. There
you have the Repository, with all its cells, classically, annually,
numerically, and alphabetically disposed. There you may see
how, when the perplexed animal, on the loss of a thought or
word, scratches his poll, every attack of his invading fingers
knocks at Nature's door, alarms all the register keepers, and
away they run, unlock all the classes, search diligently for what
he calls for, and immediately deliver it up to the brain; if it
cannot be found, they entreat a little patience till they step into
the Revolvary, where they run over little catalogues of the minutest
passages of life, and so in time never fail to hand on the thing,
if not just when he calls for it, yet at some other time.

And thus when a thing lies very abstruse, and all the rummag-
ing of the whole house cannot find it—nay, when all the people
in the house have given it over, they very often find one thing
when they are looking for another.

Next you have the Retentive in the remotest part of the place,
which, like the records in the Tower, takes possession of all
matters, as they are removed from the classes in the Repository
for want of room. These are carefully locked and kept safe,
never to be opened but on solemn occasions, and have swingeing
great bars and bolts upon them, so that what is kept here is seldom

S

lost. Here Conscience has one large warehouse and the Devil
another. The first is very seldom opened, but has a chink or
till, where all the follies and crimes of life being minuted, are
dropped in ; but as the man seldom cares to look in, the locks
are very rusty, and not opened but with great difficulty and on
extraordinary occasions, as sickness, afflictions, gaols, casualties,
and death, and then the bars all give way at once ; and being
pressed from within with a more than ordinary weight, burst as a
cask of wine upon the fret, which, for want of vent, makes all the
hoops fly. As for the Devil's warehouse, he has two constant
warehouse keepers, Pride and Conceit, and these are always at
the door, showing their wares and exposing the pretended virtues
and accomplishments of the man by way of ostentation.

In the middle of this curious part of Nature there is a clear
thoroughfare representing the world, through which so many thousand people pass so easily, and do so little worth taking notice
of, that it is for no manner of signification to leave word they have
been here. Through this opening pass millions of things not
worth remembering, and which the register keepers, who stand at
the doors of the classes as they go by, take no notice of, such as
friendships, helps in distress, kindnesses in affliction, voluntary
services, and all sorts of importunate merit ; things which, being
but trifles in their own nature, are made to be forgotten.

In another angle is to be seen the Memory's Garden, in which
her most pleasant things are not only deposited, but planted,
transplanted, grafted, innoculated, and obtain all possible propagation and increase ; these are the most pleasant, delightful,
and agreeable things, called envy, slander, revenge, strife, and
malice, with the additions of ill-turns, reproaches, and all manner
of wrong ; these are caressed in the cabinet of the memory, which
a world of pleasure never let pass, and carefully cultivated with
all imaginable art.

There are multitudes of weeds, toys, chat, story, fiction, and
lying, which in the great throng of passing affairs stop by the
way, and crowding up the place, leave no place for their betters

that come behind, which makes many a good guest be put by, and left to go clear through for want of entertainment.

There are a multitude of things very curious and observable concerning this little but very accurate thing called Memory; but above all, I see nothing so very curious as the wonderful art of wilful forgetfulness; and as it is a thing, indeed, I never could find any person completely master of, it pleased me very much to find this author has made a large essay to prove there is really no such power in Nature, and that the pretenders to it are all impostors, and put a banter upon the world, for that it is impossible for any man to oblige himself to forget a thing, since he that can remember to forget, and at the same time forget to remember, has an art above the Devil.

In his laboratory you see a fancy preserved *à la* mummy, several thousand years old, by examining which you may perfectly discern how Nature makes a poet; another you have taken from a mere natural, which discovers the reasons of Nature's negative in the case of human understanding, what deprivation of parts she suffers in the composition of a coxcomb, and with what wonderful art she prepares a man to be a fool.

Here, being the product of this author's wonderful skill, you have the skeleton of a wit, with all the readings of philosophy and chirurgery upon the parts; here you see all the lines Nature has drawn to form a genius, how it performs, and from what principles.

Also you are instructed to know the true reason of the affinity between poetry and poverty, and that it is equally derived from what is natural and intrinsic, as from accident and circumstance; how the world being always full of fools and knaves, wit is sure to miss a good market, especially if wit and truth happen to come in company, for the fools don't understand it, and the knaves cannot bear it.

But still it is owned, and is most apparent, there is something also natural in the case too, since there are some particular vessels Nature thinks necessary to the more exact composition of this nice thing called a wit, which as they are or are not interrupted in the peculiar offices for which they are appointed, are subject to various distempers, and more particularly to effluxions and vapours, deliriums, giddiness of the brain, and lapsæ or looseness of the tongue; and as these distempers, occasioned by the exceeding quantity of volatiles Nature is obliged to make use of in the composition, are hardly to be avoided, the disasters which generally they push the animal into are as necessarily consequent to them as night is to the setting of the sun; and these are very many, as disobliging parents, who have frequently in this country whipped their sons for making verses. And here I could not but reflect how useful a discipline early correction must be to a poet, and how easy the town had been had N——t, E——w, T. Brown, Philips, D—— S—— Durfy,[1] and a hundred more of the jingling train of our modern rhymers, been whipped young, very young, for poetasting; they had never perhaps sucked in that venom of ribaldry which all the satire of the age has never been able to scourge out of them to this day.

The further fatal consequences of these unhappy defects in Nature, where she has damned a man to wit and rhyme, has been loss of inheritance, parents being aggravated by the obstinate young beaus resolving to be wits in spite of Nature, the wiser head has been obliged to confederate with Nature, and withhold the birthright of brains, which otherwise the young gentleman might have enjoyed, to the great support of his family and posterity. Thus the famous Waller, Denham, Dryden, and sundry others were obliged to condemn their race to lunacy and blockheadism, only to prevent the fatal destruction of their families, and entailing the plague of wits and weathercocks upon their posterity.

The yet further extravagances which naturally attend the mischief of wit are beauism, dogmaticality, whimsification, impudensity, and various kinds of fopperosities (according to Mr. Boyle), which, issuing out of the brain, descend into all the faculties, and branch themselves by infinite variety into all the actions of life.

---

[1] Here I have only ventured to fill in the blanks of T. B——, P——s, and D——fy, as not doubtful.

These by consequence beggar the head, the tail, the purse, and the whole man, till he becomes as poor and despicable as negative Nature can leave him, abandoned of his sense, his manners, his modesty, and what is worse, his money, having nothing left but his poetry, dies in a ditch or a garret, *à la mode* of Tom Brown, uttering rhymes and nonsense to the last moment.

In pity to all my unhappy brethren who suffer under these inconveniences, I cannot but leave it on record that they may not be reproached with being agents of their own misfortunes, since I assure them Nature has formed them with the very necessity of acting like coxcombs, fixed upon them by the force of organic consequences, and placed down at the very original effusion of that fatal thing called wit.

Nor is the discovery less wonderful than edifying, and no human art on our side the world ever found out such sympathetic influence between the extremes of wit and folly till this great Lunarian naturalist furnished us with such unheard-of demonstrations.

Nor is this all I learnt from him, though I cannot part with this till I have published a *memento mori*, and told them what I had discovered of Nature in these remote parts of the world ; from whence I take the freedom to tell these gentlemen, that if they please to travel to these distant parts, and examine this great master of Nature's secrets, they may every man see what cross strokes Nature has struck to finish and form every extravagant species of that heterogeneous kind we call wit.

There Captain Steele may be informed how he comes to be very witty and a madman all at once ; and Prior may see that with less brains and more pox he is more a wit and more a madman than the Coll. Addison may tell his master my Lord —— the reason from Nature why he would not take the Court's word, nor write the poem called "The Campaign" till he had £200 per annum secured to him, since it is known they have but one author in the nation that writes for them for nothing, and he is labouring very hard to obtain the title of blockhead, and not to be paid for it. Here D. might understand how

he came to be able to banter all mankind, and yet all mankind be able to banter him; at the same time, our numerous
throng of Parnassians may see reasons for the variety of the
negative and positive blessings they enjoy; some for having
wit and no verse, some verse and no wit, some mirth without
jest, some jest without forecast, some rhyme and no jingle,
some all jingle and no rhyme, some language without measure,
some all quantity and no cadence, some all wit and no sense,
some all sense and no flame; some preach in rhyme, some sing
when they preach, some all song and no tune, some all tune and
no song; all these unaccountables have their originals, and can
be answered for in unerring Nature, though in our outside guesses
we can say little to it.   Here is to be seen why some are all
Nature, some all art; some beat verse out of the twenty-four
rough letters with ten hammers and anvils to every line, and
maul the language as a Swede beats stockfish.   Others huff
Nature, and bully her out of whole stanzas of ready-made lines
at a time, carry all before them, and rumble like distant thunder
in a black cloud.   Thus degrees and capacities are fitted by
Nature according to organic efficacy, and the reason and nature
of things are found in themselves.   Had Durfy seen his own
draft by this light of Chinese knowledge, he might have known
he should be a coxcomb without writing twenty-two plays to
stand as so many records against him.   Dryden might have told
his fate, that having his extraordinary genius flung and pitched
upon a swivel, it would certainly turn round as fast as the times,
and instruct him how to write elegies to O. C. and King C.
the Second, with all the coherence imaginable; how to write
  Religio Laici" and the "Hind and Panther," and yet be the
same man; every day to change his principle, change his religion,
change his coat, change his master, and yet never change his
nature.

   There are abundance of other secrets in Nature discovered in
relation to these things, too many to repeat and yet too useful to
omit; as the reason why physicians are generally atheists, and why
atheists are universally fools, and generally live to know it them-

selves; the real obstructions which prevent fools being mad; all
the natural causes of love; abundance of demonstrations of the
synonymous nature of love and lechery, especially considered *à
la moderne ;* with an absolute specific for the frenzy of love found
out in the constitution—anglicè, a halter.

It would be endless to reckon up the numerous improvements
and wonderful discoveries this extraordinary person has brought
down, and which are to be seen in his curious chamber of rarities.
Particularly a map of Parnassus, with an exact delineation of all
the cells, apartments, palaces, and dungeons of that most famous
mountain, with a description of its height, and a learned dissertation proving it to be the properest place next to the P——e House
to take a rise at for a flight to the world in the moon. Also
inquiries whether Noah's ark did not first rest upon it, and this
might be one of the summits of Ararat, with some confutations of
the gross and palpable errors which place this extraordinary skill
among the mountains of the moon in Africa.

Also you have here a Muse calcined, a little of the powder of
which given to a woman big with child, if it be a boy, it will be a
poet; if a girl, she will be light; if an hermaphrodite, it will be
lunatic.

Strange things, they tell us, have been done with this calcined
womb of imagination. If the body it came from was a lyric poet,
the child will be a beau or a beauty; if an heroic poet, he will be
a bully; if his talent was satire, he will be a philosopher.

Another Muse, they tell us, they have dissolved into a liquid
and kept with wondrous art, the virtues of which are sovereign
against idiotism, dulness, and all sorts of lethargic diseases; but
if given in too great a quantity, creates poesy, poverty, lunacy,
and the devil in the head ever after.

I confess I always thought these Muses strange intoxicating
things, and have heard much talk of their original, but never
was acquainted with their virtue *à la simple* before. However, I
would always advise people against too large a dose of wit, and
think the physician must be a madman that will venture to prescribe it.

As all these noble acquirements came down with this wonderful man from the world in the moon, it furnished me with these useful observations :—

1. That country must needs be a place of strange perfection in all parts of extraordinary knowledge.

2. How useful a thing it would be for most sorts of our people, especially statesmen, Parliament-men, Convocation-men, philosophers, physicians, quacks, mountebanks, stockjobbers, and all the mob of the nation's civil or ecclesiastical bone-setters, together with some men of the law, some of the sword, and all of the pen ; I say, how useful and improving a thing it must be to them to take a journey up to the world in the moon ; but above all, how much more beneficial it would be to them that stayed behind.

3. That it is not to be wondered at why the Chinese excel so much all these parts of the world, since but for that knowledge which comes down to them from the world in the moon they would be like other people.

No man need to wonder at my exceeding desire to go up to the world in the moon, having heard of such extraordinary knowledge to be obtained there, since in the search of knowledge and truth wiser men than I have taken as unwarrantable flights, and gone a great deal higher than the moon, into a strange abyss of dark phenomena, which they neither could make other people understand, nor ever rightly understood themselves ; witness Malebranche, Mr. Locke, Hobbes, the Honourable Boyle, and a great many others, besides Messrs. Norris, Asgil, Coward, and the " Tale of a Tub."

This great searcher into nature has, besides all this, left wonderful discoveries and experiments behind him ; but I was with nothing more exceedingly diverted than with his various engines, and curious contrivances to go to and from his own native country, the moon. All our mechanic motions of Bishop Wilkins, or the artificial wings of the learned Spaniard, who could have taught God Almighty how to have mended the creation, are fools to this gentleman ; and because no man in China has made more voyages up into the moon than myself, I cannot but give you some account of the easiness of the passage as well as of the country.

Nor are his wonderful telescopes of a mean quality, by which such plain discoveries are made of the lands and seas in the moon, and in all the habitable planets, that one may as plainly see what o'clock it is by one of the dials in the moon as if it were no farther off than Windsor Castle; and had he lived to finish the speaking-trumpet which he had contrived to convey sound thither, Harlequin's mock-trumpet had been a fool to it; and it had no doubt been an admirable experiment to have given us a general advantage from all their acquired knowledge in those regions, where no doubt several useful discoveries are daily made by the men of thought for the improvement of all sorts of human understanding, and to have discoursed with them on those things must have been very pleasant, besides its being very much to our particular advantage.

I confess I have thought it might have been very useful to this nation to have brought so wonderful an invention hither, and I was once very desirous to have set up my rest here, and, for the benefit of my native country, have made myself master of these engines, that I might in due time have conveyed them to our Royal Society, that once in forty years they might have been said to do something for public good, and that the reputation and usefulness of the so-so's might be recovered in England; but being told that in the moon there were many of these glasses to be had very cheap, and I having declared my resolution of undertaking a voyage thither, I deferred my design, and shall defer my treating of them till I give some account of my arrival there.

But above all his inventions for making this voyage, I saw none more pleasant or profitable than a certain engine formed in the shape of a chariot, on the backs of two vast bodies with extended wings, which spread about fifty yards in breadth, composed of feathers so nicely put together that no air could pass; and as the bodies were made of lunar earth, which would bear the fire, the cavities were filled with an ambient flame, which fed on a certain spirit deposited in a proper quantity to last out the voyage; and this fire so ordered as to move about such springs and wheels as kept the wings in a most exact and regular motion, always ascendant; thus the person being placed in this airy chariot drinks a certain dosing draught, that throws him into a gentle slumber, and dreaming all the way, never wakes till he comes to his journey's end.

### OF THE CONSOLIDATOR.[1]

These engines are called in their country language *Dupekasses,* and according to the ancient Chinese or Tartarian, *Apezolanthukanistes ;* in English, a consolidator.

The composition of this engine is very admirable, for, as is before noted, it is all made up of feathers, and the quality of the feathers is no less wonderful than their composition; and therefore I hope the reader will bear with the description for the sake of the novelty, since I assure him such things as these are not to be seen in every country.

The number of feathers are just 513, they are all of a length and breadth exactly, which is absolutely necessary to the floating figure, or else one side or any one part being wider or longer than the rest, it would interrupt the whole motion of the engine ; only there is one extraordinary feather, which, as there is an odd one in the number, is placed in the centre, and is the handle, or rather rudder, to the whole machine. This feather is every way larger than its fellows ; it is almost as long and broad again ; but above all, its quill or head is much larger, and it has as it were several small bushing feathers round the bottom of it, which all make but one presiding or superintendent feather, to guide, regulate, and pilot the whole body.

Nor are these common feathers, but they are picked and culled out of all parts of the Lunar country by the command of the prince ; and every province sends up the best they can find, or ought to do so at least, or else they are very much to blame; for

---

[1] The Consolidator is the English House of Commons, representing the collective wisdom of the nation ; the feathers are the members, the guide-feather is the Speaker.

the employment they are put to being of so great use to the public, and the voyage or flight so exceeding high, it would be very ill done if, when the King sends his letters about the nation to pick him up the best feathers they can lay their hands on,[1] they should send weak, decayed, or half-grown feathers, and yet sometimes it happens so. And once there was such rotten feathers collected, whether it was a bad year for feathers, or whether the people that gathered them had a mind to abuse their King, but the feathers were so bad, the engine was good for nothing, but broke before it was got half way; and by a double misfortune this happened to be at an unlucky time, when the King himself[2] had resolved on a voyage or flight to the moon, but being deceived by the unhappy miscarriage of the deficient feathers, he fell down from so great a height that he struck himself against his own palace and beat his head off.

Nor had the sons of this prince much better success, though the first of them was a prince mightily beloved by his subjects; but his misfortunes chiefly proceeded from his having made use of one of the engines so very long, that the feathers were quite worn out and good for nothing. He used to make a great many voyages and flights into the moon, and then would make his subjects give him great sums of money to come down to them again; and yet they were so fond of him that they always complied with him, and would give him everything he asked rather than be without him; but they grew wiser since.

At last, this prince used his engine so long it could hold together no longer, and being obliged to write to his subjects to pick him out some new feathers, they did so, but withal sent him such strong feathers, and so stiff, that when he had placed them in their proper places, and made a very beautiful engine, it was too heavy for him to manage.[3] He made a great many essays at it, and had it placed on the top of an old idol chapel, dedicated to an old Brahmin saint of those countries, called *Phantosteinaschap*

---

[1] Writs for new elections.    [2] Charles I.
[3] Difficulties of Charles II. with his Parliaments and the question of Protestant succession.

—in Latin, Chap. de Saint Stephano, or in English, St. Stephen's. Here the prince tried all possible contrivances, and a vast deal of money it cost him; but the feathers were so stiff they would not work, and the fire within was so choked and smothered with its own smoke, for want of due vent and circulation, that it would not burn, so he was obliged to take it down again; and from thence he carried it to his college of Brahmin priests, and set it up in one of their public buildings. There he drew circles of ethics and politics, and fell to casting of figures and conjuring; but all would not do, the feathers could not be brought to move; and, indeed, I have observed that these engines are seldom helped by art and contrivance; there is no way with them but to have the people spoke to to get good feathers; and they are easily placed, and perform all the several motions with the greatest ease and accuracy imaginable. But it must be all Nature; anything of force distorts and dislocates them, and the whole order is spoiled; and if there be but one feather out of place, or pinched, or stands wrong, the Devil would not ride in the chariot.

The prince thus finding his labour in vain, broke the engine to pieces, and sent his subjects word what bad feathers they had sent him; but the people, who knew it was his own want of management, and that the feathers were good enough, only a little stiff at first, and with good usage would have been brought to be fit for use, took it ill, and never would send him any other as long as he lived.[1] However, it had this good effect upon him, that he never made any more voyages to the moon as long as he reigned.

His brother[2] succeeded him, and truly he was resolved upon a voyage to the moon as soon as ever he came to the crown. He had met with some unkind usage from the religious *Lunesses* of his own country, and he turned *Abogratziarian*, a zealous fiery sect, something like our Anti-Everybodyarians in England. It is confessed some of the Brahmins of his country were very false to him, put him upon several ways of extending his power over his subjects, contrary to the customs of the people, and contrary to

---

[1] Government without Parliaments in the latter part of Charles the Second's reign.   [2] James II.

his own interest; and when the people expressed their dislike of it, he thought to have been supported by those clergymen, but they failed him, and made good that old English verse—

" That priests of all religions are the same."

He took this so heinously, that he conceived a just hatred against those that had deceived him; and as resentments seldom keep rules, unhappily entertained prejudices against all the rest; and not finding it easy to bring all his designs to pass better, he resolved upon a voyage to the moon.

Accordingly, he sends a summons to all his people, according to custom, to collect the usual quantity of feathers for that purpose; and because he would be sure not to be used as his brother and father had been, he took care to send certain cunning men express all over the country to bespeak the people's care in collecting, picking, and culling them out. These were called in their language *Tsopablesdetoo*, which being translated may signify in English, Men of Zeal or Booted Apostles. Nor was this the only caution this Prince used; for he took care, as the feathers were sent up to him, to search and examine them one by one in his own closet, to see if they were fit for his purpose. But, alas! he found himself in his brother's case exactly, and perceived that his subjects were generally disgusted at his former conduct about *Abrogratzianism* and such things, and particularly set in a flame by some of their priests, called *Dullobardians*, or Passive Obedience-men, who had lately turned their tale, and their tail, too, upon their own princes; and upon this he laid aside any more thoughts of the engine, but took up a desperate and implacable resolution, viz., to fly up to the moon without it. In order to this, abundance of his cunning men were summoned together to assist him, strange engines contrived and methods proposed, and a great many came from all parts to furnish him with inventions and equivalent for their journey; but all were so preposterous and ridiculous, that his subjects, seeing him going on to ruin himself, and by consequence them too, unanimously took arms, and if their prince had not made his escape into a foreign country, it is thought they would have secured him for a madman.[1]

And here it is observable that, as it is in most such cases, the mad councillors of this prince, when the people began to gather about him, fled, and every one shifted for themselves; nay, and some of them plundered him first of his jewels and treasure, and never were heard of since.

From this prince none of the kings or government of that country have ever seemed to incline to the hazardous attempt of the voyage to the moon, at least not in such a hare-brained manner.

However, the engine has been very accurately rebuilt and finished, and the people are now obliged by a law to send up new feathers every three years[2] to prevent the mischiefs which happened by that prince aforesaid keeping one set so long that it was dangerous to venture with them, and thus the engine is preserved fit for use.

And yet has not this engine been without its continual disasters, and often out of repair; for though the kings of the country, as has been noted, have done riding on the back of it, yet the restless courtiers and ministers of state have frequently obtained the management of it from the too easy goodness of their masters or the evils of the times.

To cure this, the princes frequently changed hands, turned one set of men out and put another in. But this made things still worse, for it divided the people into parties and factions in the state, and still the strife was who should ride in this engine, and no sooner were these Skaet-riders got into it, but they were for driving all the nation up to the moon : but of this by itself.

Authors differ concerning the original of these feathers, and by what most exact hand they were first appointed to this particular use; and as their original is hard to be found, so it seems a difficulty to resolve from what sort of bird these feathers are obtained. Some have named one, some another; but the most learned in those climates call it by a hard word, which the printer

---

[1] Revolution of 1688.  [2] Triennial Parliaments.

having no letters to express, and being in that place hieroglyphical, I can translate no better than by the name of a Collective.[1] This must be a strange bird without doubt; it has heads, claws, eyes, and teeth innumerable; and if I should go about to describe it to you, the history would be so romantic, it would spoil the credit of those more authentic relations which are yet behind.

It is sufficient, therefore, for the present only to leave you this short abridgment of the story, as follows: This great monstrous bird, called the Collective, is very seldom seen, and indeed never but upon great revolutions, and portending terrible desolations and destructions to a country.

But he frequently sheds his feathers, and they are carefully picked up by the proprietors of those lands where they fall;[2] for none but those proprietors may meddle with them; and they no sooner pick them up but they are sent to court, where they obtain a new name, and are called in a word equally difficult to pronounce as the other, but very like our English word Representative; and being placed in their proper rows, with the great feather in the centre, and fitted for use, they lately obtained the venerable title of the Consolidators, and the machine itself the Consolidator; and by that name the reader is desired for the future to let it be dignified and distinguished.

I cannot, however, forbear to descant a little here on the dignity and beauty of these feathers, being such as are hardly to be seen in any part of the world but just in these remote climates.

And first, every feather has various colours, and according to the variety of the weather are apt to look brighter and clearer, or paler and fainter, as the sun happens to look on them with a stronger or weaker aspect. The quill or head of every feather is or ought to be full of a vigorous substance, which gives spirit and supports the brightness and colour of the feather, and as this is more or less in quantity, the bright colour of the feather is increased or turns languid and pale.

---

[1] The members (feathers) are supplied in each place by general vote from the collective wisdom of the people.

[2] Territorial influence in elections.

It is true some of those quills are exceeding empty and dry; and the humid being totally exhaled, those feathers grow very use-less and insignificant in a short time.

Some, again, are so full of wind and puffed up with the vapour of the climate, that there is not humid enough to condense the steam ; and these are so fleet, so light, and so continually flutter-ing and troublesome, that they greatly serve to disturb and keep the motion unsteady.

Others, either placed too near the inward concealed fire, or the head of the quill being thin, the fire causes too great a fermenta-tion ; and the consequence of this is so fatal, that sometimes it mounts the engine up too fast and endangers precipitation. But it is happily observed that these ill feathers are but a very few compared to the whole number; at the most, I never heard they were above 134 of the whole number. As for the empty ones, they are not very dangerous, but a sort of good-for-nothing feathers, that will fly when the greatest number of the rest fly, or stand still when they stand still. The fluttering hot-headed feathers are the most dangerous, and frequently struggle hard to mount the engine to extravagant heights ; but still the greater number of the feathers being staunch and well fixed, as well as well fur-nished, they always prevail, and check the disorders the others would bring upon the motion ; so that upon the whole matter, though there have sometimes been oblique motions, variations, and sometimes great wanderings out of the way, which may make the passage tedious, yet it has always been a certain and safe voyage, and no engine was ever known to miscarry or overthrow but that one mentioned before,[1] and that was very much owing to the precipitate methods the prince took in guiding it ; and though all the fault was laid in the feathers, and they were to blame enough, yet I never heard any wise man but what blamed his discretion, and particularly a certain great man has written three large tracts of those affairs, and called them " The History of the Opposition of the Feathers," wherein, though it was expected he

---

[1] The Parliament of the Civil War that overthrew Charles I.

[2] Clarendon's History of the Great Rebellion.

would have cursed the engine itself and all the feathers to the devil, on the contrary, he lays equal blame on the prince, who guided the chariot with so unsteady a hand, now as much too slack as then too hard, turning them this way and that so hastily that the feathers could not move in their proper order ; and this at last put the fire in the centre quite out, and so the engine overset at once. This impartiality has done great justice to the feathers, and set things in a clearer light. But of this I shall say more when I come to treat of the " Works of the Learned " in this Lunar world.

This is hinted here only to inform the reader that this engine is the safest passage that ever was found out, and that, saving that one time it never miscarried, nor, if the common order of things be observed, cannot miscarry ; for the good feathers are always negatives when any precipitant motion is felt, and immediately suppress it by their number, and these negative feathers are indeed the traveller's safety. The others are always upon the flutter, and upon every occasion hie for the moon, up in the clouds presently ; but these negative feathers are never for going up, but when there is occasion for it, and from hence these fluttering fermented feathers were called by the ancients Highflying [1] feathers, and the blustering things seemed proud of the name.

But to come to their general character. The feathers, speaking of them all together, are generally very comely, strong, large, beautiful things, their quills or heads well fixed, and the cavities filled with a solid substantial matter, which, though it is full of spirit, has a great deal of temperament, and full of suitable, welldisposed powers to the operation for which they are designed.

These placed, as I noted before, in an extended form like two great wings, and operated by that sublime flame which, being concealed in proper receptacles, obtains its vent at the cavities appointed, are supplied from thence with life and motion ; and as fire itself, in the opinion of some learned men, is nothing but motion, and motion tends to fire, it can no more be a wonder if,

---

[1] Extreme politicians like the Earl of Nottingham were called High-flyers.

T

exalted in the centre of this famous engine, a whole nation should be carried up to the world in the moon.

It is true this engine is frequently assaulted with fierce winds and furious storms, which sometimes drive it a great way out of its way; and indeed, considering the length of the passage and the various regions it goes through, it would be strange if it should meet with no obstructions. These are oblique gales, and cannot be said to blow from any of the thirty-two points, but retrograde and thwart. Some of these are called in their language *Pensiona-zima*, which is as much as to say, being interpreted, a court-breeze. Another sort of wind, which generally blows directly contrary to the *Pensionazima*, is the *Clamorio*, or, in English, a country-gale. This is generally tempestuous, full of gusts and disgusts, squalls and sudden blasts, not without claps of thunder, and not a little flashing of heat and party fires.

There are a great many other internal blasts which proceed from the fire within, which sometimes not circulating right, breaks out in little gusts of wind and heat, and is apt to endanger setting fire to the feathers, and this is more or less dangerous according as among which of the feathers it happens; for some of the feathers are more apt to take fire than others, as their quills or heads are more or less full of that solid matter mentioned before.

The engine suffers frequent convulsions and disorders from these several winds, and which, if they chance to overblow very much, hinder the passage; but the negative feathers always apply temper and moderation, and this brings all to rights again.

For a body like this, what can it not do? what cannot such an extension perform in the air? And when one thing is tacked to another, and properly consolidated into one mighty Consolidator, no question but whoever shall go up to the moon will find himself so much improved in this wonderful experiment, that not a man ever performed that wonderful flight but he certainly came back again as wise as he went.

Well, gentlemen, and what if we are called High-flyers now, and a hundred names of contempt and distinction? What is this to the purpose? Who would not be a High-flyer, to be tacked and consolidated in an engine of such sublime elevation, and which lifts men, monarchs, members, yea, and whole nations, up into the clouds, and performs with such wondrous art the long expected experiment of a voyage to the moon? And this much for the description of the Consolidator.

The first voyage I ever made to this country was in one of these engines, and I can safely affirm I never waked all the way; and now having been as often there as most that have used that trade, it may be expected I should give some account of the country, for it appears I can give but little of the road.

Only this I understand, that when this engine, by help of these artificial wings, has raised itself up to a certain height, the wings are as useful to keep it from falling into the moon as they were before to raise it and keep it from falling back into this region again.

This may happen from an alteration of centres; and gravity having passed a certain line, the equipoise changes its tendency; the magnetic quality being beyond it, it inclines of course, and pursues a centre, which it finds in the Lunar world, and lands us safe upon the surface.

I was told I need take no bills of exchange with me nor letters of credit, for that upon my first arrival the inhabitants would be very civil to me; that they never suffered any of our world to want anything when they came there; that they were very free to show them anything, and inform them in all needful cases, and that whatever rarities the country afforded should be exposed immediately.

I shall not enter into the customs, geography, or history of the place, only acquaint the reader that I found no manner of difference in anything natural, except as hereafter excepted, but all was exactly as is here—an elementary world, peopled with folks, as like us as if they were only inhabitants of the same continent, but in a remote climate.

The inhabitants were men, women, beasts, birds, fishes, and insects, of the same individual species as ours, the latter excepted. The men no wiser, better, nor bigger than here; the women no handsomer or honester than ours. There were knaves and honest men, honest women and whores of all sorts, countries, nations, and kindreds, as on this side the skies.

They had the same sun to shine, the planets were equally visible as to us, and their astrologers were as busily impertinent as ours, only that those wonderful glasses hinted before made strange discoveries that we were unacquainted with. By them they could plainly discover that this world was their moon, and their world our moon; and when I came first among them, the people that flocked about me distinguished me by the name of the man that came out of the moon.

I cannot, however, but acquaint the reader with some remarks I made in this new world before I come to anything historical.

I have heard that among the generality of our people, who, being not much addicted to revelation, have much concerned themselves about demonstrations, a generation has risen up, who, to solve the difficulties of supernatural systems, imagine a mighty vast something, which has no form but what represents itself to them as one great Eye. This infinite optic they imagine to be *Natura naturans*, or power-forming; and that as we pretend the soul of man has a similitude in quality to its original— according to a notion some people have who read that so much ridiculed old legend, called Bible—that man was made in the image of his Maker. The soul of man, therefore, in the opinion of these naturalists, is one vast optic power, diffused through him into all his parts, but seated principally in his head.

From hence they resolve all beings to eyes, some more capable of sight and receptive of objects than others; and as to things invisible, they reckon nothing so, only so far as our sight is deficient, contracted, or darkened by accidents from without, as distance of place, interposition of vapours, clouds, liquid air, exhalations, &c., or from within, as wandering errors, wild notions, cloudy understandings, and empty fancies, with a thousand other interposing obstacles to the sight, which darken it and prevent its operation, and particularly obstruct the perceptive faculties, weaken the head, and bring mankind in general to stand in need of the spectacles of education as soon as ever they are born. Nay, and as soon as they have made use of these artificial eyes, all they can do is but to clear the sight so far as to see that they cannot see; the utmost wisdom of mankind, and the highest improvement a man ought to wish for, being but to be able to see that he was born blind, this pushes him upon search after mediums for the recovery of his sight, and away he runs to school, to art and science, and there he is furnished with hocoscopes, microscopes, telescopes, cœlescopes, money-scopes, and the Devil and all of glasses, to help and assist his moon-blind understandings. These with wonderful skill and ages of application, after wandering through bogs and wildernesses of guess, conjectures, supposes, calculations, and he knows not what, which he meets with in physics, politics, ethics, astronomy, mathematics, and such bewildering things, bring him with vast difficulty to a little minute spot called demonstration ; and as not one in ten thousand ever finds the way thither, but are lost in the tiresome uncouth journey, so they that do, it is so long before they come there that they are grown old, and good for little in the journey ; and no sooner have they obtained a glimmering of this universal eyesight, this *eclaircissement* general, but they die, and have hardly time to show the way to those that come after.

Now, as the earnest search after this thing called demonstration filled me with a desire of seeing everything, so my observations of the strange multitude of mysteries I met with in all men's actions here spurred my curiosity to examine if the great Eye of the world had no people to whom he had given a clearer eyesight, or at least that made a better use of it than we had here.

In pursuing this search, I was much delighted at my arrival into China; it cannot be thought strange, since there we find knowledge as much advanced beyond our common pitch as it was pretended to be derived from a more ancient original.

We are told that in the early age of the world the strength of invention exceeded all that ever has been arrived to since; that we in these latter ages, having lost all that pristine strength of reason and invention which died with the ancients in the Flood, and receiving no help from that age, have by long search arrived at several remote parts of knowledge by the helps of reading, conversation, and experience, but that all amounts to no more than faint imitations, apings, and resemblances of what was known in those masterly ages.

Now, if it be true, as is hinted before, that the Chinese empire was peopled long before the Flood, and that they were not destroyed in the general deluge in the days of Noah, it is no such strange thing that they should so much outdo us in this sort of eyesight we call general knowledge, since the perfections bestowed on Nature when in her youth and prime met with no general suffocation by that calamity.

But if I was extremely delighted with the extraordinary things I saw in those countries, you cannot but imagine I was exceedingly moved when I heard of a lunar world, and that the way was passable from these parts. I had heard of a world in the moon among some of our learned philosophers, and Moor, as I have been told, had a moon in his head; but none of the fine pretenders—no, not Bishop Wilkins—ever found mechanical engines whose motion was sufficient to attempt the passage. A late happy author, indeed, among his mechanic operations of the spirit, had found out an enthusiasm which, if he could have pursued to its proper extreme, without doubt might, either in the body or out of the body, have landed him somewhere hereabout; but that he formed his system wholly upon the mistaken notion of wind, which learned hypothesis being directly contrary to the nature of things in this climate, where the elasticity of the air is quite different, and where the pressure of the atmosphere has, for want of vapour, no force, all his notion dissolved in its native vapour called wind, and flew upward in blue strakes of a livid flame called blasphemy, which burnt up all the wit and fancy of the author, and left a strange stench behind it that has this unhappy quality in it, that everybody that reads the book smells the author though he be never so far of, nay, though he took shipping to Dublin to secure his friends from the least danger of a conjecture.

But to return to the happy regions of the Lunar continent. I was no sooner landed there and had looked about me, but I was surprised with the strange alteration of the climate and country, and particularly a strange salubrity and fragrancy in the air, which I felt so nourishing, so pleasant, and delightful, that though I could perceive some small respiration, it was hardly discernible, and the least requisite for life supplied so long that the bellows of Nature were hardly employed.

But as I shall take occasion to consider this in a critical examination into the nature, uses, and advantages of good lungs, of which by itself, so I think fit to confine my present observations to things more particularly concerning the eyesight.

I was, you may be sure, not a little surprised when, being upon an eminence, I found myself capable, by common observation, to see and distinguish things at the distance of a hundred miles and more; and seeking some information on this point, I was acquainted by the people that there was a certain grave philosopher hard by that could give me a very good account of things.

It is not worth while to tell you this man's Lunar name, or whether he had a name or no. It is plain it was a man in the moon; but all the conference I had with him was very strange. At my first coming to him, he asked me if I came from the world in the moon. I told him, No; at which he began to be angry, and told me I lied; he knew whence I came as well as I did, for he saw me all the way. I told him I came to the world in the moon, and began to be as surly as he. It was a long time before we could agree about it. He would have it that I came down from the moon, and I that I came up to the moon. From this we came to explications, demonstrations, spheres, globes, regions, atmospheres, and a thousand odd diagrams to make the thing out to one another. I insisted, on my part, as that my experiment qualified me to know, and challenged him to go back with me to prove it. He, like a true philosopher, raised a thousand scruples, conjectures, and spherical problems to confront me, and as for demonstrations, he called them fancies of my own.

Thus we differed a great many ways. Both of us were certain, and both uncertain; both right, and yet both directly contrary. How to reconcile this jangle was very hard, till at last this demonstration happened. The moon, as he called it, turning her blind side upon us three days after the change, by which, with the help of his extraordinary glasses, I that knew the country perceived that side the sun looked upon was all moon, and the other was all world; and either I fancied I saw, or else really saw, all the lofty towers of the immense cities of China. Upon this, and a little more debate, we came to this conclusion—and there the old man and I agreed—that they were both moons and both worlds, this a moon to that, and that a moon to this, like the sun between two looking-glasses, and shone upon one another by reflection, according to the oblique or direct position of each other.

This afforded us a great deal of pleasure, for all the world covet to be found in the right, and are pleased when their notions are acknowledged by their antagonists. It also afforded us many very useful speculations, such as these :—

1. How easy it is for men to fall out, and yet all sides to be in the right?

2. How natural it is for opinion to despite demonstration?

3. How proper mutual inquiry is to mutual satisfaction?

From the observation of these glasses we also drew some puns, crotchets, and conclusions :—

(1.) That the whole world has a blind side, a dark side, and a bright side, and consequently so has everybody in it.

(2.) That the dark side of affairs to-day may be the bright side to-morrow: from whence abundance of useful morals were also raised; such as :—

(a.) No man's fate is so dark but when the sun shines upon it, it will return its rays and shine for itself.

(b.) All things turn like the moon, up to-day, down to-morrow, full and change, flux and reflux.

(c.) Human understanding is like the moon at the first quarter, half dark.

(3.) The changing sides ought not to be thought so strange or so much condemned by mankind, having its original from the lunar influence, and governed by the powerful operation of heavenly motion.

(4.) If there be any such thing as destiny in the world, I know nothing man is so predestinated to as to be eternally turning round ; and but that I purpose to entertain the reader with at least a whole chapter or section of the philosophy of human motion, spherically and hypocritically examined and calculated, I should enlarge upon that thought in this place.

Having thus jumped in our opinions, and perfectly satisfied ourselves with demonstration that these worlds were sisters, both in form, function, and all their capacities—in short, a pair of moons and a pair of worlds, equally magnetical, sympathetical, and influential, we set up our rest as to that affair and went forward.

I desired no better acquaintance in my new travels than this new associate. Never was there such a couple of people met ; he was the man in the moon to me, and I the man in the moon to him. He wrote down all I said and made a book of it, and called it "News from the World in the Moon ;" and all the town is like to see my minutes under the same title. Nay, I have been told he published some such bold truths there, from the allegorical relations he had of me from our world, that he was called before the public authority, who could not bear the just reflections of his damned satirical way of writing ; and there they punished the poor man, put him in prison, ruined his family, and not only fined him *ultra tenementum*, but exposed him in the high places of their capital city for the mob to laugh at him for a fool. This is a punishment not unlike our pillory, and was appointed for mean criminals, fellows that cheat and cozen people, forge writings, forswear themselves, and the like ; and the people, that it was expected would have treated this man very ill, on the contrary pitied him, wished those that set him there placed in his room, and expressed their affections by loud shouts and acclamations when he was taken down.

But as this happened before my first visit to that world, when I came there all was over with him, his particular enemies were disgraced and turned out, and the man was not at all the worse received by his country-folks than he was before; and so much for the man in the moon.[1]

After we had settled the debate between us about the nature and quality, I desired him to show me some plan or draft of this new world of his; upon which he brought me out a pair of very beautiful globes, and there I had an immediate geographical description of the place.

I found it less by     degrees than our terrestrial globe, but more land and less water; and as I was particularly concerned to see something in or near the same climate with ourselves, I observed a large extended country to the north, about the latitude of 50° to 56° northern distance; and inquiring of that country, he told me it was one of the best countries in all the world; that it was his native climate, and he was just going to it, and would take me with him.

He told me in general the country was good, wholesome, fruitful, rarely situate for trade, extraordinarily accommodated with harbours, rivers, and bays for shipping, full of inhabitants, for it had been peopled from all parts, and had in it some of the blood of all the nations in the moon.[2]

He told me, as the inhabitants were the most numerous, so they were the strangest people that lived; both their natures, tempers, qualities, actions, and way of living was made up of innumerable contradictions; that they were the wisest fools and the foolishest wise men in the world, the weakest, strongest, richest, poorest, most generous, covetous, bold, cowardly, false, faithful, sober, dissolute, surly, civil, slothful, diligent, peaceable, quarrelling, loyal, seditious nation that ever was known.

Besides my observations which I made myself, and which could only furnish me with what was present, and which I shall take time to inform my reader with as much care and conciseness as possible, I was beholden to this old Lunarian for everything that was historical or particular.

---

[1] The counterpart of Daniel de Foe.     [2] The counterpart of England.

And first he informed me that in this new country they had very seldom any clouds at all, and consequently no extraordinary storms, but a constant serenity. Moderate breezes cooled the air, and constant evening exhalations kept the earth moist and fruitful; and as the winds they had were various and strong enough to assist their navigation, so they were without the terrors, dangers, shipwrecks, and destructions which he knew we were troubled with in this our Lunar world, as he called it.

The first just observation I made of this was, that I supposed from hence the wonderful clearness of the air and the advantage of so vast optic capacities they enjoyed was obtained. "Alas!" says the old fellow, "you see nothing to what some of our great eyes see in some parts of this world, nor do you see anything compared to what you may see by the help of some new invented glasses, of which I may in time let you see the experiment; and perhaps you may find this to be the reason why we do not so abound in books as in your Lunar world; and that except it be some extraordinary translations out of your country, you will find but little in our libraries worth giving you a great deal of trouble."

We immediately quitted the philosophical discourse of winds, and I began to be mighty inquisitive after these glasses and translations; and

1. I understood here was a strange sort of glass, that did not so much bring to the eye, as by I know not what wonderful operation carried out the eye to the object, and quite varies from all our doctrine of optics by forming several strange phenomena in sight which we are utterly unacquainted with. Nor could vision, rarification, or any of our schoolmen's fine terms stand me in any stead in this case; but here was such additions of piercing organs, particles of transparence, emission, transmission, mediums, contraction of rays, and a thousand applications of things prepared for the wondrous operations that you may be sure are requisite for the bringing to pass something yet unheard of on this side the moon.

First, we were informed by the help of these glasses of strange things which passed in our world for nonentities here to be seen, and very perceptible. For example :—

State polity, in all its meanders, shifts, turns, tricks, and contraries, are so exactly delineated and described, that they are in hopes in time to draw a pair of globes out to bring all those things to a certainty.

Not but that it made some puzzle even among these clear-sighted nations to determine what figure the plans and drafts of this undiscovered world of mysteries ought to be described in. Some were of opinion it ought to be an irregular centagon, a figure with an hundred cones or angles, since the unaccountables of this State Science are hid in a million of undiscovered corners, as the craft, subtilty, and hypocrisy of knaves and courtiers have concealed them, never to be found out but by this wonderful Devilscope, which seemed to threaten a perfect discovery of all those nudities which have lain hid in the embryo and false conceptions of abortive policy ever since the foundation of the world.

Some were of opinion this plan ought to be circular and in a globular form, since it was, on all sides alike, full of dark spots, untrod mazes, waking mischiefs and sleeping mysteries; and being delineated like the globes displayed, would discover all the lines of wickedness to the eye at one view. Besides, they fancied some sort of analogy in the rotundity of the figure with the continued circular motion of all court politics in the stated round of universal knavery.

Others would have had it hieroglyphical, as by a hand in hand, the form representing the affinity between state policy here and state policy in the infernal regions, with some unkind similes between the economy of Satan's kingdom and those of most of the temporal powers on earth; but this was thought too unkind. At last it was determined that neither of these schemes were capable of the vast description, and that, therefore, the drafts must be made single, though not dividing the governments, yet dividing the arts of governing into proper distinct schemes, viz. :—

1. A particular plan of public faith; and here we had the

experiment immediately made. The representation is qualified
for the meridian of any country, as well in our world as theirs;
and turning it towards our own world, there I saw plainly an
Exchequer shut up, and twenty thousand mourning families selling their coaches, horses, whores, equipages, &c., for bread, the
Government standing by laughing and looking on. Hard by I saw
the chamber of a great city shut up, and forty thousand orphans
turned adrift in the world; some had no clothes, some no shoes,
some no money, and still the city magistrates calling upon other
orphans to pay their money in. These things put me in mind
of the prophet Ezekiel, and methought I heard the same voice
that spoke to him calling me, and telling me, "Come hither, and
I will show thee greater abominations than these." So, looking
still on that vast map by the help of these magnifying glasses, I
saw huge fleets hired for transport service, but never paid; vast
taxes anticipated, that were never collected; others collected and
appropriated, but misapplied; millions of tallies struck to be
discounted, and the poor paying 40 per cent. to receive their
money. I saw huge quantities of money drawn in, and little or
none issued out; vast prizes taken from the enemy, and then
taken away again at home by friends; ships saved on the sea,
and sunk in the prize-offices; merchants escaping from enemies
at sea, to be pirated by sham embargoes, counterfeit claims,
confiscations, &c., ashore. There we saw Turkey fleets taken
into convoys, and guarded to the very mouth of the enemy, and
then abandoned for their better security. Here we saw Monsieur
Pouchartrain shutting up the town-house of Paris and plundering
the bank of Lyons.

2. Here we saw the state of war among nations. Here was
the French giving sham thanks for victories they never got,
and somebody else addressing and congratulating the sublime
glory of running away. Here was *Te Deum* for sham victories
by land, and there was thanksgiving for ditto by sea. Here we
might see two armies fight, both run away, and both come and
thank God for nothing. Here we saw a plan of a late war like
that in Ireland; there was all the officers cursing a Dutch general,

because the damned rogue would fight and spoil a good war, that with decent management and good husbandry might have been eked out this twenty years; there were whole armies hunting two cows to one Irishman; and driving off black cattle declared the noble end of the war. Here we saw a country full of stone walls and strong towns, where every campaign the trade of war was carried on by the soldiers with the same intriguing as it was carried on in the council-chambers; there was millions of contributions raised, and vast sums collected, but no taxes lessened; whole plate-fleets surprised, but no treasure found; vast sums lost by enemies, and yet never found by friends; ships loaded with volatile silver, that came away full and got home empty; whole voyages made to beat nobody and plunder everybody; two millions robbed from the honest merchants, and not a groat saved for the honest subjects. There we saw captains listing men with the Government's money, and letting them go again for their own; ships fitted out at the rates of two millions a year, to fight but once in three years, and then run away for want of powder and shot.

There we saw partition treaties damned, and the whole given away—confederacies without allies, allies without quotas, princes without armies, armies without men, and men without money, crowns without kings, kings without subjects, more kings than countries, and more countries than were worth fighting for.

Here we could see the King of France upbraiding his neighbours with dishonourably assisting his rebels, though the mischief was they did it not neither, and in the same breath assisting the Hungarian rebels against the Emperor; M. Ld. N. refusing so dishonourable an action as to aid the rebellious Camissars, but leaguing with the Admiral de Castile to invade the dominions of his master, to whom he swore allegiance. Here we saw Protestants fight against Protestants to help Papists, Papists against Papists to help Protestants, Protestants call in Turks to keep faith against Christians that break it. Here we could see Swedes fighting for revenge and calling it religion; cardinals deposing their Catholic prince to introduce the tyranny of a Lutheran and call it liberty; armies electing kings and calling it free choice; France conquering Savoy to secure the liberty of Italy.

3. The map of state policy contains abundance of civil trans-actions nowhere to be discovered but in this wonderful country, and by this prodigious invention. At first it shows an eminent prelate running in everybody's debt to relieve the poor and bring to God robbery for burnt-offering. It opens a door to the fate of nations, and there we might see the Duke of Savoy bought three times, and his subjects sold every time; Portugal bought twice, and neither time worth the earnest; Spain bought once, but loth to go with the bidder; Venice willing to be bought if there had been any buyers; Bavaria bought and running away with the money; the Emperor bought and sold, but bilking the chapman; the French buying kingdoms they cannot keep; the Dutch keeping kingdoms they never bought; and the English paying their money without purchase.

In matters of civil concerns, here was to be seen religion with no outside, and much outside with no religion; much strife about peace, and no peace in the design. Here was plunder without violence, violence without persecution, conscience without good works, and good works without charity; parties cutting one another's throats for God's sake, pulling down churches *de propa-ganda fide*, and making divisions by way of association.

Here we have peace and union brought to pass the shortest way, extirpation and destruction proved to be the road to plenty and pleasure. Here all the wise nations a learned author would have quoted if he could have found them, are to be seen, who carry on exclusive laws to the general safety and satisfaction of their subjects.

Occasional bills may have here a particular historical, cate-gorical description. But of them by themselves.

Here you might have the rise, original, lawfulness, usefulness, and necessity of passive obedience as fairly represented as a system of divinity, and as clearly demonstrated as by a geo-graphical description; and, which exceeds our mean understand-ing here, it is by the wonderful assistance of these glasses, plainly discerned to be coherent with resistance, taking arms, calling in foreign powers, and the like. Here you have a plain discovery of Church of England politics and a map of loyalty. Here it is as plainly demonstrated as the nose on a man's face, provided he has one, that a man may abdicate, drive away, and dethrone his prince, and yet be absolutely and entirely free from and innocent of the least fracture, breach, encroachment, or intrenchment upon the doctrine of non-resistance; can shoot at his prince without any design to kill him, fight against him without raising rebellion, and take up arms without levying war against his prince.

Here they can persecute Dissenters without desiring they should conform to the Church they would overthrow; pray for the prince they dare not name, and name the prince they do not pray for.

By the help of these glasses strange insights are made into the vast mysterious dark world of State Policy; but that which is yet more strange, and requires vast volumes to descend to the particulars of, and huge diagrams, spheres, charts, and a thousand nice things to display, is that in this vast intelligent discovery it is not only made plain that those things are so, but all the vast contradictions are made rational, reconciled to practice, and brought down to demonstration.

German clockwork, the perpetual motions, the prime mobiles of our short-sighted world, are trifles to these nicer disquisitions.

Here it would be plain and rational why a Parliament-man should spend £5000 to be chosen, that cannot get a groat honestly by sitting there. It would be easily made out to be rational why he that rails most at a court is soonest received into it. Here it would be very plain how great estates are got in little places, and double in none at all. It is easy to be proved honest and faithful to victual the French fleet out of English stores, and let our own navy want them. A long sight or a large Lunar perspective will make all these things not only plain in fact, but rational and justifiable to all the world.

It is a strange thing to anybody without doubt, that has not been in that clear-sighted region, to comprehend that those we call High-flyers in England are the only friends to the Dissenters, and have been the most diligent and faithful in their interest of any people in the nation; and yet so it is, gentlemen, and they ought to have the thanks of the whole body for it.

In this advanced station, we see it plainly by reflection that the Dissenters, like a parcel of knaves, have retained all the High Churchmen in their pay; they are certainly all in their pension roll: indeed, I could not see the money paid them there, it was too remote; but I could plainly see the thing. All the deep lines of the project are laid as true; they are so tacked and consolidated together, that if any one will give themselves leave to consider, they will be most effectually convinced that the High Church and the Dissenters here are all in a cabal, a mere knot, a piece of clockwork; the Dissenters are the dial-plate and the High Church the movement, the wheel within the wheels, the spring and the screw to bring all things to motion, and make the hand on the dial-plate point which way the Dissenters please.

For what else have been all the shams they have put on the governments, kings, states, and people they have been concerned with? What schemes have they laid on purpose to be broken? What vast contrivances on purpose to be ridiculed and exposed? The men are not fools; they had never voted to consolidate a Bill but that they were willing to save the Dissenters, and put it into a posture in which they were sure it would miscarry. I defy all the wise men of the moon to show another good reason for it.

Methinks I begin to pity my brethren, the moderate men of the Church, that they cannot see into this new plot, and to wish they would but get up into our Consolidator, and take a journey to the moon, and there, by the help of these glasses, they would see the allegorical, symbolical heterodoxicality of all this matter; it would make immediate converts of them; they would see plainly that to tack and consolidate, to make exclusive laws, to persecute for conscience, disturb and distress parties—these are all fanatic plots, mere combinations against the Church, to bring her into

U

contempt, and to fix and establish the Dissenters to the end of the chapter. But of this I shall find occasion to speak occasionally, when an occasion presents itself to examine a certain occasional bill transacting in these Lunar regions some time before I had the happiness to arrive there.

In examining the multitude and variety of these most admirable glasses for the assisting the optics, or indeed the formation of a new perceptive faculty, it was, you may be sure, most surprising to find there that Art had exceeded Nature, and the power of vision was assisted to that prodigious degree as even to distinguish nonentity itself; and in these strange engines . of light it could not but be very pleasing to distinguish plainly betwixt being and matter, and to come to a determination in the so long canvassed dispute of substance, *vel materialis, vel spiritualis,* and I can solidly affirm that in all our contention between entity and nonentity there is so little worth meddling with that, had we had these glasses some ages ago, we should have left troubling our heads with it.

I take upon me, therefore, to assure my reader that whosoever pleases to take a journey or voyage or flight up to these Lunar regions, as soon as ever he comes ashore there, will presently be convinced of the reasonableness of immaterial substance, and the immortality as well as immateriality of the soul. He will no sooner look into these explicating glasses, but he will be able to know the separate meaning of body, soul, spirit, life, motion, death, and a thousand things that wise men puzzle themselves about here, because they are not fools enough to understand.

Here, too, I find glasses for the second-sight, as our old women call it. This second-sight has often been pretended to in our regions, and some famous old wives have told us they can see death, the soul, futurity, and the neighbourhood of them, in the countenance. By this wonderful art these good people unfold strange mysteries; as under some irrecoverable disease to foretell death; under hypochondriac melancholy to presage trouble of mind; in pining youth to predict contagious love; and a hundred other infallibilities, which never fail to be true as soon as ever they come to pass, and are all grounded upon the same infallibility by which a shepherd may always know when any one of his sheep is rotten, viz., when he shakes himself to pieces.

But all this guess and uncertainty is a trifle to the vast discoveries of these explicatory optic glasses, for here are seen the nature and consequences of secret mysteries; here are read strange mysteries relating to predestination, eternal decrees, and the like; here it is plainly proved that predestination is, in spite of all enthusiastic pretences, so entirely committed into man's power, that whoever pleases to hang himself to-day won't live till to-morrow—no, though forty predestination prophets were to tell him his time was not yet come. These abstruse points are commonly and solemnly discussed here; and these people are such heretics that they say God's decrees are all subservient to the means of His providence; that what we call providence is a subjecting all things to the great chain of causes and consequences by which that one grand decree—that all effects shall obey without reserve to their proper moving causes—supersedes all subsequent doctrines or pretended decrees or predestination in the world; that by this rule he that will kill himself, God, nature, providence, or decree will not be concerned to hinder him, but he shall die; any decrees, predestination, or foreknowledge of infinite power to the contrary in any wise notwithstanding, that it is in a man's power to throw himself into the water and be drowned; and to kill another man, and he shall die; and to say God appointed it, is to make Him the author of murder, and to injure the murderer in putting him to death for what he could not help doing.

All these things are received truths here, and no doubt would be so everywhere else if the eyes of reason were opened to the testimony of Nature, or if they had the helps of these most incomparable glasses.

Some pretended, by the help of these second-sight glasses, to see the common periods of life; and others said they could see a great way beyond the leap in the dark. I confess all

I could see of the first was, that holding up the glasses against the sea, I plainly saw, as it were on the edge of the horizon, these words—

> "The verge of life and death is here.
> 'Tis best to know where 'tis, but not how far."

As to seeing beyond death, all the glasses I looked into for that purpose made but little of it, and these were the only tubes that I found defective; for here I could discern nothing but clouds, mists, and thick, dark, hazy weather. But revolving in my mind that I had read a certain book in our own country called Nature, it presently occurred that the conclusion of it to all such as gave themselves the trouble of making out those foolish things called inferences, was always, "Look up;" upon which, turning one of their glasses up, and erecting the point of it towards the zenith, I saw this word in the air, "Revelation," in large capital letters.

I had like to have raised the mob upon me for looking upright with this glass, for this, they said, was prying into the mysteries of the Great Eye of the world; that we ought to inquire no farther than He has informed us, and to believe what He had left us more obscure. Upon this I laid down the glasses, and concluded that we had Moses and the prophets, and should never be the likelier to be taught by one come from the moon.

In short, I found indeed they had a great deal more knowledge of things than we in this world, and that Nature, Science, and Reason had obtained great improvements in the Lunar world; but as to Religion, it was the same, equally resigned to and concluded in Faith and Redemption; so I shall give the world no great information of these things.

I come next to some other strange acquirements obtained by the help of these glasses, and particularly for the discerning the imperceptibles of Nature, such as the soul, thought, honesty, religion, virginity, and a hundred other nice things too small for human discerning.

The discoveries made by these glasses as to the soul are of a very diverting variety, some hieroglyphical and emblematical, and some demonstrative.

The hieroglyphical discoveries of the soul make it appear in the image of its Maker ; and the analogy is remarkable even in the very simile ; for as they represent the original of Nature as one Great Eye, illuminating as well as discerning all things, so the soul, in its allegorical or hieroglyphical resemblance, appears as a great eye, embracing the man, enveloping, operating, and informing every part. From whence those sort of people whom we falsely call politicians, affecting so much to put out this great eye by acting against their common understandings, are very aptly represented by a great eye with six or seven pairs of spectacles on. Not but that the eye of their souls may be clear enough of itself as to the common understanding, but that they happen to have occasion to look sometimes so many ways at once, and to judge, conclude, and understand so many contrary ways upon one and the same thing, that they are fain to put double glasses upon their understandings, as we look at the solar eclipse, to represent them in different lights, lest their judgments should not be wheedled into a compliance with the hellish resolutions of their wills; and this is what I call the emblematic representation of the soul.

As for the demonstration of the soul's existence, it is a plain case, by these explicative glasses, that it is. Some have pretended to give us the parts; and we have heard of chirurgeons that could read an anatomical lecture on the parts of the soul, and these pretend it to be a creature in form, whether cameleon or salamander authors have not determined; nor is it completely discovered when it comes into the body, or how it goes out, or where its locality or habitation is while it is a resident.

But they very aptly show it, like a prince in his seat, in the middle of his palace, the brain, issuing out his incessant orders to innumerable troops of nerves, sinews, muscles, tendons, veins, arteries, fibres, capillaries, and useful officers, called Organici, who faithfully execute all the parts of sensation, locomotion, concoction, &c., and in the hundred-thousandth part of a moment return with particular messages for information, and demand new instructions. If any part of his kingdom, the body, suffers a depredation or an invasion of the enemy, the expresses fly to the seat of the soul, the brain, and immediately are ordered back to smart, that the body may of course send more messengers to complain; immediately other expresses are dispatched to the tongue, with orders to cry out, that the neighbours may come in and help, or friends send for the chirurgeon. Upon the application and a cure, all is quiet, and the same expresses are despatched to the tongue to hush, and say no more of it till further orders : all this is as plain to be seen in these engines as the moon of our world from the world in the moon.

As the being, nature, and situation of the human soul is thus spherically and mathematically discovered, I could not find any second thoughts about it in all their books, whether of their own composition or by translation; for it was a generally received notion that there could not be a greater absurdity in human knowledge than to employ the thoughts in questioning what is as plainly known by its consequences as if seen with the eye, and that to doubt the being or extent of the soul's operation is to employ her against herself; and therefore, when I began to argue with my old philosopher against the materiality and immortality of this mystery we call soul, he laughed at me, and told me he found we had none of their glasses in our world, and bid me send all our sceptics, soul-sleepers, our Cowards, Bakers, Kings, and Bakewells, up to him into the moon if they wanted demonstrations, where, by the help of their engines, they would make it plain to them that the Great Eye, being one vast intellect, infinite and eternal, all inferior life is a degree of Himself, and exactly represents Him as one little flame the whole mass of fire ; that it is, therefore, incapable of dissolution, being like its original in duration, as well as in its powers and faculties, but that it goes and returns by emission, regression, as the Great Eye governs and determines; and this was plainly made out by the figure I had seen it in, viz., an Eye, the exact image of its Maker. It is true it was darkened by ignorance, folly, and crime, and therefore obliged to wear spectacles;

but though these were defects or interruptions in its operation, they were none in its nature, which, as it had its immediate efflux from the Great Eye, its return to Him must partake of Himself, and could not but be of a quality uncomatable by casualty or death.

From this discourse we the more willingly adjourned our present thoughts, I being clearly convinced of the matter; and as for our learned doctors with their second and third thoughts, I told him I would recommend them to the man in the moon for their further illumination, which if they refuse to accept, it was but just they should remain in a wood, where they are, and are like to be, puzzling themselves about demonstrations, squaring of circles, and converting oblique into right angles, to bring out a mathematical clockwork soul, that will go till the weight is down, and then stand still till They-know-not-who must wind it up again.

However, I cannot pass over a very strange and extraordinary piece of art which this old gentleman informed me of, and that was an engine to screw a man into himself. Perhaps our countrymen may be at some difficulty to comprehend these things by my dull description, and to such I cannot but recommend a journey in my engine to the moon.

This machine that I am speaking of contains a multitude of strange springs and screws, and a man that puts himself into it is very insensibly carried into vast speculations, reflections, and regular debates with himself. They have a very hard name for it in those parts; but if I were to give it an English name, it should be called the Cogitator or the Chair of Reflection.

And, first, the person that is seated here feels some pain in passing some negative springs, that are wound up effectually to shut out all injecting, disturbing thoughts, and the better to prepare him for the operation that is to follow; and this is without doubt a very rational way; for when a man can absolutely shut out all manner of thinking but what he is upon, he shall think the more intensely upon the one object before him.

This operation past, here are certain screws that draw direct lines from every angle of the engine to the brain of the man, and at the same time other direct lines to his eyes, at the other end of which lines there are glasses which convey or reflect the objects the person is desirous to think upon.

Then the main wheels are turned, which wind up according to their several offices,—this the memory, that the understanding, a third the will, a fourth the thinking faculty; and these being put all into regular motions, pointed by direct lines to their proper objects, and perfectly uninterrupted by the intervention of whimsy, chimera, and a thousand fluttering demons that gender in the fancy, but are effectually locked out as before, assist one another to receive right notions and form just ideas of the things they are directed to; and from thence the man is empowered to make right conclusions, to think and act like himself, suitable to the sublime qualities his soul was originally blest with.

There never was a man went into one of these thinking engines but he came wiser out than he was before; and I am persuaded it would be a more effectual cure to our deism, atheism, scepticism, and all other-cisms than ever the Italian's engine for curing the gout by cutting off the toe.

This is a most wonderful engine, and performs admirably, and my author gave me extraordinary accounts of the good effects of it; and I cannot but tell my reader that our sublunar world suffers millions of inconveniences for want of this thinking engine. I have had a great many projects in my head how to bring our people to regular thinking, but it is in vain without this engine; and how to get the model of it I know not; how to screw up the will, the understanding, and the rest of the powers; how to bring the eye, the thought, the fancy, and the memory into mathematical order and obedient to mechanic operation; help Boyle, Norris, Newton, Manton, Hammond, Tillotson, and all the learned race; help philosophy, divinity, physics, economics—all is in vain; a mechanic chair of reflection is the only remedy that ever I found in my life for this work.

As to the effects of mathematical thinking, what volumes might be writ of it will more easily appear if we consider the wondrous usefulness of this engine in all human affairs; as of war, peace, justice, injuries, passion, love, marriage, trade, policy, and religion.

When a man has been screwed into himself, and brought by this art to a regularity of thought, he never commits any absurdity after it; his actions are squared by the same lines; for action is but the consequence of thinking, and he that acts before he thinks sets human nature with the bottom upward.

M. would never have made his speech, nor the famous Bentley wrote a book, if ever they had been in this thinking engine. One would never have told us of nations he never saw, nor the other told us he had seen a great many, and was never the wiser.

H. had never ruined his family to marry whore, thief, and beggar-woman in one salient lady, after having been told so honestly and so often of it by the very woman herself.

Our late unhappy monarch had never trusted the English clergy when they preached up that non-resistance which he must needs see they could never practise; had His Majesty been screwed up into this cogitator, he had presently reflected that it was against Nature to expect they should stand still and let him tread upon them; that they should, whatever they had preached or pretended to, hold open their throats to have them be cut, and tie their own hands from resisting the Lord's anointed.

Had some of our clergy been screwed in this engine, they had never turned martyrs for their allegiance to the late King only for the lechery of having Dr. Sacheverell in their company.

Had our merchants been managed in this engine, they had never trusted their Turkey fleet with a famous squadron, that took a great deal of care to convey them safe into the enemy's hands.

Had some people been in this engine when they made a certain league in the world in order to make amends for a better made before, they would certainly have considered further before they embarked with a nation that is neither fit to go abroad nor stay at home.

As for the thinking practised in noble speeches, occasional bills, addressings about prerogative, Convocation disputes, turnings in and turnings out at ours and all the courts of Christendom, I have nothing to say to it.

Had the Duke of Bavaria been in our engine, he would never have begun a quarrel which he knew all the powers of Europe were concerned to suppress, and lay all other business down till it was done.

Had the Elector of Saxony passed the operation of this engine, he would never have beggared a rich electorate to ruin a beggared crown, nor sold himself for a kingdom hardly worth any man's taking. He would never have made himself less than he was in hopes of being really no greater, and stepped down from a Protestant Duke and Imperial Elector to be a nominal, mock king, with a shadow of power and a name without honour, dignity, and strength.

Had Monsieur Tallard been in our engine, he would not only not have attacked the confederates when they passed the morass and rivulet in his front, but not have attacked them at all, nor have suffered them to have attacked him,[1] it being his business not to have fought at all, but have lingered out the war till the Duke of Savoy having been reduced, the confederate army must have been forced to have divided themselves of course, in order to defend their own.

Some that have been very forward to have us proceed the shortest way with the Scots may be said to stand in great need of this chair of reflection to find out a just cause for such a war, and to make a neighbour nation making tnemselves secure a sufficient reason for another neighbour nation to fall upon them. Our engine would presently show it them in a clear light by way of parallel, that it is just with the same right as a man may break open a house because the people bar and bolt the windows.

If somebody has changed hands there from bad to worse, and opened instead of closing differences, in those cases the cogitator might have brought them, by more regular thinking, to have known that was not at all the method of bringing the Scots to reason.

---

[1] At the Battle of Blenheim, where Marshal Tallard himself was taken prisoner.

Our cogitator would be a very necessary thing to show some people that poverty and weakness is not a sufficient ground to oppress a nation, and their having but little trade cannot be a sufficient ground to equip fleets to take away what they have.

I cannot deny that I have often thought they have had something of this engine in our neighbouring ancient kingdom, since no man, however we pretend to be angry, but will own they are in the right of it, as to themselves, to vote and procure bills for their own security, and not to do as others demand without conditions fit to be accepted. But of that by itself.

There are abundance of people in our world, of all sorts and conditions, that stand in need of our thinking engines, and to be screwed into themselves a little, that they might think as directly as they speak absurdly. But of these also in a class by itself.

This engine has a great deal of philosophy in it, and particularly it is a wonderful remedy against poring, and, as it was said of Monsieur Jurieu at Amsterdam, that he used to lose himself in himself. By the assistance of this piece of regularity a man is most effectually secured against bewildering thoughts, and by direct thinking he prevents all manner of dangerous wandering, since nothing can come to more speedy conclusions than that which, in right lines, points to the proper subject of debate.

All sorts of confusion of thoughts are perfectly avoided and prevented in this case, and a man is never troubled with spleen, hypo, or mute madness, when once he has been thus under the operation of the screw. It prevents abundance of capital disasters in men in private affairs ; it prevents hasty marriages, rash vows, duels, quarrels, suits at law, and most sorts of repentance. In the State it saves a government from many inconveniences; it checks immoderate ambition, stops wars, navies, and expeditions; especially it prevents members making long speeches when they have nothing to say ; it keeps back rebellions, insurrections, clashings of Houses, occasional bills, tacking, &c.

It has a wonderful property in our affairs at sea, and has prevented many a bloody fight in which a great many honest men might have lost their lives that are now useful fellows, and help to man and manage Her Majesty's navy.

What if some people are apt to charge cowardice upon some people in those cases? It is plain that cannot be it; for he that dare incur the resentment of the English mob shows more courage than would be able to carry him through forty sea-fights.

It is therefore for want of being in this engine that we censure people because they are not knocking one another on the head like the people at the Bear-garden, where, if they do not see the blood run about, they always cry out, "A cheat!" and the poor fellows are fain to cut one another that they may not be pulled to pieces; where the case is plain, they are bold for fear, and pull up courage enough to fight because they are afraid of the people.

This engine prevents all sort of lunacies, love-frenzies, and melancholy madness; for preserving the thought in right lines to direct objects, it is impossible any deliriums, whimsies, or fluttering air of ideas can interrupt the man; he can never be mad; for which reason I cannot but recommend it to my Lord Sunderland, my Lord Nottingham, and my Lord Halifax, as absolutely necessary to defend them from the state madness which for some ages has possessed their families, and which runs too much in the blood.

It is also an excellent introduction to thought, and therefore very well adapted to those people whose peculiar talent and praise is that they never think at all. Of these, if his Grace of Bedford would please to accept advice from the man in the moon, it should be to put himself into this engine as a sovereign cure to the known disease called the thoughtless evil.

But above all, it is an excellent remedy and very useful to a sort of people who are always travelling in thought but never delivered into action; who are so exceeding busy at thinking, they have no leisure for action; of whom the late poet sung well to the purpose :—

> ". . . Some modern coxcombs, who
> Retire to think, 'cause they have nought to do ;
> For thoughts were given for action's government :
> Where action ceases, thought's impertinent.

The sphere of action is life's happiness,
And he that thinks beyond, thinks like an ass. "
—ROCHEST., *Poems*, p. 9.

These gentlemen would make excellent use of this engine, for it would teach them to dispatch one thing before they begin another, and therefore is of singular use to honest S——, whose peculiarity it was to be always beginning projects but never finish any.

The variety of this engine, its uses and improvements, are innumerable, and the reader must not expect I can give anything like a perfect description of it.

There is yet another sort of machine, which I never obtained a sight of till the last voyage I made to this Lunar orb, and these are called Elevators. The mechanic operations of these are wonderful, and helped by fire, by which the senses are raised to all the strange extremes we can imagine, and whereby the intelligent soul is made to converse with its own species, whether embodied or not.

Those that are raised to a due pitch in this wondrous frame have a clear prospect into the world of spirits, and converse with visions, guardian angels, spirits departed, and what not. And as this is a wonderful knowledge, and not to be obtained but by the help of this fire, so those that have tried the experiment give strange accounts of sympathy, pre-existence of souls, dreams, and the like.

I confess I always believed a converse of spirits, and have heard of some who have experienced so much of it, as they could obtain upon nobody else to believe.

I never saw any reason to doubt the existent state of the spirit before embodied, any more than I did of its immortality after it shall be uncased, and the Scriptures saying the spirit returns to God that gave it, implies a coming from, or how could it be called a return ?

Nor can I see a reason why embodying a spirit should altogether interrupt its converse with the world of spirits from whence it was taken ; and to what else shall we ascribe guardian angels, in which the Scripture is also plain? And from whence come secret notices, impulse of thought, pressing urgencies of inclination to or from this or that, altogether involuntary, but from some waking kind assistant wandering spirit, which gives secret hints to its fellow-creatures of some approaching evil or good which it was not able to foresee.

"For spirits without the helps of voice converse."

I know we have supplied much of this with enthusiasm and conceited revelation; but the people of this world convince us that it may be all natural by obtaining it in a mechanic way, viz., by forming something suitable to the sublime nature, which, working by art, shall only rectify the more vigorous particles of the soul, and work it up to a suitable elevation. This engine is wholly applied to the head, and works by injection, the chief influence being on what we call fancy or imagination which, by the heat of strong ideas, is fermented to a strange height, and is thus brought to see backward and forward every way beyond itself. By this a man fancies himself in the moon, and realises things there as distinctly as if he were actually talking to my old philosopher.

This indeed is an admirable engine. It is composed of a hundred thousand rational consequences, five times the number of conjectures, supposes, and probabilities, besides an innumerable company of fluttering suggestions and injections, which hover round the imagination, and are all taken in as fast as they can be concocted and digested there. These are formed into ideas, and some of these so well put together, so exactly shaped, so well dressed, and set out by the additional fire of fancy, that it is no uncommon thing for the person to be entirely deceived by himself, not knowing the brat of his own begetting, nor be able to distinguish between reality and representation. From hence we have some people talking to images of their own forming, and seeing more devils and spectres than ever appeared. From hence we have weaker heads, not able to bear the operation, seeing imperfect visions, as of horses and men without heads or arms, light without fire, hearing voices without sound, and noises without shapes, as their own fears or fancies broke the phenomena before the entire formation.

But the more genuine and perfect use of these vast elevations of the fancy, which are performed, as I said, by the mechanic operation of innate fire, is to guide mankind to as much foresight of things as, either by nature or by the aid of anything extra-natural, may be obtained; and by this exceeding knowledge a man shall forebode to himself approaching evil or good, so as to avoid this or be in the way of that. And what if I should say that the notices of these things are not only frequent, but constant, and require nothing of us but to make use of this elevator to keep our eyes, our ears, and our fancies open to the hints, and observe them?

You may suppose me, if you please, come by this time into those northern kingdoms I mentioned before, where my old philosopher was a native; and not to trouble you with any of the needful observations, learned inscriptions, &c., on the way, according to the laudable practices of the famous Mr. Bromly, it is sufficient to tell you I found there an opulent, populous, potent, and terrible people.

I found them at war with one of the greatest monarchs of the Lunar world, and at the same time miserably rent and torn, mangled and disordered, among themselves.

As soon as I observed the political posture of their affairs (for here a man sees things mighty soon by the help of such a masterly eyesight as I have mentioned), and remembering what is said for our instruction, "That a kingdom divided against itself cannot stand," I asked the old gentleman if he had any estate in that country. He told me, "No great matter," but asked me why I put that question to him. "Because," said I, "if this people go on fighting and snarling at all the world and one among another in this manner, they will certainly be ruined and undone, either subdued by some more powerful neighbour, whilst one party will stand still and see the other's throat cut, though their own turn immediately follows, or else they will destroy and devour one another." Therefore I told him I would have him turn his estate into money, and go somewhere else, or go back to the other world with me.

"No, no," replied the old man; "I am in no such fear at this time. The scale of affairs is very lately changed here," says he, "in but a very few years."

"I know nothing of that," said I, "but I am sure there never was but one spot of ground in that world which I came from that was divided like them, and that is that very country I lived in. Here are three kingdoms of you in one spot," said I; "one has already been conquered and subdued, the other suppressed its native inhabitants, and planted it with her own, and now carries it with so high a hand over them of her own breed, that she limits their trade, stops their ports. When the inhabitants have made their manufactures, these won't give them leave to send them abroad, impose laws upon them, refuse to alter and amend those they would make for themselves, make them pay customs, excises, and taxes, and yet pay the garrisons and guards that defend them themselves; press their inhabitants to their fleets, and carry away their old veteran troops that should defend them, and leave them to raise more to be served in the same manner; will let none of their money be carried over thither, nor let them coin any of their own; and a great many such hardships they suffer under the hand of this nation as mere slaves and conquered people, though the greatest part of the traders are the people of the very nation that treats them thus."

On the other hand, this creates eternal murmurs, heart-burnings, and regret, both in the natives and the transplanted inhabitants; the first have shown their uneasiness by frequent insurrections and rebellions, for nature prompts the meanest animal to struggle for liberty; and these struggles have often been attended with great cruelty, ravages, death, massacres, and ruin, both of families and the country itself. As to the transplanted inhabitants, they run into clandestine trade, into corresponding with their master's enemies, victualling their navies, colonies, and the like, receiving and importing their goods in spite of all the orders and directions to the contrary.

These are the effects of divisions and feuds on that side ; on the other hand, there is a kingdom, entire, unconquered, and independent, and for the present under the same monarch with the rest. But here their feuds are greater than with the other, and more dangerous by far, because national. This kingdom joins to the north part of the first kingdom, and terrible divisions lie among the two nations.

The people of these two kingdoms are called, if you please, for distinction sake, for I cannot well make you understand their hard names, *Solunarians* and *Nolunarians*, these to the south, and those to the north. The *Solunarians* were divided in their articles of religion ; the governing party, or the Established Church, I shall call the *Solunarian* Church ; but the whole kingdom was full of a sort of religious people called *Crolians*, who, like our Dissenters in England, profess divers subdivided opinions by themselves, and could not, or would not, let it go which way it will, join with the Established Church.

On the other hand, the Established Church in the northern kingdom was all *Crolians*, but full of *Solunarians* in opinions, who were Dissenters there, as the *Crolians* were Dissenters in the south ; and this unhappy mixture occasioned endless feuds, divisions, subdivisions, and animosities without number, of which hereafter.

The northern men are bold, terrible, numerous, and brave to the last degree, but poor, and by the encroachments of their neighbours growing poorer every day.

The southern are equally brave, more numerous and terrible, but wealthy, and care not for wars ; had rather stay at home and quarrel with one another than go abroad to fight, making good an old maxim, " Too poor to agree, and yet too rich to fight."

Between these the feud is great, and every day growing greater, and those people who pretend to have been in the cogitator or thinking engine tell us all the lines of consequences in that affair point at a fatal period between the kingdoms.

The complaints also are great, and backed with fiery arguments on both sides. The northern men say the *Solunarians*

x

have dealt unjustly and unkindly by them in several articles ; but the southern men reply with a most powerful argument, viz., they are poor, and therefore ought to be oppressed, suppressed, or anything.

But the main debate is like to lie upon the article of choosing a king, both the nations being under one government at present ; but the settlement ending in the reigning line, the northern men refuse to join in government again, unless they have a rectification of some conditions in which they say they have the worst of it.

In this case even the southern men themselves say they believe the *Nolunarians* have been in the chair of reflection, the thinking engine, and that having screwed their understandings into a direct position to that matter before them, they have made a right judgment of their own affairs, and, with all their poverty, stand on the best foot as to right.

But as the matter of the northern quarrel comes under a second head, and is more properly the subject of a second voyage to the moon, the reader may have it more at large considered in another class, and some further enlightenings in that affair than perhaps can be reasonably expected of me here.

But of all the feuds and brangles that ever poor nation was embroiled in, of all the quarrels, the factions, and parties that ever the people of any nation thought worth while to fall out for, none were ever in reality so light, in effect so heavy, in appearance so great, in substance so small, in name so terrible, in nature so trifling, as those for which this southern country was altogether by the ears among themselves.

And this was one reason why I so earnestly inquired of my Lunarian philosopher whether he had an estate in that country or no. But having told him the cause of that inquiry, he replied there was one thing in the nature of his countrymen which secured them from the ruin which usually attended divided nations, viz., that if any foreign nation, thinking to take the advantage of their intestine divisions, fell upon them, in the highest of all their feuds they laid aside their parties and quarrels, and presently fell in together to beat out the common enemy; and then no sooner had they obtained peace abroad by their conduct and bravery, but they would fall to cutting one another's throats again at home, as naturally as if it had been their proper calling, and that for trifles, too—mere trifles.

"Very well," said I to my learned self; "pretty like my own country still, that whatever peace they have abroad, are sure to have none at home."

To come at the historical account of these Lunarian dissensions, it will be absolutely necessary to enter a little into the story of the place, at least as far as relates to the present constitution, both of the people, the government, and the subject of their present quarrels.

And first, we are to understand that there has for some ages been carried on in these countries a private feud or quarrel among the people about a thing called by them *Upogyla*, with us very vulgarly called Religion.

This difference, as in its original it was not great, nor indeed upon points accounted among themselves essential, so it had never been a difference of any height, if there had not always been some one thing or other happening in the state which made the court politicians think it necessary to keep the people busy and embroiled, to prevent their more narrow inspection into depredations and encroachments on their liberties, which was always making on them by the court.

It is not denied but there might be a native want of charity in the inhabitants, adapting them to feud, and particularly qualifying them to be always piquing one another; and some of their own nation, who, by the help of the famous perspectives before mentioned, pretend to have seen farther into the insides of Nature and constitution than other people, tell us the cross-lines of Nature which appear in the make of those particular people signify a direct negative as to the article of charity and good neighbourhood.

It was particularly unhappy to this wrangling people that reasons of state should always fall in to make that uncharitableness and continual quarrelling humour necessary to carry on the public affairs of the nation, and may pass for a certain proof that the state was under some diseases and convulsions, which, like a body that digests nothing so well as what is hurtful to its constitution, makes use of those things for its support which are in their very nature fatal to its being, and must at last tend to its destruction.

But as this, however, inclined them to be continually snarling at one another, so as in all quarrels it generally appears one side must go down, the prevailing party, therefore, always kept the power in their hands, and as the under were always subject to the lash, they soon took care to hook their quarrel into the affairs of state and so join religious differences and civil differ-ences together.

These things had long embroiled the nation, and frequently involved them in bitter enmities, feuds, and quarrels, and once in a tedious, ruinous, and bloody war in their own bowels, in which, contrary to all expectation, this lesser party prevailed.

And since the allegoric relation may bear great similitude with our European affairs on this side the moon, I shall, for the ease of expression and the better understanding of the reader, frequently call them by the same names our unhappy parties are called by in England, as *Solunarian* Churchmen and *Crolian* Dissenters, at the same time desiring my reader to observe that he is always to remember who it is we are talking of, and that he is by no means to understand me of any person, party, people, nation, or place on this side the moon, any expression, circumstance, similitude, or appearance to the contrary in any wise notwith-standing.

This premised, I am to tell the reader that the last civil war in this Lunar country ended in the victors confounding their own conquests by their intestine broils, they being, as is already noticed, a most eternally quarrelling nation. Upon this new breach, they that first began the war turned about, and pleading that they took up arms to regulate the government, not to over-throw it, fell in with the family of their kings, who had been banished and one of them destroyed, and restored the crown to the family and the nation to the crown, just for all the world as the Presbyterians in England did in the case of King Charles the Second.

The party that was thus restored accepted the return the others made to their duty, and their assistance in restoring the family of their monarch, but abated not a tittle of the old rancour against them as a party, which they entertained at their first taking arms, not allowing the return they had made to be any atonement at all for the crimes they had been guilty of before. It is true they passed an Act or grant of general pardon and oblivion, as in all such cases is usual, and as without which the other would never have come in, or have joined powers to form the restoration they were bringing to pass ; but the old feud of religion continued with this addition, that the Dissenters were rebels, murderers, king-killers, enemies to monarchy and civil government, lovers of confusion, popular anarchical governments, and movers of sedition ; that this was in their very nature and principles, and the like.

In this condition, and under these mortifications, this party of people lived just an Egyptian servitude, viz., of forty years, in which time they were frequently vexed with persecution, harassed, plundered, fined, imprisoned, and very hardly treated, insomuch that they pretend to be able to give an account of vast sums of their country's money, levied upon them on these occasions, amounting, as I take it, to two millions of *lunatians*, a coin they keep their accounts by there, and much about the value of our pound sterling ; besides this, they were hooked into a great many sham plots, and sworn out of their lives and estates in such a manner, that in the very next reign the Government was so sensible of their hard treatment that they reversed several sentences by the same authority that had executed them—a most undeniable proof they were ashamed of what had been done. At last, the prince who was restored as above said died, and his brother mounted the throne ; and now began a third scene of affairs, for this prince was neither Churchman nor Dissenter, but of a different religion from them all, known in that country by the name of *Abrogratzianism ;* and this religion of his had this one absolutely necessary consequence in it, that a man could not be sincerely and heartily of this, but he must be an implacable hater of both the other. As this is laid down as a previous supposition, we are with the same reason to imagine this prince to be entirely bent upon the suppression and destruction of both the other, if not absolutely as to life and estate, yet entirely as to religion.

To bring this the more readily to pass like a true politician, had his methods and particulars been equally politic with his generals, he began at the right end, viz., to make the breach between the Solunarian Church and the Crolian Dissenters as wide as possible, and to do this it was resolved to shift sides; and as the crown had always took part with the Church, crushed, humbled, persecuted, and by all means possible mortified the Dissenters, as is noted in the reign of his predecessor, this prince resolved to caress, cherish, and encourage the Crolians by all possible arts and outward endearments; not so much that he purposed them any real favour, for the destruction of both was equally determined, nor so much that he expected to draw them over to *Abrogratzianism*, but two reasons may be supposed to give rise to this project.

1. The Lunarian Church party had all along preached up for a part of their religion that absolute undisputed obedience was due from every subject to their prince, without any reserve, reluctance, or repining; that as to resistance, it was fatal to body, soul, religion, justice, and government; and though the doctrine was repugnant to Nature, and to the very supreme command itself, yet he that resisted received to himself damnation, just for all the world like our doctrine of passive obedience. Now, though these Solunarian Churchmen did not absolutely believe all they said themselves to be true, yet they found it necessary to push these things to the uttermost extremities, because they might the better fix upon the Crolian Dissenters the charge of professing less loyal principles than they. For as to the Crolians, they professed openly they would pay obedience to the prince as far as the laws directed, but no further.

These things were run up to strange heights, and the people

were always falling out about what they would do or would not do if things were so or so, as they were not, and were never likely to be; and the hot men on both sides were every now and then going together by the ears about chimeras, shadows, maybe's and supposes.

The hot men of the Solunarian Church were for knocking the Crolians on the head, because, as they said, they were rebels, their fathers were rebels, and they would certainly turn rebels again upon occasion.

The Crolians insisted upon it that they had nothing to do with what was done before they were born; that if they were criminal because their fathers were so, then a great many who were now of the Solunarian Church were as guilty as they, several of the best members of that Church having been born of Crolian parents.

In the matter of loyalty they insisted upon it they were as loyal as the Solunarians, for that they were as loyal as Nature, reason, and the laws both of God and man required, and what the other talked of more was but a mere pretence, and so it would be found if ever their prince should have occasion to put them to the trial; that he that pretended to go beyond the power of Nature and reason must indeed go beyond them, and they never desired to be brought into the extreme, but they were ready at any time to show such proofs and give such demonstrations of their loyalty as would satisfy any reasonable prince, and for more they had nothing to say.

In this posture of affairs this new prince found his subjects when he came to the crown. The Solunarian Church caressed him, and notwithstanding his being devoted to the Abrogratzian faith, they crowned him with extraordinary acclamations.

They were the rather inclined to push this forward by how much they thought it would singularly mortify the Crolians and all the sorts of Dissenters, for they had all along declared their abhorrence of the Abrogratzians, to such a degree that they publicly endeavoured to have got a general concurrence of the whole nation in the public Cortes or Diet of the kingdom to have joined with them in excluding this very prince by name, and all other princes that should ever embrace the Abrogratzian faith.

And it wanted but a very little of bringing it to pass; for almost all the great men of the nation, though Solunarians, yet that were men of temper, moderation, and foresight, were for this exclusive law. But the high-priests and patriarchs of the Solunarian Church prevented it, and, upon pretence of this passive-obedience principle, made their interest and gave their voices for crowning or entailing the crown and government on the head of one of the most implacable enemies both to their religion and civil right that ever the nation saw; but they lived to repent it too late.

This conquest over the Crolians and the moderate Solunarians, if it did not suppress them entirely, it yet gave the other party such an ascendant over them, that they made no doubt, when that prince came to the crown, they had done so much to oblige him that he could deny them nothing, and therefore in expectation they swallowed up the whole body of the Crolians at once, and began to talk of nothing less than banishing them to the northern part of the country, or to certain islands and countries a vast way off, where formerly great numbers of them had fled for shelter in like cases.

And this was the more probable as by an unhappy stroke these Crolians attempted to strike, but miscarried in, at the very beginning of this prince's reign; for as they had always professed an aversion to this prince on account of his religion, as soon as their other king was dead they set up one of his natural sons against this king, which the Solunarians had so joyfully crowned. This young prince invaded his dominions, and great numbers of the most zealous Crolians joined him. But to cut the story short, he was entirely routed by the forces of the new prince, for all the Solunarian Church joined with him against the Crolians without any respect to the interest of religion; so they overthrew their brethren! The young invading prince was taken and put to death openly, and great cruelties were exercised in cold blood upon the poor unhappy people that were taken in the defeat.[1]

---

[1] After the defeat of Monmouth at Sedgmoor.

Thus a second time these loyal Solunarian Churchmen established their enemy, and built up what they were glad afterwards to pull down again, and to beg the assistance of those very Crolians, whom they had so rudely handled, to help them demolish the power they had erected themselves, and which now began to set its foot upon the throat of those that nourished and supported it.

Upon this exceeding loyalty and blind assistance given to their prince, the Solunarians made no question but they had so eternally bound him to them that it would be in their power to pull down the very name of Crolianism and utterly destroy it from the nation.

But the time came on to undeceive them, for this prince, whose principle as an Abrogratzian was to destroy them both, as it happened, was furnished with counsellors and ecclesiastics of his own profession ten thousands times more bent for their general ruin than himself.

For, abstracted from the venom and rancour of his profession as an Abrogratzian, and from the furious zeal of his Bramin priests, and religious people, that continually hung about him, and that prompted him to act against his temper and inclination, by which he ruined all, he was else a forward and generous prince, and likely to have made his people great and flourishing.

But his furious Churchmen ruined all his good designs, and turned all his projects to compass the introduction of his own religion into his dominions.

Nay, and had he not fatally been pushed on by such as really designed his ruin to drive this deep design on too hastily, and turn the scale of his management from a close and concealed to an open and professed design, he might have gone a great way with it. Had he been content to have let that have been twenty year a doing which he impatiently as well as preposterously attempted all at once, wise men have thought he might in time have suppressed the Solunarian religion, and have set up his own.

To give a short scheme of his proceedings, and with them of the reason of his miscarriage.

1. Having defeated the rebellious Crolians, as is before noted, and reflecting on the danger he was in upon the sudden progress of that rebellion ; for indeed he was within a trifle of ruin in that affair ; and had not the Crolians been deceived by the darkness of the night and led to a large ditch of water, which they could not pass over, they had certainly surprised and overthrown his army, and cut them in pieces before they had known who had hurt them. Upon the sense of this danger he takes up a pretence of necessity for the being always ready to resist the factious Crolians, as he called them, and by that insinuation hooks himself into a standing army in time of peace. Nay, and so easy were the Solunarian Church to yield up any point which they did but imagine would help to crush their brethren the Crolians, that they not only consented to this unusual invasion of their ancient liberties, but sent up several testimonials of their free consent ; nay, and of their joy of having arrived to so great a happiness as to have a prince that, setting aside the formality of laws, would vouchsafe to govern them by the glorious method of a standing army.

These testimonials were things not much unlike our addresses in England, and which when I heard, I could not but remember our case in the time of the late King James, when the city of Carlisle in their address thanked His Majesty for the establishing a standing army in England in time of peace, calling it the strength and glory of the kingdom.

So strong is the ambition and envy of parties, these Solunarian gentlemen not grudging to put out one of their own eyes, so they might at the same time put out both the eyes of their enemies ; the Crolians rather consented to this badge of their own slavery, and brought themselves, who were a free people before, under the power and slavery of the sword.

The ease with which this prince got over so considerable a point as this made him begin to be too credulous, and to persuade himself that the Solunarian Churchmen were really in earnest as to their pageant doctrine of non-resistance, and that as he had seen them bear with strange extravagances on the Crolian part they were real and in earnest when they preached that men ought to obey for conscience's sake whatever hardships were imposed upon them, and however unjust or contrary to the laws of God, Nature, reason, or their country. What principle in the world could more readily prompt a prince to attempt what he so earnestly coveted as this zealous prince did the restoring the Abrogratzian faith? for since he had but two sorts of people to do with, one he had crushed by force, and had brought the other to profess it their religion, their duty, and their resolution to bear everything he thought fit to impose upon them, and that they should be damned if they resisted, the work seemed half done to his hand.

And, indeed, when I reflected on the coherence of things, I could not so much blame this prince for his venturing upon the probability. For whoever was but to go up to this Lunar world and read the stories of that time, with what fury the hot men of the Solunarian Church acted against the Dissenting Crolians, and with what warmth they assisted their prince against them, and how cruelly they insulted them after they were defeated in their attempt of dethroning him, how zealously they preached up the doctrine of absolute undisputed resignation to his will, how frequently they obeyed several of his encroachments upon their liberties, and what solemn protestations they made to submit to him in any-thing, and to stand by and assist him in whatever he commanded them to the last drop, much with the same zeal and forwardness as our life-and-fortune men did here in England; I say, when all this was considered, I could not so much condemn his credulity, nor blame him for believing them, for no man could have doubted their sincerity but he that at the same time must have taxed them with most unexampled hypocrisy.

For the Solunarians now began to discern their prince was not really on their side, that neither in state matters any more than religion he had any affection for them, and the first absolute shock he gave them was in publishing a general liberty to the Crolians.[1] It is true this was not out of respect to the Crolian

---

[1] James the Second's Declaration of Indulgence.

religion any more than the Solunarian, but purely because by that means he made way for an introduction of the Abrogratzian religion, which now began to appear publicly in the country.

But however, as this was directly contrary to the expectation of the Solunarians, it gave them such a disgust against their prince, that from that very time, being disappointed in the sovereign authority they expected, they entered into the deepest and blackest conspiracy against their prince and his government that ever was heard of.

Many of the Crolians were deluded by the new favour and liberty they received from the prince to believe him real, and were glad of the mortification of their brethren; but the more judicious, seeing plainly the prince's design, declared against their own liberty, because given them by an illegal authority without the assent of the whole body legally assembled.

When the Solunarians saw this, they easily reconciled themselves to the Crolians, at least from the outside of the face, for the carrying on their design; and so here was a nation full of plots; here was the prince and his Abrogratzians plotting to introduce their religion; here was a parcel of blind, short-sighted Crolians plotting to ruin the Solunarian Establishment, and weakly joining with the Abrogratzians to satisfy their private resentments; and here were the wiser Crolians joining heartily with the Solunarians of all sorts, laying aside private resentments and forgetting old grudges about religion, in order to ruin the invading projects of the prince and his party.

There were indeed some verbal conditions passed between them; and the Solunarians, willing to bring them into their party, promised them, upon the faith of their nation and the honour of the Solunarian religion, that there should be no more hatred, disturbance, or persecution for the sake of religion between them, but that they would come to a temper with them, and always be brethren for the future. They declared that persecution was contrary to their religion in general, and to their doctrine in particular, and backed their allegations with some truths they have not since thought fit to like, nor much to regard.

However, by this artifice and on these conditions they brought the Crolians to join with them in their resolutions to countermine their designing prince. These, indeed, were for doing it by the old way downright, and to oppose oppression with force, a doctrine they acknowledged, and professed to join with all the Lunar part of mankind in the practice, and began to tell their brethren how they had imposed upon themselves and the world in pretending to absolute submission against Nature and universal Lunarian practice.

But a cunning fellow personating a Solunarian, and who was in the plot, gravely answered them thus : " Look ye, gentlemen, we own with you that Nature, reason, law, justice, and custom of nations is on your side, and that all power derives from, centres in, and on all recesses or demises of power returns to its great original, the party governed. Nay, we own our Great Eye, from whom all the habitable parts of this globe are enlightened, has always directed us to practise what Nature thus dictates, always approved and generally succeeded the attempt of dethroning tyrants. But our case differs, we have always pretended to this absolute undisputed obedience, which we did indeed to gain the power of your party ; and if we should turn round at once to your opinion, though never so right, we should so fly in the face of our own doctrine, sermons, innumerable pamphlets, and pretensions, as would give all our enemies too great a power over us in argument, and we should never be able to look mankind in the face. But we have laid our measures so, that by prompting the King to run upon us in all sorts of barefaced extremes and violences, we shall bring him to exasperate the whole nation ; then we may underhand foment the breach on this side, raise the mob upon him, and by acting on both sides seem to suffer a force in falling in with the people, and preserve our reputation. Thus we shall bring the thing to pass, betray our prince, take arms against his power, call in foreign force to do the work, and even then keep our hands seemingly out of the broil by being pretended sticklers for our former prince, so save our reputation, and bring all to pass with ease and calmness, while the eager party of the Abrogratzians will do their own work by expecting we will do it for them."

The Crolians, astonished both at the policy, the depth, the knavery, and the hypocrisy of the design, left them to carry it on, owning it was a masterpiece of craft, and so stood still to observe the issue, which every way answered the exactness of its contrivance.

When I saw into the bottom of all this deceit, I began to take up new resolutions of returning back into our old world again, and going home to England, where, though I had conceived great indignation at the treatment our passive-obedience-men gave their prince here, and was in hopes in these, my remote travels, to have found out some nations of honour and principles, I was filled with amazement to see our moderate knaves so much outdone, and I was informed that all these things were mere amusements, vizors, and shams, to bring an innocent prince into the snare.

Would any mortal imagine who has read this short part of the story that all this was a Solunarian Church plot, a mere conspiracy between these gentlemen and the Crolian Dissenters, only to wheedle in the unhappy prince to his own destruction and bring the popular advantage of the mob to a greater ascendant on the crown?

Of all the Richelieus, Mazarines, Gondamours, Oliver Cromwells, and the whole train of politicians that our world has produced, the greatest of their arts are follies to the unfathomable depth of these Lunarian policies; and for wheedle, lying, swearing, preaching, printing, &c., what is said in our world by priests and politicians, we thank God may be believed; but if ever I believe a Solunarian priest preaching non-resistance of monarchs, or a Solunarian politician turning Abrogratzian, I ought to be marked down for a fool; nor will ever any prince in that country take their word again, if ever they have their senses about them. But as this is a most extraordinary scene, so I cannot omit a more particular and sufficient relation of some parts of it than I used to give.

The Solunarian clergy had carried on their non-resistance doctrine to such extremities, and had given this new prince such unusual demonstrations of it, that he fell absolutely into the snare and entirely believed them. He had tried them with such impositions as they would never have borne from any prince in the world, nor from him neither, had they not had a deep design, and consequently stood in need of the deepest disguise imaginable. They had yielded to a standing army, and applauded it as a thing they had desired; they had submitted to levying taxes upon them by new methods and illegal practices; they had yielded to the abrogation or suspension at least of their laws when the king's absolute will required it; not that they were blind, and did not see what their prince was doing, but that the black design was so deeply laid, they found it was the only way to ruin him to push him upon the highest extremes, and then they should have their turn served. Thus, if he desired one illegal thing of them, they would immediately grant two. One would have thought they had read our Bible and the command, when a man takes away the cloak to give him the coat also.

Nor was this enough, but they seemed willing to admit of the public exercise of the Abrogratzian religion in all parts; and when the prince set it up in his own chapel, they suffered it to be set up in their cities and towns, and the Abrogratzian clergy began to be seen up and down in their very habits, a thing which had never been permitted before in that country, and which the common people began to be very uneasy at. But still the Solunarian clergy, and all such of the gentry especially as were in the plot, by their sermons, printed books, and public discourses, carried on this high-topping notion of absolute submission, so that the people were kept under and began to submit to all the impositions of the prince.

These things were so acted to the life, that not only the prince, but none of his Abrogratzian counsellors could see the snare; the hook was so finely covered by the Church artificers, and the bait so delicious, that they all swallowed it with eagerness and delight.

But the conspirators, willing to make a sure game of it, and not thinking the king or all his counsellors would drive on so fast as they would have them, though they had already made fair progress for the time, resolved to play home, and accordingly they persuaded their prince that they would not only submit to his arbitrary will in matters of state and government, but in matters of religion; and in order to carry this jest on, one of the heads of their politics, and a person of great esteem for his abilities in matters of state, being without question one of the ablest heads of all the Solunarian nobility,[1] pretended to be converted and turned Abrogratzian. This immediately took as they desired, for the prince caressed him and entertained him with all possible endearments, preferred him to several posts of honour and advantage, always kept him near him, consulted him in all emergencies, took him with him to the Abrogian sacrifices, and he made no scruple publicly to appear there, and by these degrees and a super-Achitophelian hypocrisy, so insinuated himself into the credulous prince's favour, that he became his only confidant, and absolute master of all his designs.

Now the plot had its desired effect, for he pushed the king upon all manner of precipitations; and if even the Abrogratzians themselves who were about the king interposed for more temperate proceedings, he would call them cowards, strangers, ignorant of the temper of the Lunarians, who, when they were a-going, might be driven; but if they were suffered to cool and consider would face about and fall off.

Indeed, the men of prudence and estates among his own party —I mean the Abrogratzians in the country—frequently warned him to take more moderate measures and to proceed with more caution; told him he would certainly ruin them all and himself, and that there must be somebody about His Majesty that pushed him upon these extremes on purpose to set all the nation in a flame and to overthrow all the good designs which, with temper and good conduct, might be brought to perfection.

Had these wary counsels been observed and a prudence and

---

[1] The second Earl of Sunderland pleased James II. by becoming Roman Catholic.

policy agreeable to the mighty consequence of things been practised, the Solunarian Church had run a great risk of being overthrown and to have sunk gradually in the Abrogian errors, the
people began to be drawn off gradually, and the familiarity of the
thing made it appear less frightful to unthinking people who had
entertained strange notions of the monstrous things that were to
be seen in it, so that common vogue had filled the people's minds
with ignorant aversions, that it is no absurdity to say I believe
there were 200,000 people who would have spent the last drop of
their blood against Abrogratzianism that did not know whether it
was a man or a horse.

This thing considered well, would of itself have been sufficient
to have made the prince and his friends wary, and to have taught
them to suit their measures to the nature and circumstances of
things before them; but success in their beginnings blinded their
eyes, and they fell into this Church snare with the most unpitied
willingness that could be imagined.

The first thing, therefore, this new counsellor put his master
upon, in order to the beginning his more certain ruin, was to
introduce several of his Abrogratzians into places of all kinds,
both in the army, navy, treasure, and civil affairs, though contrary to some of the general constitutions of government; he
had done it into the army before, though it had disgusted several
of his military men, but now he pushed him upon making it
universal, and still the passive Solunarians bore it with patience.

From this tameness and submission his next step was to argue
that he might depend upon it the Solunarian Church had so
sincerely embraced the doctrine of non-resistance, that they
were now ripened not only to sit still and see their brethren
the Crolians suppressed, but to stand still and be oppressed
themselves, and he might assure himself the matter was now ripe;
he might do just what he would himself with them; they were
prepared to bear anything.

This was the fatal stroke; for having possessed the prince with
the belief of this, he let loose the reins to all his long-concealed
desires. Down went their laws, their liberties, their corporations,

their churches, their colleges; all went to wreck, and the eager Abrogratzians thought the day their own. The Solunarians made no opposition, but what was contained within the narrow circumference of petitions, addresses, prayers, and tears; and these the prince was prepared to reject, and upon all occasions to let them know he was resolved to be obeyed.

Thus he drove on by the treacherous advice of his new counsels, till he ripened all the nation for the general defection which afterwards followed.

For as the encroachments of the prince pushed especially at their Church liberties, and threatened the overthrow of all their ecclesiastical privileges, the clergy no sooner began to feel that they were like to be the first sacrifice, but they immediately threw off the vizor and beat the *concionazimir.* This is a certain ecclesiastic engine, which is usual in cases of general alarm, as the Church's signal for universal tumult.

This is truly a strange engine, and when a clergyman gets into the inside of it and beats it, it roars and makes such a terrible noise from the several cavities, that it is heard a long way; and there are always a competent number of them placed in all parts so conveniently that the alarm is heard all over the kingdom in one day.

I had some thoughts to have given the reader a diagram of this piece of art, but as I am but a bad draftsman, I have not yet been able so exactly to describe it as that a scheme can be drawn, but to the best of my skill take it as follows:—It is a hollow vessel, large enough to hold the biggest clergyman in the nation; it is generally an octagon in figure, open before, from the waist upward, but whole at the back, with a flat extending over it for reverberation or doubling the sound; doubling and redoubling being frequently thought necessary to be made use of on these occasions. It is very mathematically contrived, erected on a pedestal of wood like a windmill, and has a pair of winding stairs up to it, like those at the great tun at Heidelberg.

I could make some hieroglyphic discourses upon it from these references, thus: 1. That as it is erected on a pedestal like a windmill, so it is no new thing for the clergy, who are the only persons permitted to make use of it, to make it turn round with the wind, and serve to all the points of the compass. 2. As the flat over it assists to increase the sound by forming a kind of hollow or cavity proper to that purpose, so there is a certain natural hollowness or emptiness, made use of sometimes in it by the gentlemen of the gown, which serves exceedingly to the propagation of all sorts of clamour, noise, railing, and disturbance. 3. As the stairs to it go winding up like those by which one mounts to the vast tun of wine at Heidelberg, which has no equal in our world, so the use made of these ascending steps is not altogether different, being frequently employed to raise people up to all sorts of enthusiasms, spiritual intoxications, mad and extravagant action, high exalted flights, precipitations, and all kinds of ecclesiastic drunkenness and excesses.

The sound of this emblem of emptiness, the *concionazimir*, was no sooner heard over the nation, but all the people discovered their readiness to join in with the summons; and as the thing had been concerted before, they sent over their messengers to demand assistance from a powerful prince beyond the sea, one of their own religion, and who was allied by marriage to the crown.[1]

They made their story out so plain, and their king had by the contrivance of their Achitophel rendered himself so suspected to all his neighbours, that this prince, without any hesitation, resolved to join with them, and accordingly makes vast preparations to invade their king.

During this interval their behaviour was quite altered at home, the doctrine of absolute submission and non-resistance was heard no more among them, the *concionazimir* beat daily to tell all the people they should stand up to defend the rights of the Church, and that it was time to look about them for the Abrogratzians were upon them. The eager clergy made this ecclesiastic engine sound as loud and make all the noise they could, and no men in the nation were so forward as they to acknowledge that it was a state

---

[1] William of Orange had married, on the 4th of November 1677, Mary, the elder daughter of James II., then Duke of York. Her younger sister, afterwards Queen Anne, was married to Prince George, the brother of the King of Denmark.

trick; and they were drawn in to make such a stir about the pretended doctrines of absolute submission, that they did not see the snare which lay under it; that now their eyes were opened, and they had learned to see the power and superiority of natural right, and would be deceived no longer. Others were so honest to tell the truth, that they knew the emptiness and weakness of the pretence all along, and knew what they did when they preached it up viz., to suppress and pull down the Crolians. But they thought their prince, whom they always served in crying up that doctrine, and whose exclusion was prevented by it, would have had more gratitude, or at least more sense, than to try the experiment upon them, since whatever, to serve his designs and their own, which they always though well united, they were willing to pretend, he could not but see they always knew better than to suffer the practice of it in their own case. That since he had turned tne tables upon them, it is true he had them at an advantage, and might pretend they were knaves, and perhaps had an opportunity to call them so with some reason; but they were resolved, since he had drove them to the necessity of being one or the other, though he might call them knaves, they would take care he should have no reason to call them fools too.

Thus the vapour of absolute subjection was lost on a sudden, and as if it had been preparatory to what was coming after, the experiment was quickly made; for the king pursuing his encroachments upon the Church, and being possessed with a belief that, pursuant to their open professions, they would submit to anything, he made a beginning with them in sending his positive command to one of his superintendent priests or patriarchs to forbid a certain ecclesiastic to officiate any more till his royal pleasure was known.

Now it happened very unluckily that this patriarch,[1] though none of the most learned of his fraternity, yet had always been a mighty zealous promoter of this blind doctrine of non-resistance, and had not a little triumphed over and nsulted the Crolian Dissenters upon the notion of rebellion, anti-monarchical prin-

---

[1] Archbishop Sancroft.

ciples, and obedience, with a reserve for the laws and the like, as a scandalous practice, and comprehensive of faction, sedition, dangerous to the Church and State, and the like.

This reverend father was singled out as the first mark of the king's design. The deluded prince believed he could not but comply, having so publicly professed his being all submission and absolute subjection; but as this was all conceit, he was pushed on to make the assault where he was most certain to meet a repulse, and this gentleman had long since thrown off the mask; so his first order was disobeyed.

The patriarch pretended to make humble remonstrances, and to offer his reasons why he could not in conscience, as he called it, comply. The king, who was now made but a mere engine or machine, screwed up or down by this false counsellor to act his approaching destruction with his own hand, was prompted to resent this repulse with the utmost indignation, to reject all manner of submissions, excuses, or arguments, or anything but an immediate absolute compliance, according to the doctrine so often inculcated, and this he run on so high as to put the patriarch in prison for contumacy.

The patriarch as absolutely refused to submit, and offered himself to the decision of the law.

Now it was always a sacred rule in these Lunar countries that both king and people are bound to stand by the arbitrament of the law in all cases of right or claim, whether public or private; and this has been the reason that all the princes have endeavoured to cover their actions with pretences of law, whatever really has been in their design. For this reason the king could not refuse to bring the patriarch to a trial; where the humour of the people first discovered itself; for here passive obedience was tried and cast; the law proved to be superior to the king, the patriarch was acquitted, his disobedience to the king justified, and the king's command proved unjust.

The applause of the patriarch, the acclamations of the people, and the general rejoicings of the whole nation at this transaction, gave a black prospect to the Abrogratzians, and a great many of them came very honestly and humbly to the king, and told him if he continued to go on by these measures he would ruin them all. They told him what general alarm had been over the whole nation by the clamours of the clergy, and the beating of the *concionazimir* in all parts informed him how the doctrine of absolute obedience was ridiculed in all places, and how the clergy began to preach it back again like a witch's prayer, and that it would infallibly raise the devil of rebellion in all the nation; they besought him to content himself with the liberty of their religion and the freedom they enjoyed of being let into places and offices of trust and honour, and to wait all reasonable occasions to increase their advantages and gradually to gain ground. They entreated him to consider the impossibility of reducing so mighty, so obstinate, and so resolute a nation all at once. They pleaded how rational a thing it was to expect that by degrees and good management which by precipitate measures would be endangered and overthrown.

Had these wholesome counsels taken place in the king's mind, he had been king to his last hour, and the Solunarians and Crolians, too, had been all undone; for he had certainly encroached upon them gradually, and brought that to pass in time which by precipitant measures he was not likely to effect.

It was, therefore, a masterpiece of policy in the Solunarian Churchmen to place a feigned convert near their prince, who should always bias him with contrary advices, puff him up with vast prospects of success, prompt him to all extremes, and always fool him with the certainty of bringing things to pass his own way.

These arts made him set light by the repulse he met with in the matter of the patriarch, and now he proceeded to make two attacks more upon the Church. One was by putting some of his Abrogratzian priests into a college among some of the Solunarian clergy, and the other was to oblige all the Solunarian clergy to read a certain Act of his Council, in which his Majesty admitted all the Abrogratzians, Crolians, and all sorts of Dissenters to a freedom of their religious exercises, sacrifices, exorcisms, dippings, preachings, &c., and to prohibit the Solunarians to molest or disturb them.

Now as this last was a bitter reproach to the Solunarian Church for all the ill-treatment the Dissenting Crolians had received from them, and as it was expressed in the Act that all such treatment was unjust and unchristian, so for them to read it in their temples was to acknowledge that they had been guilty of most unjust and irreligious dealings to the Crolians, and that their prince had taken care to do them justice.

The matter of introducing the Abrogratzians into the colleges or seminaries of the Solunarian priests, was actually against the sacred constitutions and foundation-laws of those seminaries.

Wherefore in both these articles they not only disobeyed their prince, but they opposed him with those trifling things called laws, which they had before declared had no defensive force against their prince. These they had recourse to now, insisted upon the justice and right devolved upon them by the laws, and absolutely refused their compliance with his commands.

The prince, pushed upon the tenters before, received their denial with exceeding resentment, and was heard with deep regret to break out in exclamations at their unexpected faithless proceedings, and sometimes to express himself thus :—" Horrid hypocrisy! Surprising treachery! Is this the absolute subjection which, in such numerous testimonials or addresses, you professed, and for which you so often and so constantly branded the poor Crolians, and told me that your Church was wholly made up of principles of loyalty and obedience? But I will be fully satisfied for this treatment!"

In the minute of one of those excursions of his passion came into his presence the seemingly revolted Lunarian nobleman, and falling in with his present passions, prompts him to a speedy revenge, and proposed his erecting a Court of Searches, something like the Spanish Inquisition, giving them plenipotentiary authority to hear and determine all ecclesiastical causes absolutely and without appeal.

He empowered these judges to place by his absolute will all the

Abrogratzian students in the Solunarian College, and though they might make a formal hearing for the sake of the form, yet that by force it should be done.

He gave them power to displace all those Solunarian clergymen that had refused to read his Act of demission to the Abrogratzian and Crolian Dissenters, and it was thought he designed to keep their revenues *in petto* till he might in time fill them up by some of his own religion.

The Commission accordingly began to act, and discovering a full resolution to fulfil his command, they by force proceeded with the students of the Solunarian College; and it was very remarkable that even some of the Solunarian patriarchs were of this number, who turned out their brethren the Solunarian students to place Abrogratzians in their room.[1]

This indeed they are said to have repented of since, but, however, these it seems were not of the plot, and therefore did not foresee what was at hand.

The rest of the patriarchs, who were all in the grand design, and saw things ripening for its execution, upon the apprehension of this Court of Searches beginning with them, made an humble address to their prince, containing the reasons why they could not comply with his royal command.

The incensed king upbraided them with his having been told by them of their absolute and unreserved obedience, and refusing their submissions or their reasons, sent them all to jail, and resolved to have brought them before his new High Court of Searches, in order, as was believed, to have them all displaced.

And now all began to be in a flame, the solicitations of the Solunarian party having obtained powerful relief abroad, they began to make suitable preparations at home. The gentry and nobility whom the clergy had brought to join with them furnished themselves with horses and arms, and prepared with their tenants and dependants to join the succourers as soon as they should arrive.

---

[1] Parker, Bishop of Oxford, became Roman Catholic, and was forced upon the Fellows of Magdalene College as President.

In short, the foreign troops they had procured arrived, landed, and published a long declaration of all the grievances which they came to redress.

No sooner was this foreign army arrived with the prince at the head of them, but the face of affairs altered on a sudden. The king, indeed, like a brave prince, drew all his forces together, and marching out of his capital city, advanced above 500 stages—things they measure land with in those countries, and much about our furlong—to meet his enemy.

He had a gallant army, well appointed and furnished, and all things much superior to his adversary, but alas! the poison of disobedience was gotten in there, and upon the first march he offered to make towards the enemy, one of his great captains[1] with a strong party of his men went over and revolted.

This example was applauded all over the nation, and by this time one of the patriarchs, even the same mentioned before that had so often preached non-resistance of princes, lays by his sacred vestments, mitre, and staff, and exchanging his robes for a soldier's coat, mounts on horseback, and, in short, appears in arms against his lord. Nor was this all, but the treacherous prelate takes along with him several Solunarian lords, and persons of the highest figure and of the household and family of the king, and with him went the king's own daughter, his principal favourites and friends.

At the news of this, the poor deserted prince lost all courage, and abandoning himself to despair, he causes his army to retreat without fighting a stroke, quits them and the kingdom at once, and takes sanctuary, with such as could escape with him, in the court of a neighbouring prince.

I have heard this prince exceedingly blamed for giving himself up to despair so soon. That he thereby abandoned the best and faithfullest of his friends and servants, and left them to the mercy of the Solunarians; that when all those that would have forsaken him were gone, he had forces equal to his enemies; that

---

[1] Lord Churchill, afterwards Duke of Marlborough, who took with him the Duke of Grafton, Colonel Berkeley, and some troops of dragoons.

his men were in heart, fresh and forward; that he should have stood to the last, retreated to a strong town where his ships rode, and which was over against the territories of his great ally, to whom he might have delivered up the ships that were there, and have thereby made him superior at sea to his enemies, and he was already much superior at land; that there he might have been relieved with forces too strong for them to match, and at least might have put it to the issue of a fair battle. Others, that he might have retreated to his own court and capital city and taken possession of the citadel, which was his own, might so have awed the citizens, who were infinitely rich and numerous, with the apprehensions of having their houses burnt, they would not have dared to have declared for his enemies for fear of being reduced to heaps and ruins; and that at last he might have set the city on fire in five hundred places, and left the Solunarian Churchmen a token to remember their non-resisting doctrine by, and yet have made an easy retreat down the harbour to other forts he had below, and might with ease have destroyed all the shipping as he went.

It is confessed had he done either or both these things, he had left them a dear-bought victory; but he was deprived of his counsellor, for as soon as things came to this height, the Achitophel we have so often mentioned [1] left him also and went away; all his Abrogratzian priests too forsook him, and he was so bereft of counsel that he fell into the hands of his enemies as he was making his escape; but he got away again, not without the connivance of the enemy, who were willing enough he should go; so he got a vessel to carry him over to the neighbouring kingdom, and all his armies, ships, forts, castles, magazines, and treasure, fell into his enemies' hands.

The neighbouring prince entertained him very kindly, cherished him, succoured him, and furnished him with armies and fleets for the recovery of his dominions, which has occasioned a tedious war with that prince, which continues to this day.

Thus far passive doctrines and absolute submission served a

---

[1] The second Earl of Sunderland.

turn, bubbled the prince, wheedled him in to take their word who professed it, until he laid his finger upon the men themselves, and that unravelled all the cheat; they were the first that called in foreign power and took up arms against their prince.

Nor did they end here; but all this scene being over, and the foreign prince having thus delivered them, and their own king being thus chased away, the people called themselves together, and as reason good, having been delivered by him from the miseries, brangles, oppressions, and divisions of the former reign, they thought they could do no less than to crown their deliverer; and having summoned a general assembly of all their capital men, they gave the crown to this prince, who had so generously saved them.[1]

And here again I heard the first king exceedingly blamed for quitting his dominions; for had he stayed here, though he had actually been in their hands, unless they would have murdered him, they could never have proceeded to the extremities they did reach to, nor could they ever have crowned the other prince, he being yet alive and in his own dominions.

But by quitting the country, they fixed a legal period to their obedience, he having deserted their protection and defence, and openly laid down the administration.

But as these sort of politics cannot be decided by us, unless we know the constitutions of those Lunar regions, so we cannot pretend to make a decision of what might or might not have happened.

It remains to examine how those Solunarians behaved themselves who had so earnestly cried up the principles of obedience and absolute submission.

Nothing was so ridiculous, now they saw what they had done; they began to repent, and upon recollection of thoughts, some were so ashamed of themselves that, having broken their doctrine, and being now called upon to transpose their allegiance, truly they stopped in the midway, and so became martyrs on both sides.

[1] William III.

I can liken these to nothing so well as to those gentlemen of our English Church, who, though they broke into the principles of passive obedience by joining and calling over the P. of O., yet suffered deprivations of benefices and loss of their livings for not taking the oath, as if they had not as effectually perjured themselves by taking up arms against their king and joining a foreign power, as they could possibly do afterward by swearing to live quietly under the next king.

But these nice gentlemen are infinitely outdone in these countries, for these Solunarians, by a true Church turn, not only refuse to transpose their allegiance, but pretend to wipe their mouths as to former taking arms, and returning to their old doctrines of absolute submission, boast of martyrdom and boldly reconcile the contraries of taking up arms and non-resistance, charging all their brethren with schism, rebellion, perjury, and the damnable sin of resistance.

Nor is this all; for as a great many of these Solunarian Churchmen had no affection to this new prince, but were not equally furnished or qualified for martyrdom with their brethren, they went to certain wise men, who, being cunning at splitting hairs and making distinctions, might perhaps furnish them with some medium between loyalty and disloyalty. They applied themselves with great diligence to these men, and they by deep study and long search either found or made the quaintest device for them that ever was heard of.

By this unheard-of discovery, to their great joy and satisfaction, they have arrived at a power which all the wise men in our world could never pretend to, and which, it is thought, could the description of it be regularly made and brought down hither, would serve for the satisfaction and repose of a great many tender consciences, who are very uneasy at swearing to save their benefices.

These great masters of distinction have learned to distinguish between active swearing and passive swearing, between *de facto* loyalty and *de jure* loyalty, and by this decent acquirement they obtained the art of reconciling swearing allegiance without loyalty, and loyalty without swearing, so that native and original loyalty may be preserved pure and uninterrupted, in spite of all subsequent oaths to prevailing usurpations.

Many are the mysteries and vast the advantages of this new invented method. Mental reservations, innuendoes, and double meanings are toys to this, for they may be provided for in the literal terms of an oath ; but no provision can be made against this ; for these men, after they have taken the oath, make no scruple to declare they only swear to be quiet as long as they can make no disturbance ; that they are left at liberty still to espouse the interest and cause of their former prince. They nicely distinguish between obedience and submission, and tell you a slave taken into captivity, though he swears to live peaceably, does not thereby renounce his allegiance to his natural prince, nor abridge himself of a right to attempt his own liberty if ever opportunity present.

Had these neat distinctions been found out before, none of the Solunarian clergy—no, not the patriarchs themselves, surely would have stood out and suffered such depredations on their fortunes and characters as they did. They would never have been such fools to have been turned out of their livings for not swearing, when they might have learned here that they might have sworn to one prince and yet have retained their allegiance to another ; might have taken an oath to the new without impeachment of their old oaths to the absent prince. It is great pity these gentlemen had not gone up to the moon for instruction in this difficult case.

There they might have met with excellent logicians, men of most sublime reasons. Dr. Overall, Dr. Sherlock, and all our nice examiners of these things would appear to be nobody to them ; for as the people in these regions have an extraordinary eyesight, and the clearness of the air contributes much to the help of their optics, so they have without doubt a proportioned clearness of discerning, by which they see as far into millstones and all sorts of solids as the nature of things will permit ; but above all, their faculties are blest with two exceeding advantages :—

1. With an extraordinary distinguishing power, by which they can distinguish even indivisibles, part unity itself, divide principles, and distinguish truth into such and so many minute particles, till they dwindle it away into a very nose of wax, and mould it into any form they have occasion for, by which means they can distinguish themselves into or out of any opinion, either in religion, politics, or civil right, that their present emergencies may call for.

2. Their reasoning faculties have this further advantage, that upon occasion they can see clearly for themselves and prevent others from the same discovery, so that when they have occasion to see anything which presents for their own advantage, they can search into the particulars, make it clear to themselves, and yet let it remain dark and mysterious to all the world besides. Whether this is performed by their exceeding penetration or by casting an artificial veil over the understandings of the vulgar, authors have not yet determined, but that the fact is true admits of no dispute.

And the wonderful benefit of these things in point of dispute is extraordinary, for they can see clearly they have the better of an argument when all the rest of the world think they have not a word to say for themselves. It is plain to them that this or that proves a thing when Nature, by common reasoning, knows no such consequences.

I confess I have seen some weak attempts at this extraordinary talent, particularly in the disputes in England between the Church and the Dissenter, and between the High and Low Church, wherein people have tolerably well convinced themselves when nobody else could see anything of the matter, as particularly the famous Mr. [S.] Wesley about the anti-monarchical principles taught in the Dissenters academies; ditto in Lesslie about the Dissenters burning the city and setting fire to their own houses to destroy their neighbours'; and another famous author who proved that Christopher Love lost his head for attempting to pull down monarchy by restoring King Charles the Second.

These indeed are some faint resemblances of what I am upon;

but alas! these are tender sort of people, that have not obtained a complete victory over their consciences, but suffer that trifle to reproach them all the while they are doing it, to rebel against their resolved wills and check them in the middle of the design; from which interruptions arise palpitations of the heart, sickness, and squeamishness of stomach; and these have proceeded to castings and vomit, whereby they have been forced sometimes to throw up some such unhappy truths as have confounded all the rest, and flown in their own faces so violently as in spite of custom has made them blush and look downward; and though in kindness to one another they have carefully licked up one another's filth, yet this unhappy squeamishness of stomach has spoiled all the design and turned the appetites of their party, to the no small prejudice of a cause that stood in need of more art and more face to carry it on as it should be with a thorough-paced case-hardened policy, such as I have been relating, is completely obtained in these regions, where the arts and excellences of sublime reasonings are carried up to all the extraordinaries of banishing scruples, reconciling contradictions, uniting opposites, and all the necessary circumstances required in a complete casuist.

It is not easily conceivable to what extraordinary flights they have carried this strength of reasoning, for besides the distinguish-ing nicely between truth and error, they obtain a most refined method of distinguishing truth itself into seasons and circum-stances, and so can bring anything to be truth when it serves the turn that happens just then to be needful, and make the same thing to be false at another time.

And this method of substantiating matters of fact into truth or falsehood suited to occasion is found admirably useful to the solving the most difficult phenomena of state, for by this art the Solunarian Church made persecution be against their principles at one time, and reducible to practice at another. They made taking up arms and calling in foreign power to depose their prince consistent with non-resistance and passive obedience; nay, they went farther; they distinguished between a Crolian's taking arms and a Solunarian's, and fairly proved this to be rebellion, and that to be non-resistance.

Nay, and which exceeded all the power of human art in the highest degree of attainment that ever it arrived to on our side the moon, they turned the tables so dexterously as to argument upon one sort of Crolians called Prestarians,[1] that though they repented of the war they had raised in former times, and protested against the violence offered their prince, and after another party[2] had in spite of them beheaded him, took arms against the other party, and never left contriving their ruin till they had brought in his son and set him upon the throne again.

Yet by this most dexterous way of twisting, extending, contracting, and distinguishing of phrases and reasoning, they presently made it as plain as the sun at noonday that these Prestarians were king-killers, commonwealth-men, rebels, traitors, and enemies to monarchy; that they restored the monarchy only in order to destroy it, and that they preached up sedition, rebellion, and the like. This was proved so plain by these sublime distinctions, that they convinced themselves and their posterity of it by a rare and newly acquired art, found out by extraordinary study, which proves the wonderful power of custom, insomuch that let any man by this method tell a lie over a certain number of times, he shall arrive to a satisfaction of its certainty, though he knew it to be a fiction before, and shall freely tell it for a truth all his life after.

Thus the Prestarians were called the murderers of the father though they restored the son, and all the testimonials of their sufferings, protests, and insurrections to prevent his death signified nothing; for this method of distinguishing has that powerful charm in it, that all those trifles we call proofs and demonstration were of no use in that case. Custom brought the story up to a truth, and in an instant all the Crolians were hooked in under the general name of Prestarians, at the same time to hook all parties in the crime.

Now as it happened at last that these Solunarian gentlemen

---

[1] The Presbyterians.　　　　[2] The Independents.

found it necessary to do the same thing themselves, viz., to lay aside their loyalty, depose, fight against, shoot bullets at, and throw bombs at their king, till they frightened him away, and sent him abroad to beg his bread, the Crolians began to take heart, and tell them now they ought to be friends with them, and tell them no more of rebellion and disloyalty ; nay, they carried it so far as to challenge them to bring their loyalty to the test, and compare Crolian loyalty and Solunarian loyalty together, and see who had raised more wars, taken up arms oftenest, or appeared in most rebellions against their kings ; nay, who had killed most kings, the Crolians or the Solunarians ; for there having been then newly fought a great battle between the Solunarian Churchmen under their new prince and the armies of foreign succours under their old king,[1] in which their old king was beaten and forced to fly a second time, the Crolians told them that every bullet shot at the battle was as much murdering their king as cutting off the head with a hatchet was killing his father.

These arguments in our world would have been unanswerable ; but when they came to be brought to the test of Lunar reasoning, alas! they signified nothing. They distinguished and distinguished till they brought the Prestarian war to be mere rebellion ; king-killing, bloody and unnatural ; and the Solunarian fighting against their king and turning him adrift to seek his fortune, no prejudice at all to their loyalty, no, nor to the famous doctrine of passive obedience and absolute subjection.

When I saw this, I really bewailed the unhappiness of some of our gentlemen in England, who stand exceedingly in need of such a wonderful dexterity of argument to defend their share in our late Revolution, and to reconcile it to their antecedent and subsequent conduct, should not be furnished from this more accurate world with the suitable powers, in order the better to defend them against the banter and just raillery of their ill-natured enemies the Whigs.

---

[1] In the Battle of the Boyne, July 1, 1690, James joined the Irish with ten thousand French troops under Lauzun.

Z

By this they might have attained suitable reserves of argument to distinguish themselves out of their loyalty and into their loyalty, as occasion presented to dismiss this prince, and entertain that as they found it to their purpose; but above all, they might have learnt a way how to justify swearing to one king and praying for another, eating one prince's bread and doing another prince's work, serving one king they do not love and loving another they do not serve; they might easily reconcile the schisms of the Church, and prove they are still loyal subjects to King James, while they are only forced bondsmen to the Act of Settlement for the sake of that comfortable importance called food and raiment; and thus their reputation might have been saved, which is most unhappily tarnished and blurred with the malicious attacks of the Whigs on one hand and the Non-Jurants on the other.

These tax them, as above, with rebellion by their own principles, and contradicting the doctrine of passive submission and non-resistance by taking up arms against their prince, calling in a foreign power and deposing him. They charge them with killing the Lord's anointed by shooting at him at the Boyne, where, if he was not killed, it was his own fault—at least it is plain it was none of theirs.

On the other hand, the Non-Jurant clergy charge them with schism, declare the whole Church of England schismatics and breakers off from the general union of the Church in renouncing their allegiance and swearing to another power, their former prince being yet alive.

It is confessed all the answers they have been able to make to these things are very weak and mean, unworthy men of their rank and capacities, and it is a pity they should not be assisted by some kind communication of these Lunar arguments and distinctions, without which, and till they can obtain which, a Conforming Jacobite must be the absurdest contradiction in Nature; a thing that admits of no manner of defence—no, not by the people themselves, and which they would willingly abandon, but that they can find no side to join with them.

The Dissenting Jacobites have some plea for themselves, for let their opinions be never so repugnant to their own interest or general vogue, they are faithful to some thing, and they will not join with these people, because they have perjured their faith and yet pretend to adhere to it at the same time. The Conforming Whigs will not receive them, because they pretend to rail at the Government they have sworn to, and espouse the interest they have sworn against; so that these poor creatures have but one way left them, which is to go along with me next time I travel to the moon, and that will most certainly do their business; for when they come down again they will be quite another sort of men, the distinctions, the power of argument, the way of reasoning they will be then furnished with will quite change the scene of the world with them; they will certainly be able to prove they are the only people, both in justice, in politics, and in prudence; that the extremes of every side are in the wrong; they will prove their loyalty preserved untainted through all the swearings, fightings, shootings, and the like, and nobody will be able to come to the test with them; so that, upon the whole, they are all distracted if they do not go up to the moon for illumination, and that they may easily do in the next consolidator.

But as this is a very long digression, and for which I am to beg my reader's pardon, being an error I slipped into from my abundant respect to these gentlemen and for their particular instruction, I shall endeavour to make my reader amends by keeping more close to my subject.

To return, therefore, to the historical part of the Solunarian Churchmen in the world in the moon.

Having, as is related, deposed their king and placed the crown upon the head of the prince that came to their assistance, a new scene began all over the kingdom.

1. A terrible and bloody war began through all the parts of the Lunar world where their banished prince and his new ally had any interest; and the new king having a universal character over all the northern kingdoms of the moon, he brought in a great many potent kings, princes, emperors, and states to take part

with him, and so it became the most general war that had happened in those ages.

I did not trouble myself to inquire into the particular successes of this war, but as what had a more particular regard to the country from whence I came and for whose instruction I have designed these sheets, the strife of parties, the internal feuds at home, and their analogy to ours, and whatever is instructively to be deduced from them, was the subject of immediate inquiry.

No sooner was this prince placed on the throne but, according to his promises to them that invited him over, he convened the Estates of the realm, and giving them free liberty to make, alter, add, or repeal all such laws as they thought fit, it must be their own fault if they did not establish themselves upon such foundation of liberty and right as they desired, for he gave them their full swing, never interposed one negative upon them for several years, and let them do almost everything they pleased.

This full liberty had like to have spoiled all, for, as is before noted, this nation had one unhappy quality they could never be broke off—always to be falling out one among another.

The Crolians, according to capitulation, demanded the full liberty and toleration of religion which the Solunarians had conditioned with them for when they drew them off from joining with the old king, and when they promised to come to a temper and to be brethren in peace and love ever after.

Nor were the Solunarian Churchmen backward either to remember or perform the conditions; but by the consent of the king, who had been by agreement made guarantee of their former stipulations, an Act was drawn up in full form, and as complete as both satisfied the desires of the Crolians and testified the honesty and probity of the Solunarians, as they were abstractedly and moderately considered.

During the whole reign of this king this union of parties continued without any considerable interruption. There were, indeed, brooding mischiefs which hovered over every accident, in order to generate strife; but the candour of the prince and the prudence of his ministers kept it under for a long time.

At last an occasion offered itself which gave an unhappy stroke to the nation's peace. The King, through innumerable hazards, terrible battles, and a twelve years' war, had reduced his powerful adversary to such a necessity of peace that he became content to abandon the fugitive king, and to own the title of this warlike prince; and upon these, among various other conditions, very honourable for him and his allies, and by which vast conquests were surrendered and disgorged to the losers, a peace was made, to the universal satisfaction of all those parts of the moon that had been involved in a tiresome and expensive war.[1]

This peace was no sooner made but the inhabitants of this unhappy country, according to the constant practice of the place, fell out in the most horrid manner among themselves, and with the very prince that had done all these great things for them; and I cannot forget how the old gentleman I had these relations from, being once deeply engaged in discourse with some senators of that country, and hearing them reproach the memory of that prince, from whom they received so much, and on the foot of whose gallantry and merit the constitution then subsisted, it put him into some heat, and he told them to their faces that they were guilty both of murder and ingratitude.

I thought the charge was very high, but as they returned upon him, and challenged him to make it out, he answered he was ready to do it, and went on thus :—

His Majesty, said he, left a quiet, retired, completely happy condition, full of honour, beloved of his country, valued and esteemed, as well as feared by his enemies, to come over hither at your own request, to deliver you from the encroachments and tyranny, as you called it, of your prince.

Ever since he came hither, he has been your mere journeyman, your servant, your soldier of fortune; he has fought for you, fatigued and harassed his person, and robbed himself of all his peace for you; he has been in a constant hurry, and run through a million of hazards for you; he has conversed with fire and blood, storms at sea, camps and trenches ashore, and given him-

[1] The Peace of Ryswick.

self no rest for twelve years, and all for your use, safety, and repose. In requital of which, he has always been treated with jealousies and suspicions, with reproaches and abuses of all sorts and on all occasions, till the treatment of the Solunarians ate into his very soul, tired it with serving an unthankful nation, and absolutely broke his heart; for which reason I think him as much murdered as his predecessor was, whose head was cut off by his subjects.

I could not, when this was over, but ask the old gentleman what was the reason of his exclamation, and how it was the people treated their prince upon this occasion.

He told me it was a grievous subject and a long one, and too long to rehearse, but he would give me a short abridgment of it; and not to look back into his wars, in which he was abominably ill served, his subjects constantly ill-treated him in giving him supplies too late, that he could not get into the field, nor forward his preparations in time to be ready for his enemies, who frequently were ready to insult him in his quarters.

By giving him sham taxes and funds that raised little or no money, by which he having borrowed money of his people by anticipation, the funds not answering, he contracted such vast debts as the nation could never pay, which brought the war into disrepute, sunk the credit of his exchequer, and filled the nation with murmurs and complaints. by betraying his counsel and well-laid designs to his enemies, selling their native country to foreigners, retarding their navies and expeditions till the enemies were provided to receive them, betraying their merchants and trade, spending vast sums to fit out fleets just time enough to go abroad and do nothing, and then get home again.

But as these were too numerous evils, and too long to repeat, the particular things he related too in his discourse were these that follow :—

There had been a hasty peace concluded with a furious and powerful enemy. The king foresaw it would be of no continuance, and that the demise of a neighbouring king,[1] who by all appear-

---

[1] Of Spain.

ance could not live long, would certainly embroil them again. He saw that prince keep up numerous legions of forces, in order to be in a posture to break the peace with advantage. This the king fairly represented to them, and told them the necessity of keeping up such a force, and for such a time at least as might be · necessary to awe the enemy from putting any affront upon them in case of the death of that prince, which they daily expected.

The party who had all along maligned the prosperity of this prince took fire at the offer, and here began another state plot, which, though it hooked in two or three sets of men for different ends, yet altogether joined in affronting and ill-treating their prince upon this article of the army.

The nation had been in danger enough from the designs of former princes invading their privileges, and putting themselves in a posture to tyrannise by the help of standing forces, and the party that first took fire at this proposal, though the very same men who in the time of an Abrogratzian prince, were for caressing him and giving him thanks for his standing army, as has been noted before, were the very people that began the outcry against this demand ; and so specious were the pretences they made, that they drew in the very Crolians themselves upon the pretence of liberty and exemption from arbitrary methods of government to oppose their king.

It grieved this good prince to be suspected of tyrannic designs, and that by a nation for whom he had done so much and ventured so far to save from tyranny and standing armies. It was in vain he represented to them the pressing occasion ; in vain he gave them a description of approaching dangers, and the threatening posture of the enemy's armies ; in vain he told them of the probabilities of renewing the war, and how keeping but a needful force might be a means of preventing it ; in vain he proposed the subjecting what force should be necessary to the absolute power, both as to time and number, of their own Cortes or National Assembly.

It was all one, the design being formed in the breasts of those who were neither friends to the nation nor to the king, those reasons which would have been of force in another case made them the more eager; bitter reflections were made on the king, and scurrilous lampoons published upon the subject of tyrants and governing by armies.

Nothing could be more ungrateful to a generous prince, nor could anything more deeply affect this king, than whom none ever had a more genuine, single-hearted design for the people's good; but above all, like Cæsar in the case of Brutus, it heartily moved him to find himself pushed at by those very people whom he had all along seen pretending to adhere to his interest and the public benefit, which he had always taken care should never be parted, and to find these people join against this proposal as a design against their liberties and as a foundation of tyranny, heartily and sensibly afflicted him.

It was a strange mystery, and not easily unriddled, that those men who had always a known aversion to the interest of the deposed king should fall in with this party, and those that were friends to the general good never forgave it them.

All that could be said to excuse them was the plot I am speaking of, that by carrying this point for that party they hooked in those forward people to join in a popular cry of liberty and property, things they were never fond of before, and to make some settlement of the people's claims, which they always had opposed, and which they would since have been very glad to have repealed.

So great an ascendant had the personal spleen of this party over their other principles, that they were content to let the liberties of the people be declared in their highest claims, rather than not obtain this one article, which they knew would so exceedingly mortify their prince and strengthen the nation's enemies. They freely joined in acts of succession, abjuration, declaration of the power and claims of the people, and the superiority of their right to the prince's prerogative, and abundance of such things which they could never be otherwise brought to.

It is true these were great things, but it was thought all this might have been obtained in conjunction with their prince, rather than by putting affronts and mortifications upon the man that had, next to the influence of Heaven, been the only agent of restoring them to a power and capacity of enjoying as well as procuring such things as national privileges.

It was vigorously alleged that standing armies in times of peace were inconsistent with the public safety, the laws and constitutions of all the nations in the moon.

But these allegations were strenuously answered, that it was true without the consent of the great national council it was so ; but that being obtained, it was not illegal, and public necessities might make that consent not only legal but convenient.

It was all to no purpose ; the whole was carried with a torrent of clamour and reflection against the good prince, who consented because he would in nothing oppose the current of the people, but withal told them plainly what would be the consequences of their heat, which they have effectually found true since to their cost, and to the loss of some millions of treasure.

For no sooner was this army broke, which was the best ever that nation saw, and was justly the terror of the enemy, but the great monarch we mentioned before broke all measures with this prince and the confederate nations—a proof what just apprehensions they had of his conduct at the head of such an army. For they broke with contempt a treaty [1] which the prince upon a prospect of this unkindness of his people had entered into with the enemy, and which he engaged in, if possible, to prevent a new war, which he foresaw he should be very unfit to begin or carry on, and which they would never have dared to break had not this feud happened.

It was but a little before I came into this country when such repeated accounts came of the encroachments, insults, and preparations of their great powerful neighbour, that all the world saw the necessity of a war, and the very people who were to feel it most applied to the prince to begin it.

He was forward enough to begin it, and in compliance with his people resolved on it ; but the grief of the usage he had received, the unkind treatment he had met with from those very

---

[1] The second Partition Treaty.

people that had brought him thither, had sunk so deep upon his spirits that he could never recover it ; but being very weak in body and mind, and joined to a slight hurt, he received by a fall from his horse, he died, to the unspeakable grief of all his subjects that wished well to their native country.

This was the melancholy account of this great prince's end, and I have been told that once every year there is a kind of fast or solemn commemoration kept up for the murder of that former prince, who, as I noted, was beheaded by his subjects ; so it seems some of the people, who are of opinion this prince was murdered by the ill-treatment of his friends, a way which I must own is the cruellest of deaths, keep the same day to commemorate his death, and this is a day in which it seems both parties are very free with one another as to raillery and ill-language.

But the friends of this last prince have a double advantage, for they also commemorate the birthday of this prince, and are generally very merry on that day ; and the custom is at their feast on that day, just like our drinking healths, they pledge one another to the immortal memory of their deliverer. As the historical part of this matter was absolutely necessary to introduce the following remarks, and to instruct the ignorant in those things, I hope it shall not be thought a barren digression, especially when I shall tell you that it is a most exact representation of what is yet to come in a scene of affairs of which I must make a short abstract by way of introduction.

The deceased prince we have heard of was succeeded by his sister-in-law,[1] the second daughter of the banished prince, a lady of an extraordinary character, of the old race of their kings, a native by birth, a Solunarian by profession, exceeding pious, just, and good, of an honesty peculiar to herself, and for which she was justly beloved by all sorts and degrees of her subjects.

This princess having the experience of her father and grand-father before her, joined to her own prudence and honesty of design, it was no wonder if she prudently shunned all manner of

---

[1] Queen Anne.

rash counsels, and endeavoured to carry it with a steady hand between her contending parties.

At her first coming to the crown she made a solemn declaration of her resolutions for peace and just government; she gave the Crolians her royal word that she would inviolably preserve the toleration of their religion and worship, and always afford them her protection, and by this she hoped they would be easy.

But to the Solunarians, as those among whom she had been educated, and whose religion she had always professed, been trained up in, and piously pursued, she expressed herself with an uncommon tenderness, told them they should be the men of her favour, and those that were most zealous for that Church should have most of her countenance; and she backed this soon after with an unparalleled act of royal bounty to them, freely parting with a considerable branch of her royal revenue for the poor priests of that religion, of which there were many in the remote parts of her kingdom.[1]

What vast consequences, and prodigiously differing from the design, may words have when mistaken and misapplied by the hearers! Never were significant expressions spoken from a sincere, honest, and generous principle, with a single design to engage all the subjects in the moon to peace and union, so perverted, misapplied, and turned by a party to a meaning directly contrary to the royal thoughts of the queen. For from this very expression, "most zealous," grew all the divisions and subdivisions in the Solunarian Church, to the ruin of their own cause and the vast advantage of the Crolian interest. The eager men of the Church, especially those we have been talking of, hastily catched at this expression of the queen, most zealous, and millions of fatal constructions and unhappy consequences they made of it, some of which are as follows :—

1. They took it to imply that the queen, whatever she had said to the Crolians, really designed their destruction, and that those that were of that opinion must be meant by the most zealous

---

[1] Queen Anne's Bounty was a birthday gift, in 1704, to the poorer clergy of firstfruits and tenths, which Henry VIII. had swept into the revenue of the crown.

members of the Solunarian Church, and they could understand zeal no otherwise than their own way.

2. From this speech, and their mistaking the words most zealous, arose an unhappy distinction among the Solunarians themselves, some zealous, some more zealous, which afterwards divided them into two most opposite parties, being fomented by an accident of a book published on an occasion, of which presently.

The consequences of this mistake appeared presently in the most zealous, in their offering all possible insults to the Crolian Dissenters, preaching them down, printing them down, and talking them down, as a people not fit to be suffered in the nation, and now they thought they had the game sure.

" Down with the Crolians ! " began to be all the cry, and truly the Crolians themselves began to be uneasy, and had nothing to rely upon but the queen's promise, which, however, her Majesty always made good to them.

The other party proceeded so far that they began to insult the very queen herself upon the matter of her word, and one of her college-priests told her plainly in print she could not be a true friend to the Solunarian Church if she did not declare war against and root out all the Crolians in her dominions.

But these proceedings met with a check by a very odd accident. A certain author[1] of those countries, a very mean, obscure, and despicable fellow, of no great share of wit, but that had a very unlucky way of telling his story, seeing which way things were a going, writes a book, and personating this High Solunarian zeal, musters up all their arguments as if they were his own, and strenuously pretends to prove that all the Crolians ought to be destroyed, hanged, banished, and the devil and all. As this book was a perfect surprise to all the country, so the proceedings about it on all sides were as extraordinary.

The Crolians themselves were surprised at it, and so closely had the author couched his design, that they never saw the irony of the style, but began to look about them to see which way they should fly to save themselves.

[1] Defoe himself in his " Shortest Way with Dissenters."

The men of zeal we talked of were so blinded with the notion, which suited so exactly with their real design, that they hugged the book, applauded the unknown author, and placed the book next their oracular writings or laws of religion.

The author was all this while concealed, and the paper had all the effect he wished for. For as it caused these first gentlemen to caress, applaud, and approve it, and thereby discovered their real intention, so it met with abhorrence and detestation in all the men of principle, prudence, and moderation in the kingdom, who, though they were Solunarians in religion, yet were not for blood, desolation, and persecution of their brethren, but with the Queen were willing they should enjoy their liberties and estates, they behaving themselves quietly and peaceably to the Government.

At last it came out that it was writ by a Crolian; but good God! what a clamour was raised at the poor man. The Crolians flew at him like lightning, ignorantly and blindly, not seeing that he had sacrificed himself and his fortunes in their behalf; they rummaged his character for reproaches, though they could find little that way to hurt him; they plentifully loaded him with ill-language and railing, and took a great deal of pains to let him see their own ignorance and ingratitude.

The Ministers of State, though at that time of the fiery party, yet seeing the general detestation of such a proposal and how ill it would go down with the nation, though they approved the thing, yet began to scent the design, and were also obliged to declare against it, for fear of being thought of the same mind. Thus the author was proscribed by proclamation, and a reward of fifty thousand hecatos, a small imaginary coin in those parts, put upon his head.

The Cortes of the nation being at the same time assembled, joined in censuring the book, and thus the party blindly damned their own principles for mere shame of the practice, not daring to own the thing in public which they had underhand professed, and the fury of all parties fell upon the poor author.

The man fled the first popular fury, but at last being betrayed, fell into the hands of the public Ministry.

When they had him, they hardly knew what to do with him. They could not proceed against him as author of a proposal for the destruction of the Crolians, because it appeared he was a Crolian himself; they were loth to charge him with suggesting that the Solunarian Churchmen were guilty of such a design, lest he should bring their own writings to prove it true; so they fell to wheedling him with good words to throw himself into their hands and submit, giving him that gewgaw the public faith for a civil and gentleman-like treatment. The man, believing like a coxcomb that they spoke as they meant, quitted his own defence, and threw himself on the mercy of the queen, as he thought; but they, abusing their queen with false representations, perjured all their promises with him, and treated him in a most barbarous manner, on pretence that there were no such promises made, though he proved it upon them by the oath of the persons to whom they were made. Thus they laid him under a heavy sentence, fined him more than they thought him able to pay, and ordered him to be exposed to the mob in the streets.

Having him at this advantage, they set upon him with their emissaries to discover to them his adherents, as they called them, and promised him great things on one hand, threatening him with his utter ruin on the other; and the great scribe of the country, with another of their great courtiers, took such a low step as to go to him to the dungeon where they had put him, to see if they could tempt him to betray his friends. The comical dialogue between them there the author of this has seen in manuscript, exceeding diverting, but having not time to translate it, it is omitted for the present, though he promises to publish it in its proper season for public instruction.

However, for the present it may suffice to tell the world that neither by promises of reward or fear of punishment could they prevail upon him to discover anything, and so it remains a secret to this day.

The title of this unhappy book was "The Shortest Way with the Crolians." The effects of it were various, as will be seen in our ensuing discourse. As to the author, nothing was more unaccountable than the circumstances of his treatment, for he met with all that fate which they must expect who attempt to open the eyes of a nation wilfully blind.

The hot men of the Solunarian Church damned him without bell, book, or candle; the more moderate pitied him, but looked on as unconcerned. But the Crolians, for whom he had run this venture, used him worst of all; for they not only abandoned him, but reproached him as an enemy that would have them destroyed. So one side railed at him because they did understand him, and the other because they did not.

Thus the man sunk under the general neglect, was ruined and undone, and left a monument of what every man must expect that serves a good cause professed by an unthankful people.

And here it was I found out that my Lunar philosopher was only so in disguise, and that he was no philosopher, but the very man I have been talking of.

From this book, and the treatment its author received—for they used him with all possible rigour—a new scene of parties came upon the stage, and this queen's reign began to be filled with more divisions and feuds than any before her.

These parties began to be so numerous and violent, that it endangered the public good, and gave great disadvantages to the general affairs abroad.

The queen invited them all to peace and union, but it was in vain; nay, one had the impudence to publish that to procure peace and union it was necessary to suppress all the Crolians, and have no party but one, and then all must be of a mind.

From this heat of parties all the moderate men fell in with their queen, and were heartily for peace and union. The other, who were now distinguished by the title of High Solunarians, called these all Crolians and Low Solunarians, and began to treat them with more inveteracy than they used to do the Crolians themselves, calling them traitors to their country, betrayers of their mother, serpents harboured in the bosom, who bite, sting, and hiss at the hand that succoured them; and, in short, the enmity grew so violent, that from hence proceeded one of the subtlest, foolishest, deep, shallow contrivances and plots that ever was hatched or set on foot by any party of men in the whole moon—at least who pretended to any brains or to half a degree of common understanding.

There had always been dislikes and distastes between even the most moderate Solunarian and the Crolians, as I have noted in the beginning of this relation, and these were derived from dissenting in opinions of religion, ancient feuds, private interest, education, and the like; and the Solunarians had frequently, on pretence of securing the government, made laws to exclude the Crolians from any part of the administration, unless they submitted to some religious tests and ceremonies which were prescribed them.

Now as the keeping them out of offices was more the design than the conversion of the Crolians to the Solunarian Church, the Crolians, at least many of them, submitted to the test, and frequently conformed to qualify themselves for public employments.

The most moderate of the Solunarians were in their opinion against this practice, and the High men taking advantage of them, drew them in to concur in making a law with yet more severity against them, effectually to keep them out of employment.

The Low Solunarians were easy to be drawn into this project, as it was only a confirming former laws of their own making, and all things run fair for the design; but as the High men had further ends in it than barely reducing the Crolians to conformity, they couched so many gross clauses into their law, that even the grandees of the Solunarians themselves could not comply with; nay, even the patriarchs of the Solunarian Church declared against it, as tending to persecution and confusion.

This disappointment enraged the party, and that very rage entirely ruined their project; for now the nobility, the patriarchs, and all the wise men of the nation, joining together against these men of heat and fury, the queen began to see into their designs; and as she was of a most pious and peaceable temper, she conceived a just hatred of so wicked and barbarous a design, and immediately dismissed from her council and favour the great scribe and several others who were leaders in the design, to the great mortification of the whole party and utter ruin of the intended law against the Crolians.

Here I could not but observe, as I have done before in the case of the banished king, how impolitic these High Solunarian Churchmen acted in all their proceedings; for had they contented themselves by little and little to have done their work, they had done it effectually; but pushing to extremities, they overshot themselves, and ruined all.

For the grandees and patriarchs made but a few trifling objections at first, nay, and came off and yielded some of them too; and if these would have consented to have parted with some clauses which they have willingly left out since, they had had it passed; but these were, as hot men always are, too eager and sure of their game; they thought all was their own, and so they lost themselves.

If they railed at the Low Solunarian Churchmen before, they doubled their clamours at them now; all the patriarchs and all the nobility and grandees, nay, even the queen herself came under their censure, and everybody who was not of their mind were Prestarians and Crolians.

As this rage of theirs was implacable, so, as I hinted before, it drove them into another subdivision of parties, and now began the mysterious plot to be laid which I mentioned before; for the Cortes being summoned and the law being proposed, some of these High Solunarians appeared in confederacy with the Crolians—in perfect confederacy with them, a thing nobody would have imagined could ever have been brought to pass.

Now as these sorts of plots must always be carried very nicely, so these High gentlemen who confederated with the Crolians, having, to spite the other, resolved effectually to prevent the passing the law against the qualification of the Crolians, it was not their business immediately to declare themselves against it as a law, but by still loading it with some extravagance or other, and pushing it on to some intolerable extreme, secure its miscarriage.

In the managing this plot one of their authors was specially employed, and that all that was really true of the Crolian Dissenters might be ridiculed, his work was to draw monstrous pictures of them, which nobody could believe. This took immediately, for now people began to look at their shoes to see if they were not cloven-footed as they went along the streets; and at last, finding that they were really shaped like the rest of the Lunar inhabitants, they went back to the author, who was a learned member of a certain seminary or brotherhood of the Solunarian clergy, and inquired if he were not mad, distracted, and raving, or moon-blind and in want of the thinking engine. But finding all things right there, and that he was in his senses, especially in a morning when he was a little free from, &c., that he was a good, honest, jolly Solunarian priest, and no room could be found for an objection there,—upon all these searches it presently appeared, and all men concluded, it was a mere fanatic Crolian plot; that this High party of all were but pretenders and mere traitors to the true High Solunarian Churchmen; that, wearing the same cloth, had herded among them in disguise only to wheedle them into such wild extravagances as must of necessity confuse their counsels, expose their persons, and ruin their cause, according to the like practice put upon their Abrogratzian prince, and of which I have spoken before.

And since I am upon the detection of this most refined practice, I crave leave to descend to some particular instances, which will the better evince the truth of this matter, and make it appear that either this was really a Crolian plot or else all these people were perfectly distracted; and as their wits in that Lunar world are much higher strained than ours, so their lunacy, where it happens, must, according to the rules of mathematical nature, bear an extreme equal in proportion.

This college fury of a man [1] was the first on whom this useful discovery was made; and having writ several learned tracts wherein he invited the people to murder and destroy all the Crolians, branded all the Solunarian patriarchs, clergy, and gentry that

[1] Sacheverell.

would not come into his proposal with the name of cowards, traitors, and betrayers of Lunar religion, having beat the *conciona-zimir* at a great assembly of the *cadirs* or judges, and told them all the Crolians were devils, and they were all perjured that did not use them as such, he carried on matters so dexterously and with such surprising success, that he filled even the Solunarians themselves with horror at his proposals. And as I happened to be in one of their public halls where all such writings as are new are laid a certain time to be read by every comer, I saw a little knot of men round a table where one was reading this book. There were two Solunarian high-priests in their proper vestments, one privy councillor of the state, one other nobleman, and one who had in his hat a token to signify that he possessed one of the fine feathers of the consolidator, of which I have given the description already.

The book being read by one of the habited priests, he starts up with some warmth. "By the moon," says he, "I have found this fellow out. He is certainly a Crolian, a mere Prestarian Crolian, and is crept into our Church only in disguise, for it is certain all this is but mere banter and irony, to expose us and to ridicule the Solunarian interest."

The privy councillor took it presently. "Whether he is a Crolian or no," says he, "I cannot tell; but he has certainly done the Crolians so much service, that if they had hired him to act for them, they could not have desired he should serve them better."

"Truly," says the man of the feather, "I was always for pulling down the Crolians, for I thought them dangerous to the state; but this man has brought the matter nearer to my view and shown me what destroying them is; for he put me upon examining the consequences, and now I find it would be lopping off the limbs of the Government and laying it at the mercy of the enemy that they might lop off its head. I assure you he has done the Crolians great service, for whereas abundance of our men of the feather were for routing the Crolians, they lately fell down to 134 or thereabouts."

All this confirmed the first man's opinion that he was a Crolian in disguise, or an emissary employed by them to ruin the project of their enemies; for these Crolians are damned cunning people in their way, and they have money enough to engage hirelings to their side.

Another party concerned in this plot was an old cast-out Solunarian priest, who, though professing himself a Solunarian, was turned out for adhering to the Abrogratzian king, a mighty stickler for the doctrine of absolute subjection.

This man draws the most monstrous picture of a Crolian that could be invented; he put him in a wolf's skin with long ass's ears, and hung him all over full of associations, massacres, persecutions, rebellions, and blood. Here the people began to stare again, and a Crolian could not go along the street but they were always looking for the long ears, the wolf's claws, and the like; until at last nothing of these things appearing, but the Crolians looking and acting like other folks, they began to examine the matter, and found this was a mere Crolian plot too, and this man was hired to run these extravagant lengths to point out the right meaning.

The discovery being made, people ever since understand him that when he talks of the Dissenters, associations, murders, persecutions, and the like, he means that his readers should look back to the murders, oppressions, and persecutions they had suffered for several past years, and the associations that were now forming to bring them into the same condition again.

From this famous author I could not but proceed to observe the further progress of this most refined piece of cunning among the very great ones, grandees, feathers, and consolidators of the country. For these cunning Crolians managed their intrigues so nicely that they brought about a famous division even among the High Solunarian party themselves, and whereas the law of qualification was revived again, and in great danger of being completed, these subtle Crolians brought over a hundred and thirty-four of the feathers in the famous consolidator to be of their side, and to contrive the utter destruction of it; and thus fell the design which the High Solunarian Churchmen had laid for the ruin of the

Crolians' interest by their own friends first joining in all the extremes they had proposed, and then pushing it so much farther, and to such mad periods, that the very highest of them stood amazed at the design, startled, flew back, and made a full stop : they were willing to ruin the Crolians, but they were not willing to ruin the whole nation. The more these men began to consider, the more furiously these plotters carried on their extravagances. At last they made a general push at a thing in which they knew if the other High men joined, they must throw all into confusion, bring a foreign enemy on their backs, unravel all the thread of the war, fight all their victories back again, and involve the whole nation in blood and confusion.

They knew well enough that most of the High men would hesitate at this; they knew if they did not, the grandees and patriarchs would reject it, and so they played the surest game to blast and overthrow this law that could possibly be played.

If any man in the whole world in the moon will pretend this was not a plot, a Crolian design, a mere conspiracy to destroy the law, let him tell me for what other end could these men offer such extremes as they needs must know would meet with immediate opposition, things that they knew all the honest men, all the grandees, all the patriarchs, and almost all the feathers would oppose.

From hence all the men of any foresight brought it to this pass, as is before noted, that either these hundred and thirty four were fools or madmen, or that it was a fanatic Crolian plot and conspiracy to ruin the making of this law, which the rest of the Solunarian Churchmen were very forward to carry on.

I heard, indeed, some men argue that this could not be, the breach was too wide between the Crolians and these gentlemen ever to come to such an agreement; but the wiser heads who argued the other way always brought them, as is noted above, to this pinch of argument, that either it must be so—be a fanatic Crolian plot—or else the men of fury were all fools, madmen, and fitter for an hospital than a state-house or a pulpit.

It must be allowed these Crolians were cunning people thus to wheedle in these high-flying Solunarians to break the neck of their dear project. But upon the whole, for ought I could see, whether it went one way or the other, all the nation esteemed the other people fools—fools of the most extraordinary size in all the moon; for either way they pulled down what they had been many years a building.

I cannot say that this was in kindness to the Crolians, but in mere malice to the Low Solunarian party, who had the government in their hands; for malice always carries men on to monstrous extremes.

Some, indeed, have thought it hard to call this a plot and a confederacy with the Crolians. But I cannot but think it the kindest thing that can be said of them, and that it is impossible those people who pushed at some imaginary things in that law could but be in a plot as aforesaid, or be perfectly lunatic, downright madmen or traitors to their country, and let them choose which character they like. I cannot in charity but spare them their honesty and their senses, and attribute it all to their policy.

When I had understood all things at large and found the exceeding depth of the design, I must confess the discovery of these things was very diverting, and the more so when I made the proper reflections upon the analogy there seemed to be between these Solunarian High Churchmen in the moon and ours here in England; our High Churchmen are no more to be compared to these than the hundred and thirty-four are to the consolidators.

Ours can plot now and then a little among themselves, but then it is all gross and plain sailing, downright taking arms, calling in foreign forces, assassinations, and the like; but these are nothing to the more exquisite heads in the moon. For they have the subtlest ways with them that ever were heard of. They can make war with a prince on purpose to bring him to the crown, fit out vast navies against him that he may have the more leisure to take their merchantmen, make descents upon him on purpose to come home and do nothing; if they have a mind to a sea-fight, they carefully send out admirals that care not to come within half a mile of the enemy, that coming off safe, they may have the boasting part of the victory and the beaten part both together.

It would be endless to call over the roll of their sublime politics. They damn moderation in order to peace and union, set the house on fire to save it from desolation, plunder to avoid persecution, and consolidate things in order to their more imme. diate dissolution.

Had our High Churchmen been masters of these excellent arts, they had long ago brought their designs to pass.

The exquisite plot of these High Solunarians answered the Crolians' end, for it broke all their enemies' measures, the law vanished, the grandees could hardly be persuaded to read it, and when it was proposed to be read again, they hissed at it and threw it by with contempt.

Nor was this all ; for it not only lost them their design as to this law, but it absolutely broke the party ; and just as it was with Adam and Eve, as soon as they sinned they quarrelled and fell out with one another, so as soon as things came to this height the party fell out one among another, and even the High men themselves were divided ; some were for consolidating and some not for consolidating, some were for tacking, and some not for tacking, as they were or were not let into the secret.

If this confusion of languages or interest lost them the real design, it cannot be a wonder. Have we not always seen it in our world that dividing an interest weakens and exposes it ? Has not a great many, both good and bad designs, been rendered abortive in this our lower world for want of the harmony of parties and the unanimity of those concerned in the design.

How had the knot of rebellion been dissolved in England if it had not been untied by the very hands of those that knit it ? All the contrary force had been entirely broken and subdued, and the restoration of monarchy had never happened in England, if union and agreement had been found among the managers of that age.

The enemies of the present establishment had shown suffi-ciently that they perfectly understand the shortest way to our infallible destruction when they bend their principal force at dividing us into parties, and keeping those parties at the utmost variance.

But this is not all, the author of this cannot but observe here, that as England is unhappily divided among parties, so it has this one felicity even to be found in the very matter of her misfortunes, that those parties are all again subdivided among themselves.

How easily might the Church have crushed and subdued the Dissenters if they had been all as mad as one party, if they had not been some High and some Low Churchmen? And what mischief might not that one party have done in this nation had not they been divided again into Jurant Jacobites and Non-Jurant, into Consolidators and Non-Consolidators? From whence it is plain to me, that just as it is in the moon, these consolidating Churchmen are mere confederates with the Whigs; and it must be so unless we should suppose them mere madmen, that do not know what they are doing, and who are the drudges of their enemies, and know nothing of the matter.

And from this Lunar observation it presently occurred to my understanding that my masters, the Dissenters, may come in for a share among the moon-blind men of this generation, since had they done for their own interest what the law fairly admits to be done; had they been united among themselves, had they formed themselves into a public body, to have acted in a public, united capacity, by general concert, and as persons that had but one interest and understood it, they had never been so often insulted by every rising party; they had never had so many machines and ntrigues to ruin and suppress them; they had never been so often tacked and consolidated to oppression and persecution, and yet never have rebelled or broke the peace, incurred the displeasure of their princes, or have been upbraided with plots, insurrections, and anti-monarchical principles; when they had made treaties and capitulations with the Church for temper and toleration, the articles would have been kept, and these would have demanded justice with an authority that would upon all occasions be respected.

Were they united in civil polity in trade and interest, would they buy and sell with one another, abstract their stocks, erect banks and companies in trade of their own, lend their cash to the Government in a body and as a body.

If I were to tell them what advantages the Crolians in the moon make of this sort of management, how the Government finds it their interest to treat them civilly and use them like subjects of consideration; how upon all occasions some of the grandees and nobility appear as protectors of the Crolians, and treat with their princes in their names, present their petitions, and make demand from the prince of such loans and sums of money as the public occasions require; and what abundance of advantages are reaped from such a union, both to their own body as a party, and to the Government also, they would be convinced. Wherefore I cannot but very earnestly desire of the Dissenters and Whigs in my own country that they would take a journey in my consolidator up to the moon; they would certainly see there what vast advantages they lose for want of a spirit of union and a concert of measures among themselves.

The Crolians in the moon are men of large souls, and generously stand by one another on all occasions. It was never known that they deserted anybody that suffered for them, my old philosopher excepted, and that was a surprise upon them.

The reason of the difference is plain. Our Dissenters here have not the advantage of a cogitator or thinking engine, as they have in the moon. We have the elevator here, and are lifted up pretty much; but in the moon they always go into the thinking engine upon every emergency, and in this they outdo us of this world on every occasion.

In general, therefore, I must note that the wisest men I found in the moon, when they understood the notes I had made, as above, of the subdivisions of our parties, told me that it was the greatest happiness that could have been obtained to our country, for that if our parties had not been thus divided the nation had been undone. They owned that had not their Solunarian party been divided among themselves, the Crolians had been undone, and all the moon had been involved in persecution, and been very probably subjected to the Gallunarian monarch.

Thus the fatal errors of men have their advantages; the separate ends they serve are not foreseen by their authors, and they do good against the very design of the people and the nature of the evil itself.

And now that I may encourage our people to that peace and good understanding among themselves which can alone produce their safety and deliverance, I shall give a brief account how the Crolians in the moon came to open their eyes to their own interest; how they came to unite, and how the fruits of that union secured them from ever being insulted again by the Solunarian party, who in time gave over the vain and fruitless attempt, and so a universal Lunar calm has spread the moon ever since.

If our people will not listen to their own advantages nor do their own business, let them take the consequences to themselves; they cannot blame the Man in the Moon.

To endeavour to bring this to pass, as these memoirs have run through the general history of the feuds and unhappy breaches between the Solunarian Church and the Crolian Dissenters in the world of the moon, it would seem an imperfect and abrupt relation if I should not tell you how and by what method, though long hid from their eyes, the Crolians came to understand their own interest and know their own strength.

It is true it seemed a wonder to me, when I considered the excellence and variety of those perspective glasses I have mentioned, the clearness of the air, and consequently of the head, in this Lunar world. I say it was very strange the Crolians should have been moon-blind so long as they were; that they could not see it was always in their power, if they had but pursued their own interest, and made use of those legal opportunities which lay before them, to put themselves in such a posture as that the Government itself should think them a body too big to be insulted, and find it their interest to keep measures with them.

It was indeed a long time before they opened their eyes to these advantages, but bore the insults of the hare-brained party with a weakness and negligence that was as unjustifiable in them as unaccountable to all the nations of the moon.

But at last, as all violent extremes rouse their contrary extremities, the folly and extravagance of the High Solunarians drove the Crolians into their senses and roused them to their own interest. The occasion was, among a great many others, as follows :—

The eager Solunarians could not on all occasions forbear to show their deep regret at the dissenting Crolians enjoying the toleration of their religion by a law; and when all their legal attempts to lessen that liberty had proved abortive—her Solunarian Majesty on all occasions repeating her assurances of the continuance of her protection, and particularly the maintaining this toleration inviolable—they proceeded then to show the remains of their malice in little insults, mean and illegal methods, and continual private disturbances upon particular persons; in which, however, the Crolians, having recourse to the law, always found justice on their side, and had redress with advantage, of which the following instance is more than ordinarily remarkable.

There had been a law made by the men of the feather that all the meaner idle sort of people who had no settled way of living should go to the wars, and the Lazognians, a sort of magistrates there, in the nature of our justices of the peace, were to send them away by force.

Now it happened in a certain Solunarian island that, for want of a better, one of their high-priests was put into the civil administration and made a Lazognian. In the neighbourhood of this man's jurisdiction one of their own Solunarian priests had turned Crolian, and whether he had a better talent at performance, or rather was more diligent in his office, is not material, but he set up a kind of Crolian temple in an old barn, or some such mechanic building, and all the people flocked after him.

This so provoked his neighbours of the Black Girdle, an order of priests of which he had been one, that they resolved to suppress him, let it cost what it would. They ran strange lengths to bring this to pass.

They forged strange stories of him, defamed him, ran him into jail upon frivolous and groundless occasions, represented him as a monster of a man, told their story so plain, and made it so specious, that even the Crolians themselves, to their shame, believed it, and took up prejudices against the poor man, which had like to have been his ruin.

They proscribed him in print for crimes they could never prove; they branded him with forgery, adultery, drunkenness, swearing, breaking jail, and abundance of crimes; but when matters were examined, and things came to the test, they could never prove the least thing upon him.  In this manner, however, they continually worried the poor man, till they ruined his family and reduced him to beggary; and though he came out of the prison they cast him into by the mere force of innocence, yet they never left pursuing him with all sorts of violence.  At last they made use of their Brother of the Girdle, who was in commission as above, and this man being high-priest and Lazonian too, by the first was a party, and by the last had a power to act the tragedy they had plotted against the poor man.

In short, they seized him without any crime alleged, took violently from him his license as a Crolian priest, by which the law justified what he had done, pretending it was forged, and after very ill treating him, condemned him to the wars, delivered him up for a soldier, and accordingly carried him away.

But it happened, to their great mortification, that this man found more mercy from the men of the sword than from those of the word, and so found means to get out of their hands, and afterwards to undeceive all the moon both as to his own character and as to what he had suffered.  For some of the Crolians, who began to be made sensible of the injury done the poor man, advised him to have recourse to the law, and to bring his adversaries before the criminal bar.

But as soon as this was done, good God! what a scene of villainy was here opened.  The poor man brought up such a cloud of witnesses to confront every article of their charge and to vindicate his own character, that when the very judges heard it, though they were all Solunarians themselves, they held up their hands, and declared in open court it was the deepest track of villainy that ever came before them, and that the actors ought to be made examples to all the moon.

The persons concerned used all possible arts to avoid, or at least to delay the shame, and adjourn the punishment, thinking still to weary the poor man out. But now his brethren the Crolians began to see themselves wounded through his sides, and above all, finding his innocence cleared up beyond all manner of dispute, they espoused his cause and assisted him to prosecute his enemies, which he did till he brought them all to justice, exposed them to the last degree, obtained full reparation of all his losses, and a public decree of the judges of his justification and future repose.

Indeed, when I saw the proceedings against this poor man run to a height so extravagant and monstrous, when I found malice, forgery, subornation, perjury, and a thousand unjustifiable things which their own sense, if they had any, might have been their protection against, and which any child in the moon might have told them must one time or other come upon the state and expose them, I began to think these people were all in the Crolian plot too.

For really such proceedings as these were the greatest pieces of service to the Crolians that could possibly be done; for as it generally proves in other places as well as in the moon, that mischief unjustly contrived falls upon the head of the authors, and redounds to their treble dishonour, so it was here. The barbarity and inhuman treatment of this man made the sober and honest part even of the Solunarians themselves blush for their brethren, and own that the punishment awarded on them was just.

Thus the Crolians got ground by the folly and madness of their enemies, and the very engines and plots laid to injure them served to bring their enemies on the stage and expose both them and their cause.

But this was not all. By these incessant attacks on them as a party, they began to come to their senses out of a fifty-year slumber ; they found the law on their side and the Government moderate and just ; they found they might oppose violence with law, and that when they did fly to the refuge of justice, they always had the better of their enemy. Flushed with this success, it put them upon considering what fools they had been all along, to bear the insolence of a few hot-headed men, who, contrary to the true intent and meaning of the queen or of the Government, had resolved their destruction. It put them upon revolving the state of their own case and comparing it with their enemies ; upon examining on what foot they stood, and though established upon a firm law, yet a violent party pushing at the overthrow of that establishment, and dissolving the legal right they had to their liberty and religion, it put them upon duly weighing the nearness of their approaching ruin and destruction ; and finding things run so hard against them, reflecting upon the extremity of their affairs, and how if they had not drawn in the High Church champions to damn the projects of their own party by running at such desperate extremes as all men of any temper must of course abhor, they had been undone : truly now they began to consider and to consult with one another what was to be done.

Abundance of projects were laid before them—some too dangerous, some too foolish to be put in practice. At last they resolved to consult with my philosopher.

He had been but scurvily treated by them in his troubles, and so universally abandoned by the Crolians, that even the Soluna rians themselves insulted them on that head, and laughed at them for expecting anybody should venture for them again. But he, forgetting their unkindness, asked them what it was they desired of him.

They told him they had heard that he had reported he could put the Crolians in a way to secure themselves from any possibility of being insulted again by the Solunarians, and yet not disturb the public tranquillity nor break the laws ; and they desired him, if he knew such a secret, he would communicate it to them, and they would be sure to remember to forget him for it as long as he lived.

He frankly told them he had said so, and it was true he could put them in a way to do all this, if they would follow his directions. "What's that?" says one of the most earnest inquirers. "It is included in one word," says he—"Unite."

This most significant word, deeply and solidly reflected upon, put them upon strange and various conjectures, and many long debates they had with themselves about it; at last they came again to him, and asked him what he meant by it.

He told them he knew they were strangers to the meaning of the thing, and therefore, if they would meet him the next day, he would come prepared to explain himself. Accordingly they met, when, instead of a long speech they expected from him as to what sort of union he meant and with whom, he brings them a thinking press or cogitator, and setting it down, goes away without speaking one word.

This hieroglyphical admonition was too plain not to let them all into his meaning; but still, as they are an obstinate people, and not a little valuing themselves upon their own knowledge and penetration, they slighted the engine and fell to offhand surmises, guesses, and supposes.

1. Some concluded he meant unite with the Solunarian Church; and they reflected upon his understanding, that not being the question in hand, and something remote from their intention or the High Solunarians' desire.

2. Some meant unite to the moderate party of the Solunarians, and this they said they had done already.

At last, some being very cunning, found it out, that it must be his meaning to unite one among another; and even there again they misunderstood him too; and some imagined he meant downright rebellion, uniting power and mobbing the whole moon; but he soon convinced them of that too.

At last they took the hint that his advice directed them to unite their subdivided parties into one general interest, and to act in concert upon one bottom; to lay aside the selfish, narrow, suspicious spirit, three qualifications the Crolians were but too justly charged with, and begin to act with courage, unanimity, and largeness of soul, to open their eyes to their own interest, maintain a regular and constant correspondence with one another in all parts of the kingdom, and to bring their civil interest into a form.

The author of this advice having thus brought them to understand and approve his proposal, they demanded his assistance for making the essay; and it is a most wonderful thing to consider what a strange effect the alteration of their measures had upon the whole Solunarian nation.

As soon as ever they had settled the methods they resolved to act in, they formed a general council of the heads of their party, to be always sitting, to reconcile differences, to unite parties, to suppress feuds in their beginning.

They appointed three general meetings in three of the most remote parts of the kingdom, to meet half yearly, and one universal meeting of persons deputed to concert matters among them in general. By the time these meetings had sat but once, and the conduct of the council of twelve began to appear, it was a wonder to see the prodigious alteration it made all over the country.

Immediately a Crolian would never buy anything but of a Crolian; would hire no servants, employ neither porter nor carman, but what were Crolians.

The Crolians in the country that wrought and managed the manufactures would employ nobody but Crolian spinners, Crolian weavers, and the like.

In their capital city the merchandising Crolians would freight no ships but of which the owners and commanders were Crolians.

They called all their cash out of the Solunarian bank; and as the Act of the Cortes confirming the bank then in being seemed to claim their support, they made it plain that cash and credit will make a bank without a public settlement of law, and without these all the laws in the moon will never be able to support it.

They brought all their running cash into one bank, and settled a sub-cash depending upon the grand bank in every province of the kingdom, in which, by a strict correspondence and crediting their bills, they might be able to settle a paper credit over the whole nation.

They went on to settle themselves in all sorts of trade in open companies, and sold off their interests in the public stocks then in trade.

If the Government wanted a million of money upon any emergency, they were ready to lend it as a body ; not by different sums and private hands blended together with their enemies, but, as will appear at large presently, it was only Crolian money, and passed as such.

Nor were the consequences of this new model less considerable than the proposer expected ; for the Crolians being generally of the trading and manufacturing part of the world and very rich, the influence this method had upon the common people, upon trade, and upon the public was very considerable every way.

1. All the Solunarian tradesmen and shopkeepers were at their wit's-end ; they sat in their shops and had little or nothing to do, while the shops of the Crolians were full of customers and their people over head and ears in business. This turned many of the Solunarian tradesmen quite off the hooks, and they began to break and decay strangely, till at last a great many of them, to prevent their utter ruin, turned Crolians on purpose to get a trade ; and what forwarded that part of it was that when a Solunarian who had little or no trade before came over to the Crolians, immediately everybody came to trade with him, and his shop would be full of customers, so that this presently increased the number of the Crolians.

2. The poor people in the countries, carders, spinners, weavers, knitters, and all sorts of manufacturers, ran in crowds to the Crolian temples for fear of being starved, for the Crolians were two-thirds of the masters or employers in the manufactures all over the country, and the poor would have been starved and undone if they had cast them out of work. Thus insensibly the Crolians increased their number.

3. The Crolians being men of vast cash, they no sooner with-drew their money from the general bank but the bank languished,

credit sank, and in a short time they had little to do, but dissolved of course.

One thing remained which people expected would have put a check to this undertaking, and that was a way of trading in classes or societies, much like our East India Companies in England; and these depending upon public privileges granted by the queen of the country or her predecessors, nobody could trade to those parts but the persons who had those privileges. The cunning Crolians, who had great stocks in those trades, and foresaw they could not trade by themselves without the public grant or charter, contrived a way to get almost all that capital trade into their hands as follows :—

They concerted matters, and all at once fell to selling off their stock, giving out daily reports that they would be no longer concerned, that it was a losing trade, that the fund at bottom was good for nothing, and that of two societies the old one had not 20 per cent. to divide, all their debts being paid ; that the new society had traded several years, but if they were dissolved could not say they had got anything ; and that this must be a cheat at last, and so they resolved to sell.

By this artifice, they daily offering to sale, and yet in all their discourse discouraging the thing they were to sell, nobody could be found to buy.

The offering a thing to sale and no bidders is a certain neverfailing prospect of a lowering the price ; from this method, therefore, the value of all the banks, companies, societies, and stocks in the country fell to be little or nothing worth, and that was to be bought for forty or forty-five Lunarians that was formerly sold at 150, and so in proportion of all the rest.

All this while the Crolians employed their emissaries to buy up privately all the interest or shares in these things that any of the Solunarian party would sell.

This plot took readily, for these gentlemen exposing the weakness of these societies, and running down the value of their stocks, and at the same time warily buying at the lowest prices, not only in time got possession of the whole trade, with their grants, privileges, and stocks, but got into them at a prodigiously low and despicable price.

They had no sooner thus wormed them out of the trade, and got the greatest part of the effects into their own hands, and consequently the whole management, but they ran up the price of the funds again as high as ever, and laughed at the folly of those that sold out.

Nor could the other people make any reflections upon the honesty of the practice, for it was no original, but had its birth among the Solunarians themselves, of whom three or four had frequently made a trade of raising and lowering the funds of the societies by all the clandestine contrivances in the world, and had ruined abundance of families to raise their own fortunes and estates.

One of the greatest merchants in the moon raised himself by this method to such a height of wealth that he left all his children married to grandees, dukes, and great folks, and from a mechanic original they are now ranked among the Lunarian nobility, while multitudes of ruined families helped to build his fortune by sinking under the knavery of his contrivance.

His brother in the same iniquity, being at this time a man of the feather, has carried on the same intriguing trade with all the face and front imaginable; it has been nothing with him to persuade his most intimate friends to sell or buy, just as he had occasion for his own interest to have it rise or fall, and so to make his own market of their misfortune. Thus he has twice raised his fortunes—for the house of feathers demolished him once—and yet he has by the same clandestine management worked himself up again.

This civil way of robbing houses, for I can esteem it no better, was carried on by a middle sort of people, called in the moon Bloutegondegours, which signifies men with two tongues, or in English, stockjobbing brokers.

These had formerly such an unlimited power, and were so numerous, that indeed they governed the whole trade of the country; no man knew when he bought or sold, for though they pretended to buy and sell and manage for other men whose stocks they had very much at command, yet nothing was more frequent than when they bought a thing cheap to buy it for themselves, if dear, for their employer; if they were to sell, if the price rose, it was sold—if it fell, it was unsold; and by this art nobody got any money but themselves, that at last, excepting the two capital men we spoke of before, these governed the prizes of all things, and nothing could be bought or sold to advantage but through their hands; and as the profit was prodigious, their number increased accordingly, so that business seemed engrossed by these men, and they governed the main articles of trade.

This success, and the imprudence of their conduct, brought great complaints against them to the Government, and a law was made to restrain them, both in practice and number.

This law has in some measure had its effect. The number is not only lessened, but by chance some honester men than usual are got in among them; but they are so very, very, very few, hardly enough to save a man's credit that shall vouch for them. Nay, some people that pretend to understand their business better than I do, having been of their number, have affirmed it is impossible to be honest in the employment.

I confess when I began to search into the conduct of these men, at least of some of them, I found there were abundance of black stories to be told of them—a great deal known and a great deal more unknown; for they were from the beginning continually encroaching into all sorts of people and societies, and in conjunction with some that were not qualified by law, but merely voluntarily, called in the moon by a long hard word, in English signifying projectors. These erected stocks in shadows, societies *in nubibus*, and bought and sold mere vapour, wind, emptiness, and bluster for money, till they drew people in to lay out their cash, and then laughed at them.

Thus they erected paper societies, linen societies, sulphur societies, copper societies, glass societies, sham banks, and a thousand mock whimsies to hook unwary people in; at last sold themselves out, left the bubble to float a little in the air, and then vanish of itself.

The other sort of people go on after all this; and though these projectors began to be out of fashion, they always found one thing or other to amuse and deceive the ignorant, and went jobbing on into all manner of things, public as well as private, whether the revenue, the public funds, loans, annuities, bear-skins, or anything.

Nay, they were once grown to that extravagant height, that they began to stock-job the very feathers of the consolidator; and in time the kings employing those people might have had what feathers they had occasion for without concerning the proprietors of the lands much about them.

It is true this began to be notorious, and received some check in a former meeting of the feathers; but even now, when I came away, the three years expiring, and by course a new consolidator being to be built, they were as busy as ever. Bidding, offering, procuring, buying, selling, and jobbing of feathers to who bid most; and notwithstanding several late wholesome and strict laws against all manner of collusion, bribery, and clandestine methods in the countries procuring these feathers, never was the moon in such an uproar about picking and culling the feathers, such bribery, such drunkenness, such caballing, especially among the High Solunarian clergy and the Lazognians, such feasting, fighting, and distraction, as the like has never been known.

And that which is very remarkable, all this not only before the old consolidator was broke up, but even while it was actually whole and in use.

Had this hurry been to send up good feathers, there had been the less to say, but that which made it very strange to me was, that where the very worst of all the feathers were to be found, there was the most of this wicked work; and though it was bad enough everywhere, yet the greatest bustle and contrivance was in order to send up the worst feathers they could get.

And indeed in some places such sorry, scoundrel, empty, husky, withered, decayed feathers were offered to the proprietors, that I have sometimes wondered any one could have the impudence to send up such ridiculous feathers to make a consolidator, which, as is before observed, is an engine of such beauty, usefulness, and necessity.

And still in all my observation this note came in my way— there was always the most bustle and disturbance about the worst feathers.

It was really a melancholy thing to consider, and had this Lunar world been my native country, I should have been full of concern to see that one thing, on which the welfare of the whole nation so much depended, put in so ill a method, and gotten into the management of such men, who for money would certainly have set up such feathers that, wherever the consolidator should be formed, it would certainly overset the first voyage ; and if the whole nation should happen to be embarked in it on the danger- ous voyage to the moon, the fall would certainly give them such a shock as would put them all into confusion, and open the door to the Gallunarian or any foreign enemy to destroy them.

It was really strange that this should be the case after so many laws, and so lately made, against it ; but in this those people are too like our people in England, who have the best laws the worst executed of any nation under heaven.

For in the moon this hurry about choosing of feathers was grown to the greatest height imaginable, as if it increased by the very laws that were made to suppress it ; for now, at a certain public place where the Bloutegondegours used to meet every day, anybody that had but money enough might buy a feather at a reasonable rate, and never go down into the country to fetch it ; nay, the trade grew so hot, that of a sudden, as if no other business was in hand, all people were upon it, and the whole market was changed from selling of bear-skins to buying of feathers.

Some gave this for a reason why all the stocks of the societies fell so fast, but there were other reasons to be given for that, such as clubs, cabals, stockjobbers, knights, merchants, and thieves ;

I mean, a private sort, not such as are frequently hanged there, but of a worse sort, by how much they merit that punishment more, but are out of the reach of the law; can rob and pick pockets in the face of the sun, and laugh at the families they ruin, bidding defiance to all legal resentment.

To this height things were come under the growing evil of this sort of people.

And yet in the very moon, where, as I have noted, the people are so exceeding clear-sighted, and have such vast helps to their perceptive faculties, such mists are sometimes cast before the public understanding that they cannot see the general interest.

This was manifest in that, just as I came away from that country, the great council of their wise men, the men of the feather, were a going to repeal the old law of restraining the number of these people; and though, as it was, there was not employment for half of them, there being a hundred in all, and not above five honest ones, yet when I came away they were going to increase their number. I have nothing to say to this here, only that all wise men that understand trade were very much concerned at it, and looked upon it as a most destructive thing to the public, and foreboding the same mischiefs that trade suffered before.

It was the particular misfortune of these Lunar people that this country had a better stock of governors in all articles of their welfare than in their trade. Their law affairs had good judges, their Church good patriarchs, except as might be excepted; their state good ministers, their army good generals, and their consolidator good feathers; but in matters relating to trade they had this particular misfortune, that those cases always came before people that did not understand them.

Even the judges themselves were often found at a loss to determine causes of negoce, such as protests, charter-parties, averages, barratry, demurrage of ships, right of detaining vessels on demurrage, and the like; nay, the very laws themselves are fain to be silent, and yield in many things a superiority to the custom of merchants.

And here I began to congratulate my native country, where the prudence of the Government has provided for these things by establishing in a commission of trade some of the most experienced gentlemen in the nation to regulate, settle, improve, and revive trade in general by their unwearied labours and most consummate understanding ; and this made me pity these countries, and think it would be an action worthy of this nation, and be spoken of for ages to come to their glory, if in mere charity they would appoint or depute these gentlemen to go a voyage to those countries of the moon, and bless those regions with the schemes of their sublime undertakings and discoveries in trade.

But when I was expressing myself thus, my philosopher interrupted me, and told me I should see they were already furnished for that purpose when I came to examine the public libraries; of which by itself.

But I was further confirmed in my observation of the weakness of the public heads of that country as to trade when I saw another most preposterous law going forward among them, the title of which was specious, and contained something relating to employing the poor, but the substance of it absolutely destructive to the very nature of their trade, tended to transposing, confounding, and destroying their manufactures, and to the ruin of all their home commerce. Never was nation so blind to their own interest as these Lunarian law-makers, and the people who were the contrivers of this law were so vainly conceited, so fond of the gilded title, and so positively dogmatic, that they would not hear the frequent applications of persons better acquainted with those things than themselves, but pushed it on merely by the strength of their party for the vanity of being authors of such a contrivance.

But to return to the new model of the Crolians. The advice of the Lunarian philosopher ran through all their affairs. "Unite" was the word through all the nation, in trade, in cash, in stocks, as I noted before.

If a Solunarian ship was bound to any outport, no Crolian would load any goods aboard ; if any ship came to seek freight abroad, none of the Crolians' correspondents would ship anything

unless they knew the owners were Crolians; the Crolian merchants turned out all their Solunarian masters, sailors, and captains
from their ships; and thus, as the Solunarians would have them
be separated in respect of the government, profits, honours, and
offices, they resolved to separate in everything else too, and to
stand by themselves.

At last, upon some public occasion, the public treasurers of the
land sent to the capital city to borrow 500,000 Lunarians upon
very good security of established funds. Truly nobody would
lend any money, or at least they could not raise above a fifth part
of that sum, inquiring at the bank, at their general societies' cash,
and other places; all was languid and dull, and no money to be
had; but being informed that the Crolians had erected a bank of
their own, they sent thither, and were answered readily that whatever sum the Government wanted was at their service, only it was
to be lent not by particular persons, but such a grandee, being one
of the prime nobility, and whom the Crolians now called their protector, was to be treated with about it.

The Government saw no harm in all this. Here was no law
broken, here was nothing but oppression answered with policy
and mischief fenced against with reason.

The Government, therefore, took no notice of it, nor made any
scruple when they wanted any money to treat with this nobleman,
and borrow any sum of the Crolians as Crolians. On the contrary, in the name of the Crolians, their head or protector presented their addresses and petitions, procured favours on one
hand and assistance on the other; and thus by degrees and
insensibly the Crolians became a politic body, settled and established by orders and rules among themselves. And while a spirit
of unanimity thus ran through all their proceedings, their enemies
could never hurt them; their princes always saw it was their
interest to keep measures with them, and they were sure to have
justice upon any complaint whatsoever.

When I saw this, it forced me to reflect upon affairs in our own
country. Well, said I, it is happy for England that our Dissenters
have not this spirit of union and largeness of heart among them,

for if they were not a narrow, mean-spirited, short-sighted, self-preserving, friend-betraying, poor-neglecting people, they might have been every way as safe, as considerable, as regarded, and as numerous as the Crolians in the moon; but it is not in their souls to do themselves good, nor to espouse or stand by those that would do it for them; and it is well for the Churchmen that it is so, for many attempts have been made to save them, but their own narrowness of soul and dividedness in interest has also prevented its being effectual, and discouraged all the instruments that ever attempted to serve them.

It is confessed the case was thus at first among the Crolians; they were full of divisions among themselves, as I have noted already of the Solunarians, and the unhappy feuds among them had always not only exposed them to the censure, reproach, and banter of their Solunarian enemies, but it had served to keep them under, prevent their being valued in the Government, and given the other party vast advantages against them.

But the Solunarians, driving thus furiously at their destruction and entire ruin, opened their eyes to the following measures for their preservation. And here again the High Solunarians may see, and doubtless whenever they make use of the lunar glasses they must see, that nothing could have driven the Crolians to make use of such methods for their defence but the rash proceedings of their own warm men in order to suppressing the whole Crolian interest. And this might inform our countrymen of the Church of England that it cannot but be their interest to treat their brethren with moderation and temper, lest their extravagances should one time or other drive the other, as it were, by force into their senses, and open their eyes to do only all those things which by law they may do, and which they are laughed at by all the world for not doing.

This was the very case in the moon. The philosopher, or pretended such, as before, had often published that it was their interest to unite; but their eyes not being open to the true causes and necessity of it, their ears were shut against the counsel till oppression and necessity drove them to it.

Accordingly they entered into a serious debate of the state of their own affairs, and finding the advice given very reasonable, they set about it, and the author gave them a model entitled "An Inquiry into what the Crolians may Lawfully do to Prevent the Certain Ruin of their Interest, and Bring their Enemies to Peace."

I will not pretend to examine the contents of this sublime tract; but from this very day we found the Crolians in the moon acting quite on a different footing from all their former conduct, putting on a new temper and a new face, as you have heard.

All this while the hot Solunarians cried out plots, associations, confederacies, and rebellions, when indeed here was nothing done but what the laws justified, what reason directed, and what, had the [Crolians but made use of the cogitator, they would have done forty years before.

The truth is, the other people had no remedy but to cry murder and make a noise; for the Crolians went on with their affairs, and established themselves so, that when I came away they were become a most solid and well-united body, made a considerable figure in the nation, and yet the Government was easy; for the Solunarians found when they had attained the utmost end of her wishes, her Solunarian Majesty was as safe as before, and the Crolians' property being secured, they were as loyal subjects as the Solunarians, as consistent with monarchy, as useful to it, and as pleased with it.

I cannot but remark here that this union of the Crolians among themselves had another consequence, which made it appear it was not only to their own advantage, but to the general good of all the nation. For by little and little the feuds of the parties cooled, and the Solunarians began to be better reconciled to them; the Government was easy and safe, and the private quarrels, as I have been told since, begin to be quite forgot.

What blindness, said I to myself, has possessed the Dissenters in our unhappy country of England, where, by eternal discords, feuds, distrusts, and disgusts among themselves, they always fill their enemies with hopes that by pushing at them they may one time or other complete their ruin, which expectation has always served as a means to keep open the quarrel; whereas had the Dissenters been united in interest, affection, and management among themselves, all this heat had long ago been over, and the nation, though there had been two opinions, had retained but one interest, been joined in affection, and peace at home been raised up to that degree that all wise men wish, as it is now among the inhabitants of the world in the moon.

It is true, in all the observations I made in this Lunar country, the vast deference paid to the persons of princes began to lessen, and whatever respect they had for the office, they found it necessary frequently to tell the world that on occasion they could treat them with less respect than they pretended to owe them.

For about this time the divine right of kings and the inheritances of princes in the moon met with a terrible shock, and that by the Solunarian party themselves; and insomuch that even my philosopher, and he was none of the *jure divino* men neither, declared against it.

They made crowns perfect footballs, set up what kings they would and pulled down such as they did not like, *pro ratione voluntas*, right or wrong, as they thought best, of which some examples shall be given by and bye.

After I had thus inquired into the historical affairs of this Lunar nation, which, for its similitude to my native country, I could not but be inquisitive in, I waived a great many material things, which at least I cannot enter upon the relation of here, and began to inquire into their affairs abroad.

I think I took notice in the beginning of my account of these parts that I found them engaged in a tedious and bloody war with one of the most mighty monarchs of all the moon. I must therefore hint that, among the multitude of things which for brevity sake I omit, the reader may observe these were some :—

1. That this was the same monarch who harboured and entertained the Abrogratzian prince who was fled as before, and whom we are to call the King of Gallunaria.

2. I have omitted the account of a long and bloody war,

which lasted a great many years, and which the present queen's predecessor managed with a great deal of bravery and conduct, and finished very much to his own glory and the nation's advantage.

3. I have too much omitted to note how barbarously the High Solunarian Churchmen treated him for all his services, upbraided him with the expense of the war; and though he saved them all from ruin and Abrogratzianism, yet had not one good word for him; and, indeed, it is with some difficulty that I pass this over, because it might be necessary to observe, besides what is said before, that ingratitude is a vice in Nature, and practised everywhere, as well as in England. So that we need not upbraid the party among us with their ill-treatment of the late king, for these people used their good king every jot as bad, till their unkindness perfectly broke his heart.

Here, also, I am obliged to omit the historical part of the war and of the peace that followed; only I must observe that this peace was very precarious, short, and unhappy, and in a few months the war broke out again with as much fury as ever.

In this war happened one of the strangest, most unaccountable, and most preposterous actions that ever a people in their national capacity could be guilty of.

Certainly if our people in England who pretend that kingship is *jure divino* did but know the story of which I speak, they would be quite of another mind; wherefore I crave leave to relate part of the history or original of this last war, as a necessary introduction to the proper observations I shall make upon it.

There was a king of a certain country in the moon called in their language Ebronia, who was formerly a confederate with the Solunarians. This prince dying without issue, the great monarch we speak of seized upon all his dominions as his right, though, if I remember right, he had formerly sworn never to lay claim to it, and after that by a subsequent treaty had agreed with the Solunarian prince that another monarch who claimed a right as well as he should divide it between them.

The breach of this agreement and seizing this kingdom put

almost all the Lunar world into a flame, and war hung over the
heads of all the northern nations of the moon, for several claims
were made to the succession by other princes, and particularly by
a certain potent prince called the Eagle, of an ancient family,
whose Lunar name I cannot well express, but in English it
signifies the men of the great lip. Whether it was originally a sort
of a nickname, or whether they had any such thing as a great
lip hereditary to the family by which they were distinguished, is
not worth my while to examine.

It is without question that the successive right, if their Lunar
successions are governed as ours are in this world, devolved upon
this man with the lip and his families; but the Gallunarian monarch brought things so to pass by his extraordinary conduct
that the Ebronian king was drawn in by some of his nobility,
whom this prince had bought and bribed to betray their country to
his interest, and particularly a certain high-priest of that country,
to make an assignment or deed of gift of all his dominions to
the grandson of this Gallunarian monarch.

By virtue of this gift or legacy, as soon as the king died, who
was then languishing, and, as the other party alleged, not in a very
good capacity to make a will, the Gallunarian king sent his grandson to seize upon the crown, and backing him with suitable forces,
took possession of all his strong fortifications and frontiers.

Nor was this all. The man with the lip indeed talked big, and
threatened war immediately, but the Solunarians were so unset-
tled at home, so unprepared for war, having just dismissed their
auxiliary troops and disbanded their own, and the prince was so
ill served by his subjects, that both he and a powerful neighbour,
nations in the same interest, were merely bullied by this Gallunarian, and as he threatened immediately to invade them, which
they were then in no condition to prevent, he forced them both
to submit to his demand, tacitly allow what he had done in
breaking the treaty with him, and at last openly acknowledge
his new king.

This was indeed a most unaccountable step, but there was a
necessity to plead, for he was at their very doors with his forces,

and this neighbouring people, whom they call Mogenites, could not resist him without help from the Solunarians, which they were very backward in, notwithstanding the earnest solicitations of their prince, and notwithstanding they were obliged to do it by a solemn treaty.

These delays obliged them to this strange step of acknowledging the invasion of their enemy and pulling off the hat to the new king he had set up.

It is true the policy of these Lunar nations was very remarkable in this case, and they outwitted the Gallunarian monarch in it; for by the owning this prince, whom they immediately after declared a usurper and made war against, they stopped the mouth of the Gallunarian, his grandfather, took from him all pretence of invading them, and making him believe they were sincere, wheedled him to restore several thousand of their men that he had taken prisoners in the frontier towns of the Ebronians.

Had the Gallunarian prince had but the forecast to have seen that this was but a forced pretence to gain time, and that as soon as they had their troops clear and time to raise more, they would certainly turn upon him again, he would never have been put by with so weak a trifle as the ceremony of congratulations; whereas had he immediately pushed at them with all his forces, they must have been ruined, and he had carried his point without much interruption.

But here he lost his opportunity, which he never retrieved; for it is in the moon just as it is here—when an occasion is lost, it is not easy to be recovered; for both the Solunarians and the Mogenites quickly threw off the mask, and declaring this new prince an usurper, and his grandfather an unjust breaker of treaties, they prepared for war against them both.

As to the honesty of this matter, my philosopher and I differed extremely; he exclaimed against the honour of acknowledging a king, with a design to depose him, and pretending peace when war is designed, though it is true they are too customary in our world; but, however, as to him, I insisted upon the lawfulness of it, from the universal custom of nations, who generally do things ten times more preposterous and inconsistent when they suit their occasions. Yet I hope nobody will think I am recommending them by this relation to the practice of our own nations, but rather exposing them as unaccountable things never to be put in practice without quitting all pretences to justice and national honesty.

The case was this :—As upon the progress of matters before related, the Solunarians and Mogenites had made a formal acknowledgment of this new monarch, the grandson of the Gallunarian king, so, as I have hinted already, they had no other design than to depose him and pull him down.

Accordingly, as soon as by the aforesaid wile they had gained breath and furnished themselves with forces, they declared war against both the Gallunarian king and his grandson, and entered into strict confederacy with the man of the great lip, who was the monarch of the Eagle, and who, by right of succession, had the true claim to the Ebronian crowns.

In these declarations they allege that crowns do not descend by gift, nor are kingdoms given away by legacy, like a gold ring at a funeral, and therefore this young prince could have no right, the former deceased king having no right to dispose it by gift.

I must allow that, judging by our reason and the practice in our countries here on this side the moon, this seemed plain, and I saw no difference in matters of truth there or here; but right and liberty both of princes and people seems to be the same in that world as it is in this, and upon this account I thought the reasons of this war very just, and that the claim of right to the succession of the Ebronian crown was undoubtedly in the man with the lip and his heirs, and so far the war was most just and the design reasonable.

And thus far my Lunar companion agreed with me, and had they gone on so, says he, they had my good wishes, and my judgment had been witness to my pretences that they were in the right. But in the prosecution of this war, says he, they went on to one of the most impolitic, ridiculous, dishonest, and inconsistent actions that ever any nation in the moon was guilty of. The fact was thus.

Having agreed among themselves that the Ebronian crown should not be possessed by the Gallunarian king's grandson, they in the next place began to consider who should have it.[1]

The man with the lip had the title, but he had a great govern·ment of his own, powerful, happy, and remote, being, as is noted, the lord of the great Eagle, and he told them he could not pretend to come to Ebronia to be a king there. His eldest son truly was not only declared heir-apparent to his father, but had another Lunarian kingdom of his own still more remote than that, and he would not quit all this for the crown of Ebronia; so it was concerted by all the confederated parties that the second son of this prince, the man with the lip, should be declared king, and here lay the injustice of all the case.

I confess at my first examining this matter, I did not see far into it, nor could I reach the dishonesty of it, and perhaps the reader of these sheets may be in the same case; but my old Lunarian friend being continually exclaiming against the matter, and blaming his countrymen the Solunarians for the dishonesty of it, but especially the Mogenites, he began to be something peevish with me that I should be so dull as not to reach it, and asked me if he should screw me into the thinking-press for the clearing up my understanding.

At last he told he would write his particular sentiments of this whole affair in a letter to me, which he would so order as it should effectually open my eyes; which indeed it did, and so I believe it will the eyes of all that read it, to which purpose I have obtained of the author to assist me in the translation of it, he having some knowledge also in our sublunar languages.

*The substance of a letter wrote to the author of these sheets while he was in the regions of the moon.*

"FRIEND FROM THE MOON,—

"According to my promise, I hereby give you a scheme of Solunarian honesty, joined with Mogenite policy, and my opinion of the action of my countrymen and their confederates in declaring their new-made Ebronian king.

[1] War of the Spanish Succession : see pages 169-171.

2 C

"The Mogenites and Solunarians are looked upon here to be the original contrivers of this ridiculous piece of pageantry, and though some of their neighbours are supposed to have a hand in it, yet we all lay it at the door of their politics, and for the honesty of it, let them answer it if they can.

"It is observed here that as soon as the king of Gallunaria had declared that he accepted the will and disposition of the crown of Ebronia in favour of his grandson, and that according to the said disposition he had owned him for king, and in order to make it effectual had him put into immediate possession of the kingdom, the Mogenites and their confederates made wonderful clamours at the injustice of his proceedings, and particularly on account of his breaking the treaty then lately entered into with the king of the Solunarians and the Mogenites, for the settling the matter of right and possession, in case of the demise of the Ebronian king.

"However, the king of Gallunaria had no sooner placed his grandson on the throne but the Mogenites and other nations, and to all our wonder the King of Solunaria himself, acknowledged him, owned him, sent their ministers and compliments of congratulation, and the like, giving him the title of king of Ebronia.

"Though this proceeding had something of surprise in it, and all men expected to see something more than ordinary politic in the effect of it, yet it did not give half the astonishment to the lunar world as this unaccountable monster of politics begins to do.

"We have here two unlucky fellows called Pasquin and Marforio, these had a long dialogue about this very matter, and Pasquin, as he always loved mischief, told a very unlucky story to his comrade of a high Mogenite skipper, as follows:—

"'A Mogenite ship coming from a far country, the custom-house officers found some goods on board which were contraband, and for which they pretended the ship and goods were all confiscated; the skipper or captain in a great fright comes up to the custom-house, and being told he must swear to something relating to his taking in those goods, replied in his country jargon, 'Ya, dat sall ick doen, myn heer;' or in English, 'Ay, ay, I'll swear.' But finding they did not assure him that it would clear his ship, he scruples the oath again, at which they told him it would clear his ship immediately. ' Hael, well, myn heer,' says the Mogen man, 'vat mot ick sagen, ick sall all swear myn skip to salvare,' *i.e.*, ' I shall swear anything to save my skip.'

" We apply this story thus :—

" If the Mogenites did acknowledge the king of Ebronia, we did believe it was done to save the skip ; and when they reproached the Gallunarian king with breaking the treaty of division, we used to say we would all break through twice as many engagements for half as much advantage.

"This setting up a new king against a king on the throne acknowledged and congratulated by them is not only looked on in the Lunar world as a thing ridiculous, but particularly infamous, that they should first acknowledge a king and then set up the title of another. If the title of the first Ebronian king be good, this must be an impostor, an usurper of another man's right. If it was not good, why did they acknowledge him and give him the full title of all the Ebronian dominions, caress and congratulate him, and make a public action of it to his ambassador ?

" Will they tell us they were bullied and frightened into it ? That is to own they may be huffed into an ill action, for owning a man in the possession of what is none of his own is an ill thing; and he that may be huffed into one ill action may by consequence be huffed into another, and so into anything.

" What will they say for doing it? We have heard there has been in the world you came from a way found out to own kings *de facto* but not *de jure*. If they will fly to that ridiculous shift, let them tell the world so, that we may know what they mean, for those foolish things are not known here.

"If they owned the king of Ebronia voluntarily, and acknowledged his right as we thought they had, how then can this young gentleman have a title unless they have found out a new division, and so will have two kings of Ebronia make them partners, and have a Gallunarian king of Ebronia and a Mogenite king of Ebronia both together?

"Our Lunar nations, princes, and states, whatever they may do in your world, always seek for some pretences at least to make their actions seem honest, whether they are so or no; and therefore they generally publish memorials, manifestoes, and declarations of their reasons why and on what account they do so or so; that those who have any grounds to charge them with injustice may be answered and silenced. It is for the people in your country to fall upon their neighbours, only because they will do it, and make probability of conquest a sufficient reason of conquest. The Lunarian nations are seldom so destitute of modesty, but that they will make a show of justice, and make out the reasons of their proceedings; and though sometimes we find even the reasons given for some actions are weak enough, yet it is a bad cause indeed that can neither have a true reason nor a pretended one. The custom of the moon has obliged us to show so much respect to honesty, that when our actions have the least colour of honesty, yet we will make reasons to look like a defence, whether it be so or no.

"But here is an action that has neither reality nor pretence; here is not face enough upon it to bear an apology. First they acknowledge one king, and then set up another king against him; either they first acknowledged a wrong king, and thereby became parties to a usurper, or they act now against all the rules of common justice in the world, to set up a sham king to pull down a true one, only because it is their interest to have it so.

"This makes the very name of a Solunarian scandalous to all the moon, and mankind look upon them with the utmost prejudice, as if they were a nation who had sold all their honesty to their interest, and who could act this way to-day and that way to-morrow, without any regard to truth or the rule of honour, equity, or conscience; this is swearing anything to save the skip; and never let any man reproach the Gallunarian king with breaking the treaty of division and disregarding the faith and stipulations of leagues; for this is an action so inconsistent with itself, so incongruous to common justice and to the reason and nature of things, that no history of these latter times can parallel it, and it is past the power of art to make any reasonable defence for it.

"Indeed, some lame reasons are given for it by our politicians. First, they say the prince with the great lip was extremely pressed by the Gallunarians at home in his own country, and not without apprehensions of seeing them before long under the walls of his capital city.

"From this circumstance of the man with the lip, it was not irrational to expect that he might be induced to make a separate peace with the Gallunarians, and serve them as he did once the prince of Berlindia at the treaty of peace in a former war, where he deserted him after the solemnest engagements never to make peace without him; but his pressing occasions requiring it, concluded a peace without him, and left him to come out of the war as well as he could, though he had come into it only for his assistance. Now finding him in danger of being ruined by the Gallunarian power, and judging from former practice in like cases that he might be hurried into a peace and leave them in the lurch, they have drawn him into this labyrinth as into a step which can never be receded from without the utmost affront and disgrace, either to the family of the Gallunarian or of the Lip; an action which, in its own nature, is a defiance of the whole Gallunarian power, and without any other manifesto may be taken as a declaration from the house of the Lip to the Gallunarian that this war shall never end till one of those two families are ruined and reduced.

"What condition the Prince with the Lip's power is in to make such a huff at this time shall come under examination by and bye; in the meantime the Solunarians have clinched the nail, and secured the war to last as long as they think convenient.

"If the Gallunarians should get the better and reduce the man with the lip to terms never so disadvantageous, he cannot now make a peace without leave from the Solunarians and the Mogenites, lest his son should be ruined also. Or if he should make articles for himself, it must be with ten times the dishonour that he might have done before.

"Politicians say it is never good for a prince to put himself into a case of desperation. This is drawing the sword and throwing away the scabbard; if a disaster should befall him, his retreat is impossible, and this must have been done only to secure the man with the lip from being huffed or frighted into a separate peace.

"The second reason people here give why the Solunarians are concerning themselves in this matter is drawn from trade.

"The continuing of Ebronia in the hands of the Gallunarians will most certainly be the destruction of the Solunarian and Mogenites' trade, both to that kingdom and the whole seas on that side of the moon. As this article includes a fifth part of all the trade of the moon, and would, in conjunction with the Gallunarians, at last bring the mastership of the sea out of the hands of the other, so it would in effect be more detriment to those two nations than ten kingdoms lost, if they had them to part with.

"This the Solunarians foreseeing, and being extremely sensible of the entire ruin of their trade, have left no stone unturned to bring the piece of pageantry on the stage, by which they have hooked in the old Black Eagle to plunge himself over head and ears in the quarrel in such a manner as he can never go back with any tolerable honour; he can never quit his son and the crown of Ebronia without the greatest reproach and disgrace of all the world in the moon.

"Now whether one or both of these reasons are true in this case, as most believe both of them to be true, the policy of my countrymen, the Solunarians, is visible indeed; but as for their honesty, it is past finding out.

"But it is objected here, this son of the lip has an undoubted right to the crown of Ebronia. We do not fight now to set up an usurper, but to pull down an usurper, and it has been made plain by the manifesto that the giving a kingdom by will is no conveyance of right; the prince of the Eagle has an undoubted right, and they fight to maintain it.

"If this be true, then we must ask these high and mighty gentlemen how came they to recognise and acknowledge the present king on the throne? why did they own a usurper if he be such? Either one or other must be an act of cowardice and injustice, and all the politics of the moon cannot clear them of one of these two charges: either they were cowardly knaves before, or else they must be cunning knaves now.

"If the young Eagle has an undoubted title now, so he had before, and they knew it as well before as they do now. What can they say for themselves, why they should own a king who they knew had no title, or what can they say for going to pull down one that has a title?

"I must be allowed to distinguish between fighting with a nation and fighting with the king. For example, our quarrel with the Gallunarians is with the whole nation, as they are grown too strong for their neighbours. But our quarrel with Ebronia is not with the nation, but with their king; and this quarrel seems to be unjust in this particular, at least in them who owned him to be king, for that put an end to the controversy.

"It is true the justice of public actions, either in princes or in states, is no such nice thing that anybody should be surprised to see the Government forfeit their faith; and it seems the Solunarians are no more careful this way than their neighbours. But then those people should in an especial manner forbear to reproach other nations and princes with the breaches which they themselves are subject to.

"As to the Eagle, we have nothing to say to the honesty of his declaring his son king of Ebronia; for, as is hinted before, he never acknowledged the title of the usurper, but always declared and insisted on his own undoubted right, and that he would recover it if he could.

"Without doubt the Eagle has a title by proximity of blood, founded on the renunciation of the king of Gallunaria, formerly mentioned; and if the will of the late king be invalid, or he had no right to give the sovereignty of his kingdom away, then the Eagle is next heir.

" But as we quit his morals and justify the honesty of his proceedings in the war against the present king of Ebronia, so in this
action of declaring his second son, we must begin to question
his understanding, and, saving a respect of decency, it looks as if
his musical head was out of tune. To illustrate this, I crave leave .
to tell you a story out of your own country which we have heard
of hither. A Frenchman that could speak but broken English
was at the court of England, when on some occasion he happened
to hear the title of the king of England read thus, 'Charles the
Second, King of England, Scotland, France, and Ireland.' 'Vat
is dat you say?' says Monsieur. Being a little affronted, the man
reads it again as before, 'Charles the Second, King of England,
Scotland, France, and Ireland.' 'Charles the Second King of
France! My foy,' says the Frenchman, 'you can no read.
Charles the Second King of France, ha! ha! ha! Charles the
Second King of France when he can catch.' Any one may apply
the story, whether it was a true one or no.

" All the Lunar world looks on it, therefore, as a most ridiculous,
senseless thing to make a man a king of a country he has not
one foot of land in, nor can have a foot there but what he must
fight for. As to the probability of gaining it, I have nothing to
say to it; but if we may guess at his success there by what has
been done in other parts of the moon, we find he has fought three
campaigns to lose every foot he had got.

" It had been much more to the honour of the Eagle's conduct,
and of the young hero himself, first to have let him have faced
his enemy in the field, and as soon as he had beaten him, the
Ebronians would have acknowledged him fast enough; or his
own victorious troops might have proclaimed him at the gate of
their capital city; and if, after all, the success of the war had
denied him the crown he had fought for, he had the honour to
have shown his bravery, and he had been where he was, a prince
of the great lip. A son of the Eagle is a title much more honourable than a king without a crown, without subjects, without a
kingdom, and another man upon his throne; but by this declaring him king, the old Eagle has put him under a necessity of

gaining the kingdom of Ebronia, which at best is a great hazard, or if he fails to be miserably despicable, and to bear all his life the constant chagrin of a great title and no possession.

" How ridiculous will this poor young gentleman look if at last he should be forced to come home again without his kingdom ? What a king of clouts will he pass for, and what will this king-making old gentleman, his father, say when the young hero shall tell him ? 'Your Majesty has made me a mock king for all the world to laugh at.'

" It was certainly the weakest thing that could be for the Eagle thus to make him a king of that which, were the probability greater than it is, he may easily, without the help of a miracle, be disappointed of.

" It is true the confederates talk big, and have lately had a great victory ; and if talk will beat the King of Ebronia out of his kingdom, he is certainly undone ; but we do not find the Gallunarians part with anything they can keep, nor that they quit anything without blows. It must cost a great deal of blood and treasure before this war can be ended. If absolute conquest on one side must be the matter, and if the design on Ebronia should miscarry, as one voyage thither has done already, where are we then ? Let any man but look back and consider what a sorry figure your confederate fleet in your world had made after their Andalusian expedition, if they had not, more by fate than conduct, chopped upon a booty at Vigo as they came back.

" In the like condition will this new king come back, if he should go for a kingdom and should not catch, as the Frenchman called it. It is in the sense of the probability of this miscarriage that most men wonder at these unaccountable measures, and think the Eagle's counsels look a little wildish, as if some of his great men were grown delirious and whimsical, that fancied crowns and kingdoms were to come and go just as the great Divan at their court should direct. This confusion of circumstances has occasioned a certain copy of verses to appear about the moon, which in our characters may be read as follows :—

'Wondelis Idulasin na Perixola Metartos,
　Strigunia Crolias Xerin Hytale sylos;
Parnicos Galvare Orpto sonamel Egonsberch,
　Sib lona Sipos Gullia Ropta Tylos.'

" Which may be Englished thus :—

' Cæsar, you trifle with the world in vain;
　Think rather now of Germany than Spain.
He's hardly fit to fill the eagle's throne
　Who gives new crowns and can't protect his own.'

"But, after all, to come closer to the point. If I can now make it out that, whatever it was before, this very practice of declaring a second son to be king of Ebronia has publicly owned the proceedings of the king of Gallunaria to be just, and the title of his grandson to be much better than the title of the now declared king,—what shall we call it then?

"In order to this, it is first necessary to examine the title of the present king and to enter into the history of his coming to the crown, in which I shall be very brief.

"The last king of Ebronia dying without issue, and a former renunciation taking place, the succession devolves on the house of the Eagle as before, of whom the present Eagle is the eldest branch.

"But the late king of Ebronia, to prevent the succession of the Eagle's line, makes a will, and supplies the proviso of renunciation by devising, giving, or bequeathing the crown to the grandson of his sister.

"The king of Gallunaria insists that this is a lawful title to the crown, and seizes it accordingly, instating his grandson in the possession.

"The Eagle alleges the renunciation to confirm his title as heir; and as to the will of the late king, he says crowns cannot descend by gift, and though the late king had an undoubted right to enjoy it himself, he had none to give it away.

"To make the application of this history as short as may be, I demand, then, what right has the Eagle to give it to his second son ? If crowns are not to descend by gift, he may have a right to enjoy it, but can have none to give it away; but if he has a right to give it away, so had the former king, and then the present king has a better title to it than the new one, because his gift was prior to this of the Eagle.

" I would be glad to see this answered ; and if it can't, then I query whether the Eagle's senses ought not to be questioned for setting up a title on the very foundation for which he quarrels with him that is in possession, and so confirm the honesty of the possessor's title by his own practice ?

" From the whole, I make no scruple to say that either the Eagle's second son has no title to the kingdom of Ebronia, or else giving of crowns is a legal practice ; and if crowns may descend by gift, then has the other king a better title than he, because it was given him first, and the Eagle has only given away what he had no right to, because it was given away before he had any title to it himself.

" Further, the posterity of the Eagle's eldest son are manifestly injured in this action ; for kings can no more give away their crowns from their posterity than from themselves. If the right be in the Eagle, it is his, for he is the eldest male branch of the house of the great Lip, not as he is Eagle, and from him the crown of Ebronia by the same right of devolution descends to his posterity, and rests on the male line of every eldest branch. If so, no act of renunciation can alter this succession, for that is a gift, and the gift is exploded, or else the whole house of the great Lip is excluded ; so that, let the argument be turned and twisted never so many ways, it all centres in this, that the present person can have no title to the crown of Ebronia.

" If he has any title, it is from the gift of his father and elder brother. If the gift of a crown is no good title, then his title cannot be good. If the gift of a crown is a good title, then the crown was given away before, and so neither he nor his father has any title.

" Let him that can answer these paradoxes defend his title if he can. And what shall we now say to the war in Ebronia ? Only this, that they are going to fight for the crown of Ebronia (?), and to take it away from one that has no right to it, to give it to one that has a less right than he; and it is to be feared that if Heaven be righteous it will succeed accordingly.

"The gentlemen of letters who have wrote of this in our Lunar world, on the subject of the Gallunarian's title, have taken a great deal of liberty in the Eagle's behalf to banter and ridicule the Gallunarian sham of a title, as if it were a pretence too weak for any prince to make use of, to talk of kings giving their crowns by will.

"Kingdoms and governments, says a learned Lunar author, are not things of such indifferent value to be given away like a token left for a legacy. If any prince has ever given or transferred his government, it has been done by solemn act, and the people have been called to assent and confirm such concessions.

"Then the same author goes on to treat the king of Gallunaria with a great deal of severity, and exposes his politics, that he should think to put upon the moon with so empty, so weak, so ridiculous a pretence as the will of a weak-headed prince, who neither had a right to give his crown nor a brain to know what he was doing; and he laughs to think what the king of Gallunaria would have said to have such a dull trick as that put upon him in any such case.

"Now when we have been so witty upon this very article of giving away the crown to the king of Gallunaria's grandson as an incongruous and ridiculous thing, shall we come to make the same incongruity be the foundation of a war? With what justice can we make a war for a prince who has only a good title by virtue of the self-same action which makes the grandson of his enemy have a bad title?

"I always thought we had a just ground to make war on Ebronia, as we were bound by former alliances to assist the Eagle in the recovery of it in the case of death of the late king of that country. But now the Eagle has refused the succession, and his eldest son has refused it, I would be glad to see it proved how the second son can have a title, and yet the other king have no title.

"What a strange sort of thing is the crown of Ebronia, that two of the greatest princes of the Lunar world should fight, not who shall have it, for neither of them will accept of it, but who shall have the power of giving it away.

"Here are four princes refuse it. The king of Gallunaria's sons had a title in right of their mother, and it was not the former renunciations that would have barred them if this softer way had not been found out; for time was it had been pleaded on behalf of the eldest son of the Gallunarian king that his mother could not give away his right before he was born.

"Then the Eagle has a right, and under him his eldest son; and none of all these four will accept of the crown. I believe all the moon could not find four more that would refuse it.

"Now, though none of these think it worth accepting themselves, yet they fall out about the right of giving it away. The king of Gallunaria will not accept of it himself, but he gets a gift from the last incumbent. 'This,' says the Eagle, 'cannot be a good title, for the late king had no right to make a deed of gift of the crown, since a king is only tenant for life, and succession of crowns either must descend by a lineal progression in the right of primogeniture, or else they lose the tenure and devolve on the people.

"Now as this argument holds good, the Eagle has an undoubted title to the crown of Ebronia. 'But then,' says his Eaglish Majesty, 'I cannot accept of the crown myself, for I am the Eagle, and my eldest son has two kingdoms already, and is in a fair way to be Eagle after me, and it is not worth while for him; but I have a second son, and we will give it him.'

"Now may the king of Gallunaria say, 'If one gift is good, another is good, and ours is the first gift, and therefore we will keep it.' And though I solemnly declare I should be very sorry to see the crown of Ebronia rest in the House of the Gallunarian, because our trade will suffer exceedingly, yet if never so much damage were to come of it, we ought to do justice in the world. If neither the Eagle nor his eldest son will be king of Ebronia, but a deed of gift shall be made, the first gift has the right; for nothing can be given away to two people at once, and it is apparent that the late king had as much right to give it away as anybody.

"The poor Ebronians are in a fine condition all this while, that nobody concerns them in the matter. Neither party has so much as thought it worth while to ask them who they would have to reign over them. Here has been no assembly, no Cortes, no meeting of the people of Ebronia, neither collectively nor representatively, no general convention of the nobility, no house of feathers; but Ebronia lies as the spoil of the victor, wholly passive, and her people and princes, as if they were wholly unconcerned, lie by and look on. Whoever is like to be king, they are like to suffer deeply by the strife, and yet neither side has thought fit to consult them about it.

"The conclusion of the whole matter is, in short, this:—Here is certainly a false step taken; how it shall be rectified is not the present business, nor am I wise enough to prescribe. One man may do in a moment what all the Lunar world cannot undo in an age. It is not to be thought the Eagle will be prevailed on to undo it; nay, he has sworn not to alter it.

"I am not concerned to prove the title of the present king of Ebronia, no, nor of the Eagle neither; but I think I can never be answered in this, that this gift of the Eagle to his second son is preposterous, inconsistent with all his claim to the crown, and the greatest confirmation of the title of his enemy that it was possible to give; and no doubt the Gallunarians will lay hold of the argument.

"If this prince was the Eagle's eldest son, he might have a just right from the concession of his father, because the right being inherent, he only received from him an investiture of time; but as this young gentleman is a second son, he has no more right, his elder brother being alive, than your Grand Seignior or Czar of Muscovy in your world.

"Let them fight, then, for such a cause, who, valuing only the pay, make war a trade and fight for anything they are bid to fight for; and as such value not the justice of the war, nor trouble their heads about causes and consequences so they have their pay, it is well enough for them.

"But were the justice of the war examined—I can see none—this declaring a new king who has no right but by a gift, and pulling down one that had it by a gift before, has so much contradiction in it, that I am afraid no wise man or honest man will embark in it.—Your humble servant,

"THE MAN IN THE MOON."

I would have nobody now pretend to scandalise the writer of this letter, which being for the Gallunarians, for no man in the moon had more aversion for them than he, but he would have had the war carried on upon a right bottom, justice and honesty regarded in it; and, as he said often, they had no need to go out of the road of justice, for had they made war in the great Eagle's name, all had been well.

Nor was he a false prophet; for as this was ill-grounded, so it was as ill-carried on, met with shocks, rubs, and disappointments every way. The very first voyage the new king made he had like to have been drowned by a very violent tempest, things not very usual in those countries; and all the progress that had been made in his behalf when I came away from the Lunar world had not brought him so much as to be able to set his foot upon his new kingdom of Ebronia; but his adversary, by wonderful dexterity and the assistance of his old grandfather the Gallunarian monarch, beat his troops upon all occasions, invaded his ally that pretended to assist him, and kept a quiet possession of all the vast Ebronian monarchy; and but at last, by the powerful diversion of the Solunarian fleet, a shock was given them on another side, which, if it had not happened, it was thought the new king had been sent home again *re infecta*.

Being very much shocked in my judgment of this affair by these unanswerable reasons, I inquired of my author who were the directors of this matter; and he told me plainly it was done by those great statesmen which the Solunarian queen had lately very justly turned out, whose politics were very unaccountable in a great many other things as well as in that.

It is true the war was carried on under the new Ministry, and no war in the world can be juster, on account of the injustice and encroachment of the Gallunarian monarch.

The queen therefore and her present Ministers go on with the war on the principles of confederacy. It is the business of the Solunarians to beat the invader out, and then let the people come and make a fair decision who they will have to reign over them.

This indeed justifies the war in Ebronia to be right; but for the personal procedure, as before, it is all contradiction, and can never be answered.

I hope no man will be so malicious as to say I am hereby reflecting on our war with Spain. I am very forward to say it is a most just and reasonable war. As to parallels between the case of the princes in defending the matter of personal right, *Hic labor, hoc opus.*

Thus, however, you see *humanum est errare.* Whether in this world or in the moon, it is all one; infallibility of counsels any more than of doctrine is not in man.

The reader may observe I have formerly noted there was a new consolidator to be built, and observed what struggle there was in the moon about choosing the feathers.

I cannot omit some further remarks here, as—

1. It is to be observed that this last consolidator was in a manner quite worn out. It had indeed continued but three years, which was the stated time by law; but it had been so hurried, so party-rid, so often had been up in the moon, and made so many such extravagant flights and unnecessary voyages thither, that it began to be exceedingly worn and defective.

2. This occasioned that the light fluttering feathers and the fermented feathers made strange work of it. Nay, sometimes they were so hot, they were like to have ruined the whole fabric; and had it not been for the great feather in the centre, and a few negative feathers who were wiser than the rest, all the machine

had been broken to pieces, and the whole nation put into a most strange confusion.

Sometimes their motion was so violent and precipitant that there was great apprehensions of its being set on fire by its own velocity; for swiftness of motion is allowed by the sages and so-so's to produce fire, as in wheels, mills, and several sorts of mechanical engines, which are frequently fired; and so in thoughts, brains, assemblies, consolidators, and all such combustible things.

Indeed these things were of great consequence, and therefore require some more nice examination than ordinary, and the following story will in part explain it.

Among the rest of the broils they had with the grandees, one happened on this occasion.

One of the tacking feathers being accidentally met by a grandee's footman, who, it seems, wanted some manners, the slave began to haloo him in the street with "A tacker, a tacker, a feather fool, a tacker!" &c., and so brought the mob about him; and had not the grandee himself come in the very interim and rescued the feather, the mob had demolished him, they were so enraged.

As this gentleman feather was rescued with great courtesy by the grandee, taken into his coach, and carried home to his house, he desired to speak with the footman.

The fellow being called in, was asked by him who employed him or set him on to offer him this insult. The footman, being a ready, bold fellow, told him, "Nobody, sir; but you are all grown so ridiculous to the whole nation, that if the one hundred and thirty-four of you were left but to us footmen, and it was not in more respect to our masters than you, we should cure you of ever coming into the consolidator again; and all the people in the moon are of our mind."

"But," says the feather, "why do you call me fool, too?" "Why, sir," says he, "because nobody could ever tell us what it was you drove at, and we have been told you never knew yourselves. Now, if one of you tacking feathers would but tell the world what your real design was, they would be satisfied; but to be leaders in the consolidator, and to act without meaning, without thought or design, must argue you are fools or worse; and you will find all the moon of my mind."

"But what if we had a meaning?" says the feather-man. "Why, then," says the footman, "we shall leave off calling you fools, and call you knaves, for it could never be an honest one; so that you had better stand as you do; and I make it out thus:—You knew that upon your tacking the Crolians to the tribute bill, the grandees must reject both, they having declared against reading any bills tacked together, as being against their privileges. Now, if you had any design, it must be to have the bill of tribute lost, and that must be to disappoint all the public affairs, expose the queen, break all measures, discourage the confederates, and, putting all things backward, bring the Gallunarian forces upon them, and put all Solunaria into confusion. Now, sir," says he, "we cannot have such coarse thoughts of you as to believe you could design such dark, mischievous things as these, and therefore we chose rather to believe you all fools, and not fit to be put into a consolidator again, than knaves and traitors to your country, and consequently fit for a worse place."

The plainness of the footman was such and so unanswerable, that his master was fain to check him; and so the discourse broke off, and we shall leave it there and proceed to the story.

The men of the feather, as I have noted, who are represented here by the consolidator, fell all together by the ears, and all the moon was in a combustion. The case was as follows:—

They had three times lost their qualifying law, and particularly they observed the grandees were the men that threw it out, and, notwithstanding the plot of the tackers, as they called them, who were, as I noted, observed to be in conjunction with the Crolians, yet the law always passed the feathers, but still the grandees quashed it.

To show their resentment at the grandees, they had often made attempts to mortify them, sometimes arraigning them in general, sometimes impeaching private members of their house. But still all would not do; the grandees had the better of them, and going on with regularity and temper, the consolidators or feather-men always had the worst, the grandees had the applause of all the moon, had the last blow on every occasion, and the other sunk in their reputation exceedingly.

It is necessary to understand here that the men of the feather serve in several capacities and under several denominations, and act by themselves. Singly considered, they are called the consolidator, and the feathers we mentioned abstracted from their persons make the glorious engine we speak of, and in which, when any sudden motion takes them, they can all shut themselves up and away for the moon. But when these are joined with the grandees and the queen, so united they make a great Cortes, or general collection of all the governing authority of the nation.

When this last fraction happened, the men of the feather were under an exceeding ferment; they had in some passion taken into their custody some good honest Lunar countrymen for an offence which indeed few but themselves ever imagined was a crime, for the poor men did nothing but pursue their own right by the law.

It is thought the men of the feather soon saw they were in the wrong, but acted like some men in our world, that when they make a mistake, being too proud to own themselves in the wrong, run themselves into worse errors to mend it.

So these Lunar gentlemen, disdaining to have it said they could be mistaken, committed two errors to conceal one, until at last they came to be laughed at by all the moon.

These poor men having lain a long while in prison for little or no crime, at last were advised to apply themselves to the law for discharge. The law would fairly have discharged them, for in that country no man may be imprisoned but he must in a certain time be tried, or let go upon pledges of his friends, much like our giving bail on a writ of *Habeas Corpus;* but the judges, whether overawed by the feathers, or what was the cause authors have not determined, did not care to venture discharging them.

The poor men, thus remanded, applied themselves to the

grandees, who were then sitting, and who are the sovereign judicature of the country, and before whom appeals lie from all courts of justice. The grandees, as in duty bound, appeared ready to do them justice, but the queen was to be applied to, first to grant a writ or a warrant for a writ, called in their country a writ of follies, which is as much as to say mistakes.

The consolidators, foreseeing the consequence, immediately applied themselves to the queen with an address, the terms of which were so undutiful and unmannerly, that had she not been a queen of unusual candour and goodness, she would have treated them as they deserved; for they upbraided her with their freedom and readiness in granting her supplies, and therefore as good as told her they expected she should do as they desired.

Those people that knew the supplies given were from necessity legal and for their own defence, while the granting their request must have been illegal, arbitrary, a dispensing with the laws, and denying justice to her subjects, the very thing they ruined her father for, were justly provoked to see their good queen so barbarously treated.

The queen, full of goodness and calmness, gave them a gentle, kind answer, but told them she must be careful to act with due regard to the laws, and could not interrupt the course of judicial proceedings, and at the same time granted the writ, having first consulted with her council, and received the opinion of all the judges that it was not only safe but just and reasonable, and a right to her people which she could not deny.

This proceeding galled the feathers to the quick, and finding the grandees resolved to proceed judicially upon the said writ of follies, which if they did, the prisoners would be delivered and the follies fixed upon the feathers, they sent their pursuivants, took them out of the common prison, and conveyed them separately and privately into prisons of their own.

This rash and unprecedented proceeding pushed them farther into a labyrinth, from which it was impossible they could ever find their way out but with infinite loss to their reputation, like a sheep in a thick wood that at every briar pulls some of the wool from

her back, till she comes out in a most scandalous pickle of naked-
ness and scratches.

The grandees immediately published six articles in vindication
of the people's rights against the assumed privileges of the feathers,
the abstract of which is as follows :—

1. That the feathers had no right to claim or make any new
privileges for themselves other than they had before.

2. That every freeman of the moon had a right to repel injury
with law.

3. That imprisoning the five countrymen by the feathers was
assuming a new privilege they had no right to, and a subjecting
the subjects' right to their arbitrary votes.

4. That a writ of deliverance or removing the body is the legal
right of every subject of the moon, in order to his liberty in case
of imprisonment.

5. That to punish any person for assisting the subject in procuring or prosecuting the said writ of deliverance is a breach of
the laws and a thing of dangerous consequence.

6. That a writ of follies is not a grace, but a right, and ought
not to be denied to the subject.

These resolves struck the languishing reputation of the feathers
with the dead palsy, and they began to stink in the nostrils of all
the nations in the moon.

But besides this, they had one strange effect, which was a prodigious disappointment to the men of the feather.

I have observed before that there was to be a new set of feathers
provided in order to building another consolidator, according to
a late law, for a new engine every three years. Now several of
these men of the feather, who thought their feathers capable of
serving again, had made great interest and been at great cost to
have their old feathers chosen again ; but the people had entertained such scoundrel opinions of these proceedings, such as
tacking, consolidating, imprisoning electors, impeaching without
trial, writs of follies, and the like, that if any one was known to be
concerned in any of these things, nobody would vote for him.

The gentlemen were so mortified at this, that even the hottest

High Church Solunarian of them all, if he put in anywhere to be re-chosen, the first thing he had to do was to assure the people he was no tacker, none of the hundred and thirty-four; and a vast deal of difficulty they had to purge themselves of this blessed action, which they used to value themselves on before as their glory and merit.

Thus they grew ashamed of it as a crime; got men to go about to vouch for them to the country people that they were no tackers; nay, one of them, to clear himself, loudly forswore it, and taking a glass of wine, wished it might never pass through him if he were a tacker, though all men suspected him to be of that number too, he having been one of the most forward that way on all occasion of any person among the south folk of the moon.

In like manner, one of the feathers for the middle province of the country, who used to think it his honour to be for the qualifying law, seeing which way the humour of the country ran, took as much pains now to tell the people he was no tacker as he did before to promise them that he would do his utmost to have the Crolians reduced and that bill to pass; the reason of which was plain, that he saw if it should be known he was a tacker, he should never have his feather returned to be put into the consolidator.

The heats and feuds that the feathers and the grandees were now run into began to make the latter very uneasy, and they sent to the grandees to hasten them, and put them in mind of passing some laws they had sent up to them for raising money, and which lay before them, knowing that as soon as those laws were passed the queen would break them up, and they being very willing to be gone before these things came too far upon the stage, urged them to dispatch.

But the grandees, resolving to go through with the matter, sent to them to come to a treaty on the foot of the six articles, and to bring any reasons they could to prove the power they had to act as they had done with the countrymen, and with the lawyers they had put in prison for assisting them.

The feathers were very backward and stiff about this conference or treaty, till at last the grandees having sufficiently exposed them to all the nation, the bills were passed, the grandees caused the particulars to be printed, and a representation of their proceedings and the feathers' foul dealings to the queen of the country, and so Her Majesty sent them home.

But if they were ashamed of being called tackers before, they were doubly mortified at this now; nay, the country resented it so exceedingly that some of them began to consider whether they should venture to go home or no. Printed lists of their names were published, though we do not say they were true lists, for it was a hard thing to know which were true lists and which were not; nor indeed could a true list be made, no man being able to retain the exact account of who were the men in his memory.

For as there were 134 tackers, so there were 141 of these, who, by a name of distinction, were called *Lebusyraneim*, in English Ailesburymen.

The people were so exasperated against these, that they expressed their resentment upon all occasions; and lest the queen should think that the nation approved the proceedings, they drew up a representation or complaint, full of most dutiful expressions to their queen, and full of resentment against the feathers; the copy of which being handed about the moon the last time I was there, I shall take the pains to put it into English in the best manner I can, keeping as near the original as possible.

If any man shall now wickedly suggest that this relation has any retrospect to the affairs of England, the author declares them malicious misconstruers of his honest relation of matters from this remote country, and offers his positive oath for their satisfaction that the very last journey he made into those Lunar regions this matter was upon the stage, of which, if this treatise was not so near its conclusion, the reader might expect a more particular account.

If there is any analogy or similitude between the transactions of either world, he cannot account for that. It is application makes the ass. And yet sometimes he has thought, as some people fable of the Platonic year, that after such a certain revolution of time all things are transacted over again, and the same people live again, are the same fools, knaves, philosophers and madmen they were before, though without any knowledge of, or retrospect to what they acted before; so why should it be impossible that as the moon and this world are noted to be twins and sisters, equal in motion and in influence, and perhaps in qualities, the same secret power should so act upon them as that like actions and circumstances should happen in all parts of both worlds at the same time.

I leave this thought to the improvement of our royal learned societies of the Anticacofanums, Opposotians, Periodicarians, Antepredestinarians, Universal Soulians, and such like unfathomable people, who without question, upon mature inquiry, will find out the truth of this matter.

But if any one shall scruple the matter of fact as I have here related it, I freely give him leave to do as I did, and go up to the moon for a demonstration; and if, upon his return, he does not give ample testimony to the case in every part of it as here related, I am content to pass for the contriver of it myself, and be punished as the law shall say I deserve.

Nor was this all. The public matters in which this nation of Solunarians took wrong measures; for about this time the misunderstandings between the southern and northern men began again, and the Solunarians made several laws, as they called them, to secure themselves against the dangers they pretended might accrue from the new measures the Nolunarians had taken; but so unhappily were they blinded by the mong themselves and beset by opinion and interest, that every law they made, or so much as attempted to make, was really to the advantage and to the interest of the northern men and to their own loss, so ignorantly and weak-headed were these High Solunarian Churchmen in the true interest of their country, led by their implacable malice at Crolianism, which, as before noted, was the established religion of that country.

But as this matter was but transacting when I took the other remarks, and that I did not obtain a full understanding of it till my second voyage, I refer it to a more full relation of my farther travels that way, when I shall not fail to give a clear state of the debate of the two kingdoms, in which the southern men had the least reason and the worst success that ever they had in any affair of that nature for many years before.

It was always my opinion in affairs on this side the moon, that though sometimes a foolish bolt may hit the point and a random shot kill the enemy, yet that generally discretion and prudence of management had the advantage, and met with a proportionate success; and things were or were not happy in their conclusion as they were more or less wisely contrived and directed.

And though it may not be allowed to be so here, yet I found it more constantly so there. Effects were true to their causes, and confusion of counsels never failed in the moon to be followed by distracted and destructive consequences.

This appeared more eminently in the dispute between these two Lunar nations we are speaking of. Never were people in the moon, whatever they might be in other places, so divided in their opinions about a matter of such consequence. Some were for declaring war immediately upon the northern men, though they could show no reason at all why, only because they would not do as they would have them. " A parcel of poor scoundrels, scabby rogues! they ought to be made submit. What! won't they declare the same king as we do? Hang them, rogues! a pack of Crolian Prestarian devils, we must make them do it. Down with them the shortest way; declare war immediately, and down with them!" Nay, some were for falling on them directly without the formality of declaring war.

Others, more afraid than hurt, cried out invasions, depredation, fire, and sword; the northern men would be upon them immediately, and proposed to fortify their frontiers and file off their forces to the Borders; nay, so apprehensive did those men of prudence pretend to be, that they ordered towns to be fortified a hundred miles off of the place, when all this while the poor northern men did nothing but tell them that unless they would come to terms they would not have the same king as they, and

then took some measures to let them see they did not purpose
to be forced to it.

Another sort of wiser men than these proposed to unite with
them, hear their reasons, and do them right. These indeed were
the only men that were in the right method of concluding this
unhappy broil, and for that reason were the most unlikely to
succeed.

But the wildest notion of all was when some of the grandees
made a grave address to the queen of the country, to desire the
northern men to settle matters first, and to tell them that when
that was done they should see what these would do for them.
This was a home-stroke if it had but hit, and the misfortune only
lay in this, that the northern men were not fools enough; the
clearness of the air in those cold climates generally clearing the
head so early, that those people see much farther into a millstone
than any blind man in all the southern nations of the moon.

There was another unhappiness in this case which made the
matter yet more confused, and that was that the soldiers had
generally no gust to this war. This was an odd case; for those
sort of gentlemen, especially in the world in the moon, did not
used to inquire into the justice of the case they fought for, but
they reckoned it their business to go where they were sent, and
kill anybody they were ordered to kill, leaving their governors to
answer for the justice of it. But there was another reason why
the men of the sword were so averse, and always talked coldly of
the fighting part; and though the northern men called it fear, yet
I cannot join with them in that; for to fear requires thinking, and
some of our Solunarians are absolutely protected from the first,
because they never meddle with the last, except when they come
to the engine, and therefore it is plain it could not proceed from
fear.

It has puzzled the most discerning heads of the age to give a
reason from whence this aversion proceeded, and various judgments have been given of it.

The Nolunarians jested with them, and when they talked of
fighting, bade them look back into history and examine what they

ever made of a Nolunarian war, and whether they had not been
often well beaten and sent short home; bade them have a care
of catching a tartar, as we call it, and always made themselves
merry with it.

They bantered the Solunarians too about the fears and terrors
they were under from their arming themselves and putting themselves in a posture of defence, when it was easy to see by the
nature of the thing that their design was not a war, but a union
upon just conditions; that it was a plain token that they designed
either to put some affront upon the Nolunarians, to deny them
some just claims, or to impose something very provoking upon
them more than they had yet done, that they were so exceeding
fearful of an invasion from them.

Though these were sufficient to pass for reasons in other cases,
yet it could not be so here, but I saw there must be something
else in it. As I was thus wondering at this unusual backward-
ness of the soldiers, I inquired a little further into the meaning
of it, and quickly found the reason was plain : there was nothing
to be got by it; that people were brave, desperate, and poor; the
country barren, mountainous, and empty; so that, in short, there
would be nothing but blows and soldier's fellows to be had; and
I always observed that soldiers never care to be knocked on the
head and get nothing by the bargain.

In short, I saw plainly the reasons that prompted the Solunarians to insult their neighbours of the north were more derived
from the regret at their establishing Crolianism than at any real
causes they had given, or indeed were in a condition to give
them.

These and abundance more particular observations I made ;
but as I left the thing still in agitation and undetermined, I shall
refer it to another voyage, which I purpose to make thither, and
at my return may perhaps set that case in a clearer light than
our sight can yet bear to look at it in.

If in my second voyage I should undeceive people in the
notions they entertained of those northern people, and convince
them that the Solunarians were really the aggressors and had put

great hardships upon them, I might possibly do a work that, if it met with encouragement, might bring the Solunarians to do them justice, and that would set all to rights; the two nations might easily become one and unite for ever or at least become friends and give mutual assistance to each other; and I cannot but own such an agreement would make them both very formidable; but this I refer to another time.

At the same time, I cannot leave it without a remark that this jealousy between the two nations may perhaps in future ages be necessary to be maintained, in order to find some better reasons for fortifications, standing armies, guards, and garrisons than could be given in the reign of the great prince I speak of, the queen's predecessor, though his was against a foreign insulting enemy. But the temper of the Solunarian high party was always such that they would with much more ease give thanks for a standing army against the Nolunarians and Crolians than agree to one legion against the Abrogratzians and Gallunarians. But of these things I am also promised a more particular account upon my journey into that country. I cannot, however, conclude this matter without giving some account of my private observations upon what was further to be seen in this country. And had not my remarks on their state matters taken up more of my thoughts than I expected, I might have entered a little upon their other affairs, such as their companies, their commerce, their public offices, and stockjobbers, their temper, their conversation, their women, their stages, universities, their courtiers, their clergy, and the characters of the severals under all these denominations; but these must be referred to time and my more perfect observations.

But I cannot omit that, though I have very little knowledge of books, and had obtained less upon their language, yet I could not but be very inquisitive after their libraries and men of letters. Among their libraries I found not abundance of their own books, their learning having so much of demonstration and being very hieroglyphical; but I found to my great admiration vast quantities of translated books out of all languages of our world.

As I thought myself one of the first, at least of our nation, that ever came thus far, it was, you may be sure, no small surprise to me to find all the most valuable parts of modern learning, especially of politics, translated from our tongue into the Lunar dialect, and stored up in their libraries, with the remarks, notes, and observations of the learned men of that climate upon the subject.

Here, among a vast crowd of French authors, condemned in this polite world for trifling, came a huge volume containing "Les Œuvres des Savans," which has nineteen small bells painted upon the book, of several disproportioned sizes. I inquired the meaning of that hieroglyphic, which the master of the books told me was to signify that the substance was all jingle and noise, and that of thirty volumes which that one book contains, twenty-nine of them have neither substance, music, harmony, nor value in them.

The "History of the Fulsomes," or a collection of three hundred fine speeches made in the French Academy at Paris, and fifteen hundred gay flourishes out of Monsieur Boileau, all in praise of the invincible monarch of France.

"The Duke of Bavaria's Manifesto," showing the right of making war against our sovereigns, from whence the people of that Lunar world have noted that the same reasons which made it lawful to him to attempt the imperial power entitle him to lose his own, viz., conquest and the longest sword.

"Jack a both Sides," or a dialogue between Pasquin and Marforio upon the subject-matter of the Pope's sincerity in case of the war in Italy. Written by a citizen of Ferrara, one side arguing upon the occasion of the Pope's general wheedling the Imperialists to quit that country; the other bantering Imperial policy, or the Germans pretending they were tricked out of Italy when they could stay there no longer.

"Louis the Invincible," by Monsieur Boileau, a poem on the glory of his Most Christian Majesty's arms at Hochstadt and Venloo.

All these translations have innumerable hieroglyphical notes and emblems painted on them, which pass as comments, and are readily understood in that climate. For example, on the volume of dialogues are two cardinals washing the Pope's hands under a cloud that often bespatters them with blood, signifying that in spite of all his pretensions he has a hand in the broils of Italy; and before him the sun setting in a cloud and a blind ballad-singer making sonnets upon the brightness of its lustre.

"The Three Kings of Brentford," being some historical observations on three mighty monarchs in our world, whose heroic actions may be the subject of future ages, being like to do little in this—the King of England, King of Poland, and King of Spain. These are described by a figure representing a castle in the air, and three knights pointing at it, but they could not catch.

I omit abundance of very excellent pieces, because remote, as three great volumes of European mysteries, among the vast varieties of which, and very entertaining, I observed but a few such as these:—

1. Why Prince Ragotski will make no peace with the Emperor, but more particularly why the Emperor will not make peace with him.

2. Where the policy of the King of Sweden lies, to pursue the King of Poland and let the Muscovites ravage and destroy his own subjects.

3. What the Duke of Bavaria proposed to himself in declaring for France.

4. Why the Protestants of the Confederacy never relieved the Camissars.

5. Why there are no cowards found in the English service but among their sea-captains.

6. Why the King of Portugal did not take Madrid; why the English did not take Cadiz; and why the Spaniards did not take Gibraltar, viz., because the first were fools, the second knaves, and the last Spaniards.

7. What became of all the silver taken at Vigo.

8. Who will be the next king of Scotland.

9. If England should ever want a king, who would think it worth while to accept of it.

10. What specific difference can be produced between a knave, a coward, and a traitor.

Abundance of these mysteries are hieroglyphically described in this ample collection, and without doubt our great collection of annals and historical observations, particularly the learned Mr. Walker, would make great improvements there.

But to come nearer home. There, to my great amazement, I found several new tracts out of our own language which I could hardly have imagined it possible should have reached so far.

As, first, sundry Transactions of our Royal Society about winds, and a valuable dissertation of Dr. Bentley's about wind in the brain.

"A Discourse of Poisons," by the learned Dr. Mead, with Lunar notes upon it, wherein it appears that Dr. Coward had more poison in his tongue than all the adders in the moon have in their teeth.

"*Nec Non,*" or lawyer's Latin turned into Lunar burlesque. The hieroglyphic was the Queen's money tossed in a blanket, dedicated to the Attorney-General and five false Latin counsellors.

"*Mandamus,*" as it was acted at Abington Assizes by Mr. Solicitor General, where the Queen had her own Solicitor against her for a bad cause, and never a counsel for her in a good one.

"Lunar Reflections," being a list of about two thousand ridiculous errors in history, palpable falsities and scandalous omissions in Mr. Collier's "Geographical Dictionary," with a subsequent inquiry by way of appendix into which are his own and which he has ignorantly deduced from ancient authors.

"Assassination and Killing of Kings proved to be a Church of England Doctrine," humbly dedicated to the Prince of Wales by Mr. Collier and Mr. Snat, wherein their absolving Sir John Friend and Sir William Parkins without repentance, and while they both owned and justified the fact, is vindicated and defended.

"*Les Bagatelles,*" or Bromley's Travels into Italy, a choice book, and by great accident preserved from the malicious design of the author, who diligently bought up the whole impression for fear they should be seen, as a thing of which this ungrateful age was not worthy.

"Killing no Murder," being an account of the severe justice designed to be inflicted on the barbarous murderers of the honest constable at Bow, but unhappily prevented by my Lord Nottingham being turned out of his office.

"*De Modo Belli*," or an account of the best method of making conquests and invasion *à la mode de* Port St. Mary, three volumes in 8vo.   Dedicated to Sir Hen. Bellers.

"King Charles the First proved a Tyrant." By Edward Earl of Clarendon, three volumes in folio.   Dedicated to the University of Oxford.

"The Bawdy Poets," or new and accurate editions of Catullus, Propertius, and Tibullus, being the maidenhead of the new printing-press at Cambridge.   Dedicated by the editor, Mr. Annesley, to the University, and in consideration of which, and some disorders near Casterton, the University thought him fit to represent them in Parliament.

"Alms no Charity," or the skeleton of Sir Humphrey Mackworth's bill for relief of the poor.   Being an excellent new contrivance to find employment for all the poor in the nation, viz., by setting them at work to make all the rest of the people as poor as themselves.

"*Synodium Superlativum*," being sixteen large volumes of the vigorous proceedings of the English Convocation digested into years, one volume to every year.   Wherein are several large lists of the heretical, atheistical, deistical, and other pernicious errors which have been condemned in that venerable assembly, the various services done, and weighty matters dispatched for the honour of the English Church for sixteen years last past, with their formal proceedings against Asgil, Coward, Toland, and others for reviving old antiquated errors in doctrine, and publishing them to the world as their own.

"New Worlds in Trade," being a vast collection out of the journals of the proceedings of the Right Honourable the Commissioners of Trade, with several eminent improvements in general negoce, vast schemes of business, and new discoveries of settlements and correspondences in foreign parts, for the honour and advantage of the English merchants, being twelve volumes in folio and very scarce and valuable books.

"Legal Rebellion," or an argument proving that all sorts of insurrections of subjects against their princes are lawful, and to be supported whenever they suit with our occasions, made good from the practice of France with the Hungarians, the English with the Camissars, the Swedes with the Poles, the Emperor with the subjects of Naples, and all the princes of the world as they find occasion ; a large volume in folio, with a poem upon the sacred right of kingly power.

"*Ignis Fatuus,*" or the occasional bill in miniature, a farce, as it was acted by his Excellency the Lord Granville's servants in Carolina.

"Running Away the Shortest Way to Victory," being a large dissertation, showing to save Queen's ships is the best way to beat the French.

"The Tookites," a poem upon the hundred and thirty-four.

"A New Tract upon Trade," being a demonstration that to be always putting the people upon customary mourning, and wearing black upon every state occasion, is an excellent encouragement to trade and a means to employ the poor.

"City Gratitude," being a poem on the statue erected by the Court of Aldermen at the upper end of Cheapside to the immortal memory of King William.

There were many more tracts to be found in this place, but these may suffice for a specimen, and to excite all men that would increase their understandings in human mysteries to take a voyage to this enlightened country, where their memories, thinking faculties, and penetration will no question be so tacked and consolidated, that when they return they will all write memoirs of the place, and communicate to their country the advantages they have reaped by their voyage, according to the laudable example of their

Most humble servant,

THE MAN IN THE MOON.

2 E

# A TRUE RELATION

OF

# THE APPARITION

OF

## MRS. VEAL,

### THE NEXT DAY AFTER HER DEATH,

TO

## MRS. BARGRAVE,

AT

## CANTERBURY, THE EIGHTH OF SEPTEMBER 1705.

WHICH APPARITION RECOMMENDS THE PERUSAL OF DRELINCOURT'S
BOOK OF CONSOLATIONS AGAINST THE FEARS OF DEATH.

# THE PREFACE.

—◆◆—

THIS relation is matter of fact, and attended with such circumstances as may induce any reasonable man to believe it. It was sent by a gentleman, a justice of peace at Maidstone, in Kent, and a very intelligent person, to his friend in London, as it is here worded; which discourse is attested by a very sober and understanding gentleman, who had it from his kinswoman, who lives in Canterbury, within a few doors of the house in which the within-named Mrs. Bargrave lived; and who he believes to be of so discerning a spirit, as not to be put upon by any fallacy, and who positively assured him that the whole matter as it is related and laid down is really true, and what she herself had in the same words, as near as may be, from Mrs. Bargrave's own mouth, who, she knows, had no reason to invent and publish such a story, or any design to forge and tell a lie, being a woman of much honesty and virtue, and her whole life a course, as it were, of piety. The use which we ought to make of it is to consider that there is a life to come after this, and a just God who will retribute to every one according to the deeds done in the body, and therefore to reflect upon our past course of life we have led in the world; that our time is short and uncertain; and that if we would escape the punishment of the ungodly and receive the reward of the righteous, which is the laying hold of eternal life, we ought, for the time to come to return to God by a speedy repentance, ceasing to do evil, and learning to do well; to seek after God early, if haply He may be found of us, and lead such lives for the future as may be well pleasing in His sight.

# A RELATION, &c.

—•—

THIS thing is so rare in all its circumstances, and on so good
authority, that my reading and conversation have not given
me anything like it. It is fit to gratify the most ingenious and
serious inquirer.[1] Mrs. Bargrave is the person to whom Mrs. Veal
appeared after her death; she is my intimate friend, and I can
avouch for her reputation for these last fifteen or sixteen years,
on my own knowledge; and I can confirm the good character
she had from her youth to the time of my acquaintance; though
since this relation she is calumniated by some people that are
friends to the brother of Mrs. Veal who appeared, who think
the relation of this appearance to be a reflection, and endeavour
what they can to blast Mrs. Bargrave's reputation, and to laugh
the story out of countenance. But by the circumstances thereof,
and the cheerful disposition of Mrs. Bargrave, notwithstanding
the ill-usage of a very wicked husband, there is not the least sign
of dejection in her face; nor did I ever hear her let fall a
desponding or murmuring expression; nay, not when actually
under her husband's barbarity, which I have been witness to,
and several other persons of undoubted reputation.

Now you must know Mrs. Veal was a maiden gentlewoman of
about thirty years of age, and for some years last past had been

---

[1] This *jeu d'esprit* was first published in July 1706. A translation of a book by
Charles Drelincourt, a French Protestant divine who died in 1669, had been published in 1675 as "The Christian's Defence against the Fear of Death," and was
very popular. Defoe's ingenious exercise in make-believe was added to the fourth
edition, its fault being that it passed for true.

troubled with fits, which were perceived coming on her by her
going off from her discourses very abruptly to some impertinence.
She was maintained by an only brother, and kept his house in
Dover. She was a very pious woman, and her brother a very
sober man, to all appearance; but now he does all he can to null
or quash the story. Mrs. Veal was intimately acquainted with
Mrs. Bargrave from her childhood. Mrs. Veal's circumstances
were then mean; her father did not take care of his children as
he ought, so that they were exposed to hardships; and Mrs. Bargrave in those days had as unkind a father, though she wanted
neither for food nor clothing, whilst Mrs. Veal wanted for both,
insomuch that she would often say, "Mrs. Bargrave, you are not
only the best, but the only friend I have in the world; and no
circumstance in life shall ever dissolve my friendship." They
would often condole each other's adverse fortunes, and read
together "Drelincourt upon Death," and other good books; and
so, like two Christian friends, they comforted each other under
their sorrow.

Some time after, Mr. Veal's friends got him a place in the
custom-house at Dover, which occasioned Mrs. Veal, by little
and little, to fall off from her intimacy with Mrs. Bargrave,
though there never was any such thing as a quarrel; but an
indifferency came on by degrees, till at last Mrs. Bargrave had
not seen her in two years and a half; though about a twelve-
month of the time Mrs. Bargrave had been absent from Dover,
and this last half-year had been in Canterbury about two months
of the time, dwelling in a house of her own.

In this house, on the 8th of September 1705, she was sitting
alone, in the forenoon, thinking over her unfortunate life, and
arguing herself into a due resignation to Providence, though her
condition seemed hard. "And," said she, "I have been provided for hitherto, and doubt not but I shall be still; and am
well satisfied that my afflictions shall end when it is most fit for
me;" and then took up her sewing-work, which she had no
sooner done but she hears a knocking at the door. She went to
see who was there, and this proved to be Mrs. Veal, her old

friend, who was in a riding-habit; at that moment of time the clock struck twelve at noon.

"Madam," says Mrs. Bargrave, "I am surprised to see you, you have been so long a stranger;" but told her she was glad to see her, and offered to salute her, which Mrs. Veal complied with, till their lips almost touched; and then Mrs. Veal drew her hand across her own eyes and said, "I am not very well," and so waived it. She told Mrs. Bargrave she was going a journey, and had a great mind to see her first. "But," says Mrs. Bargrave, "how came you to take a journey alone? I am amazed at it, because I know you have a good brother." "Oh," says Mrs. Veal, "I gave my brother the slip, and came away, because I had so great a desire to see you before I took my journey." So Mrs. Bargrave went in with her into another room within the first, and Mrs. Veal set her down in an elbow-chair, in which Mrs. Bargrave was sitting when she heard Mrs. Veal knock. Then says Mrs. Veal, "My dear friend, I am come to renew our old friendship again, and beg your pardon for my breach of it; and if you can forgive me, you are the best of women." "Oh," says Mrs. Bargrave, "do not mention such a thing. I have not had an uneasy thought about it; I can easily forgive it." "What did you think of me?" said Mrs. Veal. Says Mrs. Bargrave, "I thought you were like the rest of the world, and that prosperity had made you forget yourself and me." Then Mrs. Veal reminded Mrs. Bargrave of the many friendly offices she did in her former days, and much of the conversation they had with each other in the times of their adversity; what books they read, and what comfort in particular they received from "Drelincourt's Book of Death," which was the best, she said, on that subject ever written. She also mentioned Dr. Sherlock, the two Dutch books which were translated, written upon Death, and several others; but Drelincourt, she said, had the clearest notions of death and of the future state of any who had handled that subject. Then she asked Mrs. Bargrave whether she had Drelincourt. She said, "Yes." Says Mrs. Veal, "Fetch it." And so Mrs. Bargrave goes upstairs and brings it down. Says Mrs.

Veal, "Dear Mrs. Bargrave, if the eyes of our faith were as open as the eyes of our body, we should see numbers of angels about us for our guard. The notions we have of heaven now are nothing like to what it is, as Drelincourt says. Therefore be comforted under your afflictions, and believe that the Almighty has a particular regard to you, and that your afflictions are marks of God's favour; and when they have done the business they are sent for, they shall be removed from you. And believe me, my dear friend, believe what I say to you, one minute of future happiness will infinitely reward you for all your sufferings; for I can never believe" (and claps her hands upon her knees with great earnestness, which indeed ran through most of her discourse) "that ever God will suffer you to spend all your days in this afflicted state; but be assured that your afflictions shall leave you, or you them, in a short time." She spake in that pathetical and heavenly manner that Mrs. Bargrave wept several times, she was so deeply affected with it.

Then Mrs. Veal mentioned Dr. Horneck's "Ascetick," at the end of which he gives an account of the lives of the primitive Christians. Their pattern she recommended to our imitation, and said, "Their conversation was not like this of our age; for now," says she, "there is nothing but frothy, vain discourse, which is far different from theirs. Theirs was to edification, and to build one another up in faith; so that they were not as we are, nor are we as they were; but," said she, "we ought to do as they did. There was a hearty friendship among them; but where is it now to be found?" Says Mrs. Bargrave, "It is hard indeed to find a true friend in these days." Says Mrs. Veal, "Mr. Norris has a fine copy of verses, called 'Friendship in Perfection,' which I wonderfully admire. Have you seen the book?" says Mrs. Veal. "No," says Mrs. Bargrave, "but I have the verses of my own writing-out." "Have you?" says Mrs. Veal; "then fetch them." Which she did from above-stairs, and offered them to Mrs. Veal to read, who refused, and waived the thing, saying holding down her head would make it ache; and then desired Mrs. Bargrave to read them to her, which she did. As they were admiring "Friendship" Mrs. Veal said, "Dear Mrs. Bargrave, I shall love you for ever." In these verses there is twice used the word Elysian. "Ah!" says Mrs. Veal, "these poets have such names for heaven!" She would often draw her hand across her own eyes and say, "Mrs. Bargrave, do not you think I am mightily impaired by my fits?" No," says Mrs. Bargrave, "I think you look as well as ever I knew you."

After all this discourse, which the apparition put in much finer words than Mrs. Bargrave said she could pretend to, and as much more than she can remember, for it cannot be thought that an hour and three-quarters' conversation could be retained, though the main of it she thinks she does, she said to Mrs. Bargrave she would have her write a letter to her brother, and tell him she would have him give rings to such and such, and that there was a purse of gold in her cabinet, and that she would have two broad pieces given to her cousin Watson.

Talking at this rate, Mrs. Bargrave thought that a fit was coming upon her, and so placed herself in a chair just before her knees, to keep her from falling to the ground, if her fits should occasion it (for the elbow-chair, she thought, would keep her from falling on either side); and to divert Mrs. Veal, as she thought, took hold of her gown-sleeve several times and commended it. Mrs. Veal told her it was a scoured silk, and newly made up. But for all this, Mrs. Veal persisted in her request, and told Mrs. Bargrave that she must not deny her, and she would have her tell her brother all their conversation when she had an opportunity. "Dear Mrs. Veal," said Mrs. Bargrave, "this seems so impertinent that I cannot tell how to comply with it; and what a mortifying story will our conversation be to a young gentleman? Why," says Mrs. Bargrave, "it is much better, methinks, to do it yourself." "No," says Mrs. Veal, "though it seems impertinent to you now, you will see more reason for it hereafter." Mrs. Bargrave then, to satisfy her importunity, was going to fetch a pen and ink, but Mrs. Veal said, "Let it alone now, but do it when I am gone; but you must be sure to do it;" which was one of the last things she enjoined her at parting. So she promised her.

Then Mrs. Veal asked for Mrs. Bargrave's daughter. She said she was not at home, "But if you have a mind to see her," says Mrs. Bargrave, "I'll send for her." "Do," says Mrs. Veal. On which she left her, and went to a neighbour's to see for her; and by the time Mrs. Bargrave was returning, Mrs. Veal was got without the door into the street, in the face of the beast-market, on a Saturday (which is market-day), and stood ready to part. As soon as Mrs. Bargrave came to her, she asked her why she was in such haste. She said she must be going, though perhaps she might not go her journey until Monday; and told Mrs. Bargrave she hoped she should see her again at her cousin Watson's before she went whither she was going. Then she said she would take her leave of her, and walked from Mrs. Bargrave in her view, till a turning interrupted the sight of her, which was three-quarters after one in the afternoon.

Mrs. Veal died the 7th of September, at twelve o'clock at noon, of her fits, and had not above four hours' sense before death, in which time she received the sacrament. The next day after Mrs. Veal's appearing, being Sunday, Mrs. Bargrave was so mightily indisposed with a cold and a sore throat, that she could not go out that day; but on Monday morning she sent a person to Captain Watson's to know if Mrs. Veal was there. They wondered at Mrs. Bargrave's inquiry, and sent her word that she was not there, nor was expected. At this answer, Mrs. Bargrave told the maid she had certainly mistook the name or made some blunder. And though she was ill, she put on her hood, and went herself to Captain Watson's, though she knew none of the family, to see if Mrs. Veal was there or not. They said they wondered at her asking, for that she had not been in town; they were sure, if she had, she would have been there. Says Mrs. Bargrave, "I am sure she was with me on Saturday almost two hours." They said it was impossible; for they must have seen her, if she had. In comes Captain Watson while they are in dispute, and said that Mrs. Veal was certainly dead, and her escutcheons were making. This strangely surprised Mrs. Bargrave, when she sent to the person immediately who had the care of them, and found it true.    Then she related the whole story to Captain Watson's family, and what gown she had on, and how striped, and that Mrs. Veal told her it was scoured.    Then Mrs. Watson cried out, "You have seen her indeed, for none knew but Mrs. Veal and myself that the gown was scoured."    And Mrs. Watson owned that she described the gown exactly; "for," said she, "I helped her to make it up." This Mrs. Watson blazed all about the town, and avouched the demonstration of the truth of Mrs. Bargrave's seeing Mrs. Veal's apparition ; and Captain Watson carried two gentlemen immediately to Mrs. Bargrave's house to hear the relation from her own mouth.    And when it spread so fast that gentlemen and persons of quality, the judicious and sceptical part of the world, flocked in upon her, it at last became such a task that she was forced to go out of the way ; for they were in general extremely well satisfied of the truth of the thing, and plainly saw that Mrs. Bargrave was no hypochondriac, for she always appears with such a cheerful air and pleasing mien, that she has gained the favour and esteem of all the gentry, and it is thought a great favour if they can but get the relation from her own mouth.    I should have told you before that Mrs. Veal told Mrs. Bargrave that her sister and brother-in-law were just come down from London to see her.    Says Mrs. Bargrave, "How came you to order matters so strangely?"    "It could not be helped," said Mrs. Veal.    And her brother and sister did come to see her, and entered the town of Dover just as Mrs. Veal was expiring.    Mrs. Bargrave asked her whether she would drink some tea.    Says Mrs. Veal, "I do not care if I do ; but I'll warrant you this mad fellow" (meaning Mrs. Bargrave's husband) "has broken all your trinkets."    "But," says Mrs. Bargrave, "I'll get something to drink in for all that."    But Mrs. Veal waived it, and said, "It is no matter ; let it alone ;" and so it passed.

All the time I sat with Mrs. Bargrave, which was some hours, she recollected fresh sayings of Mrs. Veal.    And one material thing more she told Mrs. Bargrave—that old Mr. Breton allowed

Mrs. Veal ten pounds a year, which was a secret, and unknown to Mrs. Bargrave till Mrs. Veal told it her. Mrs. Bargrave never varies in her story, which puzzles those who doubt of the truth or are unwilling to believe it. A servant in the neighbour's yard adjoining to Mrs. Bargrave's house heard her talking to somebody an hour of the time Mrs. Veal was with her. Mrs. Bargrave went out to her next neighbour's the very moment she parted with Mrs. Veal, and told her what ravishing conversation she had with an old friend, and told the whole of it. Drelincourt's "Book of Death" is, since this happened, bought up strangely. And it is to be observed that, notwithstanding all the trouble and fatigue Mrs. Bargrave has undergone upon this account, she never took the value of a farthing, nor suffered her daughter to take anything of anybody, and therefore can have no interest in telling the story.

But Mr. Veal does what he can to stifle the matter, and said he would see Mrs. Bargrave; but yet it is certain matter of fact that he has been at Captain Watson's since the death of his sister, and yet never went near Mrs. Bargrave; and some of his friends report her to be a liar, and that she knew of Mr. Breton's ten pounds a year. But the person who pretends to say so has the reputation of a notorious liar among persons whom I know to be of undoubted credit. Now, Mr. Veal is more of a gentleman than to say she lies, but says a bad husband has crazed her. But she needs only present herself and it will effectually confute that pretence. Mr. Veal says he asked his sister on her death-bed whether she had a mind to dispose of anything, and she said no. Now, the things which Mrs. Veal's apparition would have disposed of were so trifling, and nothing of justice aimed at in their disposal, that the design of it appears to me to be only in order to make Mrs. Bargrave so to demonstrate the truth of her appearance, as to satisfy the world of the reality thereof as to what she had seen and heard, and to secure her reputation among the reasonable and understanding part of mankind. And then again Mr. Veal owns that there was a purse of gold; but it was not found in her cabinet, but in a comb-box. This looks improbable; for that Mrs. Watson owned that Mrs. Veal was so very careful

of the key of the cabinet that she would trust nobody with it;
and if so, no doubt she would not trust her gold out of it.  And
Mrs. Veal's often drawing her hand over her eyes, and asking
Mrs. Bargrave whether her fits had not impaired her, looks to me
as if she did it on purpose to remind Mrs. Bargrave of her fits, to
prepare her not to think it strange that she should put her upon
writing to her brother to dispose of rings and gold, which looks
so much like a dying person's request; and it took accordingly
with Mrs. Bargrave, as the effects of her fits coming upon her;
and was one of the many instances of her wonderful love to her
and care of her that she should not be affrighted, which indeed
appears in her whole management, particularly in her coming to
her in the daytime, waiving the salutation, and when she was
alone, and then the manner of her parting to prevent a second
attempt to salute her.

Now, why Mr. Veal should think this relation a reflection, as it
is plain he does by his endeavouring to stifle it, I cannot imagine,
because the generality believe her to be a good spirit, her discourse was so heavenly.   Her two great errands were to comfort
Mrs. Bargrave in her affliction, and to ask her forgiveness for the
breach of friendship, and with a pious discourse to encourage her.
So that after all to suppose that Mrs. Bargrave could hatch such
an invention as this from Friday noon to Saturday noon, supposing
that she knew of Mrs. Veal's death the very first moment, without
jumbling circumstances, and without any interest too, she must
be more witty, fortunate, and wicked too than any indifferent
person, I dare say, will allow.   I asked Mrs. Bargrave several
times if she was sure she felt the gown.   She answered modestly
"If my senses are to be relied on, I am sure of it."   I asked
her if she heard a sound when she clapped her hands upon her
knees.   She said she did not remember she did, but said she
appeared to be as much a substance as I did, who talked with
her.   "And I may," said she, "be as soon persuaded that your
apparition is talking to me now as that I did not really see her;
for I was under no manner of fear, and received her as a friend,
and parted with her as such.  I would not," says she, "give one

farthing to make any one believe it; I have no interest in it. Nothing but trouble is entailed upon me for a long time, for aught I know; and had it not come to light by accident, it would never have been made public." But now she says she will make her own private use of it, and keep herself out of the way as much as she can; and so she has done since. She says she had a gentleman who came thirty miles to her to hear the relation, and that she had told it to a room full of people at a time. Several particular gentlemen have had the story from Mrs. Bargrave's own mouth.

This thing has very much affected me, and I am as well satisfied as I am of the best grounded matter of fact. And why we should dispute matter of fact because we cannot solve things of which we have no certain or demonstrative notions, seems strange to me. Mrs. Bargrave's authority and sincerity alone would have been undoubted in any other case.

THE END.

PRINTED BY BALLANTYNE, HANSON AND CO.
EDINBURGH AND LONDON.